STRANGE GODS

STRANGE GODS

A Novel about Faith, Murder, Sin, and Redemption

PETER J. DALY
JOHN F. MYSLINSKI

RIVER GROVE
BOOKS

Published by River Grove Books
Austin, TX
www.rivergrovebooks.com

Distributed by River Grove Books

Design and composition by Greenleaf Book Group
Cover design by Greenleaf Book Group
Cover image: ©iStock/TomasSereda; ©iStock/Georgijevic;
©iStock/qingwa; ©iStock/jessicahyde

Cataloging-in-Publication data is available.

Print ISBN: 978-1-63299-050-1

eBook ISBN: 978-1-63299-049-5

First Edition

To all the good priests, religious, and laity, who toil away in obscurity, without recognition or thanks. They are the ones who keep the message of Christ alive.

And to the real-life Jack McClendon, a quick-witted Presbyterian minister who died in 2010. He gave us an example of holiness that combined sincerity with skepticism and a wild sense of humor with a passion for justice. He also demonstrated that piety need not be pompous and a dry martini goes well with evening prayer.

FOREWORD

We started this book in the dark days of winter, in the increasingly dysfunctional papacy of Benedict XVI. We finished this book in the spring, in the hopeful days of the papacy of Pope Francis.

It is too early to judge whether the Francis effect will bring any lasting change to the Catholic Church, but we see promising signs. Now, two years into Francis's papacy, we want to see more than just atmospherics. We want real change.

There is a terrible divide in the Church. Historically we would call it a schism. It is more than a difference in style or tone. It is a profound disagreement over the purpose and future of the Catholic Church.

On the one side are those who exalt theory over practice, abstractions over experience, and judgment over mercy. We hope their day is past.

On the other side are those who see the Church as a sign of love and mercy and a pathway to spiritual maturity.

Clericalism is an aspect of the sin of pride. It sees clergymen as superior to the laity. It makes possible all manner of corruption, arrogance, and even cruelty, because clerics do not see themselves as accountable. It is antithetical to the teaching and the example of Christ, who said He came to serve and to give His life as ransom for the many.

The clerical culture depicted in *Strange Gods* is real. It is pervasive in the clergy and deeply rooted. Unfortunately, we do not see it changing anytime soon.

We wrote this book not because we hate the Church, but because we love her. We want to see the Church restored to her truest and best self.

The murders in this book are fictional, but nearly everything else is based on real events. While the characters are fictitious, we have known people just like them.

There are the corrupt and cruel, like Cardinal Mendoza and the Soldados de Cristo. There are spectacular scoundrels, like Cardinals Crepi and Salazar, who represent the worst of self-dealing and self-indulgence.

There are also legions of clerical climbers, who rise up the ranks of the clerical ladder for their own sake. Their "strange god" is their career. In their ranks are tragically flawed men like Monsignor Matthew Ackerman.

But there are also good and great people in the Church.

There are saints like Father Jack McClendon and Sister Miriam, who remember that the Church is meant to be an instrument of mercy.

There are people like Cardinal O'Toole who, despite a life spent in the bureaucracy of the Church, can still bring courage and conviction to their work. All they need is the opportunity to be God's true servants.

Most common of all, there are millions of people like Nate and Brigid, whose relationship to the Church is similarly challenged. They are intelligent, educated, and capable people. They understand the challenges posed by modern science and culture. They still want to be part of this family of faith, but not part of its foolishness.

Despite all its weaknesses, the Catholic Church is still mother and teacher to millions of people. It still has a noble purpose and serves a real human need. We hope this book helps her, in a small way, to recover.

Peter Daly and Jack Myslinski

ACKNOWLEDGMENTS

We are grateful to so many people who have helped to bring this book to fruition.

We especially want to thank Ron Amiot, Mary Dwan, Charles Connor, Maureen Daly, and Mary Blaney for reading the first rough drafts of the novel and making many helpful corrections and comments.

Thanks as well to our brother priests who work in obscurity and holiness, often without much recognition or thanks. They continue to inspire in the same way all goodness inspires.

We especially want to thank Donna Myslinski, who made wonderful meals and put up with our terrible mess while we spent many hours with books and papers spread all over her dining room. Thanks for being our best cheerleader.

1

THE FUNERAL

NATE WAS IN A HURRY.

Whenever he was in a hurry, he had trouble with French cuffs and cuff links. Really, it takes three hands to put on cuff links. Most people only have two.

Nate had to get over to St. Patrick's Cathedral for the funeral of Frank Sullivan, his old boss. Only a week ago, Sullivan had dropped dead of a heart attack while waiting for a cab in the lobby of the New York Athletic Club.

Sullivan was a former US attorney general. Everybody, including the vice president of the United States, was going to be at the funeral. The cathedral and the streets around it would be jammed.

Nate was getting dressed in the modern "uniform" of the Knights of Malta: white tie and black jacket with tails, with a red sash across his chest. With the medal of the Maltese cross on his breast pocket, he looked like a faux aristocrat in a Marx Brothers movie.

Like Nate, Sullivan had been a Knight of Malta, shorthand for the formal mouthful, the "Sovereign Military Hospitaller Order of St. John of Jerusalem, Rhodes, and Malta." The knights took that name eight hundred years ago when they formed to take care of the wounded and dying Crusaders in the Holy Land.

It was Nate's first funeral as a knight since he had been asked to join the group a year ago. Both Nate and Sullivan had joined the knights for the same reason—contacts. It was a great way to network with other rich and powerful Catholics.

Today it is an exclusive "LinkedIn" for Catholic laymen powerful in politics, medicine, the military, or business. The Knights of Malta raise a lot of money for Catholic causes, especially for the Vatican. So, when they die, they get noticed by the Church hierarchy. A cardinal would say the funeral Mass. As a former colleague of Sullivan's, Nate had been selected for the honor of being a pallbearer, to carry Sullivan's casket in and out of the church.

Still fumbling, Nate called down the hall of their Park Avenue apartment to his wife, Brigid, who was reading in their library. "Brig, come in here and help me get these damned cuff links on."

She shouted back sarcastically, "Coming, master."

A few seconds later, she appeared at the bedroom door. "Do I have to come in and dress you, too?"

"Just help me with these damned cuff links," he said impatiently. Their fourteen-year marriage had deteriorated into a series of brief and sometimes irritated exchanges.

"Why don't you wear the cuff links I got you from Turnbull and Asher?" she asked, pulling out a tiny drawer in a mahogany chest in their dressing room. She took out gold cuff links with onyx centers.

"OK," he said, "but hurry. There will be a lot of security at the cathedral. I have to get there early."

"I don't understand you and your fascination with that crazy Church," she said. "You could pray for Frank Sullivan right here if you wanted to."

Even though they had both been raised as Catholics, Brigid had long ago stopped going to church. Like many women, she found the religion misogynistic and patriarchal.

"I have to be there, Brig. And don't start on the Church," said Nate. "We don't have time for that argument today."

She snapped the cuff links on his wrists. As she held up his morning coat, she said, "Do you want me to call the car service?"

"No," said Nate. "Traffic will be terrible around the cathedral. It'll be quicker to walk."

He smiled at her. "How do I look?" he asked. He didn't really wait for the answer. He knew he looked splendid.

Brigid looked at him all dressed up like a nineteenth-century diplomat. She had to admit he looked good. Nate was handsome in that Kennedyesque sort of way—lots of caramel-colored hair, a toothy grin, and a swimmer's build.

"You better run, or they won't let you in," Brigid said.

Nate walked across the marble foyer of their Manhattan apartment and called the elevator. "See you this afternoon," he said.

As the polished bronze doors of the elevator closed between them, he gave a little wave. It was what passed for affection between them these days. They both felt there should be more.

Out on the street, Nate hurried down Park Avenue to 50th Street, crossed toward Fifth Avenue, and slipped in the side door in the south transept of St. Patrick's Cathedral. The Secret Service had set up a security checkpoint there and was screening the early arrivals through metal detectors. Men in suits with earpieces were standing in pairs, talking into their sleeves.

Once in the cathedral, it took a few seconds for his eyes to adjust to the dim light. Automatically, he stepped to the holy water font just inside the door, dipped his hand in the marble bowl, and blessed himself.

In the center aisle of the cathedral, Nate saw a group of knights, dressed like he was, in formal regalia. They were gathered at the foot of the steps leading to the high altar in the sanctuary. As he walked toward them, he scanned the pews for faces he might know. Funerals like Sullivan's were not just liturgies of prayer for the dead, but networking opportunities.

The group of six pallbearers included two other knights who, like Nate, were federal prosecutors. There was also a doctor friend of Nate's who was a cardiologist at Columbia–St. Luke's Hospital. The others Nate did not know, but they looked to him like finance guys. They were all professional men, accustomed to being in charge and unaccustomed to the silent service of a pallbearer.

As Nate joined the group, he heard a little commotion coming from the front pews nearest them. The vice president, a gregarious Irishman from Delaware, was arriving, shaking hands with everyone in the vicinity. Nate knew him vaguely. Though they were not the same age, they had both attended Georgetown Law School in Washington, DC, and had met each other at alumni functions. Nate left the group for a moment to shake the vice president's hand. The two men exchanged pleasantries about priests they knew in common from their Jesuit-run alma mater. Once the vice president entered his pew, Nate rejoined the other pallbearers.

Under the direction of a bossy young priest dressed in a black cassock and lace surplice, the knights were lined up in the center aisle, in two rows of three facing the rear of the church, toward the Fifth Avenue entrance. At the main entrance of the cathedral, the seldom-used great bronze doors had been thrown open, a sign of the significance of the occasion. Sunlight streamed in through the opening. The pallbearers waited awkwardly for the priests and the bishops and finally the Cardinal Archbishop of New York to emerge from their vesting rooms in the subterranean sacristy, below the high altar. In their white ties and tails, the knights looked like the march of the penguins.

While they waited, Nate looked at the cathedral. Glancing up at the great gothic arches inside the church, it occurred to him that St. Patrick's was oddly placed, a medieval temple plunked down right in the middle of Manhattan, arguably the most godless place on the planet.

Nate took a kind of proprietary pride in this place, even though it had been dedicated in 1879, about a century before he was born. After all, St. Patrick's was the product of his people, the working-class Irish. Thousands of Irish washerwomen and dockworkers of nineteenth-century New York had built this grand church with their little sacrifices. John Hughes, the Archbishop of New York in the 1850s, chose the cathedral's Fifth Avenue location with an important purpose. He wanted St. Patrick's to be a stick in the eye to the English "swells" of Protestant New York. He wanted the Protestants to have to walk past the cathedral and be impressed by it, even envy it. The building was meant to scream at them, "Irish immigrants built this!" Hughes made his point.

Even in the twenty-first century, immigrants still made St. Patrick's their own. Every day thousands of people stopped in for "a visit," as Catholics call an informal chat with God. No longer were the new arrivals Irish. Now they were mostly Latino and African. Nonetheless, they were still the poor.

It was one of the few places in pricey Manhattan where a poor person could sit down for free. No policeman would ask you to move along. Whether they were kneeling upright or hunched over in the pews, ordinary people could talk to whatever God was out there. They could tell the divine presence about their broken hearts and shattered dreams. On happy occasions they could thank the ineffable mystery for prayers answered: a job found, a baby born, or a loved one cured. In a city hopped up on caffeine-induced stress, St. Patrick's was a sort of decompression chamber.

Churches always filled Nate with awe. As a boy, growing up in the Charlestown section of Boston, the nuns had instilled in him a reverence for Catholic churches. "Jesus is present there in the tabernacle," they told him. He believed it still with the simplicity of a child. And while this cavernous building dwarfed his parish church back home, the language of the architecture and the feeling of reverence were the same. Both churches had the same smell of incense and candle wax breathed into their stone walls by an endless round of solemn Masses and perpetually burning vigil lights.

Nate looked up at the magnificent stained glass windows, forty feet above his head. The thousands of pieces of broken bits of colored glass reminded him of the broken hearts who had sat silently in these pews. The figures in the windows could hardly be seen from where he stood. Their identity was known only to God and the artist, he guessed. Looking to his right, Nate saw an elderly man in one of the side-aisle chapels lighting a candle on the stand where the vigil lights burned in ranks before the altars of the saints. To Catholics, these candles were not magic. They were wordless prayers that persisted in petitioning heaven for days after the supplicant left the church. To Nate it all made perfect sense. Catholic religion is tactile and sensual. Prayer is expressed in gesture and substance as well as words.

Nate's contemplation of the cathedral was brought to an end by the arrival of two long lines of white-robed priests who formed up behind the pallbearers in the center aisle. The procession would start as soon as the cardinal appeared.

*   *   *

On the crypt level, twenty feet below the high altar, His Eminence, Cardinal John Michael Manning, the Archbishop of New York, was vesting for the funeral. He stood at a large dressing table in the sacristy facing vestments that had been laid out before him.

Cardinal Manning was called "Tubby" by the priests of New York, at least when they were among themselves. At nearly three hundred pounds, Manning was a cheerful package of pious platitudes. He never had anything original to say, but he always said it cheerfully.

Manning was wrapped in the scarlet watered silk of a cardinal's cassock. In such a bright red dress, he was a dramatic sight, like a New York City fire truck that needed a large turning radius.

Standing at the dressing table, the cardinal was momentarily indecisive and irritated. He vented his frustration on the two flunky monsignors, Kelly and Krakowski, who were helping him get dressed.

"Is that it?" he asked. "Just these two vestments? Don't we have anything else?"

The priests ignored his questions and pulled the cardinal's white alb over his head and down his body to cover his red cassock.

"Should I wear the white or the purple chasuble?" the cardinal asked the two monsignors who were at his ankles, tugging on the hem of the alb.

He answered himself, "Purple is more conservative." Manning's natural inclination, like most bishops, was to be conservative in all things.

"What would the Holy Father wear?" he asked the mute monsignors. Cardinals always take their cues from the pope. That's how they get to be cardinals.

Manning's dithering over costume was not unusual. St. Patrick's is several blocks off Broadway, but it is no less theatrical. Costumes were important to Manning. Like many clerics, he believed that clothes did make the man.

Kelly and Krakowski looked at each other with shared impatience. "Just wear the white one, Your Eminence," said Monsignor Kelly. "All the concelebrants are already upstairs. They are all vested in white. We have to hurry."

Manning put out his arms. The monsignors placed an ornate gold and white stole around his shoulders and then pulled a heavily embroidered matching chasuble over his head. They didn't bother with the cincture, a rope belt meant to symbolize purity. Getting a cincture around Manning was too much trouble. Besides, nobody could see it under his vestments.

Kelly hung a jeweled pectoral cross around Manning's neck. A symbol of the office of a bishop, it dangled on the cardinal's chest. He clutched it for a moment with his right hand and fingered it lovingly. On his left hand, he wore his archbishop's ring, only slightly more modest than a Super Bowl ring. His ecclesiastical "bling."

The cardinal was already moving toward the door when Krakowski handed him a silver crosier, a six-foot-long staff meant to recall a shepherd's crook. Kelly plopped a gold and white miter, a sort of pointed hat, on the cardinal's head. Manning paused for a moment in front of a full-length mirror to admire himself. The miter added at least a foot to his height of six feet. Fully vested, he looked ready for the Macy's Thanksgiving Day Parade.

Cardinal Manning struggled to get his bulk up the steps. Halfway up, he stopped to catch his breath. Wheezing a bit, the archbishop pushed himself up the last flight of stairs. He emerged from behind the high altar into the sanctuary, where the priests and a few bishops had already been lined up by the bossy young master of ceremonies.

From the loft at the rear of the cathedral, the choir director saw the cardinal arrive. He raised his baton and signaled to the small orchestra in the loft and the organist to begin the prelude to Mozart's Requiem.

Nate felt a thrill as the choir intoned, "*Requiem aeternam dona eis, Domine, et lux perpetua luceat eis.*" The two lines of pallbearers had already been moved down the center aisle to the main entrance of the church. As the music started, they moved out of the cathedral and down its front steps to the hearse waiting at the curb. By the time the procession with the cardinal reached the great cathedral door, they had lifted Sullivan's bronze casket out of the hearse and carried it to the main entrance.

It was a struggle getting the heavy coffin up the stairs. Moving slowly, they strained to keep it level as they carried it up the first set of five steps. At the landing they wobbled a little. Nate felt his sweating palms slipping on the coffin handle. Two New York City policemen raced up to help them lift the casket up the last three steps to a cart waiting to receive the coffin on the vestibule level.

Disaster averted, Nate and the other pallbearers breathed a sigh of relief as they set the coffin down on the "church truck," a cart with four rubber wheels. The undertaker pushed the coffin forward a few paces, so that it was flanked by the huge bronze doors. The pallbearers stepped back a step and allowed Sullivan's family to come up to the casket. They were all clearly visible from the street in the bright sunlight.

The two rows of priests parted like the waters of the Red Sea when Cardinal Manning approached. Winded from his walk down the aisle, Manning paused near the head of the casket to greet Sullivan's widow and family.

Cardinal Manning worked the crowd of family at the top of the steps, giving them that super-sincere politician's handshake—his left hand on their elbows, grabbing their right hands with a firm squeeze. He looked them each straight in the eye and offered some brief words of comfort.

Manning was good with people. If he hadn't been an archbishop, he would have made a great mayor or governor.

Having greeted the family, Manning stepped closer to the head of the casket and was now fully in the sunlight. Nate watched admiringly as the sunlight glinted off the cardinal's jeweled crozier. The cardinal made the sign of the cross. Nate and the others around the casket followed suit.

Catholic funerals begin with the blessing of the body with holy water to recall baptism. Manning reached to a small bronze bucket of holy water, carried by an acolyte, and grabbed an aspergillum, a brass stick with a little orb on the end that spritzed out water when Manning shook it.

Spritz, spritz, spritz, the cardinal sprinkled water on the casket as he prayed out loud, "I bless the body of John Francis Xavier Sullivan with the holy water that recalls his baptism."

Nate liked the drama of the blessing. Manning amplified the moment by walking around the casket, sprinkling it from all sides. Nate and the other pallbearers stepped back to avoid getting hit with the holy water as the cardinal circumnavigated the coffin. As Manning returned to the head of the casket, he placed the aspergillum in the bronze holy water bucket.

The undertaker stepped forward with the pall, a large white cloth bigger than a bedsheet. Manning signaled to the family to step forward and drape the cloth over the casket. As the family struggled to unfold the heavy cloth, Manning prayed, "On the day of his baptism, Francis put on Christ; on the day of Christ's coming, may he be clothed in glory."

Only a dozen feet away from the cardinal, Nate had a great view of the ceremony, but the traffic noise on Fifth Avenue made it hard to hear the prayers. Nate leaned in a little, looking at the cardinal's face, trying to hear what was being said.

A red spot of light appeared on the archbishop's forehead, looking like a Hindu bindi. It seemed to dance around for a split second. Suddenly the cardinal recoiled. Nate saw blood spurt from the place where the red spot had been. Everything seemed to be in slow motion. Nate saw Manning's mouth open wide as the cardinal's eyes rolled upward in his head, so only the whites were visible.

My God, thought Nate. The cardinal's been shot!

The impact of the bullet propelled Manning's head backward, in a kind of whiplash. His miter fell forward and tumbled to the floor. The cardinal staggered back a step or two and collapsed into the arms of the two monsignors, Kelly and Krakowski. Unable to hold his weight, they let him go, and the archbishop crashed to the floor.

Standing beside the casket, Mrs. Sullivan screamed.

The pallbearers dived into the shadows of the vestibule, seeking cover. Nate hit the deck, tripping over one of the other pallbearers as he fell to the floor, very near the body of the fallen archbishop. He could see a little pool of blood oozing out behind Manning's skull.

In the choir loft above, the choir was completely unaware that the cardinal had been shot. Seeing people running down the aisle, the choir director became confused. He signaled to the choir to intone the "Dies Irae," the solemn hymn that begins with the Latin words for "day of wrath." Oddly, it was the perfect accompaniment to the chaos unfolding below.

As everyone on the cathedral steps and in the vestibule scattered to find shelter, Frank Sullivan's bronze casket sat alone for a moment, shining in the brilliant sunlight.

After seeing the commotion, New York City police officers raced up the cathedral steps, guns drawn. They secured the area and stood facing the crowd on the street, looking for a shooter. There was no obvious gunman.

At the other end of the cathedral, the dignitaries stood in their pews, straining to see what was going on at the main entrance. It was not clear what had happened. The Secret Service at the Fifth Avenue entrance radioed their comrades guarding the vice president, who was standing at his place in the second pew. His bodyguard detail formed a human shield around him and hustled him out of the church. They went down the steps to the sacristy where Manning had vested and then through an underground passageway to the cathedral rectory on Madison Avenue.

Firemen and EMTs from the ambulances stationed on Fifth Avenue shoved their way through the panicked crowd on the sidewalk with a hydraulic stretcher, trying to reach the cardinal. Unceremoniously, they shoved Sullivan's casket aside, almost toppling it from the church truck. Policemen pushed Nate and the other pallbearers deeper into the vestibule.

Unsure if there were other wounds, the EMTs tried to undress the cardinal, but his weight made it impossible. In seconds, they cut the silk chasuble from top to bottom and all Manning's multiple layers of clothing down to the skin.

By now, blood was everywhere. The bullet had entered Manning's forehead and exited through the back of his skull, making a larger exit wound just above the cardinal's neck. The EMTs' efforts were futile.

The Archbishop of New York was dead.

2

TELLING THE POPE

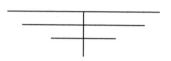

NEWS OF MANNING'S ASSASSINATION REACHED ROME before Nate could reach the lobby of his Park Avenue apartment building. Even in the chaos after the cardinal's shooting, Monsignor Krakowski managed to reach his cell phone in the pocket of his cassock and call his office. He told his secretary to notify Rome immediately of the cardinal's death.

The secretary pushed speed dial on her desk phone. Seconds later, an English-speaking operator in the Vatican answered. The call was immediately relayed to the pope's personal secretary, Monsignor Mario Ranieri. When he answered the phone with a cheerful "*pronto*," he was hardly ready for the news he received. "*O Dio*," he said breathlessly.

Pope Thomas was in the middle of a late afternoon *ad limina* meeting with twenty-eight bishops from the southeastern African countries of Malawi, Zimbabwe, and Zambia.

Only a few weeks past his eighty-fifth birthday, Pope Thomas hardly ever felt well. He suffered from gout. He also had arthritis in his hips. His perpetual cough, caused by chronic bronchitis, was made worse by the drafty rooms in his apartment in the Vatican's Apostolic Palace. And the swelling in his feet and ankles marked the beginnings of congestive heart failure.

Thomas was a nice man, but ineffectual. The religious zeal of his youth had been supplanted in old age by a desire for rest and comfort. He had been elected six years before by a group of conservative cardinals who wanted a "placeholder" pope. They mostly got what they wanted.

Basically, the Roman Curia, the papal bureaucracy, wanted a man who would do nothing and disturb no one. After a succession of non-Italian popes, they chose a "safe" Italian. They wanted no waves, no drama, and no initiatives.

Church politics, like secular politics, is divided into three camps: men who want change, men who want no change, and men who want power. Even more than secular politics, church politics is all men. No women are allowed in the biggest and most powerful "old boys' club" in the world.

When he was elected, the pope chose the name Thomas. The name itself was a surprise. He was the first in a line of 265 popes to ever bear that name.

Supposedly, he picked the name to honor St. Thomas Aquinas, the great medieval theologian. That pleased the conservatives, who love St. Thomas, because he has a settled answer to every question. His *Summa Theologica*, written in question-and-answer format, gives the illusion of dialogue, but only an illusion, since it is a dialogue with the self. The big questions about God, truth, justice, grace, and salvation are neatly answered. That's what conservatives wanted: definitive answers.

But after five years of Pope Thomas, the conservative prelates had buyer's remorse. They thought he was too weak. He had not crushed the liberals as they had hoped. They joked that he started out as Thomas Aquinas but ended up as a doubting Thomas.

What most irritated the Roman Curia were Thomas's attempts to reform the Vatican bureaucracy. Thomas wanted to take away their perks and their privileges. He wanted them to live like ordinary men. Even worse, he expected them to be followers of Jesus, the poor man of Nazareth. They had worked most of their lives to get the benefits of high office, and now he wanted to take them away. What would we be, they said to themselves in their heart of hearts, without our watered silk and jeweled pectoral crosses? Thomas's answer did not please them: disciples of Jesus.

Pope Thomas hated meetings. He especially hated afternoon meetings, because they interfered with his nap. In his little hometown, overlooking the Bay of Naples, everybody slept for a couple hours during the midday heat. They were made drowsy by a big *pranzo* with wine, topped off by the local lemon *liquore*, Limoncino. Nap time to people like Pope Thomas was more than customary; it was necessary. He was not the only person in the Vatican who liked an afternoon nap. Most Vatican clerics worked only in the mornings. Returning to your office after *pranzo* was considered optional.

Pope Thomas rested his cheek on his fist, with his elbow propped on the arm of his chair, as he listened to the African bishops drone on about places he'd never heard of and people he would never see. He was bored out of his mind.

Thomas's lackadaisical attitude toward work would have been anathema to the Polish and German popes before him. Northern Europeans generally thought that people should put in a whole workday. Thomas thought that was heresy. Humanity could not be perfected by human striving, he thought, especially after lunch.

If the pope hated afternoon meetings, his special ire was reserved for these *ad limina* visits that filled most weeks of the year. Each of the more than three-thousand Catholic bishops in the world is required to make a trip to Rome every five years. The pious reason is to visit the tombs of St. Peter and St. Paul, to go *ad limina apostolorum*, "to the threshold of the apostles." However, *ad liminas* are more administrative meetings than pilgrimages. Bishops make a pit stop at the tombs of the apostles, but they spend most of their time making the rounds of the Vatican offices.

Ad liminas are not frank exchanges between equals. They are more like a visit to the principal's office where bishops are called in to account for themselves.

The Vatican is a monarchy, and bishops are its courtiers. Like courtiers everywhere, they flatter the monarch.

They kiss the pope's ring. They make a great fuss over how well he looks, even though they gossip among themselves that he looks like death warmed over.

They laugh at all the pope's feeble jokes. They pretend they are inspired when he reads an address to them that they usually have written themselves. When it is all over, they praise the pope for his brilliant statement to them.

Bishops from poor countries want *ad limina* visits, because they are an opportunity to raise money or curry favor with Vatican bureaucrats. Sometimes, they angle for jobs in Rome. Mostly, they promote special projects back home for which they need money.

Bishops from rich countries, like the United States or Germany, have a shorter agenda. They want to influence Rome. They bring gifts, generally checks for Vatican foundations or papal charities. Their money gets them respect in the Vatican. For them, the money flows to Rome.

In some ways, the Vatican operates as a giant currency exchange, passing money from one part of the church to another, generally from rich to poor. That is why it needs a bank, or at least thinks it does.

During World War II, when money was hard to move around the world, Pope Pius XII started the *Instituto per le Opere di Religione*, the Institute for Religious Works. Sometimes it is referred to by its initials, IOR, but mostly people just call it the Vatican Bank.

The setting for this afternoon *ad limina* meeting was the pope's private library, an elegant room on the top floor of the papal palace. The coffered ceiling thirty feet above Pope Thomas's head was gilded, and the massive crown molding featured chubby cherubim mounted in each corner.

The pope sat at one end of the room, on a raised carpeted dais. His cream-colored armchair was similar to the chairs the bishops sat in, but it was raised up above them to indicate his superiority. Though Pope Thomas had tried to change this atmosphere, the Vatican remained

resistant to change. Certainly, none of the bishops in that room entertained the idea that they were equal to the pope, despite the fact that he
called them brothers.

On the pope's right-hand side sat Cardinal Michael O'Toole, an
American and a native of Boston. He was the head of the Congregation
for the Evangelization of Peoples, the Vatican's missionary office. African bishops wanted to keep Cardinal O'Toole happy, since he was the
guy who held the purse strings for the third world.

O'Toole was the consummate insider. He knew the bureaucratic
game and played it well. That was how he had risen to be the most influ-
ential American in the Vatican Curia. At sixty-five years old, he was just
a little overweight. His face was reddish, but not wrinkled. His manner
was reserved. Only when he went home to Boston did he ever really
relax. In Boston he was just plain Mike. There he could drink a beer
and cheer for the Red Sox. He might even tell an off-color joke. But in
Rome, he was always on his game.

O'Toole had endured dozens of these meetings. He feigned interest
while the Bishop of Lilongwe, in Malawi, was standing at the microphone, droning on about the conflict in his country between the Chewa
and Tumbuka tribes. O'Toole knew the dispute. It was like tribal dis-
putes everywhere. We have the same thing in Northern Ireland between
the Protestants and Catholics, he thought.

Behind the pope, a door opened noiselessly. The pope's secretary, Monsignor Mario Ranieri, glided silently into the room. A good servant, he had
mastered the art of making himself invisible. His feet, concealed under his
black cassock, moved across the polished floor as if they were in slippers.

Monsignor Ranieri was not only the pope's secretary, he was also his
boyhood friend. As children, they had worked in the lemon groves near
their hometown of Sant'Agata, a tiny spot on a hill overlooking Sorrento
and the Bay of Naples. When they were fourteen, they went off to the high
school seminary together in Naples. Later, they studied at the Capranica
in Rome, the school that produced most Italian bishops. Ranieri was the
only one in the room who could speak to the pope as an equal.

He moved to the pope's side and leaned in close to his ear. The Bishop of Lilongwe stopped talking, curious about the interruption. "Paolo," breathed Ranieri, using the pope's boyhood name, "*Abiamo una crisi.*"

The pope raised his eyebrows and sat up straight. He leaned closer to Mario.

"Cardinal Manning in New York is dead," he said in Italian. "Assassinated in his cathedral. *Sparito.*" Ranieri puffed out a little bit of air to make a gunshot sound.

The pope blanched. "*Perche?*" he asked.

"*Non sapiamo,*" said Ranieri.

Almost as a reflex to the news, the pope stood stiffly, steadying himself on the armchair. Without hesitation, the African bishops all jumped up.

Pope Thomas made the sign of the cross and began the Our Father in English. The bishops followed along, perplexed. Nobody asked why he was leaving mid-meeting, even mid-sentence. Popes don't have to explain themselves, and they seldom do.

Leaning on Ranieri, the pope stepped off the dais and left the room by the same door from which Ranieri had emerged. It led to a private office. The pope gestured for Cardinal O'Toole to follow.

With the door closed, Ranieri briefed the pope and O'Toole. They spoke in Italian. After many years in Rome, O'Toole was comfortable in the language. He even spoke with the "sh-sh" accent of the Roman street. O'Toole could see that Ranieri was choosing his words carefully.

The monsignor repeated himself. "Manning is dead. Shot in his cathedral at the start of a funeral for un *pezzo grosso.*" Mario gestured with his hands, stretching his arms wide to indicate just how big a *pezzo* Frank Sullivan had been. He used the Italian term for a VIP, "one of the big pieces." It reflects the Italian presumption that life is a giant jigsaw puzzle, and some people are bigger pieces than others.

Ranieri continued, "We don't know who or why, but this might be part of a pattern. There is a whole '*sacco*' of cardinals dead under strange circumstances lately."

The pope reached for a decanter of water on the desk. "*Madonna Santa*," he said, "What in God's name is happening?"

Ranieri reminded the pope and the cardinal of all the deaths of cardinals in the past year or so. Deaths among the cardinals were not surprising, the priest pointed out. All of them were old, after all. Forty of the 150 cardinals were over eighty. But five had died unexpectedly at a relatively young age or from violent causes or under suspicious circumstances. Now Manning was dead, obviously a murder.

Ranieri ticked off the list of deaths from memory.

"Cardinal Alfonse Lohrman of Santiago, Chile, died in a Chilean clinic where he had gone for a routine operation.

"Only three months ago Cardinal Ignacio Garcia of Guadalajara was killed in a shoot-out at Monterrey airport, where he was attending a meeting of Mexican bishops. The police speculated that he was caught in a fight between rival drug cartels, but no one else was killed in that incident.

"Then there was Cardinal Modesto Rondo, the Archbishop of Manila, who died in a car accident on one of Manila's expressways.

"Cardinal Patrice Musaku from Kinshasa in the Congo died in a fire, when his retirement home burned to the ground.

"Cardinal Antonio deCapo, from Milan, died strangely from food poisoning at a restaurant in Milano Centro.

"And now Manning in New York, shot between the eyes in broad daylight."

Ranieri put his index finger to his forehead to indicate more dramatically where Manning was shot.

"The police are investigating these deaths in each country," said Ranieri. "But nobody has tied all of this together, at least not yet."

He paused for emphasis.

Pope Thomas took a pill from a little pillbox in his pocket and popped it into his mouth, washing it down with water. "Why would somebody do this? How could they do this? Maybe your imagination is just running away with you, Mario. Maybe these were accidents. Maybe the food was bad. Maybe this is a fantasy."

The three men sat in silence for a moment. Then Ranieri spoke up. "No, Holiness, this is no fantasy. There is a pattern here."

"*Madonna Santa*," said the pope again. "This is evil."

The pope turned to O'Toole. "What do you think, Michael? With Manning's death, the American authorities will be involved. Maybe you have some *amici* in America who can help us?"

In Italy, everything is accomplished through the "friend network." A useful man is a man who has many friends. O'Toole was a useful man. He was legendary in the Vatican for his extensive friend network. It came naturally to him. He just imitated the Irish politicians of Boston. His network included a great many lawyers, judges, and government officials in the United States, mostly contacts from O'Toole's service as the chaplain to the Knights of Malta.

"Maybe I can find an *auxiliaro* from the knights," O'Toole volunteered.

The pope nodded. "Do it. We need somebody who knows what is *sotto acqua*." The pope used the Napolitano expression for the "black market," the things "under water."

Pope Thomas added, "If these deaths are connected, somebody has real power. We need to know who and why."

O'Toole nodded. He was frightened and fascinated at the same time. Frightened, because someone might be killing cardinals like himself. Thrilled, because he was entrusted with the gravest task of his career.

"I will give this to you, Michael, as a special portfolio. You are my plenipotentiary." The pope waved his hand vaguely in the air to indicate that O'Toole had his full authority.

"Now I don't feel so well," said the pope. "If you will excuse me, I will go for a *riposo*."

Ranieri and O'Toole stood as the pope shuffled out.

Poisoning, burning, and shootings of cardinals, thought O'Toole. "We haven't seen this since the Borgias."

O'Toole and Ranieri looked at each other for a moment.

"I'll call you tomorrow, Monsignor, once I figure out whom to contact in the States."

"*Va bene,*" said Ranieri.

They left the study.

As he headed for the back stairs out of the papal apartments, O'Toole thought of the historical irony. Some people wanted to take the Church back to the sixteenth century. With all this murderous intrigue, maybe they'd actually done it.

O'Toole felt a little weak as he made his way down five flights of stairs to the street-level back door of the Belvedere Palace.

As he reached the street, he had a moment of fear and wondered, should I hire a bodyguard?

3

THE DINNER

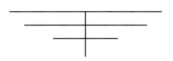

CARDINAL O'TOOLE'S BLACK ITALIAN LOAFERS MADE A clip-clop sound on the steps as he descended the back stairs from the papal apartment. Could I be next? he thought, as he pushed open the unmarked door that led to a narrow cobblestone street in Vatican City. O'Toole turned right to walk toward the Porta Sant'Anna, the business entrance of the Vatican. He hugged the high stone wall on his right side as he walked, to avoid getting hit by the cars speeding past him toward the Vatican gate. Sidewalks had not existed when that little street was built. Neither had cars.

The wall to his right was part of a fortification built in the eleventh century as a defense against the Saracen invaders of Rome. At the end of the wall was a massive round tower where papal guards could have poured down boiling oil on approaching enemies. O'Toole knew that stone tower as a financial fortress, the home of the Vatican Bank.

The solidity of the tower gave a false impression about the bank. It made people think it held a lot of money. Actually, the Vatican bank is only a mid-level financial institution, the size of a bank headquartered in a small Midwestern city.

O'Toole didn't give the bank a moment's thought as he walked past. He was intent on getting home, unnoticed. That evening he had an appointment for dinner with old friends who were in town for a few days. Maybe, he thought, I can share this news with them. They might have some idea about what to do.

O'Toole clip-clopped a hundred yards or so down the cobblestone road toward an ornate iron gate that led out of the Vatican. On his left was the Vatican visitors' office, where people registered to enter the working parts of the Vatican. As O'Toole approached the gate, two young Swiss guards snapped to attention as the cardinal passed, clicking their heels in military fashion and saluting. Simultaneously they addressed O'Toole by his title, "*Eminenza*."

Ordinarily, O'Toole loved the attention he got from the guards. Who wouldn't? Power and prestige are a sex substitute for clerics. These little marks of respect make up for a lot of what is lacking in the life of a celibate male. It may be small compensation for a lonely life, but it usually gave O'Toole an ego rush to be greeted with a title of Italian nobility. Today, however, he was less eager to call attention to himself as a cardinal.

Being a cardinal had been O'Toole's boyhood fantasy. When he was twelve years old, he had played priest in the basement of his parents' home in Salem, Massachusetts. He dressed up in vestments and made his friends kneel down for communion. Even then, he knew that an American could probably never be elected pope, so he contented himself with the fantasy of becoming the Cardinal Archbishop of Boston.

In O'Toole's boyhood world, the most powerful man in Boston was Cardinal Richard Cushing. Massachusetts politicians catered to him. They called him "Number One." Cushing's nasal voice came into the O'Toole home every Sunday night when his family turned on the radio and knelt down in the living room to say the rosary with the cardinal.

O'Toole never got the nod to be Archbishop of Boston, but he got the next best thing. He became a cardinal in Rome. Every now and then he had to remind himself that this dentist's son was a "prince" of the church. The fact that Jesus warned against loving titles of respect and places of honor at banquets did not dampen O'Toole's enthusiasm for the honors of aristocracy. He flattered himself into thinking that his office had not corrupted him. In his moments of self-criticism, he took comfort in the thought: I am far from the worst.

As he passed through the gate, O'Toole stepped across the invisible line between Vatican City State and the Republic of Italy. It is the most inconspicuous international border in the world. He was now on the Via Angelica, a busy Roman street lined with souvenir shops, tacky restaurants, and religious goods vendors.

Two blocks away from Saint Anne's Gate, on the edge of a rabbit warren of narrow streets called the Borgo Pio, he emerged into the small square, Piazza Leonina, named for Pope Leo XIII.

O'Toole's apartment was on two upper floors of a building that faced that little square. It was not an elegant location, but it was very convenient. He could walk to most places he wanted to go in and around the Vatican.

Tourists know Piazza Leonina as the last stop on the number 64 bus route that runs from Rome's main railroad station, Stazione Termini, to the Vatican. Every ten minutes another 64 bus arrives in the square, carrying an endless flow of tourists to the Vatican. Route 64 is also where Roman pickpockets ride back and forth, emptying tourists' wallets, backpacks, and purses. When O'Toole was a student in Rome, he would have ridden the buses. Today, as a cardinal, he wouldn't even consider setting foot on a bus, especially the 64 buses.

O'Toole's building was four floors tall and ran the length of the Piazza Leonina. The ground floor held some shops, including a travel agency and a cell phone store that flanked either side of the apartment house entrance.

Just above the entrance to the apartment house, an Egyptian flag flew from a pole bolted to the wall at a forty-five-degree angle. The entire second floor of the building was occupied by the Egyptian Embassy to the Holy See.

The cardinal's quarters occupied the third and fourth floors of the building. Actually, his apartment was the spacious third floor. The much smaller fourth floor was occupied by the three Mexican nuns who served as his housekeepers.

Apart from the diplomatic flag over the entrance, O'Toole's apartment house was a fairly typical Roman Renaissance-style palazzo. It was constructed in the 1950s in a gray stone in what the Romans call "fascist style," boxy and barren with enormous doors. Evidently Benito Mussolini had been partial to this design.

The second and third floors were the most elegant, with high ceilings and large rooms. They were called the *piano nobili*, literally the floors of the nobles. In Renaissance Rome, these middle floors would have been occupied by the noble families.

The top floors, with lower ceilings and smaller rooms, were reserved for servants. Roman nobility did not want to be at street level, where they would have the smell of horses and the danger of thieves. And they did not want to have to climb stairs to the top of the building in hot weather. That was for the servants. The middle floors were just right.

Twentieth-century palazzos had made the accommodation to modernity by the addition of elevators. Cardinal O'Toole reached his apartment in a tiny stainless steel elevator that he entered just off the lobby. Usually the elevator made him feel claustrophobic, but today it made him feel safe. He was glad to be encased in a bulletproof metal box. At least there no one could shoot him.

When the elevator doors opened, O'Toole saw Sister Emilia, one of three Mexican sisters of St. Joseph who served as his housekeepers, standing at his apartment door. The sisters were perpetually cheerful and reliably discreet. He nodded to her with a perfunctory *Buona sera* and handed her his hat. She responded, "*Buona sera, Eminenza.*"

The cardinal moved quickly to his bedroom down a long corridor of tan-colored marble. O'Toole wanted to change quickly out of his cardinal's cassock and into a black clerical suit. He was in a hurry to meet three priests for dinner—all old friends from Boston and his seminary days. He was anxious to see them after the disturbing news about Manning. Perhaps, he thought, I can confide in them "under the seal." When priests want something to remain secret, they use the reference to the seal of confession.

On his way down the corridor, the cardinal passed his private chapel. It adjoined his bedroom. The chapel was small, the size of a large walk-in closet. It had a small altar for private Masses, but O'Toole rarely used it. It didn't make any sense to him. It was like talking to himself. He preferred saying Mass for some convent, or at least for the nuns in his apartment.

The cardinal paused in the chapel. Despite his hurry to change, he felt the need of a moment of peace and prayer. O'Toole sat down in the chair facing the altar and flipped through his breviary, the priest's prayer book. Even in his long career of ambition, he kept the custom of daily Mass and morning and evening prayer. A ribbon marked the page for Monday evening prayer. Absentmindedly, he read the psalms for the evening. After forty years of practice, the words were so familiar that he didn't really need the book. But when he got to Psalm 15, the second psalm for the night, he paused.

> *Lord, who shall be admitted to your tent,*
> *Who shall dwell on your holy mountain?*
> *He who acts without fault;*
> *He who acts with justice and speaks the truth from*
> *   his heart . . .*

Maybe, thought the cardinal, we are being punished for our sins. It was not the sort of thought he entertained often. He always had thought of himself as one of the good guys. But if people were shooting cardinals right in their own cathedrals, there had to be a reason.

After his prayer, O'Toole stepped next door to his bedroom and changed quickly into the suit that Sister Emilia had laid out. After he put on his silk-lined suit coat, he draped his pectoral cross around his neck and dropped the crucifix neatly into the breast pocket. The gold chain of the cross was still showing. To those sensitive to ecclesiastical vesture, the chain showed that he was no ordinary priest. He was a bishop. After so many years as a bishop, it was hard for him not to have some sign of his office on his person. Cardinals spent so much of their lives rising to the top, they really did want people to notice.

The ancient part of the city of Rome is fairly compact. It was a short walk from O'Toole's apartment in the Borgo Pio to the restaurant on the other side of the Tiber River in the most ancient part of the city. O'Toole was headed for La Pentola, a discreet little restaurant near the river that was a favorite of high-ranking clerics.

At the front door of the restaurant, O'Toole suddenly remembered that a cardinal had died in La Pentola, in the very room where he was going to meet his friends.

According to legend, the Archbishop of Chicago, Samuel Cardinal Stritch, was dining at La Pentola in 1958 when he died of a heart attack in the private dining room at the back. Stritch had been out to dinner with several priest friends from Chicago. Just after the pasta was served, the Chicago cardinal turned as red as the sash on his cassock and suddenly slumped over face-first into a steaming dish of spaghetti alla carbonara. He was dead when his face hit the noodles, probably from an aneurysm.

His companions, streetwise Chicago priests, realized that a dead cardinal would trigger a major investigation by Italian authorities. Better, they reasoned, that Stritch should have died in the Vatican, where the Church was the authority and they could control the investigation. That way there would be no civil investigation and no delay in getting the cardinal's body home to Chicago.

So, two burly monsignors from the South Side grabbed Cardinal Stritch under his armpits and hustled his corpse into a waiting taxi for the short ride up to the Gianicolo Hill to the North American College. The college was legally Vatican territory, even though the seminary grounds are outside the Vatican City walls.

Once back at the college, the priests stripped the cardinal naked and put his body in warm water in the giant bathtub in the sixth-floor infirmary of the seminary. The warm water made the time of death difficult to determine. A cooperative doctor was summoned, who pronounced the cardinal dead of a heart attack on Vatican soil. The freight office of TWA was immediately summoned. The body was shipped home for a massive funeral, no questions asked.

O'Toole chuckled to himself. The only priests craftier than Boston priests were Chicago priests, he thought. Jesus said his followers should be as "cunning as serpents and gentle as doves." Chicago priests got the first part, anyway, he thought, as he pulled open the oak and glass door with a brass handle.

Despite the morbid legend, La Pentola remained popular with clerics. When he entered the restaurant, a waiter escorted O'Toole to the back, where four men in their mid-sixties were already seated around a large circular table in the legendary "Stritch room." They were nearly done with their first drink. Three of the men wore Roman collars, and the fourth had on a necktie. They all stood as the cardinal entered. O'Toole went around the table greeting them.

The first man he came to was Jim Kelleher, S.J., a Jesuit from Boston and a boyhood friend of O'Toole's from Salem. "Good to see you, old man," said Kelleher. They had the easy familiarity of friends who shared a long history. They had grown up in the same parish, Immaculate Conception. As kids they had ridden their bikes together down Hawthorne Boulevard, past the Salem Witch Trial memorial to the waterfront.

After grade school, they had taken slightly different paths. Kelleher entered the Jesuits. O'Toole entered the seminary for the Archdiocese of Boston. Both later studied in Rome. Kelleher was now a professor of theology at the notoriously liberal Boston College. Wags said that BC stood for "barely Catholic." Like most Jesuits, Kelleher was an independent thinker who prided himself on his skepticism.

"Still in the church, I see," said O'Toole, slapping Kelleher on the back and pointing to his Roman collar.

"Yeah," said Kelleher, "for at least one more day."

The next man at the table was Joe Dorney, a classmate of O'Toole's from the North American College. They had been students there in the late 1970s, a decade after the Second Vatican Council. It was a turbulent time in seminary life. People were leaving the priesthood en masse, as if somebody had shot a gun and all the pigeons in St. Peter's Square took off at once. One of their classmates put up a sign at the seminary gate: "Last one out, turn off the lights."

Dorney and O'Toole had taken different paths. Dorney was a "workhorse" parish priest, having spent more than thirty-five years in Chicago parishes. O'Toole was a "racehorse" of a Church politician, climbing the ladder in Church offices.

The stresses of parish life in the post–Vatican II period made Dorney more liberal, while the office politics of the Vatican had made O'Toole more conservative. Joe had gone home to Chicago and eventually became pastor of the parish near the University of Chicago, St. Thomas the Apostle. It was a famously contrarian place where the intellectuals from the nearby university debated everything in the parish, which was aptly named for doubting Thomas. It was a congregation full of skeptics.

O'Toole and Dorney were polite, but not chummy. "Good to see you, Joe."

"Likewise, Mike," said Dorney.

Next in order as O'Toole rounded the table was Father Raymond Schoenhoffer, who had a high forehead and thinning hair. Ray had been the brightest student in their class at the North American College, which had a reputation for bright students. He never went to a parish. After ordination he went on for a doctorate at Yale Divinity School and then taught Biblical Studies at the Biblicum, the Vatican's scripture school. The "Bib," as they call it, is full of language geeks and is a school where people tell jokes in ancient Ugaritic or Sanskrit and other people actually get them.

Schoenhoffer was now at the end of his career. He had gone back to Yale, where he was writing about scripture and developing an avant-garde "theology of process." Teaching at a non-Catholic school gave him the freedom to say what he wanted. He said some pretty radical things for a Catholic priest, but he could get away with it, because nobody had the language skills to argue with him.

O'Toole pumped his hand like a politician. "Can we speak in English tonight, Ray?" he asked. "*Optimum*," smirked Schoenhoffer in Latin.

Finally O'Toole came to the man in a necktie, Patrick McMann. O'Toole was actually surprised to see him. He had expected only three friends. But he was glad to see Pat. In seminary, forty years ago, they had been close friends. Pat was an acid-tongued guy from Brooklyn, New York. He was literally wicked smart.

Pat and Mike were ordained in the same year, 1978. Six or seven years after their ordination, a pedophile priest had been assigned as a pastor in the parish where Pat was the assistant. Pat knew the man was a pedophile because, as an altar boy, he had been molested by the priest on a camping trip to Lake George in upstate New York. Pat went to the bishop in Brooklyn to protest the assignment of the pastor to his parish and to tell the bishop of the man's crimes. The bishop, however, did nothing. "It's all in the past," he said.

Pat left the priesthood the next year, bitter. Thirty years later, his anger had not abated. After he left the priesthood, Pat had come out as gay, taken a lover, and moved to California from New York, where he was the administrator of an AIDS clinic in Oakland. Pat had done all right for himself. He was a happy man, except when he talked about the Church.

"Patrick," said the cardinal, "what a surprise."

"Mike," said McMann, "a surprise for me, too."

O'Toole couldn't tell if Patrick was being sarcastic. He noticed that Patrick had a wedding ring on his finger. The cardinal had heard that McMann had married his male partner, a former monk, as soon as gay marriage had been legalized in New York.

McMann explained that he was in Rome for an international AIDS conference. "Glad you're still at it, doing great work," said O'Toole. He was sincere about that. With all of O'Toole's involvement with the church in Africa, he knew of the huge need for AIDS treatments and research.

The five men sat down and ordered a new round of drinks. Having all lived part of their lives in Rome, they knew their Italian wines. "How about three bottles of the new Frascati?" suggested O'Toole.

"Shall we have the carbonara in honor of Cardinal Stritch?" asked McMann slyly. O'Toole winced. This was not the evening to recall the killing of cardinals.

Before the food came, O'Toole gave a rather lengthy and formal blessing. Schoenhoffer interrupted with a critique of his language and theology. McMann kept repeating, "Thank you, Jesus." Finally, Joe Dorney, the only real parish priest, put an end to the foolishness with a definitive "Amen." O'Toole enjoyed their disrespect. Cardinals don't have many friends, and it was good to be around people who could just call him by his name.

After the waiter cleared out of the room, the doors were closed, and the five men settled into serious conversation.

"How are things, Mike?" asked Kelleher.

"Tense," said O'Toole. "You heard the news about Manning." They nodded. Even McMann appeared somber about it.

"Who did it?" asked Schoenhoffer.

"We don't know," said O'Toole, "but things are worse than we thought." He looked around to see who was listening and leaned in toward the round table. The others leaned in a bit in imitation. "I want to put you under the 'seal.' You, too, Patrick. You're still a priest, you know."

McMann grimaced.

Secrecy is the standard operating mode of the Vatican. It is a form of control. Closely held information binds those who share it together into a clan of confidants. But Vatican secrets never held for very long. It was said that a Vatican secret was something that you only told to one person at a time.

"I was with the pope today when Ranieri told him about Manning's murder. It seems that it might be part of a pattern. We now have had six suspicious deaths of cardinals. This one is the most recent and notorious." O'Toole explained about the suspicious deaths of the other five cardinals. There was stunned silence at the table after he finished the grim litany. Joe Dorney was the first to speak.

"Damn it, Mike," said Dorney, "you could be next!" Realizing what he had said, Dorney blushed and added, "I'm just saying. God forbid."

"I've thought of that," said O'Toole. He was more than a little relieved to talk about his fear openly. "But it seems to me that they're only killing papabile. I'm not a likely candidate to be pope, so I'm safe . . . At least from everyone except you liberals." He waved a hand in the direction of Schoenhoffer and McMann. They chuckled.

"The pope wants me to find somebody to investigate this for the Holy See," continued O'Toole. "The local police around the world are looking into their own cases, but the investigations are stovepiped. No one is putting all the pieces together to see if there is a pattern, at least not yet. The Vatican does not really have anybody who could do this investigation. The Swiss guards are mostly decorative. The Vatican police are not detectives. They're really just a security force. The Holy Father asked me to find someone in America who can help with this. We have to move fast. The press will jump on it soon enough, and we need to know what is happening first."

Without thinking, the five men around the table leaned farther inward. They were now literally a conspiracy, a "breathing together." They spoke barely above a whisper.

"Who is the Judas here?" asked Schoenhoffer.

"What do you mean?" asked O'Toole.

"Who hates the Church enough to do this?"

"Who doesn't hate the Church?" sneered McMann. "Seems to me there are legions of candidates. Let's see: gays, feminists, liberals, liberation theologians, poor people, scripture scholars, Protestant evangelicals, or anyone with half a brain in his head." He waved his fork toward the ceiling, signaling the infinite.

Patrick was on a roll. It seemed to O'Toole it was pent-up anger. "After what he said about gay marriage, I would have done Manning in myself, if I'd had any guts."

O'Toole wondered if Patrick was joking. There was a little gasp at the table. McMann realized he had gone too far. Manning's death was too raw.

"I don't mean that literally," he said. "Just that there are millions of people who are angry at the Church, some of them enough to commit crimes. There is no shortage of suspects."

The mood had turned tense, and O'Toole was not accustomed to such blunt talk, especially at meals. Curial cardinals seldom hear any opinion that does not agree with their own. Flattery is the most common form of discourse and deception in hothouse environments like the Vatican. Aides to bishops and cardinals are more courtiers than they are advisors.

"Don't forget the victims of pedophilia," added Kelleher. "No priest from Boston could leave that out. They probably would be prime candidates for rage."

"It is not necessarily a liberal," said Schoenhoffer. "It could be Opus Dei or that other crazy group, the Soldados de Cristo. Judging from my mail, there are more crazies on the right than on the left."

O'Toole bristled a little. "I doubt Opus Dei or the Soldados would threaten cardinals or the pope. They may not like this pope, but they wouldn't kill him. At least publicly they profess respect for the hierarchy. Maybe they would like to see a more conservative Church, but I can't imagine they would turn to murder." There was a moment of silence at the table.

Joe Dorney broke the tension. "Don't start off your investigation by ruling out suspects, Mike," said Dorney. "Besides, what about that Pius X crowd in Switzerland? Holocaust deniers and racists—real nut jobs. I think they could do it. Their founder, what's his name? Lefebvre. He left the Church over Vatican II. Maybe he would off a cardinal or two if he thought it would reset the ecclesiastical calendar to the 1950s. Didn't they say publicly that they don't regard anyone after Pius XII as validly elected? I'd say they are ripe for schism or murder. I've got a few in my parish. They are an endless pain in the ass."

O'Toole clinked his spoons together nervously. He wished he had never raised the topic of dead cardinals.

Just then a waiter entered from the main dining room to take orders for dessert. He left the double doors open behind him. A man dressed in clerics was seated by himself at a corner table near the window at the far corner of the restaurant. He was reading a newspaper. The priest looked up from his paper toward O'Toole. After a moment he made his way across the dining room in the direction of their private room, looking right at O'Toole. The five friends looked nervously at the intruder, who extended his hand toward the cardinal.

"Your Eminence," said the priest in an American accent. "I'm Monsignor Ackerman, Matthew Ackerman, from the Congregation for Bishops. I just wanted to say that it's terrible news about Cardinal Manning. If there is anything I can do, let me know."

"Oh, of course, I remember you," said O'Toole, relaxing a bit. "Thank you for your kindness. I think the most important thing we can do for poor Cardinal Manning is to pray for him."

Outwardly O'Toole was cordial, but inwardly he wondered if the Vatican rumor mill was already churning, gossiping about his new portfolio to investigate the murders of cardinals. Ranieri could have talked already, and the word would be all over the Vatican Secretary of State's office by morning. But, O'Toole wondered, how would a lower-level monsignor at the Congregation for Bishops know what was going on? Maybe he was just being paranoid. But Mike O'Toole was starting to wonder whom he could trust. To the outside, the Vatican is opaque, but inside it is a sieve.

"I may have to call on your services if we need a contact in the Congregation for Bishops," said O'Toole. He wanted to break off the conversation with the monsignor as quickly as possible.

"Just let me know," said the young monsignor. "Good evening, gentlemen." The priest went back to his solitary corner table and his newspaper.

The waiter brought the dessert and coffee and a Roman after-dinner liqueur, Sambuca. Then he closed the doors.

The conversation resumed, but it took a different tack. Talk of conservative factions prompted O'Toole to ask, "Do you think we went too far at Vatican II?"

"What prompted that question?" asked Kelleher.

"Well," said O'Toole, "maybe we let the world set the agenda. We pushed relevancy to its extreme and ended up with irrelevancy. Maybe we need to get back to the eternal. You know, maybe we should run a tighter ship, trying to do less in society. The Holy Father has laid plans for Vatican III to tighten things up."

"That's pure bullshit!" said Schoenhoffer. "The problem is that we didn't go far enough at Vatican II. The whole world, except for maybe the Taliban and a few Islamic crazies, has found a way to include women and accept gays into their societies. We can't even accept divorced people coming to communion unless they get an annulment, which we make impossible.

"Look at my students at Yale," continued the professor. "They think Catholics are nuts on anything to do with sex. They don't hear us at all. They just walk away. Even their parents are ignoring us. Ninety percent of Catholic couples use contraception, and we tell them they are going to hell for it.

"No, Vatican II wasn't the problem. The only problem with Vatican II is that it only did half the job," said Schoenhoffer with finality.

Joe Dorney jumped in. As the only parish priest at the table, he felt he needed to say something for the priests in the trenches. "Maybe priests are killing the cardinals. Priests certainly have plenty of reasons to be angry at the hierarchy, especially their own bishops. Look at our seminary class, Mike. Over half our class has left the priesthood, mostly because of celibacy. We are impaling the Church on a cross of celibacy for no reason. They are talking about a Eucharistic 'desert' now in Ireland. They have nobody to celebrate Mass. Maybe the reason that priests are so angry is that they see their lives going down the drain.

"And don't get me started on the Irish referendum on gay marriage. That was the final nail in the casket. Nobody is paying attention to us."

Dorney continued, "Look at my diocese, Chicago. Like most of the Midwest and Northeast, we are circling the drain. All over the United States we are closing functioning parishes, because we won't ordain married men or women. All around the Midwest, we have priests pastoring two or three parishes. You have 'em in Boston, too, Mike. You've got pastors who have two and three parishes, while you guys over here in Rome say private Masses in your private chapels.

"I know priests who have a funeral every day, five days per week, for years on end. We have married deacons running parishes across town from me, because we have nobody else to run them. Why can't we just ordain the deacons and make them priests? Just because they go to bed with their wives? This is insanity. We are letting the ship run aground for want of a crew. I'll bet ya there are more than a few angry priests who would like to get a gun and shoot a bishop."

Dorney took a breath. He was just getting started. "On top of that, we have all these luxury-loving bishops wasting money on themselves. My cardinal lives in a fourteen-million-dollar mansion, for God's sake. Why does he have to live like a greedy CEO? We have parishes that can't even pay the light bill, and he has a chauffeur! A chauffeur! Can you imagine?"

As he ended his speech, Joe realized he might have gone too far. Once again, there was an awkward silence. Even among old friends, the divisions in the Church cut deep.

Patrick McMann jumped into the void, anxious not to let the fire die out. "I think it all goes back to the Church's attitude toward sex," he said. "Nobody takes the Church seriously anymore about this. The Church is hung up on women and married men because of sex. The Church is hung up on gay people like me. But we don't care. Gay people are just walking away. All my friends have. I don't know a single gay man who goes to church anymore, unless they are priests or monks."

O'Toole flinched a little at the reference to gays in the priesthood.

"The problem is all the women who want to be priests," said O'Toole, trying to make a joke out of it.

"No, Mike," countered Patrick with a smile. "The problem is the priests who want to be women."

Everybody laughed at the turn of phrase. Talking to Patrick was like sparring with Oscar Wilde. But there was a grain of truth in it. Too many priests loved to dress up in fancy vestments. They may not have wanted to be women, but they dressed up as much as Edwardian dowager countesses.

"Back to the crimes," said Dorney. "I know some people in Chicago who could help with your investigation."

"Don't think I want to bring the Chicago police into this, Joe," said O'Toole. "We don't want to rough anybody up."

"Very funny, but I was thinking of someone who could follow the money," Dorney said. "If someone is doing these killings, they probably are not doing it themselves. They are probably hiring somebody. Generally it's best to follow the money trail."

Kelleher injected a thought. "Say, Mike, don't you know Bill Tracy from the Knights of Malta? Remember him? He's a Boston boy. He went to BC High with us. I would think that the former head of the CIA could point you in the right direction."

"Not a bad idea," said O'Toole, making a mental note to call Tracy as soon as he got back to his apartment. Tracy had been head of the CIA for nearly a decade, and he still got national security briefings from the NSA as a courtesy. At least, that was what O'Toole had heard. The cardinal and the former CIA director shared the same cultural DNA, the Boston bond. Perhaps Bill would know somebody who could ferret out secrets and connect the dots. It would be much better to have somebody from completely outside the Church doing the investigation.

"Good idea, Jim. Bill might have a lead."

Sensing an end to the meal, the men got up and began the round of good-byes. Dorney asked, "Who wants to walk over to Piazza Navonna? We could get a *tartuffo* at Tre Scalini . . . "

"No, thanks," said O'Toole. "I'm a moving target tonight. I wouldn't want to put your lives in danger. Besides, at this time of evening Navonna is a little too crowded for me."

O'Toole insisted on paying the bill.

On the way out the door, they passed two more priests deep in conversation at a table near the window. O'Toole and company hadn't noticed them before. One of the priests, a gaunt and rather severe-looking fellow, stood up and bowed slightly toward O'Toole in that odd half bow that Italian professionals accord to each other. O'Toole bowed slightly in return. "*Eminenza,*" they said stiffly to each other, almost simultaneously.

Once outside, Kelleher asked, "Who was that, Mike? Another cardinal?"

"Yeah," said O'Toole, "Alejandro Mendoza from Mexico. He is a Soldado de Cristo."

"Really?" said Kelleher. "I hear he's off the charts on the conservative scale. Isn't he the guy who likes to parade around in the Capa Magna?"

Kelleher was referring to the twenty-foot-long red silk cape that cardinals had once worn when riding in procession on horseback. The cape was designed to cover the horse's rear end.

"You know," said Kelleher, "at least it is still serving the original purpose—covering the horse's ass."

O'Toole laughed. "Jimmy, you always did cut through the crap. Don't worry, my boy, Mendoza and I are not close. We run in different circles."

"Good," said Kelleher. "I wouldn't want you hanging out with his kind." Then Kelleher added, smiling, "Before you go walking anywhere tomorrow, Mike, put on your Kevlar vest."

"You know me, Jimmy boy," answered O'Toole. "Faster than a speeding bullet."

"You haven't run that fast in a long time," said Kelleher. He added, "See you next time you're in Boston, Mike. Take care of yourself."

"Nice being with you guys," said O'Toole. They hugged and waved good-bye. O'Toole walked briskly away from the other four, crossing the Tiber River on the Ponte Sant'Angelo in the direction of the Vatican. The remaining four men strolled off toward Piazza Navonna in search of gelato.

Rome is lovely after dark, especially in May. The streetlights had come on while they were at dinner. They gave the city a softer glow. Rome is a city with layers of mystery, never fully revealed, especially at night. The murky waters of the Tiber River reflected the street lamps on the Ponte Sant'Angelo. A cool breeze came off the water.

O'Toole didn't notice Rome's charms tonight. He had to hurry home to call Washington, DC.

4

THE PHONE CALL

O'TOOLE LEFT THE RESTAURANT JUST AFTER 11:00 P.M. IT was just after 5:00 p.m. in Washington.

The streets near the Vatican were deserted except for a few tourists. The cardinal walked briskly, anxious to get home and catch Tracy before the dinner hour in Washington. As a former CIA director, William Tracy was much in demand on the social circuit.

When the cardinal reached his apartment, he went directly to his study. The nuns had long since gone to bed in their quarters one floor above. He closed the door to his study and locked it. Then he flipped through his Rolodex for Bill Tracy's telephone number.

Political life in the Church is like political life everywhere. It is all about personal connections and the friend network. O'Toole was a Bostonian. Even though he had spent many years in Rome, he kept his Boston connections current with frequent calls and visits home. He always hoped that one day he might get the nod to be archbishop of his hometown.

Tracy was an old friend from Boston College High School alumni gatherings. O'Toole's contact with Tracy had proven useful over the years.

Bill Tracy was what Bostonians call a "triple Eagle," an allusion to Boston College's mascot. He had gone to Boston College High School,

Boston College, and Boston College Law School. As a consequence, he was hardwired to Boston, the Catholic Church, and the Jesuits. Like Boston Catholics of his youth, Tracy was ethnically and religiously clannish and deeply conservative. To him that meant you took care of your own first.

O'Toole found Tracy's number, a 202 area code for Washington. He picked up the phone and entered 001, smiling at the thought that Italians always made much of the fact that the international exchange for the United States was "uno," a measure of American prestige.

*　*　*

Across the Atlantic, the phone rang in William Tracy's house on Foxhall Road in Washington, DC. The former CIA director was just coming in from a game of tennis on the court in his secluded backyard. His housekeeper met him in the hallway. "There is a call from Rome," she said. "It's Cardinal O'Toole from the Vatican. He says it's urgent."

"I'll take it in my study," said Tracy. He bounded up the circular stairs to his private quarters and closed the door. Like O'Toole, he was conscious of privacy. He knew firsthand how to invade people's privacy, and he was protective of his own.

He picked up the phone. As a lifelong Catholic and Knight of Malta, Tracy knew the niceties of ecclesiastical address.

"Your Eminence," he said deferentially. "To what do I owe the pleasure of your call?"

O'Toole got right to the point. Cardinals are seldom deferential to anyone else.

"Bill, I've got a serious problem. I hope I can count on your help. You already know about what happened to Cardinal Manning."

"Yes," said Tracy. "It's all over the news."

"Well, there is more to it than just Manning's murder," said O'Toole. "We have reason to believe there is a pattern here. Someone is killing off cardinals."

"Yes," said Tracy. "I've read about the other deaths in the papers. They even talked about it as part of my security briefing last month. You might be in danger, Mike. I suggested to the regional Master of the Knights that he might want to look into this. Though I'm not sure what we could do, except give moral support."

"That would be a good idea, Bill," said O'Toole. "But we need something more than moral support." O'Toole pronounced idea in the Boston way, as "idear." Whenever he talked with someone from back home, he fell back into his North Shore accent. It was a sign of intimacy and trust.

"Listen, Bill. The pope asked me to do something. The local police are focused on their own investigations, but to our knowledge nobody is communicating with anybody else on this. What do you guys call it in government, stovepiping? We need someone to connect the dots and see if there is a conspiracy."

"Familiar story," said Tracy. "Our intelligence agencies still don't communicate with each other, even after 9/11. I was talking to the DIA about this just this morning."

O'Toole cut him off. He didn't have time for bureaucratic war stories.

"Bill, I need your help now. Give me the name of somebody we can trust. Somebody who can carry out an investigation on behalf of the Holy See. We have our own jurisdiction on this. All cardinals have dual citizenship under international law.

"We have our own police powers. We need someone who knows law enforcement and the Church. Someone we could deputize immediately to start an investigation."

"I assume you want a Catholic," said Tracy.

"Helpful, but not essential," said O'Toole. "The most important things, besides knowledge, are speed and secrecy. We need to get on this now. We are not on the usual Vatican timetable. *Domani* is not good enough. Also, it would be nice if our Sherlock Holmes were a practicing Catholic. A Knight of Malta would be even better. It would make it easier to sell him to the folks here in Rome. But we need somebody who is not afraid to chase down all the dark alleys. I want someone who is more cop than choirboy."

"Nobody springs to mind immediately," said Tracy. "I assume you would need to do a background check."

"Not much time. We'll trust you on this," said O'Toole.

"How 'bout somebody from our own circle, then?" said Tracy. When threatened, Boston Irishmen revert to their clan identity. "Somebody from back home."

"That would be fine," said O'Toole. "Who?"

"What about Nate Condon? Remember his dad? Brendan, a fireman, from Charlestown. Brendan was a close friend of that fireman, Marty Fitzpatrick. I think you buried Marty's son at St. Catherine's years ago. Remember? That was the kid who killed himself because he was molested by a priest."

"Oh, yeah," said O'Toole. "Didn't Brendan leave the Church over that?" The cardinal remembered the incident well. It was front-page news in Boston, and one of the most embarrassing moments in the history of the Church in New England. He could hardly forget that terrible incident.

Tracy continued, "Anyway, Brendan's son Nate was an FBI agent for a while. He was also a US attorney in Manhattan. Made quite a name for himself prosecuting mob cases. Now I think he is with Baker and Black in New York, a real WASP's nest of a New York law firm. Probably making piles of money."

Tracy paused for a second.

O'Toole asked, "Can the Church trust him? Is he as angry at the Church as his father was? I don't need some angry Catholic working out their own vendetta."

"I think you can trust him," said Tracy. "After all, Nate is a Knight of Malta, so he must still be a Catholic. I saw him at his installation in the knights at the Waldorf last year. You have to be a practicing Catholic to be a knight.

"I don't think he has forgotten his Charlestown roots. Still one of us,

I would guess, Mike." The cardinal noted the change to the familiar in Tracy's tone. He knew what "one of us" meant. Still Boston Irish.

"OK," said O'Toole warily. "Let's ask him if he is interested in helping us. You call him, since he saw you recently. Tell him it is a personal favor to the pope."

"Do you want to talk to him on the phone?" asked Tracy.

"We probably should meet face-to-face." The cardinal paused, remembering he had to fly to Washington at the end of the week.

"Listen, Bill, are you going to that Papal Foundation reception at the Nunciature on Friday?"

"Yeah," said Tracy. "I go every year. It's how I'm working off my purgatory."

"Good, I'll be there too. I'm representing the foundation. Then I'll certainly go up to New York for Manning's funeral. Maybe we could arrange to talk with Condon at the Nunciature in DC. It will be less of a circus than the funeral. Ask him if he can hop a train and come down to meet us. I'll get him on the guest list."

"OK, Your Eminence. I'll get the ball rolling. See you on Friday."

"Good, Bill. See you then. Ciao."

When Tracy hung up the phone, he took a deep breath. Even after a life as a government spook, Church intrigue still seemed more exotic to him.

Maybe it was because he was raised in the Catholic crucible of Boston. People his age still respected the Church. Tracy's five children had walked away from the Church. Their reaction to their father's religiosity was a mixture of derision and disdain, especially after the pedophilia scandals. Tracy's kids could not see how anybody could take a bunch of lard-assed clerics seriously.

But the skepticism of Tracy's children, who were probably about Nate Condon's age, ran deeper than disgust over scandal. They also thought of religion as a grand delusion. They didn't even think religion was worth arguing about with their father. It was just an anachronism in the old man.

After he hung up the phone, Tracy walked down the hall to the master bedroom. His house, a grand old Tudor-style home built in the 1930s, had once belonged to Lyndon Johnson, when he was majority leader of the Senate. Lady Bird's money had bought it.

In the bedroom suite, Tracy's wife, Peggy, was getting dressed for their evening at the Kennedy Center. "What did the cardinal want?" she asked.

Ordinarily, Peggy never asked her husband about business, but she was curious about a call from the Vatican. Even in the house of a CIA director, the servants talked. The housekeeper had told her that Cardinal O'Toole was on the phone.

"Sorry, can't talk about it just yet," said Bill. He added, "But it's serious."

He went into the dressing room to strip for his shower. "Say, listen," he called out, changing his tone a bit. "Do you remember Nate Condon from Boston? He became a Knight of Malta last year. We met him at that dinner at the Waldorf. What was his wife's name?"

"Brigid," said Peggy. "She's from Long Island. Huntington, I think. Or maybe Manhasset. They have an apartment on Park Avenue, so there must be some money in the family somewhere."

"Do you know how to get in touch with them?" asked Bill. "I need to ask a favor."

Peggy was intrigued to be included in a mystery. "I think I have their phone number in my cell. I had to call Brigid for the Dames meeting this year. She didn't seem very enthusiastic about it."

Peggy was proud to be a leader in the Dames of Malta, the female auxiliary of the knights. Her generation thought it made sense for women to be an "auxiliary" to their men. But women of Brigid Condon's generation could not take that role seriously. To them it seemed absurd to join an organization in which they were expected to stand around while men did all the talking.

"I'll call them when I get out of the shower," said Bill. After a couple of minutes of hot water and soap, Bill toweled off and dressed in his tux.

Peggy came in with a glass of Woodford Reserve on the rocks. He had one every evening before dinner. She handed him a little slip of paper with the Condons' home number.

"Thanks," said Bill.

Even though she was curious, Peggy did not hang around. A lifetime as the wife of a spy taught her there were many things she could not know.

Tracy called the Condons' apartment. Brigid answered. "This is Bill Tracy. I met you last year at the Knights of Malta dinner at the Waldorf, in New York."

"Oh, yes, Mr. Tracy," said Brigid. "I remember. How could I forget meeting the former director of the CIA? What can I do for you?"

"I need to speak to your husband, Nathaniel. Could you have him call me at this number?"

"You can speak to him right now," said Brigid. "He's right here on the other end of the couch. We're watching the news." She handed the phone to Nate.

Tracy dived right in. "Nate, this is Bill Tracy. You know about the Cardinal Manning killing, of course."

"Know about it?" said Nate. "I was there! I was standing right beside Sullivan's casket. It was horrible. Complete pandemonium. Once the police locked down the cathedral, everyone inside was trapped for hours. We got interviewed by the police at least twice."

No time for the whole play-by-play, Tracy pressed on.

"Manning's death may not be an isolated case," said Bill. "There are several other cardinals dead in the past year, under suspicious circumstances. The Vatican wants to see if the deaths are related. They want to know the who and the why. Are you interested in some international police work?"

"Whew, I don't know," said Nate, a little taken aback by the question. "I've got a lot on my plate here at work."

"Listen," said Tracy. "Cardinal Michael O'Toole is coming over from Rome for a reception in Washington on Friday. The pope wants the Vatican to have its own investigation. He asked O'Toole to make it happen.

I suggested that you lead it. Can you come down to meet with the cardinal on Friday evening?"

"What could I do that the police can't?" asked Nate.

"Connect the dots," said Tracy. "The Church needs to know if there is some kind of conspiracy. Are you interested?"

"I might be," said Nate. "I'd have to talk to Brigid. When would I start?"

"Friday," said Tracy. "If the cardinal approves, you'd go to Rome right away. Are you game?"

Nate looked over at his wife, wondering how he'd break the news to her. "Yes," said Nate, intrigued by the possibility of being a sleuth for the Vatican. "I'll hear the cardinal out, but I'll have a lot of rearranging to do."

Tracy jumped in and took that as a yes. "Good," he said. "I'll see you Friday." He added, "Not a word to anyone except the missus. The code of *omerta* applies. Understand?"

Tracy used the Italian word for a conspiracy of silence. Nate caught the allusion to the Italian mob.

"I understand," he said.

"Great," said Tracy. "Meet me at the Papal Nuncio's on Mass Ave. You know where it is?"

"Sure," said Nate. "I used to bike by it when I was a law student at Georgetown. If I remember correctly, it's just across from the vice president's house, near the British Embassy."

"Right," said Tracy. "Bring a tux. There is a reception at the Nunciature. Your wife might like to come along. It will be a good cover to have her there. I'll put you both on the guest list."

Nate thought it odd that Brigid would be cover for him. Brigid did not rearrange her schedule for his social engagements. It was just luck that her work with the Federal Reserve was taking her to Washington that week.

"We can find a quiet corner there at the Nunciature to huddle with Cardinal O'Toole."

When they rang off, Tracy hustled downstairs to his car parked in the circular drive in front of the house. Peggy was already down at the front door, trying to coax their two yapping Bichons back into the house.

Their Lincoln headed down leafy Foxhall Road, toward the Kennedy Center, for a performance of *Rigoletto*. It was Bill Tracy's favorite opera, full of intrigue and sudden death. It was just the sort of thing to entertain the former head of the CIA.

5

THE NUNCIATURE ENCOUNTER

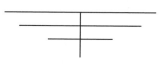

NATE AND BRIGID CLIMBED INTO A CAB UNDER THE CAN-
opy at the Four Seasons Hotel in Georgetown. It was only a ten-minute
ride to the Vatican Embassy, where they would meet up with the Tracys.

Superficially, the Condons and the Tracys were identical couples.
Both were Irish Catholic. Both were educated in the Catholic Ivies—
Boston College, Holy Cross, Georgetown, and Fordham. Both had
money. Both were confident and attractive.

The men were both secretive and clannish. For them, religion was
part of being in "the club." They played by the rules and enjoyed the
perks. They had never challenged the Church much, and it returned the
favor by not challenging them.

The women, however, were different. The generation that separated
them also defined them.

Peggy Tracy was raised on St. Paul's letter to the Ephesians, "Wives
be subordinate to your husbands." She saw herself playing a supporting
role to Bill. Advancing his career was her work, too.

Brigid Condon, on the other hand, was her own woman. She was
attractive, like Peggy, exuding a tennis-club sort of athleticism. Her natural beauty was complemented by an easy, charming smile.

But unlike Peggy, she was not content to be the second sex. Brigid had read *The Feminine Mystique* in Women's Studies in college. Her favorite women authors were more contemporary, Nora Ephron and Anne Tyler. Like Hillary and Bill Clinton, Brigid and Nate Condon had gone to law school together. Again like Hillary, Brigid was the better student. She was the note editor on the law review at Georgetown. She outranked Nate and edited his articles for the review. In professional life and achievement, Brigid was not the sidecar on Nate's motorcycle.

The Catholic Church was a comfort to Peggy Tracy. To Brigid it was more of a challenge, or perhaps an obstacle. Brigid admired the few nuns who had taught her and the few female saints she knew about, but she chafed against the medieval patriarchy of the Church. For women like Brigid, the Church was irrelevant and insulting.

Nowhere else in Brigid's world were women so completely excluded from any significant discussion or decision-making. Nowhere else were they treated as unworthy. To her generation, the Catholic Church seemed like an old boys' club, with emphasis on the old. Independent nuns were censured. Women theologians were silenced. Women's experience—especially with regard to the pelvic issues like birth control, sex, and abortion—was completely discounted.

Brigid and her friends had no desire to be ordained priests, but they resented that women could not be. Evidently the Church thought menstrual blood had rendered them ritually impure, like some Old Testament taboo.

So, while Peggy Tracy was thrilled to be going to the Nunciature, Brigid Condon wasn't.

*   *   *

The ten-minute ride from Georgetown to the Nunciature gave Nate a chance to fill Brigid in on the reason for their attendance at the reception. Since they had come down to Washington on separate trains, they had not had a chance to discuss the evening.

"Officially, it is a fund-raiser for the Papal Foundation," said Nate. "It raises money for the pope's charities. The Vatican has a party every year in the States to prime the money pump."

"Like the pope needs money!" said Brigid.

"Don't start," said Nate. "The Church is one of the largest private charities in the world. They need money."

"Of course they are," said Brigid. "But they need to do a little charity to make themselves look good."

"That's pretty cynical," said Nate.

"Maybe," said Brigid, "but it seems like the sale of a few museum artifacts would raise more money than a cocktail party."

The lawyer in Brigid was warming to the debate. "I don't see the cardinals and bishops in Port au Prince feeding the poor. They leave that for the nuns."

Nate could see that rebuttal would do no good. He glanced at the rearview mirror to see if the driver was paying attention to their conversation. He looked bored, so Nate figured he could tell Brigid a little more about the real reason for their trip.

"Actually, we are here tonight to meet Cardinal O'Toole. He is the top American in the Vatican. That's the guy Tracy told me about on the phone." Nate lowered his voice and added, "He wants to talk to me about investigating Cardinal Manning's death."

Nate looked at the driver again nervously. "Everybody is tense after what happened this week." His voice trailed off.

"Are the CIA and the Vatican working together?" Brigid whispered, half-serious and half-sarcastic.

The cab pulled into the circular drive in front of the Vatican Embassy. Paying the driver allowed Nate to suspend the conversation before it got testy. They climbed out of the air-conditioned car into a muggy Washington evening.

Brigid looked up at the gold and white Vatican flag flying over the entrance with its three-tiered tiara of the popes and the crossed keys of the See of Peter, symbols of the power to bind and loose sins in the name of Christ.

"Nice place they have here," said Brigid.

It was nice. The Vatican's embassy is gray stone in the Palladian style. It is part of a line of vaguely similar gray stone embassies along one side of Massachusetts Avenue, Washington's Embassy Row.

Directly across the street is the park-like campus of the Naval Observatory, with two huge old anchors at the entrance. On its grounds is the official residence of the vice president of the United States. Uniformed Secret Service police cars are always parked near the vice president's gate. Following the Manning assassination, there was heightened security on Massachusetts Avenue. Police were everywhere.

Officially, the Vatican Embassy is called the Apostolic Nunciature, a corruption of the Old Italian word *nuntius*, or messenger. The Palladian mansion in front of Brigid and Nate was part of a grand illusion, sort of like a Hollywood set. The Vatican's pretensions to being a country are all a façade. Nation-state status is the last echo of the Papal States that ruled most of Italy for more than 1,000 years.

The tiny fortress of the Vatican, about the size of a golf course, would not exist as a country at all if not for Benito Mussolini. In 1929, the Italian fascist dictator needed to make peace with the Catholic Church in order to consolidate his grip on Italy. The Lateran Concordat was signed in the Lateran Palace, the onetime home of popes and Roman emperors. Mussolini recognized the postage-stamp sovereign country. In exchange, the Church dropped its territorial claims to Italy.

The hierarchy loves their little Potemkin village. It makes them princes and lords. It allows bishops to pose as ambassadors among the great nations. They not only render unto Caesar, they have become Caesar, or at least a little Caesar.

Brigid and Nate knew little of this history as they walked up the three steps to the front door of the Nunciature. Most American Catholics don't realize that the United States and the Vatican have had a rocky relationship over the years.

For most of its history, the United States had no official relations with the Holy See. The nineteenth-century Know-Nothing Party raged and rioted against papist immigrants. To them, the United States was a Protestant country.

It was only in 1984 that Ronald Reagan established diplomatic relations with the Vatican. Reagan wanted the Church's help in fighting communism. He also wanted the Church to rein in liberal bishops. John Paul II wanted the same things.

As Nate and Brigid stood on the steps, waiting for the door to open, they saw an elderly man on the sidewalk in front of the embassy. He was wearing a sandwich board sign and was part of a little knot of demonstrators.

One side of his sandwich board said, "The Church lies! Stop child abuse." On the other side was a picture of a young boy with the caption "I was abused by a priest."

The old man had been keeping vigil there in front of the Nunciature for years. He claimed he was molested by a priest when he was a boy at a summer camp in Wisconsin. He wanted an apology and an admission of guilt from the Church. He got neither. So, he came back every day to demonstrate.

"That man has been out there forever," said Brigid. "I remember him from when we were in law school."

"I think he is a fixture here," said Nate.

"Let's go over and talk to him," said Brigid.

Nate looked at her quizzically. "Dear, I make it my policy not to talk to lunatics in sandwich boards when I'm in black tie," said Nate rather condescendingly. "I find it only leads to trouble."

"Oh, the Church of hard hearts," said Brigid. "That's why people have to wear sandwich boards. Nobody will talk to them."

The main door of the embassy opened to reveal the smiling face of an Italian American monsignor, Dominic Petrini. He had the fleshy look of a man who regularly went to embassy parties. His black clerical cassock was stretched tight over him. Around his belly was a sash called a fascia. The red piping around the edges of his cassock may have looked like a bishop's, but the knowledgeable knew he was not so important. He was only a minor lordship, a monsignor.

Petrini was the kind of priest that Brigid knew from her childhood in a big Italian American parish on Long Island. He was a politician in a collar. His hands were smooth—made for "chalices, not callouses." He had a nice smile.

He claimed to be a follower of Jesus, but his real religion was epicureanism. He loved the sensual pleasures, especially food. He knew every fine restaurant in Washington. If he hadn't been a priest, he might have been a chef on a celebrity cooking show.

Brigid took an instant dislike to him. Nate was indifferent.

"Good evening," said Petrini, beaming at the attractive couple in evening dress. "Welcome to the Nunciature. The reception is at the top of the staircase, in the grand *aula*." He used the Italian word for a large room, an insider's pretension.

"I am Nathaniel Condon. This is my wife, Brigid. Have you seen Director Tracy and his wife? We are supposed to meet them and Cardinal O'Toole here."

Petrini clapped his hand to his chest dramatically, five lily-white fingers touching his breastbone. "Oh, His Eminence," he said gushingly, his shoulders rising. "Are you meeting him here? Let me escort you."

Brigid sensed that Petrini was curious about this attractive couple. He wanted to know what business they might have with Cardinal O'Toole. She also suspected that the monsignor made it his habit to attach himself to beautiful and powerful people, the better to advance his ecclesiastical career.

The three of them headed up the red-carpeted circular staircase. Along the wall to their left were portraits of the past *nuncios*, or apostolic delegates.

At the top of the stairs, Brigid stopped to look at a portrait of a strikingly handsome cleric.

"Who is that?" she asked.

"Oh," said Petrini, "that is Monsignor Francisco Satolli, our first apostolic delegate. He was from my hometown of Lucca in Tuscany."

Petrini did not mention that Satolli bore an uncanny resemblance to Pope Leo XIII. Rumor had it that he was the pope's son. In any case, he certainly was a favorite of Leo XIII, and that was enough to make him the first Apostolic Delegate to the United States, in 1892. Nate and Brigid passed the portrait and turned toward the reception room. The Tracys were waiting for them near the door.

"Brigid," said Tracy, "you look ravishing. The Latin ambassadors' wives will be envious." That sort of flattery was required at these receptions, and Tracy was good at it.

"Director Tracy," said Nate, "nice to see you again. Mrs. Tracy, you look lovely." Peggy nodded appreciatively. Lovely was the sort of word reserved for older women. No longer ravishing, they had to content themselves with lovely.

The two couples entered the reception room. In the receiving line near the windows, they saw four men who were dressed more dramatically than any of the women in the room, no matter how lovely or ravishing. Four cardinals in red watered silk were greeting the guests. It's hard to outdress a cardinal.

"Which one is O'Toole?" asked Nate.

"The last one," said Tracy, leading the way to the receiving line.

Brigid, still escorted by Monsignor Petrini, was the last in line of their foursome. It gave her the opportunity to ask Petrini questions.

"Who is the first one?" Brigid whispered to Petrini.

"Cardinal William Kelly, Archbishop of Washington," Petrini answered.

"How did he get to be archbishop?" asked Brigid.

"He was secretary to the cardinal in Philadelphia," said Petrini.

"Who is the next one in line?" Brigid whispered.

"That's Cardinal Lawrence Williams of Baltimore. He was secretary to the former Archbishop of Washington."

Brigid raised her eyebrows.

"Who's the next one?" she asked. "And who was he secretary to?"

"That's Cardinal Baumgartner. He's retired. He was secretary to the Bishop of Dallas. Then they made him a cardinal."

Brigid smirked.

"What about the last one?" she asked, nodding her head toward O'Toole.

"That's Cardinal O'Toole, the Prefect of the Congregation for the Evangelization of Peoples."

"How did he get to be a cardinal?" Brigid was enjoying the litany.

"Again, a secretary to a cardinal," said Petrini. "He worked for the cardinal who was Secretary of State."

"There is one guy who is not in red. Who is that one?" asked Brigid.

"The Nuncio, Archbishop Lorenzo Cappelletti," breathed Petrini. Then, without waiting for her to ask, he added, "He was secretary to several archbishops before they made him nuncio to the United States. He will no doubt be a cardinal one day."

"Are all bishops and cardinals secretaries to bishops first?" asked Brigid innocently.

"Well, yes," said Monsignor Petrini. "That is pretty much how it works. First a secretary, then a bishop."

"Not a parish priest?" asked Brigid.

"Oh, no," said Petrini with mock horror. "We don't want our bishops contaminated by too much contact with the sheep." Brigid studied the monsignor's expression, but she could not tell if he was serious or not.

The Tracys and the Condons made their way down the receiving line. When Tracy came to O'Toole, he said, "Your Eminence, this is the man I told you about, Nate Condon. I'm sure you remember his dad, Brendan, from the Boston Fire Department. Their family lived in St. Catherine's in Charlestown. This is Nate's wife, Brigid. And you remember my wife, Peggy."

"Eminence," said Nate, with a slight bow. "It's a pleasure to see you again. The last time I saw you was years ago. I was an altar boy at the funeral of Tommy Fitzpatrick."

"Oh, yes," said O'Toole, "I remember. That young man's death was a terrible tragedy. He committed suicide, as I remember."

"He was the son of my father's best friend," said Nate. Nothing bonds two Irishmen like a shared memory of death.

O'Toole shook hands and exchanged the obligatory pleasantries with the wives, then he leaned in close and said to Bill and Nate, "We'll meet in the visiting parlor over there, as soon as I'm done here with the grip-and-grin." He nodded his head toward a set of double doors at the end of the reception room.

"OK," said Tracy. The foursome moved on, passing through the doors to a small sitting room. It was decorated with the formality of a funeral parlor, with four leather chairs arranged around a large coffee table of inlaid wood.

Monsignor Petrini stayed with them. The priest hailed a passing waiter, and they each accepted a wine glass filled with pinot grigio. They took their seats. Petrini stood nearby, like a valet in waiting.

After a few minutes, O'Toole entered the room in a rustle of silk. They all stood. It was immediately apparent that there were not enough chairs for the two couples and the cardinal.

Still standing, O'Toole said to the wives, "Would you ladies please excuse us?"

"Yes, of course," said Peggy Tracy immediately. She was used to being excluded. But Brigid looked a little stunned and said with a touch of sarcasm, "We probably won't understand anyway."

Nate glared at her. The ladies went back to the reception room, followed by Petrini, who closed the doors.

When they were in the next room, Brigid said, "Isn't it just like the Church? When there is something serious to discuss, the women are excused."

"Oh, well," said Peggy, "I'd rather talk to Father Murphy from the Soldados. He has such a charming Irish brogue. He's over there by the buffet table. Come on, I'll introduce you. I went on a retreat with him last year. He was brilliant."

Peggy took Brigid by the arm and led her off across the reception room to speak to a dark-haired young Irish priest in a Roman collar so stiff it looked like it would choke him.

* * *

Back in the sitting room, O'Toole wasted no time with small talk. He pulled the three men into a seated huddle around the coffee table.

"Mr. Condon," said the cardinal, "the Church is in crisis and needs a favor. Someone appears to be killing cardinals. We have six dead all around the globe, counting Cardinal Manning earlier this week. We are not sure they have all been murdered, but they certainly all died under surprising circumstances. I have a special interest in this, since I could be next." He chuckled nervously at his macabre admission.

"Perhaps someone is trying to narrow the choices for the next pope. Or, perhaps, some group has a vendetta against the Church. We just don't know. But we need to."

O'Toole paused and took a deep breath. "By custom, Vatican officials are not supposed to speak of the Holy Father's death, but the laws of nature tell us that it won't be long until a new man is chosen. Maybe someone is trying to position themselves for the next conclave.

"It's only a matter of time until the police around the world realize these deaths might be connected. If there is some sort of conspiracy, we need to know before it gets into the press and the courts."

Like any good salesman, O'Toole moved quickly to the close. Nate knew it was coming. "Are you interested in helping the Church find out who did it?"

Nate thought it clever the way the cardinal phrased his question. O'Toole knew that a Knight of Malta could say no to an individual but would have a hard time saying no to the Church.

Nate paused for only a moment. This was a unique case and a once-in-a-lifetime opportunity. It didn't even occur to him to consult Brigid.

He answered immediately, "Of course, Your Eminence. I'm at your disposal."

O'Toole turned to Tracy. Nate was struck at how much the cardinal and the spy looked alike. They were both flush-faced Boston Irishmen. Their build could be seen in any bar in Southie or police precinct in Boston. "Bill has already done a little research on possible suspects. He can fill you in, so you can start immediately."

Tracy nodded. "I've used a few of my contacts to put together a background dossier. Maybe we could meet tomorrow to go over what we know so far."

O'Toole turned back to Nate. "And maybe some of your friends at the FBI could help us as well. We need all the help we can get."

Nate nodded.

"This will be your full-time job for now," said Tracy to Nate. "I can help you with intelligence sources, but this will be your investigation. Take it where it leads. Could be as tough as going after the mob." Then Tracy added, "Maybe it actually is going after the mob. But you've done it before."

Nate smiled at the reference to his past triumphs in New York. Certainly Manning's murder was executed with the precision of a mob hit.

"I have clients, of course," said Nate. "I'll have to give them notice."

"Short notice," said Tracy. "I will square it with your partners. We can arrange leave for you. I can tell them this involves national security. Any group powerful enough to kill six cardinals is probably a group the US government should know about.

"You can stay in touch with your clients by phone, but you have to get going on this now." Tracy was pushing hard. Nate assumed that Bill was just anxious to be a loyal son of the Church. Unlike Nate, Bill was of the generation that gave nearly blind obedience.

A side door, leading to a hallway, opened, and Monsignor Petrini entered the sitting room. He cleared his throat. "It's time for the prayer service for Cardinal Manning," he said.

O'Toole acknowledged the monsignor with a quick nod and then leaned in for his close. "So, gentlemen, we're in agreement?" The two Irishmen nodded. Then the cardinal stood and headed for the large reception room, followed by Condon and Tracy.

As they entered the reception, the ladies broke off their conversation with Father Murphy and rejoined their husbands.

The cardinal joined the other clerics by a little podium set up at one end of the room. The Tracys and the Condons joined a large semicircle of laypeople standing behind the clerics. Nate stood on the fringe. He liked to observe from the rear.

The nuncio, Archbishop Cappelletti, came to the microphone, tapped it twice, and cleared his throat.

"As you know, we have suffered a terrible loss this past week in the Church. We are grieved for the loss of our dear brother, Cardinal Manning, from New York." He spoke in a heavy Italian accent. His voice trembled in a moment of genuine sorrow. "We thought we should remember him this evening with a brief prayer for the repose of his soul."

The nuncio made the sign of the cross and began to pray, quoting from St. Paul:

> *Praise be the God and father*
> *Our Lord Jesus Christ,*
> *the father of all mercy and the God*
> *of all consolation.*

Just as the archbishop said the word "consolation," a woman let out a piercing scream, like Una O'Connor in one of those old Frankenstein movies. The guests in the reception room turned toward the scream. One of the nuns who worked at the Nunciature was standing near the windows that faced out onto Massachusetts Avenue. She pointed out the window, screaming, "*O Dio, O Dio.*"

*   *   *

People rushed to the windows. Brigid got there before Nate. She could see thick black smoke and flames rising. The guests let out a collective gasp.

Below, on the sidewalk, the man with the sandwich board was on fire. He must have doused himself with gasoline from a large bottle that stood nearby. He was screaming and running. Then he threw himself on the ground, still burning, trying to extinguish the flames by rolling on the concrete.

He was shouting something, but his words were not clear. Finally, they were just screams of agony.

The police came running from across the street, where they were stationed at the vice president's house. Two EMTs from the ambulance stationed at the gate of the residence came running with a fire extinguisher.

They sprayed him with foam. They ran back to the ambulance and got water-gel fire blankets to extinguish the flames and relieve the pain. But the man was already charred flesh. Looking on from the windows, the Nunciature guests were paralyzed in horror.

Once the man was rolled up in the blanket, the EMTs lifted him onto a gurney. As they moved him, the man was still screaming. Then the screaming stopped. They must have given him some kind of painkiller.

Even though there were a dozen priests and another dozen bishops and cardinals, not one of them ran out to anoint the man and give the last rites. That mundane duty, second nature to parish priests, was not the sort of thing that Vatican diplomats and cardinals were prepared to administer. They didn't even know how.

The memorial service for Cardinal Manning was now completely forgotten. The guests at the Nunciature stood at the window in silence, transfixed by the horror below.

Once the ambulance pulled away, the police rushed into the embassy and up the stairs. "Everybody, please leave quickly!" they ordered.

They ushered the cardinal and archbishops into an interior room for protection. After the Manning assassination, they could take no chances.

The Condons and the Tracys were herded down the stairs along with the other guests. They exited the embassy through the back doors and into formal gardens. Then they all filtered out onto 34th Street.

As they spilled onto the street, Nate asked Tracy, "Do you think this is connected to the cardinal's death?"

"Who knows?" said Tracy. "I'll try to find out."

Traffic had come to a halt all around the embassy, as they cordoned off the crime scene, and police arrived from all directions.

"Nothing is moving around here," said Nate to Brigid. "We'd better walk up to Wisconsin Avenue to get a taxi."

The four of them walked up 34th Street to Fulton and cut over to Wisconsin. Just as the Tracys climbed into a cab, Bill looked back at Nate.

"I have a meeting at Georgetown University tomorrow morning. Let's meet at Milano's for lunch. I'll bring what I have so far. Meet me at noon."

"Fine," said Nate.

Tracy slammed the taxi door.

Brigid and Nate stood in stunned silence on the street corner.

6

MILANO'S

ON SATURDAY MORNING THE *WASHINGTON POST* WAS delivered to the Condons' room at the Four Seasons. The front page had a picture of the burned man from the Nunciature, wrapped in a gel blanket and being loaded into an ambulance. The paper said that he had died at the hospital. No family was present, but a priest from the nearby parish of St. Stephen's was with him, the paper reported. Despite his years of protest, he still got the last rites. The story noted speculations that there may have been a connection between the self-immolation and Manning's assassination, but offered no evidence.

Nate scanned the paper briefly, then tucked it into his briefcase and left the hotel. It was only a twenty-minute walk through leafy Georgetown to Milano's, where he planned to meet Tracy. It was a perfect May morning, bright, clear, and pleasantly warm.

When Nate and Brigid were law students in Washington, they might have gone for the walk together, but now their jobs kept them apart. Brigid stayed in their hotel room working on a presentation for her job at the Federal Reserve. She worked in the Fed's Criminal Investigation Division. Her expertise was money laundering. The following week her job was taking her to Belgium to coordinate with her counterparts at the European Central Bank.

Nate vividly remembered the first time he saw Brigid. It was finals week at the end of their first semester at Georgetown. He was studying in the law library. Across the main reading room, he saw a beautiful woman emerge from behind a huge pile of Supreme Court reports stacked up on her study carrel. She stretched and yawned. Even in the exhaustion of cramming for exams, she'd been so beautiful. He remembered thinking, I'm going to marry her. Sometimes, people just know. The attraction had never faded, but irritation had crept in after fourteen years of marriage. Religion was a big part of the friction between them.

Now both thirty-nine years old, they were professionally ambitious. After law school, Nate had worked as an FBI agent for five years, then as a US attorney for another six. For the past three years he had concentrated on making money, working for Baker and Black, the world's largest law firm. In pursuit of mammon, he had switched sides. Now he worked on criminal defense for big shots.

A typical Catholic couple of an earlier generation would have been parents to at least three children after fourteen years of marriage. But like most American women, Brigid was on the pill. She didn't really care about the Church's disapproval. In fact, it never really occurred to either her or Nate that there was any problem with using birth control. The Vatican prohibition was a dead letter. They paid no attention to it.

Truth be told, even the Church didn't care all that much. Priests never brought it up in confession. It was hardly ever mentioned at the pulpit. The only people who cared about their use of birth control were Nate's and Brigid's parents. They wanted grandchildren.

Nate left the Four Seasons, crossing M Street. He then walked up 29th and weaved his way through Georgetown's side streets.

Car tires made a muffled rumble on the cobblestones. The brick sidewalks were picturesque, if uneven.

Tracy had picked Milano's as a meeting place. *The New York Times* called the restaurant "the closest thing to a celebrity palace to be found in Washington." In polarized Washington, it was one of the few bipartisan places. Both Republicans and Democrats enjoyed spending other people's money on pricey lunches.

When Nate reached the restaurant, an early lunch crowd had filled most of the sidewalk tables, so he went inside. Tracy was already at a table in the back corner. Like a Mafia don, he sat with his back to the wall and his face to the street. He waved Nate over to the table.

"My meeting at Georgetown ended mercifully early," he said. "I got a jump start on lunch. Here, have some bruschetta."

They ordered salads, veal medallions, and mineral water. The lunch of the weight-conscious.

Tracy pulled a thick folder from his battered leather briefcase and placed it on the table between them.

Nate observed that really powerful men often had really beat-up old briefcases. It was a mark of their experience. Like an old steamer trunk, covered with travel stickers, it said they were well traveled.

On the cover of the leatherette folder was the eight-pointed cross of the Knights of Malta. Nate took note of the symbol. Was Tracy better connected in the Church or in the State? Tracy had obviously assembled a lot of material. It was amazing what a few phone calls from a really powerful man could do in only four days.

"Did the agency do this or the Knights of Malta?" asked Nate.

"I'm retired from the agency," said Tracy, "but I still have connections. However, the knights are better sources when it comes to the Church." He grabbed a piece of bread. "You'll find out what a labyrinth the Church is. Makes the Kremlin look transparent." Tracy laughed, more of a snort, really. The laugh was infectious, so Nate laughed too.

Tracy was proud of being a Knight of Malta. For more than 250 years the knights had ruled the tiny island of Malta, a fortress smack in the middle of the Mediterranean Sea. It was a hotbed of intrigue. They got the island from the Holy Roman Emperor, Charles V, in 1530 after they lost to the Turks in Rhodes. The knights paid a strange rent for their island—one trained falcon each year to the Austrian emperor. Hence, the famous "Maltese falcon."

When the knights lost their island to Napoleon, their "country" was reduced to a couple of buildings in central Rome. But they punched way above their geographic weight, because all their members were well connected. Their network was unsurpassed, at least in the Church. Just the sort of group a retired spy like Tracy should belong to.

As he flipped through the stack of papers in the file, Tracy said, "The Church has some real enemies. Not all of them are nonviolent. And not all of them are outside the Church."

Nate noticed the reference to internal enemies.

He found the paper he was looking for. Bill looked at ease, as if he were back in his old career, giving an intelligence briefing.

"So, who's at the top of the enemies list?" said Nate, breaking a bread-stick. The waiter delivered their mineral waters and salads. They paused the conversation for a moment. When the waiter left, they resumed.

"Well, there could be state actors. Israel is upset with the Vatican. They think it tilts toward the Palestinians. Rumors have been swirling around for months that the Vatican is thinking of recognizing the Palestinians as a separate state. Israel wants the next pope to be more pro-Israel. They would love to see our friend O'Toole as the pope. They probably think that an American would lean their way."

Tracy popped another piece of bread in his mouth.

"Israel needs Catholic tourists in the Holy Land, but it does not want a Vatican Embassy in Ramallah." Tracy pulled a two-page brief out of the leatherette folder. "Mossad has been known to play dirty, but I don't think they are dirty enough to kill bishops. Besides, for them, the Catholic Church is just a sideshow. The people they are really worried about are in Iran and Syria."

Tracy continued his briefing.

"Next on the list of suspects is organized crime. That's home turf for you. The Vatican Bank is basically unregulated. Since nobody is watching, it would be a great way to move funny money around the world."

"How big is the bank?" asked Nate.

"Small, really. Like a regional bank in the States. Its real power is prestige and independence. People like the cachet of doing business with the Holy See. Just think of our Knights of Malta pals," said Tracy.

"Second, it is virtually unregulated. For all intents and purposes there are no bank regulators. It's useful because you can move money with practically no one looking.

"Maybe your wife could look into the bank's operations through her contacts at the Fed," said Tracy. He had obviously researched Brigid, too.

"Wouldn't the most obvious bad guys be inside the Church?" said Nate. "People who are really angry at the hierarchy?"

"Yeah," said Tracy. "Top of that list should be the victims of pedophilia. They have the motivation to kill some bishops." Tracy pulled out another list from the folder on the table.

"Here is a list of victim advocacy groups. There is a splinter group called the Avengers. They broke off from SNAP a few years ago. They vowed vengeance on any bishop who transferred pedophile priests around to avoid prosecution. They also blamed Manning for stuff he did when he was Archbishop of Milwaukee."

Tracy used the acronym SNAP for Survivors Network of those Abused by Priests. He was obviously familiar with the players in Church politics.

"Were other dead cardinals on their list, besides Manning?" asked Nate.

"No," said Tracy. "Only Manning. They are focused exclusively on the United States, so they probably would not care about the Philippines or Chile."

"My father left the Church over child abuse," said Nate. "Remember Tommy Fitzpatrick? He killed himself because of it. Victims have a strong motive to kill, even if they don't have the means."

Tracy nodded.

"Back in Charlestown a child molester would have been a dead man. We would have had an extrajudicial procedure." Tracy made a motion with his finger across his neck. "Maybe that would be true elsewhere.

Their families have reasons to be angry, especially if some bishop turned a blind eye to molesters."

The waiter delivered plates of tiny medallions of veal, with dollops of pureed potatoes. Nobody gets fat eating in really expensive restaurants like Milano's. If Tracy were anything like Nate, he would probably go home and eat a bowl of cereal to fill up.

"Who else is on the list?" asked Nate.

"Radical feminists," said Tracy. "They are angry about abortion, birth control, the all-male priesthood, and divorce. Take your pick. There is a long list of lefty liberals who think they have plenty of reasons to pull a trigger."

The phrase lefty liberals struck Nate as inapt. Tracy was thinking American politics, not Church politics.

"After the feminists, I suppose the gays would have reason to kill a few bishops, especially in New York," continued Tracy. "There are radical gay groups that are filled with rage at the Church. Here is some of their literature." Tracy put down comic books depicting bishops and priests in gay bars.

"Manning was strongly opposed to gay marriage. He threatened to excommunicate the governor of New York if he signed the bill, but nothing ever came of that threat. He once did an exorcism of the New York legislature. Dramatic stuff. I think they deserved it."

Nate was beginning to wonder if Tracy had his own agenda.

"I don't think gay groups would go after the Church," said Nate. "They think religion is irrelevant. I'm not sure the *Washington Blade* could even name a single Catholic bishop. Besides, gays are doing well in the courts and at the ballot box. They don't really worry about the Church."

"Maybe," said Tracy. He took a drink of mineral water. "You know, today things are different. Nobody really cares if someone is gay anymore. Even at the agency we don't care. Not like we used to."

Tracy chuckled to himself. Nate was surprised to hear that from Tracy.

"Check out this list of gay groups," said Tracy. "Some of them are mad at the Church, and they are well organized in the United States and Europe."

Nate nodded. Perhaps he was wrong about Tracy. He seemed to have a pretty good grasp of contemporary culture. Maybe Nate was the one who had cultural blinders.

Just then Nate's mobile phone vibrated in his jacket pocket. "Sorry," he said to Tracy as he pulled it out and looked at the screen. It was a text from Brigid. "Call me! Urgent!" Brigid was not the type to use exclamation points.

"Excuse me for a moment, Bill. Got to call the office."

Nate slipped out of their corner table and headed out the front door of the restaurant onto Prospect Street. He called Brigid as he walked down the block, away from the ears of the people lunching at the sidewalk cafe.

"What's up? What's so urgent?" he asked.

"Maybe it's nothing," said Brigid. "Maybe I'm just being too suspicious, but I thought you should know.

"I finished some of my work, and I went downstairs to the dining room to get something to eat at the buffet lunch. I ran into Peggy Tracy leaving the dining room. She was with two men: One was dressed as a priest, and the other was dressed in regular clothes. The priest was that Father Murphy from the Soldados de Cristo. I met him last night at the Vatican Embassy when Peggy and I left you with the cardinal and Bill.

"The other guy was a layman, I assume, dressed in slacks and a polo shirt. He had very big arms, like a weight lifter.

"Peggy was very friendly, you know the obligatory kiss on the cheek and all that. She introduced me to the two men. I knew Father Murphy from last night, of course, but I didn't catch the name of the other man. She said he was a member of the Soldados de Cristo or Reinado de Dios or something like that. Anyway, he was a big guy, sort of Latin-looking."

"So, what's urgent about all that?" asked Nate, irritated. He was all the way to the end of the block and turning around to retrace his steps.

"The thing that struck me was that Peggy introduced me as the wife of the man who was leading the Vatican's investigation of the Cardinal Manning murder. That raised their eyebrows. Odd way to introduce me to two strangers, don't you think?"

"Did they say anything?" asked Nate.

"No, just the regular sort of remark. Something like 'Oh, yes, horrible thing.'"

"So, is that it? What's so urgent about that?"

"Let me finish," said Brigid, herself a little impatient. "After they left, I got my lunch from the buffet. I asked the waiter to bring me a newspaper. When he finally brought it over, I realized that I'd left my reading glasses in the room. So, I took the elevator back up to our floor. Just as I was getting off, I met that layman, the one with the big arms, who had been with Peggy. He seemed surprised to see me, and a little nervous. He barely acknowledged me. I said, 'Oh, hello, again.' He just grunted and then got right on the elevator."

"Well," said Nate, "so what?" This tale seemed to be going nowhere.

"Well, when I went into our room, your laptop was open on the desk. You never leave it open. You always click it shut when you're done, to shut it off. Did you leave the laptop open?"

"I don't know," said Nate. "Maybe. It could be just a coincidence. Maybe he was staying at the hotel."

"I don't think so," said Brigid. "The Soldados have a house here in Bethesda. That's where that Father Murphy lives. Even if he were staying here, why wouldn't he do more than just grunt hello? I had just met him. Very strange, like he didn't expect to see me there. Besides, what is Peggy doing telling people about your investigation? I thought it was hush-hush. Do you want people to know?"

"People are eventually going to know anyway," said Nate. "That guy on the elevator, that could be something, or it could be nothing. My laptop is password-protected, so he probably couldn't get on it."

"But I think he was in our room," said Brigid. "That is something."

"How much time elapsed between the time you saw Peggy in the dining room and when you got off the elevator?" asked Nate.

"Maybe fifteen or twenty minutes," said Brigid.

"If he was going in our room, he probably figured he had more time since he knew you were at lunch," said Nate. By this time he was back at Milano's front door. "I'll see you in an hour." They hung up.

Back at the table he told Tracy, "My office. They were calling me back about my request for leave. Seems like we can work it out."

Tracy nodded. The old man knew some of Nate's partners.

They got back to the discussion, but Brigid's call made Nate wonder about Tracy and who else might be interested in this investigation.

"Aren't there any conservative groups who might be angry at the Church?" asked Nate. "Or what about just plain old criminals? Maybe it's the mob. They certainly have the global reach. And they have a lot of power in Italy."

"With conservatives in the Church the picture is murkier," said Tracy. "The right-wingers are publicly supportive of the hierarchy. For them, the litmus test is loyalty to the magisterium. I don't think they would kill any bishops, unless they were liberals. Hell, I might want to kill some of the liberal ones myself." Tracy chuckled again. Nate wondered who else Bill might have killed throughout his career.

"There was a real scandal in Rome this time last year," said Tracy. "The pope's butler went to the newspapers with documents on corruption in the Vatican and money laundering through the Vatican Bank. The Mafia was implicated. Here are some articles. There was a monsignor who was caught flying sacks full of euros into Italy from Switzerland."

Tracy pulled out a file of newspaper clippings. Nate saw that the Camorra in Naples was mentioned in some of the articles. He thought, certainly they could pull off murder. That's their specialty.

"The mob would not hesitate to kill if a major interest was threatened," Tracy said.

Nate made a mental note to ask Brigid about mob money laundering.

"What about insiders?" asked Nate. "In my experience, the most vicious players in any organization are the insiders who really care the most about the outcome."

He continued, "If this were a Dan Brown novel, Opus Dei would be the bad guys."

Tracy nodded but didn't respond immediately. Nate surmised that Tracy kind of liked groups like Opus Dei. Nate knew a little about the secretive group. He knew they had their own priests. They answered to nobody but the pope. He thought they were austere, to the point of being weird, wearing hair shirts and beating themselves with whips. He'd heard a rumor that they counted a US Supreme Court Justice in their camp.

"Yeah," answered Tracy. "They're on the list. Them and the Soldados de Cristo." Nate raised his eyebrows and leaned forward.

"Tell me about the Soldados," he said.

"A pretty traditional bunch," said Tracy. "They seem like nice, young guys. They have a house here in Bethesda. Peggy goes up there on retreat. She thinks they are just wonderful. I think she's attracted to them because they are young and handsome."

"Swept along by their smiles?" said Nate.

"Maybe," answered Tracy. He signaled the waiter for their bill.

"Peggy and I met their cardinal from Mexico last year. I think his name is Mendoza. Very formal, but a nice enough guy, I guess. He has a job at the Vatican. I was impressed. He really wants to bring back the disciplined, unified, and purer church."

"Maybe the Soldados have an agenda too," suggested Nate.

"I don't think so," said Tracy. "They just seem like bright young men trying to make a difference. Like the Jesuits in their early days."

Nate nodded. He felt like he was being steered again. But he didn't let on.

"What about the Vatican Bank?" asked Nate. "Money is a powerful motivator."

"I think the Vatican Bank is a good place to start turning over rocks," agreed Tracy. "Back in the 1980s there was a huge scandal there."

Tracy settled into a storytelling mood.

"There was a guy, Roberto Calvi, who did a lot of business with the Vatican Bank. They found him dead, swinging from a rope under Black-friars Bridge in London. At the time, he was president of Banco Ambrosiano, Milan's biggest bank." Tracy waved a hand in the air, pointing heavenward to indicate the size of Banco Ambrosiano.

"Some archbishops were caught up in the scandal. There was a guy from Chicago, Marcinkus. Ask your wife to pull that file at the Fed. He let Calvi use the Vatican Bank to launder money for the Contras in Nicaragua. I was head of the agency then, so I know it was true. We were grateful to the Church for their cooperation. Officially, we knew nothing about it, of course."

"Of course," said Nate with a smile.

"I don't know," said Nate. "If these deaths are connected, it could be some mundane explanation. What if someone has their hopes set on the next papal election? Pope Thomas is old. Someone could be eliminating rivals."

"Certainly, the liberals don't want white smoke for a conservative, and conservatives don't want a liberal," said Tracy.

"There is a real 'nut bunch' called the 'Society of Pius X,'" said Tracy. "They make Opus Dei look normal.

Nate was impressed. Tracy really had done his homework.

"Those people go way past disapproval. They want schism. They're so steamed about ecumenism. They hate religious liberty in general. They also want a new crusade against Muslims."

It was clear to Nate that he would have no shortage of suspects. Tracy handed over the whole stack of papers to Nate, who put them in his briefcase. As he did so, he pulled out the *Washington Post* and showed Tracy the photo on the front page.

"Grisly thing, that fire," said Nate.

"Yeah," said Tracy. "Sad." They sat there for a few seconds, remembering

the horror of the scene the night before. After a brief pause, Tracy continued. "Peggy told me that a priest from St. Stephen's, the church near the
hospital, went over to GW's emergency room to give the man his last rites.
She is pretty well connected with priests, you know. Evidently the priest
from the ER told some priest friend of Peggy's that the man talked a little
before he died. He seemed to be repeating the same word over and over.
Maybe it was a name, not a word."

"What name?" asked Nate.

"It was not very clear," said Tracy. "Something like Menoza."

Nate wrote it down. "Interesting," he said. "Menoza."

Nate had one more question. "Do you think any other cardinals are
in the crosshairs? What about O'Toole?"

"I think all the cardinals are presumed to be in danger at the moment,"
said Tracy. "It is a small but powerful club. Somebody doesn't like them."

Tracy threw down a fifty-dollar bill. "That should cover the tip,"
he said to Nate with a grin. To the waiter he said, "Put it on my tab,
Giorgio."

They stepped out into the May sunshine. "My car is up at the university. Walk with me to Healy Hall, and I'll drive you back to the Four
Seasons," suggested Tracy.

They continued their discussion as they headed up 33rd Street
toward campus.

"What about lone wolves?" asked Nate. "It could be one or two guys
on the inside. This could be the Vatican version of 'going postal.'"

"We don't know that much about the inside politics," said Tracy.
"The Vatican is secretive. In your files are the names of some Americans
who work in the Vatican. There is a Monsignor Matthew Ackerman who
works in the Congregation for Bishops. Give him a call."

"Did the police turn up anything in the Manning investigation?"
asked Nate.

"Evidently the cardinal was wearing a Kevlar vest. He must have had
some reason to be afraid. He knew something was up," said Tracy.

"Well, he was obviously right to be afraid," said Nate. "Just before he was shot, I noticed a red spot on his forehead, like it was a laser-targeted weapon."

"Could be," said Tracy. "Obviously a sophisticated group if they have that kind of weapon. The police said the trajectory of the bullet indicated that it came from the balcony of the Rockefeller Center building across the street. Maybe you could find out some more once they pinpoint the location."

They had walked up Prospect to 36th Street. Tracy lit a cigarette.

Nate said, "When I was a boy serving Mass back in Charlestown, I never dreamed there was so much intrigue in the Church."

They stood at the top of a steep staircase that led down to M Street, the famous staircase from *The Exorcist*.

"No?" asked Tracy incredulously. "Didn't you ever see the movie filmed right here? Evil has always been part of the landscape of the Church. Devils and angels are all mixed up together—always have been. Sometimes it's hard to tell them apart. After all, the devils are fallen angels."

Nate nodded. Despite the spring sunshine, he felt a chill as they looked down those infamous steps.

"Come on," said Tracy. "I'll drive you back to your hotel."

7

SUNDAY IN NEW YORK

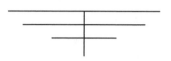

ON SUNDAY MORNINGS, THE CITY THAT NEVER SLEEPS AT least rests its eyes. For a few hours on either side of dawn, a contemplative calm blankets the streets of Manhattan, which is a blessed silence.

Nate slipped out early into that silence, walking to the 7:00 a.m. Mass at St. Patrick's. He didn't wake Brigid. She hardly ever went to Mass anymore. She said she was spiritual, but not religious.

Mass bored her. She told Nate once, "I left the Church more out of boredom than anger." But there was also a fair amount of anger in Brigid. In her world, women were taken seriously. In the Church, they were not.

Brigid's religious heroes were the nuns who had taught her, not the priests and bishops. The saints she admired were the ones who did the things that she herself did not do. They lived poor. They made lasting social change.

Nate was resigned to praying alone. He never really understood the power that the Church had over him. He associated it with his longing for mystery, peace, and order.

Ever since he was a boy, he had gone to Sunday Mass. Sometimes, he'd even gone alone when his mother was drinking and his father had stopped going. Mass was the one hour of the week that he was most at peace.

Serving Mass seemed like a significant responsibility to a boy of twelve years. It was something that older people thought was important. When they held the early Mass, he rode his bicycle through quiet streets at 5:30 a.m. The Church at dawn in the summer seemed mysterious. Back then, he'd put on his cassock and surplice in the dimly lit sacristy. The fact that he wore these odd clothes at the age of twelve made the job seem important.

Then he set up for Mass. It was the same routine each time: Light the candles. Fill the cruets with water and wine. Put out the priest's chalice. Get the big host out and put it on the paten. Check to be sure the book was in place. Then, when he was all done, he would sit in the silence of the big church and wait for the priest, like a sentry.

It was orderly. Nate liked things to be orderly. At home there was often chaos. His parents fought all the time, especially when his mother drank. But in church, there was order. Years later, in college, he read St. Thomas Aquinas's comment that "order is heaven's first law." Nate liked thinking about it that way. Order was heavenly. The Church put his life in order. And he liked that.

This Sunday, Nate was again glad for a moment of solitude. It had been a traumatic week. He had seen two people killed right before his eyes: one shot, one burned to death. He needed a moment of peace. The Church gave it to him.

Nate had not been back to St. Patrick's since the cardinal's murder six days earlier. The front entrance of the cathedral was draped in black bunting, in mourning for Manning. But inside, Sunday Masses carried on as usual. Nate went around to the Fifth Avenue entrance. He wanted to get a look at the actual spot where the cardinal fell. In the material Tracy had given him, there was a report from the NYPD that indicated that the trajectory of the bullet had been from across the street at Rockefeller Center.

Positioned on the top step of St. Patrick's, at the great center door, Nate looked across Fifth Avenue. On an axis with the main entrance to the church was the statue of a very muscular Atlas holding the world on his shoulders, guarding the main entrance to Rockefeller Center.

As Nate pivoted a little to the right, he saw a five- or six-story low-rise building that formed part of the Rockefeller Plaza complex. On the fourth floor was a terrace that faced Fifth Avenue. The terrace was generally closed to the public. It was on the terrace that the police had found a remote-controlled, high-powered rifle mounted on a tripod, the barrel facing the front door of St. Patrick's. The gun had a tiny camera and a laser attached to the sight. These could have been used to aim the gun with deadly accuracy.

Someone had fired the gun with the remote control, but the actual shooter could have been halfway across town, using GPS technology. It was a sophisticated setup and obviously required time and access to the terrace. It was probable, thought the police, that the shooter had positioned the gun perhaps two or three days ahead of Sullivan's funeral. The killer would have to know the funeral schedule.

Using the remote-controlled gun, there was no need to worry about an escape route. Obviously this was the work of killers who had money and high-tech sophistication. Probably not some lone gunman.

The police had checked to see who had access to that terrace. A friend of Nate's in the New York City Police Department told him that only maintenance people, the security staff, and tour guides had terrace keys. All the maintenance and security staff had been interviewed and accounted for. But one tour guide had disappeared. He was a foreign national from Belgium. No link had been established, but the police wanted the tour guide for questioning.

Nate had asked his policeman friend why a Belgian was working at Rockefeller Center. Evidently he was hired because he was multilingual, like all the Belgians. He gave tours in English, French, German, and Dutch.

Nate studied the Rockefeller Center building for a few seconds more, then turned and pulled open the heavy bronze door to the cathedral. He found a seat near the rear, maybe fifty pews away from the altar, and waited for Mass to begin. From his seat, the priest looked like a tiny stick figure as he stood in the pulpit to read the gospel. Nate didn't really listen to the homily. It was mostly platitudes anyway.

After Mass, Nate went back into the vestibule of the church. He stood at the spot where Manning had fallen. A little stain of blood remained on the floor, despite the best efforts of the cleaners. A vestibule is basically an entrance hall. Now it had become something of a shrine. Mourners had left flowers and candles. The maintenance staff had moved the mementos off to the side, so people could come and go.

Nate turned and faced the high altar at the other end of the cathedral, a football-field length away. He walked up the center aisle, in the reverse direction Manning had taken.

Nate got up to the communion rail at the front of the cathedral. He started up the steps to the sanctuary but was stopped by a distinguished-looking black man in a blue blazer with the cathedral crest on the breast pocket and the word Security stitched above the crest.

"May I help you?" asked the security man. An offer of help is the universal challenge to the unwanted customer.

Nate stepped down.

"I'm Nate Condon," he said, reaching out his hand to the security guard and handing him his business card. "I was here last week when the cardinal was shot. I'm doing an investigation on behalf of the Church. Can I go down and look at the sacristy?"

"What for?" asked the guard.

"Just to see if there might be any clue the police missed."

"I'll walk you down," said the guard, removing the velvet rope at the entrance of the sanctuary.

They went down the stairs behind the high altar to the sacristy in the basement. Halfway down the stairs there was a landing with a darkened flight of steps leading to a dark crypt with a gate across the entrance.

"What's down there?" asked Nate.

"The crypt where the bishops are buried," said the guard. "All the former Archbishops of New York and one saint."

"An archbishop was a saint?" asked Nate, curious.

"Not hardly," said the guard. "The saint was a black man, Pierre Toussaint. He came here as a slave from Haiti after the rebellion there and bought freedom for his whole family and a bunch of orphans, too. He was a famous hairdresser, the Vidal Sassoon of his day. He went every day to communion after the white folks had received it. He's up for canonization. He couldn't have sat in a front pew when he was alive, but now they bury him with the archbishops. Isn't that just like what Jesus said? We stone the prophets when they are alive and build them tombs when they die."

Nate had never heard the intriguing history.

"Let me ask you something," said Nate, turning to the security guard. "Were you here the day the cardinal was killed?"

"Yep," said the guard. "I'm always in the sacristy and in the shadows around here when the cardinal is here, in case there is trouble. There are always a few crazies in the church."

"Was there anything unusual about Manning on the day he was killed? Did he say or do anything that people thought out of the ordinary?" asked Nate.

"Not really," answered the guard as they went down to the sacristy and stood by the counter where Manning had vested. "He had started wearing the Kevlar vest in the past few months. He always went out to the street at the beginning of funerals. Monsignor Krakowski suggested it might not be a good idea if there were crazy folks around. But Manning always met the family at the door. It was his custom. He always did that."

Nate thought, if the cardinal had done what the other bishops do, and waited for Sullivan's body to be brought up the aisle to the steps of the altar, he probably would still be alive. Obviously somebody knew Manning's habits.

The remote-controlled gun across the street would have been useless if Manning had waited at the communion rail. Somebody knew that Manning always went to the door at funerals. Somebody was well informed about liturgy and the habits of this cardinal. During Mass, Nate had noticed cathedral employees preparing for Manning's funeral.

Beginning at noon on Sunday, the cardinal's body would lie in state in front of the high altar for twenty-four hours. Contrary to custom, the coffin would be closed.

The funeral would begin at noon on Monday, with a forty-five-minute procession of dozens of hierarchs from all around the world. O'Toole would be there, along with a couple dozen cardinals. Security would be massive. Traffic in midtown would grind to a halt for hours. Nate planned to leave for Rome immediately after the funeral, on a late flight on Monday evening.

After Mass, Nate walked down to a bakery on 48th Street to get bagels and *The New York Times*. Sunday mornings had evolved into a ritual for Brigid and Nate. They always had bagels and coffee. They always read the Sunday *Times*. Then they went jogging together in Central Park.

When he got back to their apartment, Brigid was standing at the kitchen counter making coffee. She was dressed to go jogging.

"How was Mass?" she asked, not looking up as she pushed down on the plunger of the French press to strain the coffee. Her voice indicated she didn't really care.

"OK," said Nate. "I got a good look at the scene of the crime. The gun had a clear shot at the cardinal from Rockefeller Center, so long as nobody got in the way. "

He was actually excited to be investigating a crime again. It was much better than the paper shuffling for the rich that he'd been doing at the law firm.

They moved to the living room of their apartment with the bagels and coffee on a silver tray. By New York standards, their apartment was gargantuan. They actually had separate rooms for each purpose. But Sunday was just about the only day they used the living room. Brigid sat at one end of the couch, Nate at the other, with the paper spread out between them. He took the sports and business sections; she took the front page and the travel sections.

"Manning's all over the front page," said Brigid. "*The Times* is practically canonizing him." The headline was "Cardinal's Death a Mystery!"

Below the fold on page one, the story about the man who had immo-
lated himself in front of the Nunciature appeared. *The Times* had a photo
of the man's body being loaded into the ambulance by the EMTs. It was
from a different angle than the one they'd seen the day before in the
Washington Post.

Brigid adjusted her glasses and pulled the paper closer, studying
something closely in the photo. Then she said, "That's him!"

"Who?" asked Nate.

"The man with the big arms. The man I saw with Peggy Tracy. The
man who might have been in our room at the Four Seasons."

"So what?" said Nate.

"There he is in the photo. He's standing right there in the crowd
watching as the man burned. Look." She passed the paper to Nate's end
of the couch.

"See him? Standing right there by the stretcher."

Nate looked at the photo.

Nate went to the desk in his study and got a magnifying glass and
scissors. He looked at the photo through the glass. He could see the big-
armed man, with a shaved head, standing near the stretcher.

"I'll cut this out for future reference," said Nate. "It could be nothing,
or it could be something. Odd that he would be outside the Nunciature
and then with Peggy the next day."

"Odder still that he should be in our room," said Brigid.

"We don't know that for a fact," said Nate. "Still, he's worth
remembering."

"Who do you think killed Manning?" asked Brigid. "Did Tracy have
any idea?" Apparently, she couldn't help her curiosity, now that he was
investigating the most notorious murder of the year.

"Bill gave me a long list of suspects, from the Israelis to drug dealers.
I don't think it's the Israelis. They don't care enough about the Church.
It had to be somebody who really cares about the Church—some group
that has good reasons to be angry."

"You mean like victims of pedophilia?" asked Brigid.

"Yeah," said Nate. "Maybe. Or somebody who wants to use the Church. It has to be somebody with a global concern. Otherwise, why would they kill cardinals in Chile or Mexico City? That wouldn't make sense for a purely American group."

"The Mafia has a global reach," said Brigid. "And they do a lot of money laundering. So do drug dealers. At the IMF we're running down the movement of their money all the time.

"When I go to Brussels, I'll keep my ear to the ground," she continued. "One thing about the euro, it gave criminals a whole new alternative currency."

"How long do you think you'll be there?" Nate asked.

"One meeting Thursday and Friday. Then another one Monday."

"Why don't you come down to Rome when you're done? I could use the help. It would be a lot more fun to be in Rome if you're there."

"You're not there for fun, honey. Besides, my expense account wouldn't pay for a detour to Rome."

"Pay for it yourself," said Nate. "When am I ever going to have a reason to be in Rome again?"

"You might be there quite a lot, from the looks of it," said Brigid. "Come on, let's go running before it gets too hot outside."

From their apartment on Park Avenue, it was a couple of long blocks and about eight short ones to Central Park. They were your classic upper-class jogging couple, with matching iPods strapped to their arms and Under Armour outfits.

Even back at Georgetown law school, they had already begun to chase after the good life. Their move to New York reflected their goals. The glamor and energy of New York provided a better backdrop for their lifestyle than the gray bureaucracy of Washington, DC.

They announced their engagement at their favorite watering hole in New York, the Papillon Bistro and Bar, a two-story French restaurant in midtown Manhattan. Fourteen years later, it remained their favorite place to meet with friends after hours of being "on" at work. Men and women alike gathered at a seventy-foot-long oak-paneled bar, saluting the good life with a cigar from Davidoff's and a glass of Chivas. Did they live superficial lives based too much on appearances? Nate wondered to himself, but they never talked about it.

They entered the park near the pond across from the Plaza Hotel. Both in their late thirties, they were in great shape. Running came effortlessly. They jogged along at a pretty good pace without talking, past the pond and along East Drive. Then they cut over to the great mall that went straight up through the park to the elaborately ornamented Bethesda Fountain. Winded, they sat down on the low wall surrounding the fountain, facing the statue of the Angel of the Waters.

New Yorkers call it the Bethesda Fountain. Most would be stunned to know that the angel statue is a reference to the pool of Bethesda mentioned in the Bible, in the Gospel of John. The sick used to lie beside the waters of the pool of Bethesda, at the sheep gate entrance to Jerusalem, waiting for the angel to disturb the waters. They believed that when the angel moved the waters, the first person into the pool would be cured. In the Bible, Jesus met a poor, paralyzed man who had lain there for thirty-eight years. Because of his paralysis, he was never able to be the first in the water. Jesus cured him on the Sabbath and told the paralytic to pick up his mat and walk.

The significance of the fountain's name was lost on most passing New Yorkers. They just thought it was a nice statue of an angel. Brigid knew the fountain was designed by a woman, Emma Stebbins, and that it was the first major piece of public art in America done by a woman. Brigid liked the statue because of that. Nate liked the pool, because it was a place to rest.

"You know," said Brigid, "you are going to need an angel on this job. You are going to be in a much bigger and troubled pond than this one."

"Yeah," said Nate. "If these deaths are linked, there is some kind of struggle going on in the Church."

"In most mysteries they say 'cherchez la femme,'" said Brigid. "What would they say in the Vatican, I wonder?"

"Maybe they would blame it on the butler," said Nate. "That's what they did in the last scandal."

"This has to be somebody pretty high up to pull off murders on four continents. Somebody is pretty pissed off," said Brigid.

They sat there watching the fountain for a while. Then they jogged across the brick-paved mall and up the elaborate steps that led to the terrace that framed the fountain.

"Come on," said Nate. "I'll race you to the club. We can shower and change there and have lunch in the bar." The club was the New York Athletic Club on Central Park South, private and favored by rich and powerful Catholics in government and business. Nate's Knights of Malta pals were all members.

Brigid and Nate had to go around the back entrance on 58th Street, because they weren't dressed properly for a lobby entrance. They climbed the back stairs and then took the service elevator to the locker rooms, where they kept a change of clothes for these Sunday outings.

After a sauna and shower, they met in the Tap Room overlooking Central Park for lunch. Nate was in a jacket and tie. Brigid was in a dress and light sweater. The club had a strict dress code. People looked like they stepped right out of the 1950s.

Nate liked the club, but Brigid thought it unbearably stuffy. For a working-class fireman's kid from Charlestown, Massachusetts, it was a head trip to be a member of the elite New York Athletic Club. His membership told others that he had arrived in New York. Just as importantly, it told Nate and Brigid that they had arrived.

"Tomorrow will be a mess around midtown," said Nate. "What with the cardinal's funeral and all. Before the funeral, I'll have to go into the office to close up a few things. Then I'll head back to St. Patrick's."

"You'd better pack tonight," said Brigid. "Maybe on the way home we can stop and buy you an Italian phrase book. Something tells me you might need it."

"I'm looking forward to the wine and the pasta," said Nate. "Thank God St. Peter had the good sense to die in Rome. If the Church is going to have a headquarters, it might as well be where they know how to live la dolce vita."

"From what I've seen of the clergy," said Brigid, "they certainly know about la dolce vita.

"But then," she said as she put a thick linen napkin on her lap, "so do we."

8

ALL PUSILLANIMOUS TWITS

ABOUT THE SAME TIME BRIGID AND NATE SAT DOWN TO lunch at the New York Athletic Club, Monsignor Matthew Ackerman exited the front door of the Villa Stritch on the Via della Nocetta in Rome.

The American monsignor was dressed as a layman, in mufti, as clerics like to say. His white polo shirt, tan linen slacks, and Gucci loafers could have been the uniform of any Roman metrosexual.

Even though he was not dressed as a monsignor, he loved the title, which means "my lord" in Renaissance-style Italian. He never let five minutes pass in any conversation without making people aware of his status. His was the most insidious form of clericalism, pretending to be just a regular guy but constantly reminding others of his superiority.

Ackerman wanted to be incognito for the later part of his spring evening out in Rome. Being dressed as a priest in Rome is sometimes an advantage, but often an irritation. It makes you a target for the pious and the profane.

The first part of Ackerman's evening would be ordinary enough, dinner with other English-speaking priests who also were working in Rome. The second part of his evening remained relatively unplanned. However, if past were prologue, Monsignor Ackerman's appetites would lead him to the place where he felt most comfortable, Angelo Azzurro,

Rome's venerable gay bar in Trastevere, the medieval neighborhood just across the Tiber River from the ancient city.

Spring evenings in Rome are glorious. They're warm enough to go without a coat, but cool enough to be pleasant. In late May, the setting sun paints the sandstone façades of the buildings a warm pink. The sun is also reflected in the upper-story windows. The Romans say they are glowing eyes looking down on the street.

Romans usually dine late, but on Sunday evenings they go out a little earlier. By the first of May, the *trattorie* have put their tables in the streets of Trastevere. The patrons dine al fresco, just inches from the passing cars in the narrow streets. The outdoor tables fill up first. Nobody wants to sit inside and miss the life of *la strada*.

Ackerman walked rapidly. He knew the streets of Rome well. He had lived there for nearly eighteen years. A native of St. Louis, he had been sent over to Rome to study at the North American College at the age of twenty-two, just after he finished college at St. Louis University.

In his better moments, Ackerman still had some of the air of the naïve Midwesterner about him. He was Germanic-looking, with blond hair and blue eyes. But his hair was beginning to thin, and his waist was beginning to thicken as he pushed forty.

When he'd arrived in Rome, he'd been intoxicated by the international atmosphere of the city and entranced by the power of the Church. At the time, he thought himself destined to become a bishop, "on the fast track to the purple sash," as Roman seminarians say. But now Ackerman was a disappointed careerist and a self-loathing homosexual. Both those attributes made him part of a substantial confraternity within the Vatican bureaucracy. The Roman newspapers sometimes referred to it as the gay lobby within the Vatican: jaded, cynical, and sad.

Students at the American seminary, the North American College, tend to have an elevated opinion of themselves. Some buy into a myth that they are chosen to be ecclesiastical climbers. They even have a name for it—"Alpiners." Matt Ackerman had been a champion Alpiner.

He had been a bright student, but not a brilliant one. Like everyone else, he'd completed his basic degree in theology. After ordination, he got his bishop's permission to stay on in Rome to study canon law at the Pontifical Gregorian University, the Jesuit university in Rome that Americans simply called "the Greg."

Ackerman's good looks and charming manner brought him to the attention of his professors. They recommended him for admission to the Academia, the school for Vatican diplomats. It didn't hurt that he was handsome. It was widely reported that the archbishop who ran the Academia liked to have some eye candy in each class. That was probably the actual extent of the Vatican's gay lobby.

For a boy from St. Louis, the diplomatic school was a rarefied atmosphere. Five popes had gone to the Academia. Several more had been professors there. Walking through the silver-plated doors of the Academia chapel seemed to put those students on the Vatican escalator to higher office.

However, Ackerman had problems at the Academia. He was not good in languages. At the Academia, language proficiency is essential. Everyone is expected to speak at least three modern languages: Italian, English, and French. Plus, students need a reading knowledge of Latin. Other European languages are helpful. Increasingly, Asian and African languages are needed, as the center of gravity in the Church shifts to the global south and east.

Despite his academic difficulties, Ackerman would have been fine, if not for his own demons. He was conflicted sexually. He medicated the pain of his self-hatred with alcohol. Afternoons began with Campari and soda at *pranzo*. In the evenings he had a triple martini before *cena*. Of course, in Rome every meal includes wine.

Two years after he graduated from the Academia, Ackerman collapsed. His first diplomatic assignment, in Nairobi, was also his last. He washed out of the diplomatic corps on a wave of alcohol.

Recalled to Rome, his career had been derailed. He was sent to dry out at an alcoholic rehab center in Bergamo, Italy.

After more than a decade of living in Rome, he felt himself more a

Roman than a Midwesterner. So, he stayed in Rome after rehab, and life in Rome became both his comfort and his company.

Ackerman worked at the Congregation for Bishops, just another one of the hundreds of Vatican bureaucrats. He became one of the gate-keepers to the episcopacy. For the past ten years he had put together background files on men who were candidates to be bishops in the English-speaking world. Even Cardinal O'Toole's file had to pass the review of Monsignor Matthew Ackerman.

Always the bridesmaid and never the bride, Ackerman could look forward to a couple of decades more of paper shuffling. Then he would be put out to pasture in a parish in Missouri.

Just as Ackerman knew all the secrets of all the episcopal candidates, his own secrets were also known to the Congregation for Bishops. The contents of his own dossier kept his name from ever being seriously considered for bishop.

This made him furious. He knew full well that men who shared the same demons were becoming bishops. The only difference being they'd kept their dossiers clean.

Most days he controlled his rage. Some days he nursed it. But tonight he intended to drown it. That prospect made him quite happy.

Ackerman almost danced down the steps from the Gianicolo Hill to Trastevere. As cars squeezed past in the narrow lanes, he glided into doorways and then back out again. It was the dance of a man who needed a drink and knew where to find one.

For dinner, he was meeting three priests, also in mufti, at the Buc-catino d'Oro, the Little Golden Bite. It was a clerical favorite. When Ackerman arrived, he found his dinner companions seated outside at a table perilously close to traffic. Passengers in the passing cars could easily have reached out their windows and taken a breadstick from their table. These Roman priests were so accustomed to the narrow streets, they didn't even notice.

All three of Ackerman's friends were bureaucratic gnomes in the Vatican. Truth be told, they all suffered from low-grade depression. Each of them was spending their entire careers in gray little offices, sometimes located in damp Vatican basements. There was nothing glamorous about their work. As with so many people, it was enough to drive them to drink. For them, medication had long since replaced meditation as their preferred path to peace.

"*Senta*," shouted Ackerman at the waiter, "*whiskey e giacco, senza acqua*." He was ready to drink, and there was no sense in filling half the glass with water.

One of the priests already at the table, a New Yorker named Anthony Barbieri, looked at Ackerman. "Damn it, Matt, slow down. You haven't even paused to sit down yet."

"Oh, Tony," said Ackerman, "I'm just catching up to you." The two men had always been in competition. Barbieri's flawless Italian, learned in Brooklyn, gave him a professional edge over Ackerman. Tony could easily have passed for a Roman. He spent his days writing letters in the Vatican Secretary of State's office in English and Italian.

"What do you hear about the funeral for Manning?" asked Barbieri. "All the cardinals have flown off to New York. We probably all could take the week off and nobody would notice."

"Where you work, you could take the year off and nobody would notice," said Ackerman. Most Vatican bureaucrats will probably not die from overwork.

The priest sitting next to Barbieri spoke up in a nasal voice. "*Salvatote*," said Teddy Gibson, a skinny beanpole of a guy from Indiana, who worked as a Latinist on official Vatican documents. Gibson had a perpetually worried look on his face. His speech was peppered with Latinisms. He hardly had any living friends. His best friends were Cicero and Pliny and other long-dead ancient Romans. As linguistically challenged as Ackerman had been, Teddy was gifted. He once learned Swahili while sitting in a canon law class taking notes in Italian.

"Oh, can it, Teddy," barked Ackerman. He was irritated by Gibson's Latin pretensions. "We are speaking in the vernacular this evening."

"*Scusi*," said Gibson. "Somebody is out of sorts."

The last to arrive was an Australian, Jim Collins. He came around the corner of the restaurant and pulled up a chair just a few seconds after Ackerman sat down. Collins taught moral theology. He was always happy. Ackerman detested him for his perpetual cheerfulness. Collins slapped them all on the back and greeted them with a "Hello, blokes." Ackerman did not want to be cheered up. "You damn Aussies are always too fuckin' happy," he said.

The waiter knew them all. They didn't even have to order. He brought the pasta puttanesca, the "whore's pasta." It was the house specialty.

Ackerman turned to Barbieri, picking up on his question again. "Nobody is deader than a dead archbishop. Manning is not even in his grave, and people are already calling about his successor. Black is the color of vultures and priests," said Ackerman, breaking off a piece of bread.

All through dinner the three priests plied Ackerman for information about who might replace Manning in New York. Like in most bureaucracies, gossip is the preferred recreation in the Vatican.

By the time the pasta and wine came, they were throwing out possible names. While Ackerman might have been a little drunk, he wasn't stupid drunk, at least not yet. He didn't give away any information. Besides, he didn't know much beyond the usual speculation.

"One thing is for sure," said Ackerman. "It's certainly not going to be any of you assholes. I stand a better chance than any of you. And it certainly isn't going to be me."

"You never know," said Collins hopefully. "You could be on the terna someday."

"Don't patronize me," snapped Ackerman. "Besides, I don't have the necessary episcopal qualities. To be a bishop you have to be a pusillanimous twit. If you guys work at it, you could make the short list. You pretty much fit the bill." They chuckled. They all had a low opinion of their superiors and a not much higher one of themselves.

"There are so few qualified people these days," he said cynically. "After all, nobody who has more than two years' pastoral experience is allowed to be a bishop. It's a damn rule added in the 1917 Code of canon law, I think. 'Bishops must know next to nothing about pastoral work,'" he said in a mocking voice. "Nobody who has the smell of the sheep can be a shepherd."

Ackerman was on a roll. "Hell, the three of you would be a perfect terna. I should put your names in for New York. After all, not one of you has actual experience being a priest. Hey, Tony, you don't believe in God, no matter. You want to be Archbishop of New York?"

"Matt," said Tony, "you're drunk."

"Not yet," said Ackerman. "But you know that I follow Lillian Hellman's dicta, 'I only drink to get drunk.' It's the only way I can make sense of my miserable existence." Clearly, Ackerman was not in a festive mood. A momentary silence descended on the table. Jim Collins tried to cheer things up with some observation about passing tourists. Nobody paid any attention.

Ackerman spoke up again. "They are killing cardinals all over the world. Maybe the Church will finally make some progress when we get rid of some of the detritus of clerical princes."

There was another awkward silence after this pronouncement. Rumors had been floating around that these cardinals' deaths might be connected, but this was the first that the three other priests had heard of it from an inside source. They were shocked.

"What do you mean?" said Barbieri. "Who is killing them?"

"Nobody," said Ackerman, suddenly realizing he had said too much. "I need some air."

"Matt, we are sitting outside," said Gibson helpfully, pointing out the air all around them.

"*Stai zitto*," snapped Ackerman. "I need to walk."

"Wait a minute, Matt," said Barbieri. "What do you mean *they* are killing cardinals?"

"Well," said Ackerman, "I overheard Cardinal Visconti tell the cardinal from Napoli that his ass could be next."

Barbieri said, almost to himself, "This story has legs. What else do you know, Matt?"

"I only know what I hear in the rumor mill," answered Ackerman. "And you know how accurate that is."

"No, no, no, Matt. It seems like you know more than you are letting on," said Barbieri.

Ackerman exhaled. "Like I said, I need some air." He got up from the table and threw some euros down for the check.

"Don't you want to stay for *dolce*?" said Collins.

"No, the dessert I have in mind they don't serve here. I have nothing else to say to you ass-kissers."

"Speak for yourself, Matt. You NAC guys are the experts in knowing what to kiss and when," Gibson shot back.

"It's time to go," sighed Ackerman. "This conversation has taken a nasty turn." Ackerman possessed just enough narcissism to think he was above the nastiness.

He pushed away from the table and stumbled a bit on the cobblestones as he headed down the Via Farmacia. The sun had almost set and the wrought-iron lamps of Trastevere were lit. They made a pinkish glow on the stone building. Romance was in the air. Ackerman could smell it.

He paused at the end of the street for a moment to steady himself on one of the old bollards that were once used to tie up horses. His several drinks had begun to kick in.

Just around the corner from the restaurant, a street magician performed for passing tourists. "*Guarda, guarda*," he said, as he pulled a silk handkerchief out of a little child's ear. That magician had been doing the same tricks somewhere in the neighborhood every night for years. He was something of a local celebrity. Even the local Romani stopped to watch. They loved magic.

Superstition has always been the real religion of the Romans. In the seminary, Ackerman and other seminarians used to play on this superstition of the streets. Roman men believed that if you walked between two priests you would be sterile. Ackerman and a friend often used to trap a guy and make him walk between them. Sometimes, nervous men would run the other way rather than walk between two priests.

Ackerman moved on from the magician and picked up the pace a bit. The conversation with his brethren had made him edgy. He had, perhaps, said too much.

A couple of hundred meters down the narrow street, the lane emptied out into a huge square, the Piazza of Santa Maria in Trastevere. On the square stands the oldest continuously functioning parish church in Rome and the first one ever dedicated to the Virgin Mary. The parish dates back to 300 AD and the Emperor Constantine.

Monsignor Ackerman hardly noticed the old church. It was just part of his familiar landscape. But he couldn't help but notice a large crowd of young people standing on the church portico and spilling out into the square. The massive front doors of the church were open, and he could hear the end of vespers being sung by the young people inside. The sound of the chanted prayer, mixed with the sound of vendors and street performers, created an odd counterpoint of the sacred and the profane.

Santa Maria in Trastevere was one of the few vital parishes left in central Rome. It was kept alive, not by the clergy, but by the young people Ackerman could hear praying inside. They are social activists who meet in the old convent of San Egidio next door to the Church. These youth dedicate their free time to serving the poor and making peace around the world.

The San Egidio community feeds the hungry in their soup kitchen. It also runs the homeless shelters around Rome and has become the social conscience of the city. They even negotiated peace treaties to end war in places like Ethiopia.

If the gospel of Jesus is still a living presence in the streets of Rome, it is more because of the San Egidio community than the Vatican fortress a mile away.

Matt Ackerman felt a little guilty and jealous as he passed the activist youth. Maybe twenty years before, he had been like them, full of idealism and virtue. But an iron curtain of guilt and loneliness had surrounded his heart. He no longer felt the same enthusiasm he once felt. The monsignor was on a mission, but it had nothing to do with the faith.

Ackerman headed across the Piazza of Santa Maria, past the old apartment building where Gore Vidal spent his declining years, and plunged into the shadows of a dark side street. Once again, he could hear music, this time the driving beat of European techno-pop.

Another group of mostly young people stood in line outside a nondescript steel door marked with a No Parking sticker and the words *Lasciare libero questo passagio*. Over the door a small neon sign in bright blue script read simply *Angelo Azzurro*. A neon blue angel hovered over the establishment name.

Outside the door in the little narrow street stood a bouncer with biceps as big as most people's thighs. He blocked the entrance and screened the patrons. "*Si, no, si, si,*" he said, culling the sheep from the goats. If you were pretty, or rich, or well known to him, or well connected, you got in. Your chances improved enormously if you tipped.

"*Buona sera, Monsignore.*" The bouncer nodded to Ackerman as he detached the velvet rope and let him in. Matt Ackerman was a regular.

The doorway led to an ancient stone staircase, wide enough for two people to pass. It curved down twenty feet below the modern street level of Rome, to the ancient subterranean street. Ackerman stumbled a bit on poorly lit, uneven steps as he descended into the cavern-like disco below. Purple black-light tubes running along the stairs seemed to irradiate the teeth, shirts, and white socks of patrons, making them glow in the dark. Deafening techno dance music pulsed up the staircase toward the street.

For the first time that evening, Matt Ackerman relaxed. He was as much at home here as in his office or chapel. He went directly to the bar in the corner. Shafts of light from tiny pinpoint spots illumined the glass ashtrays on the bar. The cut glass ashtrays glimmered with a reflected light that made everyone around the bar look both mysterious and alluring.

The bartender, Stefano, nodded toward Ackerman and brought him a Jack Daniels with ice. He paused to say hello.

"*Ciao, Mateo,*" said Stefano. "*Come va?*"

"Horrible."

"Why?" said the bartender.

"It is all coming apart," said Ackerman.

"What's coming apart?" asked the bartender in Italian. "The Church?"

"No," said the monsignor. "Me. I'm coming apart. I don't know how much longer I can stand this."

Stefano had other customers, but he ignored them for a moment and leaned in to hear Ackerman.

"Ever since Manning got shot, everybody is talking. Even the pope suspects something. They've started an investigation in the Vatican. They hired an American investigator. They are looking at everyone."

Stefano signaled to another bartender to cover the bar for him. Ackerman had already finished his Jack Daniels, so Stefano poured him another shot. "What are you talking about?" asked Stefano.

Ackerman started to slur his words, but he didn't stop talking. He babbled on, seemingly irrational.

"I can't keep this ball in the air," said Ackerman. "They all deserved what they got, you know. But I suppose somebody could follow the money. People will be looking everywhere. They will even be looking here, Stefano." He pointed with his finger around the bar and then toward the bartender's face.

"Watch what you are saying," growled Stefano. "*Stai calma.*" He leaned back from Ackerman. The monsignor gave him a boozy stare and stumbled to his feet from the barstool.

"I came here for sweets," said Ackerman. "And I'm going to find some." He wandered off into the dark recesses of the disco.

The bartender turned toward a mirror-covered door behind the bar and slipped through into the tiny manager's office.

"*Don Franco,*" said Stefano to the large man seated at the desk, "*abbiamo un problema.*"

9

CIAO, ROMA

CARDINAL MANNING'S FUNERAL WAS AS BIG AS HE HAD been, right down to his double-wide casket. The entry procession took forty minutes, with clerics, press, and dignitaries taking up most of the cathedral. There wasn't any room for the ordinary Catholic. In a way, that was appropriate. Like most cardinals, Manning didn't have any room in his life for the ordinary faithful. No reason his funeral should be any different.

Funerals are meant to be a consolation to the living and a spiritual help to the dead. Manning's funeral was both of these things but mostly a show. When the show was over, Nate headed to the airport.

While he waited for his flight to be called, Nate watched as several archbishops and cardinals negotiated with the gate attendant to get themselves bumped up to first class. Odd, he thought, they look more like CEOs than priests. If you took off their collars and put on a tie, they would be like any other frequent flyer—pushy, bored, and impatient.

Brigid was often critical of the priests she had known growing up on Long Island. "Worldly men," she called them. Nate's own father had once called bishops "politicians in a dog collar."

After the meal was served, Nate took a Benadryl to knock himself out. He slept the next six hours to Rome. On the approach to Fiumicino

Airport, the flight attendant came around with hot towels and told people to prepare for landing. The warm terry cloth helped take the pressure creases out of his face made from leaning against the seat next to him.

Nate raised the window shade. Below was the sparkling water of the Mediterranean. The plane made a wide arc over the sea and flew over the beaches of Ostia. From his window on the port side, Nate could see the Eternal City, bathed in pink light as the sun rose over the Colli Albani, the hills of the dawn, just to the east of Rome.

It was a thrilling sight. Nate had only been to Rome once before, on a pilgrimage with the Knights of Malta. He was excited to be back.

Everywhere in the world, the morning brings a kind of rebirth. Rome's streets were still relatively quiet as Nate's taxi made its way into *centro* on the autostrada. For a place that had been a city since 700 years before Christ, Rome looked remarkably good. Spring rains had washed the cobblestones, and Rome's *netturbini* were out in force with their long-handled witch's brooms, gathering up the refuse deposited by three million Romans and a million tourists. Coffee shops were opening. The Romani, congenitally unable to stand in an orderly line, elbowed each other out of the way to order their morning *cappuccini* and *cornetti* from the baristas.

Tracy had recommended to Nate that he stay at the Columbus Hotel. "Close to everything," he'd said. He was right.

As the taxi turned onto the Via della Conciliazione, the dome of St. Peter's appeared through the windshield. Like most Catholic tourists, Nate felt a thrill at the sight.

A grand avenue leading from the Tiber River to St. Peter's Square, the "Way of Conciliation" was built by Benito Mussolini as a "gift" to the city of Rome. It provides a magnificent entrance to St. Peter's Square. Unfortunately, its construction required the complete demolition of an entire medieval neighborhood. Romans are still bitter about it.

The Columbus Hotel is halfway down the avenue between the river and the Vatican. It is a palazzo built in the late 1400s to house Cardinal Giuliano della Rovere, a man accustomed to luxury. The cardinal lived there only a few years. Shortly after his house was finished, he moved down the street when he became Pope Julius II.

Della Rovere was a man who loved to decorate. The Columbus Hotel still has the frescoed ceilings he commissioned for his personal apartments. When he moved to the Vatican, he got busy redecorating there, too. He commissioned Michelangelo to paint the Sistine Chapel.

Nate's taxi pulled under the archway carriage entrance that led into the hotel's central courtyard. The old-fashioned reception desk just inside still had little letter boxes for each room with a brass number above each. The porter at the door wore white gloves.

After check-in, the tiny elevator carried Nate and the porter to the second floor, the *piano nobile*. Nate's room had once been part of della Rovere's private apartment. The ceiling fresco showed cherubs guiding a chariot heavenward, the apotheosis of some Greek hero. Nate had no idea who was in the fresco, but he suspected it was the cardinal himself. It occurred to him that the painting had nothing to do with Christianity.

After a shower and a change of clothes, Nate went right to work. He had a 10:00 a.m. appointment with Monsignor Matthew Ackerman, the priest Tracy had suggested as a contact. Ackerman worked at the English language desk in the Congregation for Bishops.

Even after an eight-hour flight and only six hours of sleep, Nate stepped out of his room looking like he was about to do a photo shoot for *GQ*. In a black Canali suit and a starched, custom-made white shirt, with a red silk Ferragamo tie, he would have been more at home in fashionista Milan than in a dreary dicastery of the Vatican.

Most men buy suits to wear to work. Nate bought suits simply because he liked them. At six-foot-one and weighing 183 pounds, Nate made clothes look good. Brigid sometimes still seductively reminded him that he looked best in nothing at all.

Nate and Brigid both played the game of appearances. Their true operating philosophy was more Greek epicurean than Christian ascetic. Brigid was better at the game than Nate. He was blue collar from Charlestown. She was striving middle class from Long Island.

But they both had traded the child-centered marriage of their Catholic parents for the career-centered life of a professional couple. Living well had become the reward for a life of discipline and hard work. Children were not part of their long-term plan.

After breakfast, Nate made the ten-minute walk to Monsignor Ackerman's office. The Congregation for Bishops was outside the Vatican walls, in a nondescript office building fairly close to Cardinal O'Toole's apartment.

Many Catholics have the mistaken impression that working at the Vatican is glamorous. In reality, for most Vatican bureaucrats, life is fairly dreary. There are some elegant offices inside the Vatican, but the English language desk of the Congregation for Bishops was not one of them. Nate stepped through the glass doors into a whitewashed room with gunmetal gray desks and hard wooden chairs.

* * *

Monsignor Ackerman was hung over. Hunched over his desk, he cradled his throbbing head in his hands. He drank alone at home on Monday night, out of caution. He was unable to recall completely the events of Sunday night. He could remember dinner with his friends at the trattoria. He also could remember the walk to Angelo Azzuro through Trastevere. After that, everything blurred.

When he awoke on Monday, he found a business card in his shirt pocket from a writer at *Panoramio* magazine. Ackerman hoped he hadn't said anything foolish. He also hoped he hadn't done anything incriminating. He called in sick on Monday and went to bed. But Tuesday he absolutely had to be back at work, with all the tension of the Manning murder in the Vatican.

When Ackerman's secretary tapped on his door and stuck her head into the room, he raised his head slightly and looked at her with bleary eyes. She had seen that look before. She said crisply, "*Monsignore*, your appointment has arrived. Mr. Condon from America."

Ackerman sighed and said to her, dry mouthed, "Water, please." The secretary returned with a pitcher of water. Nate Condon followed.

"*Monsignore*, this is Mr. Nathaniel Condon from New York." Nate stepped through the doorway.

Ackerman inhaled, suddenly revived.

"Mr. Condon," said Ackerman, stuttering a bit, "I was expecting . . . well, I don't know what I was expecting. Please, sit down. I hope you had a pleasant flight from New York?" Ackerman extended his hand, and Nate shook it firmly.

"Thank you for seeing me, Monsignor. I was given your name by the Nunciature in Washington, DC, as a contact for my investigation on behalf of the Holy See."

"Call me Matt," said Ackerman flirtatiously. "May I call you Nate?"

"Please do," said Nate, confusion showing on his face.

Ackerman, however, was pleased.

"As you may know," continued Nate, "I have been asked by the Holy See to investigate the deaths of the cardinals. Former CIA Director Tracy thought I could use the help of an American working at the Vatican. I need the personnel files on each of these six cardinals. I also need whatever you may have on them, no matter how trivial. On occasion, I may need files on others as well."

Nate slid a piece of paper across Ackerman's desk with the names of the six dead cardinals. The priest looked at the paper and raised his eyebrows.

"*Pezzi grossi*," said Ackerman.

"Pardon me?" asked Nate.

"VIPs. These are high-level people. I can't just release their files without some authorization."

"I have the highest level of clearance in the Church," said Nate, using terminology more suited to the US government than the Church.

Nate could see he was not getting through, but he was a quick learner. "I have a letter from Cardinal O'Toole," he added. "My authorization comes directly from His Holiness. You may call Cardinal O'Toole's office to verify my commission."

"Well, of course," said Ackerman nervously. "As soon as I can verify your credentials, I will get the files. We don't keep them here in this office. I could bring them around to your hotel." Ackerman was curious to know where Nate was staying anyway.

"I'm staying at the Hotel Columbus," said Nate. "Perhaps you could have a courier drop them off."

"Oh," said Ackerman, seizing an opportunity, "I would be delighted to bring them by as soon as they are ready. This will be a fairly large set of files. We will have to photocopy them. Most of our files are not stored digitally."

Nate could see the fatigue in the priest's eyes. "You look tired, Father. Are you sure it won't be too much trouble?"

"No trouble at all. I get off at six. I could come by then."

"That's great. Why don't you let me buy you dinner at my hotel? It's the least I could do to thank you. Perhaps you could give me some additional insight into the investigation." Nate knew how to make people feel important.

"Anything I can do to be of service to the Holy Father," said the priest breathlessly. "It would be my honor. I'll bring a paper copy and a flash drive for what we have electronically. I'll get you a password for the cloud. "

Nate smiled. It amused him to think that the Church kept documents in the "cloud." No doubt they were guarded by angels.

Ackerman seemed reluctant to end the conversation. "Will your wife be joining us?" he asked.

"No, my wife is traveling on business in Belgium. It will be just the two of us," said Nate.

Ackerman smiled with obvious delight. Nate got up to leave for his next appointment downtown, at the Questura, the offices of the Carabinieri, the national police of Italy. Tracy had arranged for him to have access to Interpol records.

"Thanks, Matt," said Nate, extending his hand to the priest. He squeezed Ackerman's hand and said, "See you at six." Nate was not oblivious to the power he had over the monsignor.

"I'll look forward to it," said the monsignor. As Nate turned to close the door behind him, he saw Ackerman collapse into his chair.

On the way to his appointment at the Questura, Nate pulled out his mobile phone to call Tracy back in Washington. He had arranged for international service and wanted to see if it was working.

It was 6:00 a.m. in DC. Tracy answered promptly. He was up already. The Roman traffic made it impossible to hear clearly, so Nate stepped into the doorway of a shop and covered his ear.

"Bill, it's Nate. I'm making some progress here in Rome. I talked to that priest whose name you gave me. Did you find out anything on your end? What about your contacts at the agency or on the hill?"

"Zero on the hill," said Tracy. "We'll get no help from Senator Reynolds at the intelligence committee. He's a Catholic, but he is pissed off at the Church. His bishop in Kentucky refused him communion because of his stand on gay marriage, at the funeral Mass for his sister, no less. These bishops are screwing themselves. They don't understand politics. Unless you are one hundred percent pure on certain issues, they cut you off."

Nate didn't have time for a transatlantic tirade about the hierarchy. He pressed on. "What about your contacts at the agency?"

"We did better there," said Tracy. "The cardinal in Chile was killed in a private clinic in Santiago where he went for a varicose vein operation. Hard to believe you could die from that. May have been a botched surgery or a reaction to the anesthesia. Perhaps it was a drug overdose. Anyway, what should have been same-day surgery turned out to be eternal." Tracy chuckled, pleased with his own joke.

"The agency doesn't have any other leads. There are no common threads, except that all are cardinals. Whoever is behind these deaths must have global reach. The agency thinks we should be looking at organized crime."

Nate felt like he could have reached that conclusion without the CIA's vaunted analysis.

Nate stepped back out onto the sidewalk and started walking toward the Tiber. "Did your pals at the agency weed out any suspects?"

"Well," said Tracy, "just like you said in Georgetown, it's probably not the Israelis. They don't care about the Church all that much. They wouldn't have reason to kill bishops in Chile, and certainly not in New York. No chatter at the agency about Israel and the Church."

"Who else is out?" asked Nate, sitting down on a park bench near the Castel Sant'Angelo. He could just barely hear over the traffic. Behind Nate was the massive fortress of the Castel, a place where popes had taken refuge when Rome was under siege. Centuries ago, when people wanted to kill the top echelons of the Church, they sent an army to do it.

"It's probably not the victims of pedophilia either," said Tracy. "They would rather drag the bishops into court or through the mud in the newspapers. Not kill them. Like that priest from Chicago—what's his name—Andrew Greeley said, they wouldn't be satisfied even if the pope ordered every priest in the world castrated."

Nate could hear the loyal Knight of Malta in Tracy's voice. Tracy usually defended the hierarchy, even when they were wrong, especially about the child abuse scandals. Nate guessed Tracy was speculating.

"Why wouldn't child abuse victims be suspects?" asked Nate.

"Oh, they're just crazy," said Tracy. "Angry and crazy."

"Anger and insanity seem like pretty good qualifications for serial murder," said Nate. "They would give you good motivation anyway."

"They couldn't do it," answered Tracy. "They're just not that organized. This would take organization."

It seemed like Tracy wanted to steer him away from child abuse victims. He made a mental note—keep that avenue open.

"So, who does that leave us?" asked Nate.

"Well, I hate to say it," said Tracy, "but probably it's probably an inside job—somebody in the Church who wants control. Whoever would kill six cardinals must know the Church pretty well and has to care about it a whole lot. Why, I'm not sure. The only place more secretive than Langley is the Vatican." Tracy chuckled at the irony.

"You've been helpful," said Nate. "This narrows the scope."

"By the way," added Tracy, "that American monsignor's name I gave you at Milano's as a contact . . . what's his name . . . Ackerman? Be careful with him. One of the people at the agency found his name on a list of possible Mafia contacts, the Naples branch of the Camorra."

"I know the Camorra well," said Nate. His work as a prosecutor in New York had brought him into contact with them. "They have a lot of contacts in the States. Maybe the FBI might know something. What kind of connection do they suspect to Ackerman?"

"Well, he hangs out at a gay bar in Rome that is known to be run by the mob. He may be doing a little freelance work. Agency people said he might be a messenger for the mob. Just be careful about what you tell him."

"I'm meeting him tonight for dinner," said Nate. "I'll be circumspect."

"By the way," added Tracy, "Peggy suggested another contact in Rome. That friend of hers, Father Murphy, from the Soldados de Cristo says that the vice rector at their seminary in Rome is an American who knows his way around the Vatican. She thought you might want to contact him, too. His name is Jim Farrell. As soon as Peg gets up, I'll get his contact info and email it to you."

Again Nate felt steered. Peggy seemed to be enamored of the Soldados. "OK," said Nate. "Any help is welcome."

They hung up. Nate hailed a taxi for the ride down to the Questura.

He only lasted a couple of hours at the police headquarters. Jet lag crept in, and Nate found himself falling asleep as he puzzled over the files on Italian mob bosses. He realized that his rudimentary Italian prevented him from understanding everything. Nate made a mental note to hire an Italian-speaking assistant. Surrendering to the fatigue, he asked the officer at the desk to make some copies for him from the files. Then he went out on the street and hailed a taxi for the ride back to the

Columbus, intent on getting a couple of hours of rest before his dinner meeting with Ackerman.

* * *

Six o'clock is early for dinner in Rome. The dining room at the Columbus Hotel was practically empty, which suited Nate just fine. He didn't want to have people listening in on their conversation.

Monsignor Ackerman had arrived right on time, carrying with him a large cardboard box filled with files on the dead cardinals. They took it up and locked it in Nate's room, then went down to dinner.

Ackerman looked all cleaned up. He gave off a pleasing aroma, one Nate recognized. Jaipur by Boucheron. Brigid had bought it for him last year for their anniversary. The scent put Nate on the alert. Perhaps Ackerman thought this was more than a business dinner?

They ordered wine and dinner from a white-coated waiter. Nate got right down to business. "What did these six men have in common, besides the fact that they were all cardinals?"

Ackerman seemed flattered to be seen as a source. A glass of wine also loosened his tongue. "Well, they were all papabile," he said.

"What's that?" asked Nate, mystified by all this Italian on his first day in Italy.

"Papabile are men capable of becoming pope," said Ackerman with a sort of patronizing tone. "They are, or were, all eligible to be pope. Italians love to speculate on who might be pope." Ackerman lowered his voice. "It's no secret that the Holy Father is old and frail. It's just a matter of time, maybe only a few weeks. Then there will be a conclave and one of them will be elected. These six guys would be on anybody's short list."

"Is there anybody else who might be on the short list?" asked Nate, wondering who else might be in danger.

"Sure," said Ackerman. "You mentioned one of them this morning: Cardinal O'Toole. He would be a likely candidate."

Ackerman broke a breadstick artfully into three pieces. "That's a sign that you will return to Rome," he said to Nate. "In my case, it probably means that I'll never leave."

The monsignor got back to the topic. "O'Toole could be elected if there weren't so much resistance to an American. He is certainly conservative enough for the current climate. I'd say he's one of the most conservative."

"What else do these guys have in common besides being candidates to be pope?"

"Well," replied the priest, getting more puffed up as he spoke, "they share the Vatican Bank connection. Three of the six who died were on the board, including the cardinals from New York, Santiago, and Milan."

"How many cardinals serve on the board of the Vatican Bank?" asked Nate.

"Six, at present," said Ackerman.

"Who are the others?"

"Well, there is the cardinal from London and two guys here in Rome, Cardinals Crepi and Salazar. They are very involved in the bank. The guy from London never attends the meetings, I'm told. There is a complete list in the Vatican directory I included in your box."

Nate was making notes. "Who are Crepi and Salazar?" he asked.

"Luciano Crepi is the governor of Vatican City. He runs the day-to-day stuff at the Vatican. Julio Salazar is the prefect of the Knights of the Holy Sepulcher. They own this hotel." Nate could tell Ackerman loved possessing insider information.

"They own this hotel?" said Nate, a bit surprised.

"Yeah," said Ackerman. "They own lots of stuff. Salazar has his own financial empire. Crepi has the Vatican machinery. They are peas in a pod, those two. Always together, been pals for years." Now the good monsignor was descending into Vatican gossip, but this could be useful.

"Anything else common to the deceased cardinals?" asked Nate.

Ackerman thought for a second. "They are all Roman trained. They all have contacts here and a history here. That's good and bad. They have a Roman pedigree, which is helpful if you want to be pope. They all have friends here. But of course, they also all have enemies."

Nate raised an eyebrow at the mention of enemies. He poured Ackerman a second glass of wine from the bottle by the table and urged him on. "Are there rivalries in the Church?" Nate asked with feigned innocence.

"It's a brood of vipers," said the monsignor through a mouthful of bread. "Especially when the pope is weakening, then the venom comes out. Nobody is deader than a dead pope. The Romans have a saying, '*Il Papa è morto, fai un altro.*'"

"Which means?" said Nate, a bit irritated with the Italian again.

"The pope is dead; make another one." Ackerman slapped the table, pleased with his irreverence, and took a sip of his wine. "People are making moves now for the inevitable. When the pope dies, things change. But then again, nothing really changes."

Their food arrived at the table, and they dived into the pasta. Nate noted that they didn't say a blessing. Ackerman talked as he ate.

"There are two groups here in Rome who are nervous about the pope's death—the people who will lose their jobs when he dies, and the people who will get new jobs when he dies. They are opposite sides of the same coin."

"What changes threaten people in the Vatican?" asked Nate. Ackerman leaned in closer. He clearly loved being the expert.

"Well, things have been going on for a long time over here. People like stability. It's human nature. They also like their own little sinecures.

"Take the Vatican Bank. As things go, it is not such a big bank by world standards. Not such a big part of the Vatican either. But," he said, pointing a finger upward for emphasis, "the bank is very important to a few people. It gives them a good life and lots of access to ready cash."

Nate was intrigued that Ackerman mentioned the bank so much without prompting. It was obviously on the priest's mind.

"Tell me about the bank," said Nate, flipping his notebook to a clean page. Ackerman looked around to see if anyone was listening. He lowered his voice, apparently as a precaution against discovery, and cleared his throat like he was going to give a speech. "Over the years," he began, "the bank has been at the center of major scandals.

"Back in the 1980s, a big scandal took down the bank director, Archbishop Paul Marcinkus from Chicago.

"Marcinkus got the bank involved in doing a lot of favors for a guy named Roberto Calvi, who was the president of the largest bank in Milan, the Banco Ambrosiano. Eventually Calvi's dead body was found hanging from a rope under Blackfriars Bridge in London, where he had gone to beg London bankers for a loan. It was probably the Mafia who did it." Ackerman was warming to his tale of the bank. It was a well-known scandal. Tracy had even mentioned it. But Nate found this insider's version quite interesting.

The waiter came over to pour more water into their glasses. Ackerman seemed irritated by his intrusion and paused until the waiter stepped away.

"The Calvi scandal cost the Vatican millions. Calvi's bank folded in Milano. The creditors there sued the Church, because it had induced them to do business with Calvi. Eventually, it was reported in the press here that the Church paid out 244 million dollars to settle with the creditors, including the Mafia."

"Where did they get the money to pay out such a big settlement?" asked Nate.

"The Vatican didn't have that much cash," answered Ackerman. "We have art but not much in the way of liquid assets.

"Most people think they got the money from Opus Dei, which has real deep pockets. It's also said that the Soldados de Cristo kicked in some of the money."

Nate had also heard the rumor about Opus Dei having given the bulk of the money for the settlement, but he had not heard the Soldados mentioned in connection with the bank before.

"Why would Opus Dei pay out so much money to save the bank?" asked Nate.

"They didn't do it to save the bank," answered Ackerman with a hint of condescension. "They did it to save the Holy See from embarrassment, and they wanted something in return.

"They wanted independence from all bishops. And they got it. Immediately after the giant payout was made in Switzerland, Rome recognized Opus Dei as an independent diocese, called a personal prelature. It is the only one in the world. It has no territory, just people in its jurisdiction. They got what the bank has—no supervision."

Ackerman nodded as if to drive home the point. "It may surprise you, Mr. Condon, but even in the Church, money talks."

Ackerman was not done with his tale of the bank. Nate signaled for some more wine. The monsignor continued.

"Then in the 1990s the bank was again implicated in several bribery scandals. One witness claimed that he laundered fifty million dollars through the bank every year. He used it to bribe Italian politicians.

"Recently you probably heard about Monsignor Nunzio Scarano, an accountant who was working for a Vatican foundation, who got arrested attempting to launder money through the Vatican Bank. He was doing some favors for friends in Naples by flying sacks of euros into Italy from Switzerland. It was valued at more than twenty-six million dollars. He ran the cash through the Vatican Bank and cleaned it up by running it through charities he controlled in Naples. Nunzio took a tip for himself, of course," said Ackerman.

Nate remembered Tracy talking about this, but he was surprised that a Vatican monsignor would speak so openly about such bald-faced corruption.

"Nunzio got caught, but there might be others," said Ackerman, sotto voce. He chuckled to himself for a moment, enjoying his scandal history.

"There have even been some humorous moments," he said. "This past year, the ATMs run by the Vatican Bank were shut off by the German bank that managed them, because the Vatican was not cooperating with international money laundering regulations.

"You see, Mr. Condon, the bank is fertile ground for scandal here in Rome, but it's not all bad.

"Sometimes the Vatican Bank is used to accomplish a political purpose, like when the Vatican funneled money to aid Solidarity in Poland in the 1980s. Every now and then it does a favor for some government trying to ransom someone in some part of the world."

"Who runs the bank day to day?" asked Nate, trying to make Ackerman focus a little more on his investigation.

"Well, there is the board of directors composed of cardinals, but they are all busy men who live a long way off. Cardinal Crepi is the real boss of the bank, and Monsignor Donato Renzi is his right-hand man.

"According to the organizational chart, Donato works for the lay director, but in the Vatican, when there is a contest between a suit and a cassock, the cassock wins."

Ackerman smiled broadly, delighted for the moment that he was on the winning team in Vatican politics because of his rank.

"It is said that Donato can escort anybody he wants right past the director's office and up the stairs to the vault with sacks of cash."

The waiter came over again to pour more water into their glasses. Ackerman glared at him at this second intrusion.

"Who is the biggest beneficiary of the bank?" asked Nate.

"The depositors, for one," said Ackerman. "It's like having a Cayman Islands bank right here in Europe. The employees and the directors also benefit. They get good pay and sometimes a little piece of the action."

Nate got the picture and wanted to shift the topic. "How would you characterize the dead cardinals? Were they conservative?"

"You don't get to be a cardinal unless you are conservative," said Ackerman, breaking apart another breadstick. "That is partly what makes them papabile, but that's only the first test. They also have to be acceptable to us here in the curia. The Vatican bureaucracy doesn't like outsiders. The most acceptable candidate to us here is someone from the inside, like the diplomatic corps or one of the departments here. It's OK if the new pope has a couple of years in a diocese, but two years in pastoral work is the limit. That's all Benedict XVI had. We don't want our popes tainted by pastoral concern. We don't really want them having the smell of the sheep. Pope Thomas has had a little too much of that odor for curia taste."

Nate was shocked. "I thought they were supposed to be pastors. Isn't that the whole idea?"

Ackerman let out a guffaw. "That is a lovely idea, Nate. Lovely, but completely naïve. Most popes have never spent a single day in a parish."

Somehow it had never occurred to Nate that popes and cardinals could get to a place where they never directly served the people. He had thought that all priests served in parishes at some time during their career. Not so, he was discovering. He recalled the receiving line at the Nunciature in Washington. The common thread there seemed to have been who was secretary to whom.

Nate refocused. "What are the factions here in Vatican bureaucracy?"

"Well, of course," said Ackerman, "there are more than three thousand people working in the Vatican. Most just do their jobs. I suppose the curators in the museum or archivists in the library don't care much about Vatican politics. It doesn't matter to them who's in charge.

"But people like me, in jobs like mine," he continued, "we certainly have factions. We have enemies and friends, because we decide who gets to be bishop and who gets to run the Church."

"What factions exist?" Nate asked again.

"Two big factions," said Ackerman, pushing his plate away. "In shorthand, I suppose you could call them the 'liberals' and the 'soldados.'" The liberals don't really count for anything. We put them in peace and justice stuff and ignore them. They can do dialogue with other religions and stuff like that, which nobody here really cares about."

"Who are the soldados?" asked Nate.

"The Soldados de Cristo? You've never heard of them?" Ackerman was incredulous.

"Vaguely, I think," said Nate, remembering Peggy Tracy and Brigid's alarm after seeing Peggy at the hotel in Washington. For a group he had never even heard of a week ago, they certainly were popping up everywhere.

"The Soldados are basically just one of the many players on the right. They are a Mexican order rapidly going global, at least until the current pope put their founder under house arrest. They have lots of money and lots of people. They're quasi-military, sort of like the Jesuits in their early days. Everywhere they go, conspiracy theories and strange rumors abound."

Nate was intrigued. "What sort of rumors?"

"Rumors of sexual impropriety," said Ackerman. "And rumors of financial corruption. That's why Pope Thomas put their founder, Marcel Marcelino, under house arrest. Seems like he's well acquainted with the seven capital sins, especially lust and greed."

"Who would know about these Soldados?" asked Nate. This seemed like something he should follow up on.

"A friend of mine knows a lot about them," said Ackerman. "Actually, he has been assigned by the pope to babysit the Soldados' founder and to manage the order. They are kind of in receivership, sort of like the Jesuits were a few years back."

"Marcelino is being held here at the Vatican under lock and key. That's the closest thing to a prison sentence that he's likely ever to get."

Ackerman took out a pen and pad from his jacket pocket and wrote a name and phone number on a piece of paper. He handed it to Nate. "Here, call this guy, Monsignor Henry Rodriguez. He knows all about the Soldados. It would be worth your while."

Nate put the paper into his leather folder.

"Henry—really, it's Enrico Rodriguez," said Ackerman. "He's Mexican American. He's the perfect guy to look into them. He speaks idiomatic Spanish, with a Mexican accent, and he looks like Mario Lopez. He probably would have been a good candidate for the Soldados himself, except for one thing. He's sane." Ackerman and Nate chuckled together. Nate was surprised by the priest's candor.

"Henry told me once that he thinks that their lay group, Miles Cristi, is dangerous. They are like a group of automatons. They all talk alike, look alike, and think alike. It is scary, actually. Kind of like a religious

version of *The Stepford Wives*. If there is one radical and scary group in
the Church, it's them." Ackerman seemed sincere.

"I thought Opus Dei was the radical and scary group in the Church,"
said Nate, wanting to show his knowledge.

"Oh, not anymore. Opus Dei is yesterday's news," answered Ackerman dismissively. "*The Da Vinci Code* neutered them by ridicule and
exposure. But now the Soldados and the Miles are more nefarious. I
suppose, really, nothing changes from century to century. The characters
are basically the same, just the names change."

Just then, the waiter came over to clear the plates. He had been
watching them from a nearby serving station. With so few patrons in
the dining room, they had a lot of attention from the waiter. He spilled
a glass of water right into Ackerman's lap.

"*Che stupido*," said Ackerman, irritated. The waiter immediately
started drying up the table and daubing the priest with a napkin. He
slapped at the man's hand, saying, "*Basta cosi*."

The waiter did not respond like the usual obsequious Italian servant.
He looked Ackerman directly in the eye and spoke only one soft syllable,
more like a groan, really. "*Oma*." Ackerman's eyes got big.

A chill ran down Nate's spine. He recognized the word, *oma*, the
slang contraction for *omerta*, a Sicilian word for "silence." It was both
an admonition and a warning. The code of *omerta* is the Mafia's code
of silence. Violating it meant death. Ackerman had just been warned to
shut his mouth.

There was a change in Ackerman's demeanor. The loquacious cleric
went abruptly silent. He finished his espresso and, politely but quickly,
took his leave.

"*Buona sera*," said Ackerman, dropping his napkin on the table. "Don't
forget to call Henry. He will be a big help to you." The priest got up and
walked out of the dining room. Nate watched him go, a bit surprised at
the sudden departure.

"*Oma*," Nate said to himself.

Jet lag overcoming him again, Nate went upstairs and collapsed into the giant bed in the room that had once been Cardinal della Rovere's bedchamber, under the fresco depicting the cardinal riding a chariot into the heavens. Probably the only way that the cardinal would ever get there.

10

SOLDADOS DE CRISTO

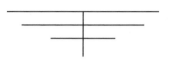

THE MORNING AFTER HIS DINNER WITH ACKERMAN, NATE called Rodriguez and asked for an appointment. He explained the commission he had from the Holy See and made sure to drop O'Toole's name to open the door. Nate was discovering that everything in the hierarchy of the Church is the network of connections.

"Sure," said the American monsignor. "Come on over now. Anything for an investigation sponsored by the Holy Father. After all, we are sort of in the same business."

"What business is that?" asked Nate.

"Fighting the bad guys," said Rodriguez.

Monsignor Rodriguez's office was located within the Vatican Secretary of State, in the Apostolic Palace, very near the papal apartments. It is the most elegant and storied part of the Vatican.

A young woman from Rodriguez's office met Nate at the Porta Sant'Anna. "I'm Sandra Orsuto," she said, introducing herself rather formally. "I'll take you up to Monsignor Rodriguez's office. It is a bit of a labyrinth, and he was afraid you would get lost."

On the way up, Nate was led through the series of rooms painted by Raphael of Urbino, the famous Stanze of Raphael. He vaguely remembered them from *Janson's History of Art*, which he read in college.

The Stanze of Raphael are designed to impress visitors with the power and historical reach of the papacy. Second only to the frescoes in the Sistine Chapel, the stanze are among the most impressive works of art in the Vatican. Like the ceiling of the Sistine Chapel, the stanze were commissioned by Julius II.

The rooms had their desired effect on Nate, who slowed his gait as he passed through them. He figured he might never get a chance to see them again, since this was not a public part of the Vatican.

He turned to Miss Orsuto and asked her, "What's it like working around such art?"

"Well," she said, "you get used to it. It would be a good place if you were an art student."

"Are you an art student?" asked Nate.

"No," said the rather formal Miss Orsuto. "I actually came to Rome as a theology student at the Gregorian. I work here part-time to help pay the bills while I am doing postdoctoral work. Monsignor Rodriguez wanted someone who could read English, Italian, and Spanish, so I got the job."

"What do you know about these rooms?" asked Nate.

"Well," she said, "I know this room is called the Sala Constantino, after the Emperor Constantine. It shows Constantine on his knees giving power over the city of Rome to the popes just before he moved the capital of the empire to Constantinople. It's called the donation of Constantine. A pretty good donation, I'd say—the western Roman empire."

"Ever since Constantine," said Orsuto, "the popes have claimed dominion over Western Europe, and consequently the right, for more than one thousand years, to appoint its monarchs. If you are going to tell a lie, might as well make it a whopper. No one will dare contradict you," she added with an ironic smile.

Nate was impressed as much with her candor as with her historical knowledge and delighted by his private tour. "What's this?" Nate asked, pointing to a wall with a man in military dress on a white horse, with angels flying above him.

"It's the Battle of the Milvian Bridge," she said. "Legend has it that Emperor Constantine heard the words *In hoc signum*, 'in this sign,' in his dream. He saw the cross in his dream, so he assumed that it meant that he would win the battle at the bridge and conquer the city of Rome in that sign. So he had crosses put on the top of his battle standards. Later he discovered that the cross was the sign of the Christians' god. He was so grateful that he became a Christian." She added, "He hedged his bets, though. He didn't actually get baptized until he was on his deathbed."

They both chuckled. "Not a bad idea," said Nate. "That way you don't have to confess your sins."

They passed into another room and stopped in front of a painting of the coronation of Charlemagne. "All Western European kings took their lineage from Charlemagne," she said. "And he was crowned by the pope, who derived his authority from God. So basically this reminds kings that they get their authority from God through the pope."

By the time they got to the next room, she was warming to her role as tour guide.

"This room is called the Eliodoro, or the room of Heliodorus. He was a Greek general mentioned in the book of Maccabees. He was sent to take over the temple of Jerusalem and put an end to Jewish worship. He was stopped by the prayer of a priest. An angel came down and beat the Greek general and threw him out of the temple. I guess it's a metaphor saying, "Don't mess with us priests."

She turned to another fresco in the same room. "Over here," she continued, "is Pope Leo the Great persuading Attila the Hun not to sack Rome. Leo was only partially successful. Attila merely postponed the sacking for a while."

"What's this?" asked Nate, pointing to another wall.

"It's the deliverance of St. Peter from prison," she said. "There is an account of it in the Acts of the Apostles. I guess it's here to show that the papacy can't be kept prisoner by anyone."

They came to a final frescoed room. "I like this room the best," said Ms. Orsuto. "It's called the Sengatura, because it was once the Vatican tribunal. I'm told that it is the only one that Raphael actually painted himself.

"This fresco is called *The School of Athens*. I only know that because they had a copy of it in a lecture hall at the University of Virginia, where I did my BA. It shows the philosophers of the ancient world, like Aristotle and Plato. I guess they are seen as antecedents of Christian wisdom."

Nate was impressed with her use of the word "antecedent." He also made note of the fact that she could read English, Italian, and Spanish.

Taken together, the paintings had one message to any visitor, thought Nate. *The papacy was around before your ancestors were born and will be around long after your children are mere dust.*

Raphael's frescoes had their desired effect on Nate. He almost forgot the reason for his visit.

When they arrived at Monsignor Rodriguez's office, the handsome Latino priest was standing at the door. He seemed to suspect the reason for the long delay. "Been getting an art lesson on the way up?" he asked with a smile.

Miss Orsuto closed the door separating the priest's office from hers and left the two men alone.

"Welcome, Mr. Condon. I'm Father Henry Rodriguez."

Nate didn't really hear the priest for a moment, he was so transfixed by the view of St. Peter's Square from Rodriguez's office. This is some impressive office, thought Nate, still a kid from Charlestown.

Rodriguez noticed Nate looking out the window, so he gave him a little tour. "Out there is an Egyptian obelisk brought here to Rome by one of the Caesars. Beyond the square, up there on the hill, is the North American College, where I went to seminary. I haven't moved very far since I was ordained."

Father Rodriguez motioned Nate to one of two armchairs near the desk. Rodriguez sat in the companion chair facing him. "How can I help you, Mr. Condon?" asked Rodriguez.

After a moment Nate said, "I'm here to find out a little about the Soldados de Cristo. Monsignor Ackerman thought you could help me."

"Smart man, that Matt Ackerman," said Rodriguez with a mixture of irony and honest praise. "You've come to the right place. Do you want the Wikipedia version or a doctoral dissertation?"

Nate liked Rodriguez's deadpan delivery and world-weary tone. The priest reminded Nate of the guys he worked with at the federal prosecutor's office in New York—no bull, just straight talk.

"I think the Wikipedia version would be fine for now," said Nate. Then he added, "I've heard of the Soldados before, but only know them vaguely. My wife met a soldado priest at the Vatican Embassy in Washington last week. But that's about all I know. Why does Monsignor Ackerman think the Soldados might have something to do with the deaths of the cardinals?"

"I've found it risky to speculate on Matt Ackerman's thoughts," said Rodriguez. Nate gathered that there was no love lost between the two monsignors.

"Let me pour you a cup of coffee," said Rodriguez. "Even the Wikipedia version is complicated. This might take a while." He went across the room to a Mr. Coffee type of coffeemaker. "I drink Cafe Americano," said the California priest. "If I drink the local brew, I'm wired all day. I like to sleep at night."

He poured two cups of black coffee and gave one to Nate. He didn't offer cream and sugar. Then he sat down again in the armchair.

"I hope that you are not easily scandalized, Mr. Condon," said Rodriguez.

"I have a reasonably high tolerance for scandal. I spent a decade as a federal prosecutor."

"Good," said Rodriguez. "You'll need a high tolerance for scandal if you are dealing with the Church. We have more than our share." Nate liked him better and better.

Rodriguez continued, "First a little history. The Soldados de Cristo is a religious congregation founded in Mexico in the late 1940s by a guy named Marcel Marcelino. He fancied himself another Ignatius of Loyola."

As a graduate of Georgetown, Nate vaguely recognized the reference to the founder of the Jesuits.

Rodriguez paused for a moment, apparently weighing his words.

"Marcelino had a love of three things: power, money, and sex—not uncommon things for men to love, of course. But his love of those three sins was an obsession. Of course, he cloaked everything in what he claimed was his love of Jesus Christ and the Church."

Rodriguez let out a little "ha." Then he took a breath and looked away for a second before he continued.

"Marcelino wanted to build a big religious order. His ambition was to set the direction of the Catholic Church for the next few hundred years, not just in Mexico, but around the world. Marcelino always thinks big."

"So, he's still alive," said Nate.

"Oh, yes," answered Rodriguez. "He is under house arrest here at the Vatican. He has a little apartment on the other side of the gardens. I'm his jailer, so to speak. He even wears an ankle bracelet." Nate's eyes widened. Rodriguez wasn't kidding about being Marcelino's jailer.

Rodriguez picked up the story again. "To tell you the truth, I think that Marcelino just wanted to use the Church. He saw it as a necessary, if inconvenient, vehicle for his own ambition. If he could have been a Mexican politician, he would have done that instead. But Mexican politics was closed to him. Politics in Mexico in those days was only open to the few who were part of the inner circle of the ruling party, the PRI. To be part of the PRI you needed to have money. Marcelino didn't have money, so he couldn't play in that game, so he turned to politics in the Church, the next best thing. The Church welcomed Marcelino as a player. I'm not sure he was ever really religious. In fact, the more I come to know him, the more I wonder if he even believed in God at all."

Nate raised his eyebrows. It was a revelation to him to think that a priest might not even believe in God.

Rodriguez continued with a smile, "An old Jesuit once told me, 'If you can't be guided by morals, at least be deterred by shame.' Marcelino had neither morals nor shame. He was an unguided Mexican missile."

Rodriguez chuckled to himself, pleased at his little touché.

"One thing about Marcelino is that he is a very charismatic man. Even today, under house arrest, he charms his visitors and gets them to do him favors. I always have to watch that. He is not supposed to be running anything anymore, but he is hard to contain."

Nate noticed that Rodriguez never referred to the founder of the Soldados by his title of monsignor. He just called him Marcelino.

"What's he under house arrest for?" asked Nate.

"Everything," said Rodriguez. "Sex crimes, theft, fraud, pedophilia, you name it. Pope Thomas assigned him to a life of penance and removed his faculties as a priest."

Rodriguez took a sip of his coffee and then continued. "Marcelino was well connected in Mexico, but to carry out his great plans, he needed two things: people and money. Mexico is a big Catholic country. It had the people. But the United States had the money. It has a rich Catholic community."

"So, Marcelino and the Soldados were more about money than sex?" asked Nate.

"No," answered Rodriguez. "Not exactly. It was really about both—money and sex.

"In Mexico, Marcelino recruited young men, mostly from devout middle-class families. He had a very clear physical profile for any young man entering his order. He told his recruiters, 'No fat guys, no ugly guys, no effeminate guys, and no poor guys.' He wanted only the most handsome guys, if you get my drift."

Rodriguez paused and smiled. Nate nodded. The monsignor did not need to spell out Marcelino's love of handsome young men.

"Money was a bigger problem for Marcelino than people. So, he looked *al otro lado*, as we Mexicans say, to the other side of the border. Marcelino founded seminaries and houses in the United States. He was blunt about it. He said he was looking for 'fountains of dollars,' as he told his local superiors. All his houses were in places like Greenwich, Connecticut, or Grosse Pointe, Michigan."

"And, I suppose, in Bethesda, Maryland, and Palm Beach, Florida," interjected Nate.

"You catch on quickly, Mr. Condon. Marcelino never founded a house in a poor neighborhood. He was not Mother Teresa."

Rodriguez continued, "Marcelino even bought the old Watson estate in Greenwich from the founder of IBM. He said he wanted to do 'youth' ministry in the United States. Evidently, he was only interested in the kind of youth who played polo. What he was looking for, of course, was wealthy young men."

Nate chuckled and thought to himself, Now I know why Peggy Tracy is drawn to the Soldados. Nate realized that he had actually run into the Soldados a lot over the years, without knowing who they were. Some of his friends from the Knights of Malta had once tried to get him to go up to Greenwich on a retreat there.

"Money was not an absolute requirement," continued Rodriguez, "but he wanted his seminarians to bring a big donation with them when they entered the order. It was like a dowry. In a way, Marcelino was very much like Ignatius and the early Jesuits, focused on the elites. Of course, the Jesuits would be offended by the comparison today."

Nate nodded. Who wouldn't be offended? he thought.

"Did most of his recruits come from the States?" asked Nate.

"No, actually," said Rodriguez. "He did best in Mexico and Latin America. Colombia was a big recruiting ground for him. Never underestimate the power of a common language bond. There is quite a Latino confraternity in the Soldados. But Ireland was also big for him for a while. Marcelino realized that Americans like Irish priests, and Irish boys want to go to America."

Rodriguez stood up and went over to a file cabinet behind his desk. He pulled out a file folder containing newspaper clippings as he continued talking.

"Marcelino also made it his business to cultivate rich widows. He ministered to grieving women, who felt forgotten by God. He let them know he had not forgotten them. Sometimes they were even allowed to live in guesthouses on his estates and pretend they were nuns or hermits. People with money get lonely, too."

Rodriguez handed Nate a clipping from the *Hartford Courant.*

"Look at this. He got this lady to leave all her money to the Soldados while she was living in a guesthouse on the old Watson estate in Greenwich."

Nate looked at the clipping. There was a headshot of an elderly Connecticut socialite in pearls. There was also a companion shot of her in a modest dress, like a nun's habit. The headline on the article read "Area Socialite Leaves Fortune to Priest." The article said that she had left thirty million dollars to the Soldados.

Rodriguez gave Nate a second to read the article, then continued, "Her children are still suing the Soldados to get it back. I hope they win. What a bastard!"

Rodriguez clearly hated this guy, but he was just warming up.

"But what the Church didn't know was that Marcel was a sexual omnivore. He liked men and women. Nobody was safe."

Rodriguez handed Nate another clipping from *The New York Times* detailing a lawsuit brought by several former members of the Soldados, who were claiming they were sexually molested by Marcelino when they were in the seminary.

"There had been rumors about him and boys for a long time. He summoned seminarians to his private rooms, where he would get them drunk and proposition them. When they left, they were often too terrorized to say anything." Rodriguez paused and shook his head.

"He had it all figured out. See, the Soldados take a special vow beyond the ordinary ones of poverty, chastity, and obedience. They promise never to speak ill of their superiors. He felt he was safe, but rumors were around for a long time about sex with seminarians.

"Eventually, however, we found out that he also liked women—several women, in fact. He had children by them. He had not one, but two secret families. He fathered a total of five children."

"Wow," said Nate.

"Marcel kept them the way upper-class men keep mistresses in Mexico. He set them up in houses and paid for the child support. The neighbors thought he was a wealthy businessman who traveled a lot. Neither mistress knew about the other until recently. He paid for them out of the funds of his order." Rodriguez handed Nate another clipping from the *National Catholic Reporter*.

"No one suspected?" Nate asked.

"People must have suspected," answered Rodriguez. "Officially, of course, the order says it never knew about his mistresses. But the comptroller, who was a pal of Marcelino's, must have known. Sometimes Marcel would draw out ten thousand dollars in cash for travel expenses just before he went to visit his families. If the order didn't know, they were just plain stupid."

"Amazing," said Nate. "This guy Marcelino has brass balls."

Rodriguez chuckled in agreement. "The man has solid brass cojones. When John Paul II came to Mexico in 1979, Marcelino even got his mistresses and children into the front-row seats at a papal Mass. Afterward he took them to a reception, so they could get their pictures taken with the pope. Yes, sir, solid brass balls. When he dies, we should make them first-class relics of the patron saint of con artists."

The two men sat there laughing for a moment. Nate liked Rodriguez's bluntness. "I know mob bosses that have more shame," said Nate.

"Like I said," continued the priest, "Marcelino has several children. Five that we know of, anyway. There may be more. He was a good Catholic father, though. He never used birth control, and he made sure they all went to Catholic schools."

They laughed again. Rodriguez was clearly enjoying the storytelling. So was Nate.

"Marcelino brought three of his kids to Rome for schooling. He put them in the international school out by the Via Aurelia. One of them has recently written a book, *Mi Padre, El Sacerdote*."

Rodriguez went over to the bookshelf behind his desk and pulled a copy of the memoir from the shelf and handed it to Nate. "I guess the apple doesn't fall too far from the tree. Even his kids are exploiting the Church connection."

Nate took the book and leafed through the pages, looking at the pictures of Marcelino with his kids and mistresses.

"You know," said Rodriguez reflectively, "you just can't make this stuff up. I admire his audacity. Train robbers are more timid."

Nate was beginning to see what Rodriguez meant about a strong stomach for scandal. The average Catholic has no idea about such things, thought Nate.

"All of that was only rumor for years," said Rodriguez. "Nobody high up in the Church believed the rumors. Marcelino was protected in Rome. He had powerful friends in the curia like Cardinals Crepi, Salazar, and Mendoza."

Nate was busily taking notes. "I've heard those names before," said Nate. "Tell me about them."

"Well, Crepi is the governor of Vatican City. In a sense, he is my landlord. He controls everything within the walls of the Vatican and its Roman properties. If you want something done in the Vatican, talk to Crepi.

"Salazar is the prefect for the Knights of the Holy Sepulcher. It's a nothing job these days, but it lets him travel around the world and talk to rich people. He raises money for the charities of the Holy See. Salazar had the Latino bond with Marcelino. He was largely responsible for all the recruits the Soldados got in Colombia. He certainly opened doors for the Soldados in Latin America.

"Mendoza." Rodrigquez paused, breathing in and putting his folded hands to his lips. "Well, now there is a piece of work. Mendoza is one of the original Soldados. He rose through the ranks in Mexico and then got himself appointed a cardinal here in Rome. He really is their cardinal protector. He is the perfect soldado in the mold of Marcelino: secretive, conspiratorial, conservative, and mean. Don't underestimate Mendoza."

Rodriguez was not done. "Remember, Marcelino still has friends in the Roman Curia. Mendoza is his first friend, but there are others. After all, Marcelino gave millions of dollars to papal charities. Back in the 1980s when the Vatican Bank was in trouble, it is rumored that he kicked in money for an out-of-court settlement made in secret in Switzerland. But what really impressed them here in Rome was the growth of his order. He got vocations to the priesthood at a time when all the other orders like the Jesuits were going out of business.

"Eventually, he moved his seminary from Mexico to Rome to give himself more visibility. He bought the old Christian Brothers' place on the Via Aurelia. It was convenient to his kids' school. He sent his seminarians to the Gregorian University for philosophy. Every morning, he delivered them to the front door of the Greg in a Mercedes bus with each seminarian perfectly dressed in a tailored, clerical black suit. He ordered them to read their breviary while they were on the bus, so as not to be tempted by what was out on the street. They even had to draw the curtains in the bus, so the seminarians could not see the corrupting world of Rome. What a show! The curia was completely snowed, even your patron O'Toole."

Nate was intrigued to hear O'Toole referred to as his patron. He realized that Rodriguez saw Nate as an ecclesiastical insider.

"And conservative!" said Rodriguez, throwing up a hand. "The man was more conservative than the pope, any pope. He was more conservative than the Latin Mass crowd. They loved him. Everybody said he was the modern Ignatius of Loyola. Marcel ate that stuff up. The only one more conservative than Marcel is Mendoza.

"Marcelino made sure that all the ordinations of the Soldados were done here in Rome, in Latin, so that everybody around here would notice. He had more ordinations than the North American College. He had more than the Mexican College. Hell, he had more than both of them combined."

"What did Marcelino want? Was he setting himself up to be pope?" asked Nate.

"No," answered Rodriguez. "He knew he would never be pope. It was all about ego, I guess. He wanted to be a power player in Church politics.

More than that, he wanted to leave a legacy with his religious order. He figured that the Soldados would set the direction for the Church for the next five hundred years, like the Jesuits did for most of the past five hundred years. But mostly it was about power. He wanted to show that they had power.

"In Church politics, people are sensitive to symbols. Let me give you an example. When I was a student over there at the North American College, the Soldados bought the old NAC summer villa in the hills outside Rome, near Castel Gandolfo, right next door to the pope's summer place. The Soldados could look down on the pope from their windows. Marcelino wanted to be sure that the popes noticed him. That real estate sent a message."

"A message?" asked Nate.

"Yeah," said Rodriguez, raising a finger and pointing out the window again toward the North American College. "It told the American bishops that this little Mexican guy had more money and power than they did. It told anybody who was looking that the Soldados were neighbors of the pope and that they had a villa bigger than the pope's."

"Who did Marcelino want to impress?" asked Nate.

"Anyone who was looking," answered Rodriguez.

"But why was he so insecure?" asked Nate. "What was he trying to prove?"

"Look," said Rodriguez, "my family is Mexican American. I know how it feels to be put down by the gringo. It feels good to us Mexicans to take you Anglos down a peg or two. It's a little payback for the condescension of the gringo toward us."

Nate nodded.

Rodriguez looked out the window again and said reflectively, "Marcelino was on a roll so long as he had the popes hoodwinked. They kept telling other religious orders that they should be more like the Soldados. When I was in the seminary, our rector invited the Soldados over to the college for dinners and plays. He was always saying, 'You guys should be more like the Soldados.' If he only knew what the Soldados were really like.

"In the past few years," continued Rodriguez, "some of the former members of the Soldados have been suing their order. You might have seen some of them on *60 Minutes* last year."

"Oh, yeah," said Nate. "I saw part of that, but I didn't really know who they were then."

"The big newspapers and scandal sheets in Mexico ran exposés on Marcelino's families. He was unashamed. I guess he thought he was untouchable."

"So, what did him in?" asked Nate.

"Sex with women," said Rodriguez. "When Pope Thomas found out about the mistresses and the secret families, that was it. The pope put him under house arrest in the Vatican and took away his faculties. He's no longer allowed to say Mass. Basically, Marcelino is supposed to live a life of prayer and penance.

"I was appointed to supervise the order and clean up the mess," said Rodriguez. "Believe me, it's a mess. Basically I'm what you lawyers would call a trustee in bankruptcy."

"Well, if Marcelino is under house arrest and you're in charge, why would Monsignor Ackerman say that the Soldados have so much influence?"

"'Cause they still do," said Rodriguez. "They have cardinals here in the curia. They still have lots of friends in high places—friends with money. They might even have connections to the Mafia."

Nate smiled as he realized Monsignor Rodriguez's "dissertation" was definitely a bit more than the Wikipedia version promised.

Nate looked at his watch. It was past noon. "Why don't you let me buy you lunch? Then we can walk and talk a bit more." Nate sensed this priest would be a good source.

"Fine," said Rodriguez. "In the seminary they told us never to turn down a free meal. I know a little trattoria in the Borgo Pio that serves great penne arrabbiata."

They stood up together. Rodriguez put on his suit coat. He was dressed in a clerical suit, not a cassock. Nate took that as a sign that he was a more "modern" priest than the ones wearing cassocks.

On their way out of the office, they said good-bye to Miss Orsuto.

Walking down the stairs of the Belvedere Palace, Nate mentioned that he was looking for an assistant, someone who could read English, Italian, and Spanish. "Do you know anybody like your assistant, Miss Orsuto? Someone who knows the Church, and languages, and who could be discreet."

"People like her are hard to find, even in Rome," said Rodriguez. "But I'll tell you what. Why don't I just detail her over to your investigation for a while? I have other staff who can look after Marcelino. Besides, I'm going on vacation for the next couple of weeks. She is very knowledgeable."

"Thank you," said Nate, realizing that he didn't have the vaguest idea how to search for an assistant in Rome. "That would help me get things moving." Nate liked the idea that his assistant already knew her way around Rome and had intimate knowledge of the underbelly of the Church.

"We don't really need to say anything to Cardinal Crepi, since she is already on the Vatican payroll. That way Crepi won't be able to put a mole in your investigation," said Rodriguez.

Nate was beginning to realize that the Vatican was full of intrigue. It was best not to trust too many people. He hoped he could trust Rodriguez, though.

"I'll ask Sandra to come work for you for a while. If she agrees, we can work it out for next week."

When they got settled in the little trattoria, Nate started the interview again. "Tell me a little more about who the Soldados can count on in the curia," said Nate.

"Well, you already know about Crepi and Salazar," said Rodriguez. "And their best friend is, of course, Cardinal Mendoza."

"I thought that when you became a cardinal, you left your order," said Nate.

"Technically, that's true," answered Rodriguez. "But people are people. If they came up through their order, they maintain their allegiance."

"Does Mendoza have any real power?" asked Nate.

Rodriguez looked around the small restaurant, apparently checking for people who might be listening. After all, they were only a couple of blocks from the Vatican gate.

"Mendoza is the head of the Sacred Penitentiary," said Rodriguez. "That's not a prison. That's the office that gives out dispensations and indulgences. They also can impose penances. It has been very hard to discipline Marcelino, because his pal Mendoza is always looking over my shoulder.

"The other thing about Mendoza's job is that he is one of two guys in the Vatican who does not lose his job when the pope dies. It's no secret that Pope Thomas is not well. Mendoza will be in charge of Marcelino when Pope Thomas dies. We aren't supposed to even talk about the pope's death, but you can imagine where that would put me. I'd probably be out on my ass."

Nate realized that Rodriguez had real reason to fear Mendoza.

When their pasta arrived, Rodriguez dived into it with enthusiasm. Nate pushed it around on his plate before starting up the questioning again. "What do you know about the dead cardinals?" he asked. He figured that it was all the gossip of the Vatican and that Rodriguez would know the speculation.

"Well, I don't know anything for sure," said Rodriguez cautiously, looking around again.

"Knowledgeable speculation is welcome," prodded Nate.

"There are rumors," said Rodriguez, lowering his voice a bit. "You know that the cardinal from Mexico, Ignacio Garcia of Guadalajara, was killed three months ago in a shootout at the airport in Monterrey. At the time, the papers reported that he just happened to get caught in the cross fire between the Zetas and Sinaloa drug cartels."

Nate nodded. He knew there was open warfare between the cartels in Mexico.

"But," said Rodriguez, lowering his voice another notch, "now we are not so sure."

"What aren't you sure about?" Nate prodded.

"Well, nobody else was killed in that shootout. The cartels are reckless, but they are not stupid. It makes no sense for the drug cartels to shoot up an airport and kill a high-profile guy like a cardinal, unless they are going after somebody really big. They don't want any unnecessary trouble with the Mexican police. You wouldn't take a risk killing people at the airport unless you were going after a pretty big fish."

"So, who would do it?" asked Nate. "Do you think it was the Soldados?"

"I wouldn't put it past them," said Rodriguez, absolutely deadpan. For the first time, Nate really was shocked. "But they probably needed help. Maybe the Sinaloa or the Zetas were hired by someone to do the job—someone who wanted Cardinal Garcia dead. I can't imagine that drug cartels really care much about cardinals. I don't know." Rodriguez fell silent. Nate noticed him looking out the window.

Nate shook his head in amazement. "Priests killing priests! It's hard to imagine."

Monsignor Rodriguez arched an eyebrow and asked, "Haven't you heard of the Borgias?"

"But why kill this cardinal?" asked Nate.

"Well, Ignacio was on to Marcel years ago. He was also the biggest threat to Mendoza. He evidently knew something about Mendoza. I'm not sure what. Maybe sex, maybe money.

"Also, Cardinal Garcia knew about Marcelino's mistresses and their families. He knew a lot about the Soldados' finances. He told me once that there were a lot of wire transfers around the world. Suspicious transfers to strange groups in Belgium and Italy. The cardinal also interviewed former soldado seminarians for the investigation of their order. He once came over to Rome to see John Paul II. He even tried to shut down the Soldados. Obviously, he wasn't successful. But if there is anyone that Marcelino really hated, it was his countryman Ignacio."

"What would be the motive to kill somebody?" asked Nate.

"Silence," said Rodriguez. At first Nate was not sure if he was telling Nate to be silent or that silence was the motive for the killing.

Suddenly Rodriguez stopped talking while some people squeezed past them in the tiny trattoria.

After a couple of minutes, Rodriguez whispered, "It's probably not safe to talk any more. But I will tell you this: Maybe the drug cartels pulled the trigger at the airport. But to me it seems the Soldados had a lot more motive to kill the cardinal from Guadalajara than the cartels. Whoever pulled the trigger, they did a favor for Marcelino."

"Why would the cartels do Marcelino a favor?" Nate asked in a low voice.

Rodriquez shrugged and continued quietly, "Maybe they just did it for money. I don't know. Marcelino has been friendly with everyone in Mexico who had money, which certainly includes some drug dealers. Maybe they were using him to launder money. He certainly could travel freely. Maybe they just killed Ignacio as a favor to their old pal Marcelino."

The inner workings of the Vatican left Nate speechless for a moment.

After they finished their wine, Rodriguez collected his coat while Nate paid the bill. The monsignor stood at the restaurant entrance waiting, looking out the window. Nate noticed him peering out the glass at a black Mercedes parked in front of the restaurant. Two men were sitting in the car, looking straight ahead.

"What is it?" asked Nate, nodding toward the car.

"Oh, nothing, probably," said the monsignor. "It looks like somebody is interested in where we are having our lunch."

They turned right out of the trattoria and walked back through the Borgo Pio. As they walked, Rodriguez began to talk in a normal voice again.

"Really," he said, "we've had a lot worse scandals than this in the history of the Church."

"Worse than this?" asked Nate. He could hardly imagine how you could get any worse than a philandering pedophile who kept two secret mistresses and consorted with drug cartels to kill a cardinal. But then, the Church has a long history. "How do you figure?"

"Oh, my dear Mr. Condon, it has been a lot worse. Just take my department, as an example. Five hundred years ago the Vatican Secretary of State was called the office of the Cardinal Intimus. It was set up to handle correspondence with foreign governments. Pope Julius III gave the job to his *intimus* 'cardinal nephew,' a fourteen-year-old boy ironically named Innocenzo. The pope's brother had adopted the boy as his son, at the pope's request. They had seen Innocenzo when he was a beggar on the streets of Parma. The boy was illiterate, but exceedingly handsome. Julius showered him with gifts and money, and even bragged about the boy's prowess in bed.

"Imagine," said Rodriguez, "the pope bragging about how somebody was in bed. All of Europe at the time was scandalized. The Calvinists and the Lutherans at the time jumped all over the scandal. But the Church survived. We even reformed. We haven't really had any big scandal in my office for five hundred years, so I guess we're due."

Nate thought to himself, This guy has become cynical.

Rodriguez looked back down the street toward the black Mercedes that was crawling after them through the narrow street of the Borgo.

"You know," he said, "I don't think I'll go back to the office right now. Nobody does much work right after lunch in the Vatican anyway. I think I'll go home for a little nap. I will talk to Miss Orsuto about working for you, Mr. Condon. If she is agreeable, I'll have her call you at the Columbus. Ciao. I wish you well in your investigation."

The monsignor abruptly turned left and jogged down a narrow side street, passing under a high archway that looked like it was once part of a Roman aqueduct.

Nate watched him go, surprised by the priest's abrupt departure. After a few steps, Rodriguez broke into a run. He dodged a car on the Via dei Corridori, just beyond the archway, and flagged down a passing city bus. Once on board, the priest waved back to Nate from the window.

Meanwhile, the black Mercedes had paused at the corner where the monsignor had abruptly turned left. Then it started to crawl past Nate, who watched the car turn right at the corner and disappear from view.

Nate walked back to the Columbus Hotel, aware that his presence in Rome was a matter of curiosity to others.

11

THE ORACLE OF GLOUCESTER

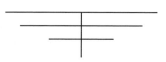

BEING A NORTH SHORE BOY, THE RIDE BROUGHT BACK A lot of memories as Cardinal O'Toole drove north from Boston through the towns of his youth—Salem, Marblehead, Beverly Farms, and finally Gloucester. He was on his way to see his old friend, confessor, and spiritual advisor, Jack McClendon.

O'Toole had stayed in the States after Cardinal Manning's funeral. He was pretty shaken by the death, and he always felt safer at home.

When he allowed himself to think about it, he was even more shaken by the probability of a worldwide conspiracy to kill cardinals. Such a threat triggered some soul searching. A trip to Gloucester and a visit with his old friend and mentor was the best way he knew to find his bearings again.

Father Jack McClendon was in his mid-eighties, twenty years older than O'Toole. He had been a parish priest all of his adult life, except for a few years when he worked as a spiritual advisor at St. John's Seminary in Boston. When O'Toole was a teenager, McClendon had been the assistant priest at O'Toole's home parish, Immaculate Conception in Salem. Later, at St. John's Seminary, he had been O'Toole's spiritual director and advisor.

Whenever O'Toole needed some sense of grounding, he went back to see McClendon. Jack was the one person who could still speak to the cardinal as an equal. He probably knew Michael O'Toole better than anyone else on earth.

The drive out of Boston was refreshing. It brought him to a place of peace. The morning sun danced on the ocean water to his right. O'Toole stopped at Salem Willows, on the waterfront in Salem, to buy two chop suey sandwiches to take to McClendon's house for lunch. That strange delicacy is unique to Salem. In his honest moments, Cardinal O'Toole would have to admit that chop suey sandwiches were an acquired taste. But they were one of McClendon's favorite foods, and the sandwiches were part of their ritual whenever they met. They always had chop suey sandwiches for lunch and lobster at the Gloucester House for dinner.

Jack McClendon was a free man. He was too old to care what people thought about him, so he spoke his mind freely, but with charity. In his eighty-sixth year, his fidelity was not to an institution, but to the truth. He had learned not just from books, but from experience.

McClendon's career in the Church had been one of humble service. He had almost always been in poor parishes, not rich ones. There he comforted the grieving, counseled the doubting, visited the sick, baptized the babies, and buried the dead. To McClendon, that was the work of the Church, not the publishing of documents and the jockeying for position that went on in Rome.

In nearly sixty years as a priest, he had developed a disdain for the pomposity and pretension of the Catholic Church. He had seen its hypocrisy and its cruelty close up. But he had also seen its generosity and kindness.

To McClendon, life was all about love. He figured we were just supposed to love the people that God, or fate, put in our path. He had no ambition for greater things. Ambition is the clerical sin. The opening lines of Psalm 131 applied to Jack:

> *O Lord, my heart is not proud, nor my eyes haughty.*
> *I have not sought after great things.*

Most of the time, people didn't call McClendon "Father." He was content to be just Jack. To him it was much better to be a companion on the journey through life than the captain of the expedition.

O'Toole had no trouble finding McClendon's house. All he had to do was get to Gloucester on the highway and then drive downhill to the waterfront and turn right. The McClendon family had occupied the same tiny row house on the waterfront for three generations. It sat directly across the street from the monument to the Gloucester fisherman. McClendon's father had been a lobsterman.

Once, these waterfront houses had been occupied by the families of the fishermen. Their roofs had widow's walks, so the wives could watch for their husbands' return. Now, they were becoming chic because of their ocean views. Boston yuppies who wanted to get out of the city would probably now pay half a million dollars for one of these little homes.

The McClendon house not changed much in fifty years. The furniture was still in the same place it had been half a century before. There were still lace doilies on the arms of the overstuffed chairs, and a Sacred Heart of Jesus picture still hung on the wall in the living room.

Jack moved back to Gloucester after he retired and lived with his sister Donna and their chocolate Labrador, aptly named Chocolate. Twice a day, winter and summer, Jack walked Chocolate up and down the breakwater past the monument.

It took McClendon a little while to shuffle to the door when Cardinal O'Toole rang the bell. His step had slowed a lot—a mixture of old age and the early stages of congestive heart failure.

The two men embraced at the door. Jack said affectionately, "Sit down here, you asshole, and let me look at you." The only person in the world who could get away with calling Cardinal Michael O'Toole an asshole was Jack. The cardinal grinned with delight, happy to be in the presence of a man who knew him completely and loved him unconditionally, despite his pomposity.

Jack was concerned about the cardinal. "How are you, Michael, you fathead?" Fathead was Jack's affectionate name for everybody he liked. "This is terrible news about Manning. I know you must be worried."

"I'm shattered," said O'Toole. "It is even worse than what you read in the papers. This may be a pattern. Someone is killing cardinals, and we don't know why. What is happening to the Church, Jack?"

"First, I want to know what is happening to you," said Jack. "Are you taking care of yourself? Are you still happy there in Rome?"

"I don't know. I don't feel the same way I used to about the Church. Where did all this vitriol come from? I always thought we were speaking for God and for good, but people seem to hate us today. They don't just disagree with us; they hate us. What did we do to deserve this?" O'Toole leaned back in the rocker and looked at the ceiling.

There was a long silence. Jack had learned over the years to listen to people's troubles. You don't always have an answer. Often there isn't really an answer, but it's always good to listen.

"There is such animosity even among the cardinals," O'Toole continued. "We don't seem to be on the same page anymore. The Church does a lot of good around the world. We feed the poor. And yet people hate us."

Jack took a deep breath. "Well, Mike, maybe what we lack is real love. Remember what St. Vincent de Paul said: 'If you feed the poor and don't do it out of love, they will hate you for it.'"

O'Toole looked at Jack's wrinkled face. "You're probably right, Jack. Maybe we are too impersonal, too institutional."

The table clock across the little room chimed noon.

Jack spoke up when it finished. "Mike, remember when you were at seminary in Boston? You came to me and said that the archdiocese wanted to send you to Rome. Do you remember my reaction?"

"You were opposed to me going."

"Not so much opposed as cautious. I told you that it would be seductive. All the history, the beauty, the power, the wealth, the titles, the sense of being at the center of it all. These things are seductive. You wind up serving strange gods instead of the real one. Remember the first commandment, Mike. 'I am the Lord your God. You shall not have strange gods before me.'"

"I don't know, Jack, that seems a little harsh," protested O'Toole.

"No," said Jack. "Those things seduce us into thinking we are something. But really, we are nothing. We are all passing away. Even St. Peter's Basilica will one day fall down in ruins. That Vatican will be dust. St. Paul told us only three things last: faith, hope, and love."

Jack patted O'Toole's hand that was resting on the arm of the chair next to him and finished his thought. "The only lasting or important thing we can do is love. That is what it is about."

"What about truth?" said O'Toole. "Isn't that lasting or important? Aren't we supposed to preach truth? Aren't we supposed to reveal to the world the truth of Christ and His Church?"

Jack could see that he had touched a nerve, so he backed off. "What is it you are trying to achieve, Mike, in evangelizing the world? What is your idea of success? If the whole world became Catholic tomorrow, what would it look like?"

"Well, there would be peace," answered Michael, "because we would all be on the same page. We would all be playing by the same rules."

"Really?" said Jack, pursing his lips for a second. "Do we have peace in the Church now? If we can't have peace now with one billion Catholics, what makes you think we would have it if there were seven billion Catholics? Does peace come from having the same rule book? Is the peace you seek a peace born of love or a peace born of law? I think St. Paul said we live by a law of love."

The cardinal was a little irritated by his old friend.

"I am a canon lawyer," said O'Toole. "I believe in the law of the Church. I think everybody should obey the law of the Church, because it's the law of Christ. Doesn't St. Paul also say we should be obedient to higher authorities?"

Father McClendon replied gently. "True, Mike, but in the end, it is not about rules. It's about relationships. People don't sacrifice their lives as missionaries or martyrs, or even as parish priests, because of obedience to rules. They sacrifice because they fall in love. They fall in love with the people God has put in their path, not some theory about how human beings should behave. Our job is first of all to love people as they are, just as Jesus loved the woman taken in adultery or the tax collectors or the centurion. Remember what Luke's gospel says, 'This man welcomes sinners and eats with them.'"

O'Toole was ready with his objection. "But Jesus did not approve of their behavior. He told them to go and sin no more. He called them to change."

"True," said Jack, "but first he loved them.

"How often does the Roman Curia discuss how they can show love to the world?" Jack asked. "It seems to me that we spend more effort reminding people of what is wrong with them than we do telling them that God loves them. We make the sacraments into rewards for good behavior rather than medicine for the soul."

"But doesn't St. Paul say we should only come to the Eucharist worthily?" objected Cardinal O'Toole.

"He was talking about people coming to communion drunk," said Jack matter-of-factly. "The Church seems to think it is supposed to be the toll booth on the way to heaven."

"But," objected O'Toole, "are we supposed to forget about their sin?"

"Not forget, but forgive," answered Jack. "The Church seems to be hung up on things that have nothing to do with Christ—things on which Jesus was absolutely silent.

"We tell gay people they are 'intrinsically disordered' when Jesus said absolutely nothing about them. All they want to do is love each other.

"We tell women that they are unworthy to serve the Church as priests when Jesus said no such thing. We make them feel bad not because of something they have done, but because of who they are.

"We tell married men that their participation in the vocation of marriage and the love of a woman excludes them from priesthood. Yet Jesus chose St. Peter, a married man, to be the first leader of the church.

"We tell people who get divorced and remarried that they are cut off from communion forever, no matter how tragic or abusive their supposedly valid marriage may have been.

"So many rules, so little love."

They both sat there in silence for a while. Finally, after a couple of minutes, Jack turned to the cardinal and said, "Let's eat that chop suey sandwich."

They moved to the kitchen table and unwrapped the sloppy sandwiches. The noodles spilled out of the soaked white bread onto the paper. Jack made coffee and got out some plates. They said a little prayer of thanks and then concentrated on eating, in a sort of informal communion.

When the sandwiches were almost gone, Mike started talking again.

"I always thought the bishops spoke for Christ. I always thought it would be the finest thing in the world to be a bishop. But today people don't see us as shepherds. It seems like half the people in the Church are hostile to us. Why?"

Jack looked at Mike as he shuffled around the kitchen cleaning up.

"Don't you read the newspapers, Mike? Don't you remember what happened here in Boston? Remember all the children who were molested by priests? Remember all the bishops who just turned a blind eye? Were they shepherds of the flock or were they wolves? Maybe that is why people are so angry."

O'Toole was stung. "Oh, Jack," he moaned. "That seems so unfair. The bishops were just trying to protect the Church."

"Yeah, that's it," answered Jack. "They were trying to protect the Church, not the people."

"That's not what I meant," protested O'Toole.

"You're a bishop, Mike, a teacher of the Church. Why is it that the bishops pay more attention to Church documents than we do to the lived experiences of people? I was a parish priest for more than fifty years. I heard confessions, and I talked to people endlessly. They were all struggling. Why can't we first be close to them in their struggles before we wag our fingers at them?

"What do all our reams of documents have to say to their struggles?

"We have no encouragement to offer to the battered wife who finally picks herself up and leaves her alcoholic husband and finds a man who will respect her.

"We have nothing to say to the gay man who finally stops torturing himself about his sexuality and falls in love.

"We have nothing to say to a mother of five children who has diabetes and might die from another pregnancy. Is she wrong when she gets on the pill to save her life so her children will have a mother?

"What do we say to a gay couple that rescues a child from abuse in foster care by adopting it? Do we say thank you for that act of love?

"We have nothing to say to all these people except criticism. All we ever say is 'Obey the rules. Tough it out.'"

O'Toole was irritated. "But we do care. We say we are sorry, but we can't ignore the truth, the truth of the faith."

"Is it the truth, or is it just our own point of view?" asked Jack.

"How come we are expected to put our faith in documents written by men who have never shared our struggles, but we are told to pay no attention to our own experiences?"

"Oh, Jack. You're reducing everything to subjective nonsense."

"No, Mike. I'm taking seriously the evidence of my eyes and ears.

"Mike, you are a good man. I know your heart. You care about people. Do you remember when you were at St. Catherine's in Charlestown? You buried a young man who was gay. He committed suicide because he had been molested by a priest when he was fourteen or fifteen. Who was the sinner? The young man?

"You knew that the Church had sinned against him. But his so-called pastor would not bury the poor boy or even comfort the family, because from his perspective the 'truth' required him to condemn both homosexuality and suicide." Jack made air quotes with his fingers.

"But you buried the poor guy and went to the man's house to comfort the family. That is the Mike O'Toole I know, a man with a big heart."

For the second time in a week, O'Toole was reminded of that event from his long-ago past. It was something he felt good about, even though he had disobeyed his pastor and broken the rules of the Church at that time.

"Funny, Bill Tracy reminded me of that young man last week when I called him for help investigating these deaths. He put me in touch with Brendan Condon's son to help us out. Remember him?" asked O'Toole.

"Poor Brendan," said Jack. "Sure, I remember him. He was a Boston fireman. He left the Church over that incident. You know firemen stick together."

"Yes," said O'Toole, "certainly more than bishops and priests."

Jack squeezed the cardinal's hand. "There are millions of Brendans out there, Mike. They leave us because of our hardness of heart. How could we get to this place?"

O'Toole felt like he should object, but he couldn't think of anything to say. The two friends sat looking at each other across the kitchen table, lost for a while in memories. The break in the conversation seemed like a good time to move to the living room. When they were settled in the armchairs again, the conversation started back up.

"How do we get it back?" asked Jack.

"Get what back?" said the cardinal.

"Our heart," said the priest. "When will we stop looking over our shoulders at the past and realize there never was a perfect time in the history of the Church or the world? Jesus said that His kingdom is not of this world.

"That Vatican you work in is a fortress, Mike. Fortresses are meant to keep people out, not to engage them.

"People have a lot to offer us despite their sinfulness, you know," continued Jack. "The Sistine Chapel is covered with sublime paintings about the mystery of God and man, which were done by a gay man who lived his life of love in secret and in shame. Bernini intended that colonnade surrounding St. Peter's Square to be a symbol of the arms of a mother embracing the people of the world, not vise grips squeezing them."

"Oh, Jack. Come down off your high horse. It's not like that. There are good men working over there, just like in the parishes. We really do have people's interests at heart, but we have to preach the truth."

"I know there are good men over there," said Jack. "But you bishops can't even agree among yourselves. How can the world see your truth, if you can't agree on it?

"Remember the bishop from Australia a few years back who said he would ordain married men, because he had no priests to serve his enormous diocese? Rome removed him. They would rather have celibacy than the Eucharist.

"And remember when some African bishops a few years back said it was OK to distribute condoms to married people because of the huge risk of AIDS in Africa? Rome rebuked them. Is the prohibition on condoms more important than human life?"

"I agree with you there, Jack," said O'Toole. "Even Pope Benedict was changing his mind on that."

"Mike, you once told me about a bishop you knew here in the States who had spent twenty-five or thirty years working in parishes. What was his name? Turin or Curling or something like that. He wasn't a great scholar, but he was a good pastor. He dissented when the bishops issued some statement on homosexuality, because he said it did not express the truth of those relationships as he had seen them. The other bishops shunned him, like the Amish do. When he came down to breakfast, nobody would sit with him. When he rode on the bus to your meetings, he had to sit by himself. Thirty years of service to the people of God counted for nothing, because he had the courage to say what he saw to be true."

O'Toole nodded. "True."

"Mike, I am an old man," said Jack. "I will die soon. We all get things wrong about the mystery of faith, and everyone will certainly get some correction when we meet our maker. But I know one thing for sure. When I stand before the throne of grace, I hope God will say that I preached His mercy more than His justice."

The late afternoon sun came in through the front window, and a breeze off the sea blew the lace curtains covering the open window. Air-conditioning was unnecessary in Gloucester.

O'Toole and McClendon sat in silence. After a while Mike looked over at Jack. He had nodded off to sleep. Mike quietly slipped out the front door and went out for a walk. Dressed in black slacks and a clerical shirt, he passed some girls in Catholic school uniforms. "Good afternoon, Father," they said, giggling.

He wondered, did I miss the point of priestly life? Should I have stayed here with these people and shared their love? Maybe the real success was here in Gloucester, not the Vatican.

O'Toole walked the length of the breakwater. When he came back to the house, Jack was still sleeping, so the cardinal sat in the other chair and nodded off himself. The table clock woke him when it chimed five o'clock. Jack was up, looking out the window. The afternoon was mostly gone.

McClendon suggested that they pray the evening prayer together. "Evening prayer always goes better when followed by a vodka martini," said Jack.

They started their prayers. When they got to the Magnificat, McClendon struggled to stand up for the words of the gospel. But his old legs would not cooperate, so they both just sat back down and read the words together.

> He has cast down the mighty from their thrones
> and has lifted up the lowly.
> He has filled the hungry with good things,
> and the rich he has sent away empty.
> He has come to the help of his servant Israel
> for he has remembered his promise of mercy,
> the promise he made to our fathers,
> to Abraham and his children forever.

After prayer, they sipped their martinis and watched the evening news. Then they got their jackets. Neither of them asked where they were going. Their ritual was unchanged. They always went to the Gloucester House for a lobster dinner.

At dinner, they sat looking at the Atlantic.

"What should we do, Jack?" asked O'Toole. "What should we do to bring the Church back?"

Jack thought for a minute, looking out at the gray ocean. It occurred to him that the ocean was a good metaphor for God. We can only know a little about the ocean. We can only splash around the edges and skim over the surface.

Jack looked back at Mike.

"Maybe," he said, "we should talk less. Instead of publishing all those documents that sink without a trace under the ocean, we should just do something that would make people know they are loved."

"What do you mean?" O'Toole asked.

"Something dramatic. Let's give the museum away. Close the Vatican Bank. Give away all the money. Trade your watered silk for an ordinary suit of clothes. Stop having bishops' coats of arms like you are medieval lords. Give up on your titles like excellency and eminence. Stop pretending the Church is a country with diplomats and embassies. Give it all away for the sake of the kingdom. Don't take anything for the journey, just like Jesus told us."

"Then we would be just like the rest of the world," said the cardinal.

"Exactly," said Jack.

12

HOLY MOTHER THE CHURCH

THE PORTER FOR THE METROPOLE HOTEL IN BRUSSELS
slipped noiselessly into the grand meeting room and made his way up
the side aisle to the second row of tables and chairs, where Brigid Condon was sitting. His white-gloved hand reached in over two empty chairs
and handed her a note. In English it said simply, "Important telephone
call, front desk."

She was not accustomed to being called out of important meetings,
but her cell phone did not work in Europe, so there was no other way
to reach her.

Brigid looked at the porter quizzically. He pointed to the lobby.
His uniform made him look like a Napoleonic general, complete with
epaulets. One did not argue with such a commanding presence. Brigid
gathered her papers up from the green cloth-covered seminar table and
stuffed them into her big briefcase.

She was attending a conference on money laundering sponsored by
the European Union. She was representing the Federal Reserve. It was
her department at the Fed that kept tabs on illegal money flowing in and
out of the European Union. It was actually interesting stuff, because it
meant tracking everybody who moved lots of currency. That included

everybody from Italian mobsters to Colombian drug lords. The EU tracked the euros. The Federal Reserve tracked the dollars.

Brigid had a hard time getting out of the meeting room as silently as the porter had come in. Her heels made a click-click sound on the polished marble floor that reverberated off the gilded coffered ceiling twenty feet above. Just as she got to the door, the giant three-ring-binder briefing book she carried fell to the floor. The crash sent up an echo and made everyone turn their heads. It was hardly a graceful exit. She was embarrassed. By the time she got to the front desk, she was more than embarrassed; she was irritated. Whoever this was, it had better be important.

The desk of the Metropole was a giant oak counter in the Beaux-Arts style. Everything at this nineteenth-century palace was in the over-the-top style of the Belle Époque, when the tiny kingdom of Belgium ruled the Congo and grew wildly rich from its trade in diamonds, rubber, and gold. Given its origins, the Metropole was a good place to think about illegal and immoral transfers of wealth.

The uniformed desk clerk, standing in front of a whole wall of old-fashioned room keys hanging from pearl-handled key chains, saw the porter and motioned Brigid to pick up the telephone on the counter. Even the phone was gaudy, like something from an opera set. Brigid had never used a phone so elaborate. It was encased in red enamel, trimmed with gold leaf. It looked like something Maurice Chevalier might have used in *Gigi*.

"Hello," said Brigid. "This is Brigid Condon."

"Brig," Nate said. "Hope I didn't interrupt your meeting."

"As a matter of fact," she answered, "you did. Everybody noticed my exit."

Nate continued, unfazed. "Come to Rome for the weekend. We are both in Europe. Nothing happens in the Vatican over the weekend, and it would be nice to spend some time with you. We could go for pasta and vino, and I could get us a private tour of the Sistine Chapel." This last little detail he was not sure of, but he thought he could entice her with art.

"No," said Brigid. "I have to be back here for work on Monday. I would be exhausted from traipsing halfway across Europe. I would hardly get there, and then I would have to turn around and come back."

"Oh, come on, Brig. It would be fun." Nate was almost pleading.

"No," she said. "It's too far. Would you fly from New York to Atlanta for an overnight?"

"I would if you were going to be there," said Nate. He was a hopeless romantic. That was what she had always loved about him.

"I've got work to do. I have a presentation to make at 8:00 a.m. on Monday. These Northern Europeans are not like that *domani* culture down there in Rome. When they say we start at eight, they mean it."

"Ah, Brig, come on. The food is better here. I have a giant room with a frescoed ceiling covered with winged nymphs."

"No, Nate. I'm not coming. My work is just as important as yours. We can see each other back in New York."

"I don't know when that will be," said Nate. "Why can't you say yes?"

"Stop it, Nate. I'm standing in the middle of a hotel lobby. This is getting embarrassing. The answer is no. What part of no don't you understand?"

"OK," said Nate. "I just thought I would try. Sometimes it's good to be a little spontaneous."

"You mean like you were when you said yes to this cloak-and-dagger thing for the Church? If I had asked you to quit your job and go off for God knows how long on a project for me, you would have said, 'Are you crazy?' But for Holy Mother the Church, you drop everything, including me."

Where was all this anger coming from? She was really on a roll. "I think you should do your detective work solo and leave me to my work here."

"I get the point," said Nate. "By the way, while you are up there, I want you to run down a lead in Belgium for me."

"Nate, are you serious? One minute you're romancing me. The next minute you're giving me work?"

"You're right, honey. But if you do get out of Brussels, there's a former priest in a little town near Bruges. His name keeps coming up in the files here. If you've got a pen, write this name down. Bernard Willebroeck."

She took a pen off the counter and wrote the name on a Metropole Hotel notepad by the phone. "What do you want me to find out?" she asked.

"Not sure," said Nate. "It looks like he might have wired money to people in all the cities where these cardinals have died. Seems like too much of a coincidence for me. Where would a former parish priest get that kind of money? The people he is sending the money to are not missionaries. I thought you could find out something through your money laundering sources."

"OK," said Brigid. "Anything else? I've got to go back to my meeting." Actually, that was not true. The meeting was breaking up, and the participants were beginning to emerge from the meeting room across the lobby. But she wanted to get off the phone. For some reason, he was irritating her.

"No," said Nate. "That's all. Sorry you won't come to Rome."

"We both have work to do," said Brigid. "Bye, Nate. See you back in the States."

"*Ciao, bella,*" said Nate, trying to win her over with flattery.

"Bye," said Brigid, undeterred.

They hung up. No I love yous were exchanged. It was all business. Brigid stood leaning on the counter for a moment, reflecting on the call. Nate could be so charming and simultaneously infuriating. He expected her to drop what she was doing and come to him, but he would never do the same for her. She felt taken for granted.

Brigid turned around, not sure what the next move should be, in the moment or in life. Things were not great between them. Nate had this allegiance to the Church that both perplexed and irritated her. She knew he wanted a more traditional marriage and definitely wanted children. They had postponed all that by mutual agreement, but now the agreement was frayed.

Across the lobby she saw one of the reps from the European Union coming toward her: Maria Erfurt, a Belgian who worked in the banking regulation department at the EU.

"Brigid," she said, in perfectly accented Oxford English, "come join me in the bar for a drink before I take my train home to Bruges." Brigid was glad for the invitation. She wanted to talk to another professional woman. Maria seemed intelligent and empathetic. They had been to a lot of meetings together in the past few years.

They headed off to Le 31, the piano bar off the grand lobby. It had high-back leather chairs and red-shaded brass floor lamps. Hercule Poirot would have felt right at home in the nineteenth-century elegance. They ordered two glasses of wine and some cheese.

"Are you married?" asked Brigid as they waited for the wine.

"Yes," said Maria. "Why?"

"Well, how do you manage a job like this and a husband?" asked Brigid.

"My husband is proud of my work," said Maria.

"But is he proud of you?" said Brigid. "My husband likes the way I look and likes the idea that I work, but he wants something more. We used to have shared friends, but now we just share social obligations, and most of his are connected with the Church. He wants me to be both the professional woman and the traditional wife. Are you a Catholic, Maria?"

"All Belgians are *catholique*," said Maria, slipping into the French pronunciation. "We are *catholique* in name, anyway, if not in practice. That is the European way."

"My husband is a twenty-first-century lawyer, but at these church functions I'm treated more like a nineteenth-century Catholic wife. I don't understand his deference to the Church. In my mind, the bishops are damaged goods after the scandals of the past decade. I can't take them seriously."

"That kind of Catholic hardly exists in Belgium anymore," said Maria. "We are evolving our own version of Catholicism. The hierarchy has been so discredited here. The bishop of my own home diocese, Bruges, was forced to resign when it came out that he had been sexually abusing his own nephew for years. He said it was all a 'game,' the stupid bastard. It was no game to his nephew."

They both sat in silence for a moment, looking at their wine glasses.

"No, Brigid," continued Maria, "nobody can take that part of the Church too seriously. But there is a good part of the Church, too. There are people who remind us of its beauty and its charity and its prayer. Like the nuns."

"Not like most of the nuns I knew. They didn't remind me of beauty, charity, or prayer," said Brigid.

Maria looked at Brigid. "Why don't you come down to Bruges this weekend, and I will show you my parish. If you like, you can even come to Mass with me."

Brigid was surprised. Nobody in her circle of friends ever invited her to Mass. They would be more likely to invite her to a séance. But there was something sincere and direct about Maria. Brigid liked her. This was a professional woman like herself, but a believer. That intrigued Brigid.

"I don't know," demurred Brigid. "Like I said, I'm not much for going to church these days. I got turned off on the way it treated women years ago."

"Well," said Maria, "I think you would like this parish. It is almost all women. I go to a convent chapel in Bruges. Sometimes we don't have any men present."

"Don't you need a priest?" said Brigid.

"No. We haven't paid much attention to the hierarchy on refusing to ordain women. If we don't have a regular priest, we have decided we should not go without the Eucharist, so one of the nuns leads us."

Brigid was intrigued. She liked Maria's progressive spirit. Maybe it would be good to spend some of her free time with her.

"Besides, you can go shopping for chocolates and lace in Bruges if you come. I'll even take you to see the relic of the Holy Blood," said Maria.

"The what?" asked Brigid.

"The Holy Blood," said Maria with a smile. "We Belgians have a vial of Christ's own blood brought back from the Crusades. People come from the whole world over just to touch it."

One thing Brigid did like about the Catholic Church was the stories. Evangelical Protestants were so relentlessly serious about all their sin and redemption. Catholics had great stories, saints, and relics. Who else had a whole vial of Christ's own blood?

"I don't know. You make a pretty good argument," said Brigid.

"It's decided, then. Come on down with me on the train. You can get a room in the old city, and we can go to Mass on Sunday. And I promise, you'll even have time to shop."

"I can't believe I'm saying yes to this, but OK," said Brigid, suddenly feeling spontaneous after brushing Nate off. "Wait in the lobby, and I'll get my bag."

13

SISTER MIRIAM

SUNDAY MORNING IN BRUGES IS QUIET. EVEN THOUGH
sixty percent of all Belgians are baptized as Roman Catholics, only about
five percent actually go to church. Consequently, Brigid and Maria had
the streets of Bruges to themselves as they made their way to the convent for Mass.

The convent of the Sisters of Our Lady is a sturdy stone building
sandwiched between a little side street and a canal, near the cathedral.

The building had been a convent off and on since the sixteenth century, with a long interruption around the time of the French Revolution,
when most convents and monasteries were closed by the revolutionaries.
This left a bad taste for liberty in the mouth of the Catholic Church.

Maria rang the bell at the convent door. The chimes could be heard
echoing down the corridors. Eventually, a short woman dressed in a simple black dress answered the door. She wore no makeup. Her gray hair
was pulled back in a neat bun. She spoke impeccable English.

Maria did the introductions. "Sister Gertrude, this is Brigid. Brigid,
Sister Gertrude." They stood smiling and nodding at each other. "We
are here for the Mass," said Maria. Gertrude nodded.

Silently, the nun led the two guests down a long corridor, past a
Baroque-style chapel and into a large dining room furnished with

wooden tables. Chairs were arranged in a semicircle at the center of the room.

Brilliant sunlight poured through the peaked Gothic windows on one side of the room. The diamond-shaped glass panes illuminated the refectory in geometric patterns. Brigid found herself stepping from diamond to diamond like she was a schoolgirl. She could almost hear her grandmother say, "Don't step on the cracks."

"This is spectacular!" said Brigid. She walked over to the windows and looked out at the canal. Tourist boats were passing, going both directions, with twenty-five or thirty people in each boat and a guide sitting up front. Flower boxes beneath the windows gave a splash of color. It was like a postcard of tourist Bruges. Isn't it just like the Church to have the best real estate? thought Brigid cynically.

Women dressed in varying styles began to filter into the room and took seats in the semicircle. Brigid and Maria joined them. The chairs were arranged facing a large dining table covered in a clean white cloth. Brigid could see a standing crucifix on the table. On a side table were a silver chalice and cruets of wine and water. It looked like the preparations for an ordinary Mass.

"How many of these women are nuns?" whispered Brigid to Maria.

"Maybe half. Most are guests like us," Maria answered, putting her finger to her lips for silence.

A bell rang. Then everyone stood. A tall, dignified woman entered. She was dressed in a floor-length white alb. Over her shoulders, she wore a white stole, a symbol of priestly office.

Apart from the fact that the priest was a woman, the Mass was just as Brigid remembered. The nun began with the sign of the cross. As a courtesy to their guests, she spoke English, the new *lingua franca* of Belgium. "Peace be with you." They all responded, "And with your spirit."

Brigid was impressed. She had heard about Episcopalian women being priests, but she had never seen a Catholic ceremony with a woman presiding.

As a homily, the sister gave a reflection on the mystery of the Eucharist for the feast of *Corpus Christi*. Brigid had not thought much about the mystical meaning of the Eucharist since high school. In fact, she had not really heard much theological talk since. For a moment, she was back in school listening to the nuns she had once loved so much.

At the consecration of the Mass, the woman in the alb said the words of consecration, just like any priest. "This is my body, given up for you. This is my blood, the blood of the new and eternal covenant . . . Do this in memory of me."

At communion the women all lined up to receive the consecrated bread and wine. Then they sat in silence. One of the women began to sing, a high and clear version of Mozart's *Ave Verum*. It is one of those hymns for which tears are the only appropriate response.

After Mass, Brigid was transfixed. "This Mass was beautiful," she whispered to Maria.

"Yes, a Mass like any other," said Maria, "but without collections, babies, and men."

After Mass the women gathered around a buffet table with sweet breads and coffee for conversation. The woman who had presided at the liturgy came over to Maria and Brigid. She had changed out of her alb into the same simple black dress that many of the other women were wearing. Brigid realized this was their habit. On her shoulder was a little pin with a cross.

"Sister Miriam," said Maria, "this is my friend Brigid Condon from the United States. She is at a meeting with me in Brussels for the week, so she came to Bruges. I told her about our community here." Maria turned to Brigid. "Sister Miriam is the superior of this convent."

"Welcome," said Sister Miriam. The two women shook hands. Brigid noticed that it was a strong handshake, like she expected in the business world but not from a nun.

Miriam was one of those dignified but friendly people who made you feel immediately at ease. "Would you like to sit down? We could take our coffee over there."

The three women picked up a coffee cup and moved to a small

table at the end of the room, near one of the big windows overlooking the canal.

Brigid had a million questions she wanted to ask. First and foremost she asked, "How come there was no priest for the Mass?"

Miriam raised her eyebrows for a moment and said, "Well, dear, we haven't been able to get a priest to come to the convent for Mass for years. There just aren't any. They tell us that if we want to have Mass we should come out to the parish church. We did that for a while, but realized that the only day we were all together in our community was Sunday. We wanted a homily and liturgy that was directed to our community.

"If the Church won't ordain enough priests, we can't wait around. The only reason there is no huge outcry in a Catholic country like Belgium is that hardly any of the laity go to Mass anymore. But we are a community of sisters. We should celebrate in community at least once a week to preserve our identity. For daily Mass we go to various parish churches near our work, but on Sundays we worship here. The ancient Church had female deacons for sure, why not priests?"

"I never knew that," said Brigid. She wasn't sure if all this was true, but it certainly was intriguing.

"Oh, yes," said Maria. "Just another case of the men writing history from the man's point of view. It wasn't until women started to do the research that these things were uncovered.

"A few years ago we realized that the Church gave us a bad choice. We could either go out to parish churches and have no community here, or we could have community here but no Eucharist. We were unwilling to make that choice. So, we decided we could have both," she said emphatically.

"Well, what does the bishop say?" asked Brigid.

"Nothing," said Sister Miriam. "He knows, but he turns his back on it. He can't acknowledge what we are doing, or he would be in trouble with Rome. He probably does want us to stop, but he also wants us to keep up our work in his diocese. He doesn't want to drive us away. It benefits him to keep us here."

"What kind of work do you do?" asked Brigid.

"Mostly, we are teachers and nurses," said Miriam. "We teach the mentally handicapped. We work with the street people—the alcoholics and drug addicts. We have a clinic for people with AIDS. One of our sisters is an archivist. She works on the archives of the diocese. Actually, we are a pretty traditional order, despite the Sunday liturgy."

"What does Rome think?" asked Brigid, even more intrigued at this group of independent women.

"Of course they don't like it. But Rome knows this is happening all across Europe and North America. We are not so unusual." Sister Miriam stopped and took a sip of coffee. "As I said," she continued, "we can't wait around for the old boys' club in Rome. It is this, or nothing. Most of our guests are women who are completely turned off by the male-dominated church. They just want a place to pray in peace."

"The Church really is an old boys' club, isn't it?" said Brigid. "I was at the Vatican Embassy in Washington recently, and when there was something serious to discuss, they dismissed the women like servants."

"Here things are different," observed Maria, who had remained pretty silent during the discussion. "Here women are taken seriously."

Sister Miriam nodded. "We form a little community of service. We collect money for a mental hospital in the Congo. We run a little hospice for women who have been victims of rape in Bruges. Even Rome does not want to stop those things. The Church needs a little redemption in the eyes of Belgians after the scandals of recent years."

Sister Miriam finished her coffee and set the cup on the table.

Suddenly Brigid was full of questions. "Do the Catholics in Belgium still practice the faith?"

Miriam exhaled. "Do you want the truth, or do you want the Vatican press release?"

"The truth, of course," said Brigid.

"No, they don't. The Catholic faith used to be what united Belgium and bridged the gap between the Dutch-speaking Flemish and the French-speaking Walloons. But today, the faith is practically dead.

People want their children in Catholic schools, which are paid for by the government, but they don't really care about the Church or its teachings."

"So, why do they put their children in Catholic school?" asked Brigid.

"Mostly they just want disciplined and educated children. They think Catholic schools are safer, free from drugs and sex. It's all illusion, of course. No school is perfectly safe. Drugs and sex are everywhere in Belgium, even Catholic schools."

Brigid nodded. "We have the same thing back home. I think half the girls in my high school on Long Island were sent there because their parents thought they would remain virgins longer. If our parents had only known what was really going on . . ."

"They probably did know," said Sister Miriam. The three women chuckled.

"We all like to have our illusions undisturbed," said Miriam.

"Are there many nuns in Belgium today?" asked Brigid, curious about Miriam.

Miriam shook her head. "We sisters are dying out. You can look at us and see that. Every head in this convent is gray. We are all within twenty years of death. What will come after us, only the Holy Spirit knows. We have to live out our last years the best way we know how."

Sister Miriam stared out the window for a moment, obviously reflecting.

"Do you regret becoming a nun?" asked Brigid.

"No," said Miriam. "I don't, but it is different today. When I was a girl, the convents were crowded with young sisters. But today, that's done. Some new form of religion will take the place of what we have lived here. There is no going back. We can't roll the clock back to 1900, despite what Rome might say. I think that whatever is coming will be better for women than what I have lived."

She was very definitive in her last statement.

Miriam looked around. Most of the sisters in the room had finished their coffee and were leaving. Miriam suggested that she and Brigid and

Maria get up and go for a walk along the canals. The sun was bright, and the late spring weather was glorious. The three women left the convent and walked along the narrow street to a little bridge that arched over the canal. They stopped and sat on a bench.

"Sister," asked Brigid, "do you pray?"

"All the time. St. Paul says to pray ceaselessly, and that's what I do. But my prayer is not just with words. It is also my work and my thoughts. It is what gives me peace."

"But don't you feel angry at the Church? Lots of women in the States are angry about the patriarchy of the Church. They are never consulted about anything, even about things that have to do with women."

Miriam held up her hand. She had heard all those critiques before.

"God is bigger than us. God is bigger than the Church or any religion. God is not the prisoner of any group of people or any set of rituals. God is God. Not male or female, not Christian or Muslim, not Catholic or Protestant. God is mystery. We serve a mystery, not an institution. The mystery will continue to live, even when the institution dies. Rome has not yet gotten the message, but the old Church is over. It is finished. A few conservatives are hanging on, out of nostalgia or fear. But it's over. Those days are long gone."

She turned and looked directly at Brigid. "Brigid, we don't need man-made mysteries. Just look out here at the water and the flowers and the sky. That is mystery enough. Look at the simple data," said Miriam. "Our churches are empty in Europe. Look at Vienna. A few years ago, it closed four hundred of its six hundred Catholic churches. This is happening throughout the world. If some company like your Starbucks closed two-thirds of its stores, you Americans would say it was time to sell that stock. Would you not?"

Brigid nodded. "We probably would have dumped it long ago if it were a stock, except for our sentimental attachment. I don't think any of my friends from Catholic high school are still going to church regularly—only with their moms on holidays."

"Sad, isn't it?" responded Miriam almost wistfully. "There is beauty in the Church. We just have to focus on the teachings of Christ and forget about all the negative baggage. It will survive, but it will be changed, no matter what the people in Rome think."

Brigid could see that Miriam was a free woman.

"What will save the Church?" asked Brigid.

"Saints," answered Miriam, now very definitive. "Saints will save the Church. They always have. We needed St. Francis to save the Church in the Middle Ages."

Miriam thumbed through her prayer book held in her left hand and pulled out a little holy card with a picture of a man in a priest's robe and a broad-brimmed hat. On the reverse side was a prayer to Damien of Molokai.

"Look at this man," said Miriam. "It's Damien of Molokai, the priest who worked with the lepers."

Brigid took the card and held it, considering the photo of the disease-ridden man.

Miriam continued, "A few years ago, a poll was taken here in Belgium. One of our newspapers asked who was the most revered Belgian of all time. The answer was Father Damien. Imagine, even in secular Belgium.

"Why? Because he gave up his life for the most wretched people on earth. That's why he was the most admired Belgian—not a movie star, not a writer, not a politician or a scientist, but a saint is the man we admire most."

Miriam waved her hand toward the scene of Bruges around them. "Even in skeptical, unbelieving, chocolate-loving, and beer-obsessed Belgium, it is a Flemish peasant who was born poor and died poor that most people admire. Not because he was a priest, but because he was a holy man, a saint.

"There will always be people like Damien," continued Miriam. "They will save the Church from itself. Saints just live the gospel. But even if they save the Church, saints cannot take it back to what it was fifty or even a hundred years ago, which is what the conservatives want. That's gone. We can no more go back to the Church of 1920 than we can insist that people travel by steamships instead of airplanes or give up their mobile phones and go back to the telegraph.

"The world has moved on from the old Church, but not from holiness. We still need our saints. The only tragedy in life is for us not to become a saint."

Brigid looked at this simple woman, sitting in the bright sunlight. She seemed positively luminous. Sister Miriam was not angry or bitter. She was resigned to change and was happy in her own skin—exactly what Brigid wanted for her own life.

Maria spoke up. Brigid had almost forgotten she was there. "Now you see why I like coming here. I feel at peace with these sisters."

Brigid looked at her watch. It was just past noon. "Look at the time," she said. "I have an errand I need to do before going back to Brussels. I promised my husband I would look up a man who lives near here. Maybe one of you knows of him. I think he is an ex-priest, Bernard Willebroeck."

"Father Bernard," nodded Miriam. "I know him well. I remember when he was a young priest in the Congo."

Maria, who had been quiet all this time, spoke up. "I've heard of him. He's not a priest anymore. I hear he has started some radical group, aimed at exposing the pedophiles in the Church."

"Why do you want to see Bernard?" asked Miriam.

"My husband is doing an investigation in Rome for the Vatican and wants me to check him out," answered Brigid vaguely.

"He has a radical reputation here," said Miriam. "He hates the bishops, especially the way they handled the pedophile priests here in Belgium. I hear his nephew was molested."

"What does he do for a living?" asked Brigid.

"He founded his own little group, New Church, I think he calls it. They have demonstrations. They get contributions, evidently. At times they have been very violent in their protests. Once, a church was burned near Bruges and they were accused of starting the fire. Threats have been made to priests," said Miriam. "Nothing was proven, though."

"Hmm," said Brigid. "Do I have any reason to be afraid of him?"

"I can't imagine Bernard would be a threat to you," said Miriam. "His anger is directed at the Church. But I don't think you should go see him alone."

"Where does he live?" asked Brigid.

"I hear he lives out near Ostende, on the way to the French border," said Maria. "It's less than a half hour away. I don't mind the drive. If you are interested, I can take you."

"If you're sure you don't mind, that would be great," said Brigid. Then, turning to Miriam, Brigid said, "Sister, why don't you join us? You could make introductions. He might be more receptive if you were there."

"I'm sure Sister has a full day," said Maria.

"Actually," said Miriam, "I was hoping to finalize my plans for a meeting in Rome at our mother house. I'll be leaving in a few days. But I'm sure I can take care of it tomorrow. Besides, it would be nice to see Bernard again, if he wants to see me. I knew his mother."

"Good," said Brigid. "It's settled, then. You'll come with us."

The three women drove out of old Bruges in Maria's Peugeot. Like most Belgians, Maria was a fast driver. Once out of the old city, they headed west toward Ostende, which means west end in Dutch.

They sped along, mostly in silence, looking at the lush fields, the fat cows, and the system of dikes meant to hold back the North Sea. Maria passed most of the cars and all of the trucks on the highway. Her driving was almost reckless. After about half an hour, they came to a little town called Jabbeke. At the center of the town was a big stone church on Kapellestraat, Chapel Street, surrounded by a parish graveyard. As they pulled up in front, Miriam said, "This was the parish where Bernard was once assigned before he left the priesthood."

Brigid was impressed at the grand building. "If nobody goes to church in Belgium, how can they manage to keep up all these buildings?" she asked. Brigid remembered her monsignor back home on Long Island always asking for money.

"The government pays," said Maria. "How much longer is anyone's guess. But for now, the Church can continue without parishioners."

Brigid rolled her eyes. To an American, the idea of the government paying for the Church seemed strange.

A few blocks from the town center, they found an ordinary-looking townhouse with Bernard's address. A small sign at the garden gate said in French and Dutch: Eglise Nouvelle, Neu Kirche, meaning New Church. "This is it," said Miriam. "This is his house."

Maria dropped Brigid and Miriam at the curb outside the house and then drove off in search of a parking space. The two women rang the doorbell.

After thirty seconds or so, they heard some jangling of keys. A man in his sixties opened the door. He had a dinner napkin in his left hand, clearly just coming from the table. He did not look pleased. Brigid saw that he was a robust and fairly handsome man. Oddly, he wore his hair long, pulled back in a ponytail. He looked like some aging hippie.

"Jab," he said in Dutch. Then, seeing that Brigid didn't understand, he switched to English. Belgians think they can easily spot an American.

"What do you want?" he asked.

Brigid spoke up. " Are you Bernard Willebroeck?"

"Who wants to know?" he said.

"Sorry," said Brigid. "I'm Brigid Condon from New York." She extended her hand to him, but he did not reciprocate.

Miriam stepped in front of Brigid. To break the ice, she said, "Bernard, it's me, Miriam."

He looked at her with surprise and said in Dutch, "Miriam! What the hell are you doing here? And who is she?" He appeared confused, almost angry.

"Brigid is a friend of mine from America," answered Miriam, still in Dutch. "Could we come in?"

"No," he said. "I'm eating dinner."

"Oh, Bernard, stop being so disagreeable. Give us a few moments of your time," answered Miriam.

Raising his voice, he asked, "Why should I?"

"Because you owe me a favor. When you were in the Congo and your mother was dying, who sat with her?" asked Miriam.

Bernard's eyes narrowed. Miriam countered, "Five minutes."

Defeated by Miriam's rebuke, Bernard stepped back and opened the door, speaking to them in English. "Very well, come in," he said with an exasperated scowl. He made it clear to Brigid that he was feeling manipulated into offering hospitality. "Five minutes, no more."

The two women entered the house. Brigid looked around quickly, with a lawyer's eye for detail. It was an ordinary little home, but the front parlor was not furnished as a sitting room. Instead, it held high-tech office equipment, including two expensive CPUs, scanners, fax machines, and several phones. New Church was obviously doing a lot of communicating with someone. She also noted a fairly large safe against the wall.

Bernard stood in the office, leaning against a computer desk that held a monitor bigger than any Brigid had ever seen. It appeared to be set up for Skype calls.

Brigid noticed a lot of vinyl bags with bank logos stacked to one side of the desk. Good for cash deposits, she thought.

"So, what do you what to know?" said Bernard testily.

"My husband asked me to come by and visit you," said Brigid. "He's doing some work for the Vatican."

Bernard raised his eyebrows. "What's your husband's name?" he demanded.

"Nathaniel Condon," answered Brigid. "Your name and New Church have come up in his research. He read about your group in several reports."

Bernard visibly recoiled at the mention of reports. "What reports?" he asked angrily. "The Vatican is doing reports on us?"

Brigid could see that the meeting was going downhill quickly, so she opted for directness. "Well, the Vatican is looking into groups that have made threats against local churches," she said.

He scoffed derisively, "They think I've made threats against the local Church? Ha! I'm not the threat. It's the bishops who are the threat."

Miriam interjected firmly, "Bernard, you know your group was in the news this past year about a church burning."

"That was investigated," he shouted. "They found nothing!"

Brigid began to think that their visit had been a mistake. Bernard's face was getting red. He clenched and unclenched his fists.

He almost shouted, "You came all the way from America to investigate something that was in the newspapers? Why didn't your husband come? Why would the Vatican investigator send his wife?"

"I was here on business," answered Brigid. "My husband merely suggested I speak with you while I was here."

Brigid could see the interview was going nowhere. She looked around the room quickly to see if she could learn anything else from its furnishings. On the walls of the office someone had taped newspaper articles in various languages. They had markings on them in blue ink. There was one article in English from the *International New York Times* about Manning's assassination.

Bernard's mood shifted from angry to threatening.

"This conversation is over," he said. "That's all I have to say to you or your husband, whoever he is. And I certainly have nothing to say to the Vatican or even to you, Miriam." He pointed his finger at the nun. "If you want to talk to me, call my lawyer or come back here with the police."

Brigid wanted to delay a few minutes so she could get a better look at the place. She used the classic stall tactic. "May I use the toilet before we leave?" she asked. Miriam looked at her quizzically.

"Down the hall," Bernard said with some irritation, unable to refuse her request.

Brigid crossed the room and went down the hall. She noted two rows of phone jacks on the wall with at least eight lines each. Why would some little organization need sixteen phone lines? she wondered. The phone lines added to her suspicion that New Church was more than just a local church group headed by an angry ex-priest.

When Brigid came out of the toilet, Miriam was already standing by the front door. Just over the door was a little plaque with a prayer to Our Lady of Guadalupe.

"Have you ever been to Mexico?" Miriam asked, pointing to the image of the Virgin.

"No," he said. "I've never been to Mexico. Now, if you'll excuse me, my dinner is growing cold. Good day, ladies."

The two women stepped outside, and Bernard closed the door behind them with a thud.

As they walked down the street to where Maria was waiting for them in the car, Miriam said to Brigid, "Too bad we didn't discover what you were looking for."

"Who knows?" said Brigid. "Maybe we did."

14

THE MAFIA CONNECTION

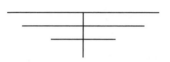

GOOGLE SEARCHES ARE A WONDERFUL THING. THE WHOLE world can be sorted out with a few clicks of the mouse. They have made police work a lot easier. But a good policeman still needs a memory for detail and the ability to make judgments.

During their dinner at the Columbus Hotel the week before, Monsignor Ackerman had referred to all the dead cardinals as papabile. One hundred twenty cardinals were under the age of eighty. Technically, all of them were eligible to be pope, but only a handful were really papabile, or contenders.

Sitting at a desk in his borrowed office in a Vatican office building, Nate did a Google search. He entered "papabile cardinals." He immediately received thousands of results, including some about baseball in St. Louis and some about bird-watching.

Refining his search a bit, he entered "papabile Roman Catholic cardinals." He also entered the city names for each of the dead clerics.

This time there were a few thousand more results. But at the top of the list was a year-old article in *Panoramio*, the Italian news magazine. It had an amazing number of cross-references with Nate's entry, including all the city names. He clicked on the article to open it.

Panoramio is the kind of magazine that Italians love—the perfect balance between gloss and gossip. It has lots of pictures of bikini-clad socialites on the beach at Monte Carlo with salacious tidbits about their private lives. Occasionally, the magazine covers the Church, still with an eye toward scandal. The title of the article Nate had opened was "I Papabili, Quali Sono Loro Oggi?" or "Papabile: Who Are They Today?" The subtitle was about corruption in the Vatican.

Nate could not read Italian well, but he could certainly make out the names of the cardinals. There were fourteen papabile cardinals listed in the article—all men who had a reasonable prayer of becoming pope if the election were held soon. O'Toole's name was on the list. So were all the names of the six dead cardinals. It had been published before any of them had died, a year ago.

From what Nate could make out, it seemed that all six of the dead cardinals were considered *stranieri* by the Vatican bureaucracy. Two other cardinals were also considered *stranieri* by the article, but they were still alive, as far as Nate knew.

Nate looked up the word *straniero/i* in his Mondadori Italian-English dictionary. The first meaning was foreigner, but an alternative meaning was outsider.

Since one of the six dead cardinals, the Archbishop of Milan, was an Italian, Nate figured that the word, as used in the article, could not mean foreigner. Evidently the article considered all the dead cardinals to have been outsiders to the Vatican bureaucracy in some sense. Nate noted that, at least as far as he could tell, while O'Toole was considered papabile, he was not considered *straniero* by *Panoramio*.

Since six of the eight outsider cardinals mentioned in the article were dead, Nate wondered if this might be some sort of hit list. If so, then the two cardinals who were still alive, the Archbishop of Recife, Brazil, and the Archbishop of Sydney, Australia, might be next.

Nate wanted a better understanding of the article.

He pushed the intercom to call Sandra Orsuto, the secretary he had hired through Monsignor Rodriguez. Orsuto had come to Rome as a student, but after she received her degree she remained because she fell in love with the city. After only a few days, she had established herself as invaluable to Nate.

"Sandra," he said, "please come in here for a moment and help me translate this article." When she entered the room, Nate handed her his printout of the *Panoramio* article. "What does this mean?" asked Nate, pointing to the term *stranieri*.

"The thing that unites the *stranieri*," read Sandra, "is a deep suspicion of the Vatican bureaucracy. They all think that it is corrupt and badly in need of a complete housecleaning."

"This is good," said Nate, deeply interested.

Sandra continued, "The *stranieri* are not liberals. They are not generally in favor of sweeping changes in the Church, such as an end to celibacy or the ordination of women. However, they all are outspoken critics of the dealings of the Vatican Bank, its secrecy, and its lack of compliance with international banking standards. All the *stranieri* have been publicly critical of the management of Vatican City itself, and in particular its governor, Cardinal Luciano Crepi. These prelates have broken the unwritten code that dictates that cardinals should always speak well of one another, at least in public. Their criticism is a sign of the weakness of the present pope and the chaos in the Vatican bureaucracy itself."

Sandra paused. "Shall I continue?" she asked.

"Go on," said Nate.

"Cardinal Manning of New York," continued Sandra, "is the strongest of the *stranieri*. He is the strongest critic of the Vatican Bank. He is also the most significant threat to the Vatican establishment, because he is chaplain to the American group, the Knights of Columbus, which has a seat on the board of the bank and is the largest single supplier of money to Rome. If Cardinal Manning turns off the money fountain, Rome goes dry." Sandra paused as she concluded the article.

"Who wrote this article?" Nate asked.

"Umberto Tochi," she said. "He is a well-known journalist who writes a lot for *Panoramio*."

"Does he quote anyone as his source for all this information?" asked Nate.

"Yes," said Sandra. "He quotes an anonymous monsignor in the Vatican. He calls him only Monsignore Anonimo."

"Call the magazine," said Nate. "See if you can find out who Tochi's Monsignore Anonimo really is."

Sandra left the room. Half an hour later she rang Nate on the office phone. "I talked to Tochi at the magazine," she said. "He refused to identify his source."

"Naturally," said Nate. "That's what a good journalist should do."

"But," continued Sandra, "he let slip a little detail. He said, 'You might know, Sandra, since all you American expats in Rome seem to know each other.' So it appears that our Monsignore Anonimo is an American."

"Good job," said Nate. "That narrows it down considerably. I think this article gives us a common thread. All of the *stranieri* were a threat to the Vatican bureaucracy, especially the Vatican Bank."

As Nate hung up the phone, he thought to himself, Money and power: the classic combination for corruption. The Church was no exception.

Nate picked up the phone on his desk and called the only American monsignor in the Vatican bureaucracy he knew, Monsignor Ackerman.

"*Pronto*," said Ackerman, in that strange way Italians have of answering the phone. They always say, "Ready." What are they ready for?

"Do you read *Panoramio*?" asked Nate.

"Not often," said Ackerman. "Why do you ask?"

"There was an article last year in the May issue, listing the papabile. There were eight names on a list of outsider candidates to be pope. Six of them are now dead. The source for the article was a Monsignore Anonimo. Do you know who that might be?"

"No idea," said Ackerman. He seemed impatient. "Anyone could speculate on who might be the next pope. It's one of the favorite indoor sports for Italians."

"Well, *Panoramio* could have just said, 'anonymous source,'" pressed Nate. "Clearly Umberto Tochi wanted to give the impression that his contact was an insider."

"Three thousand people work at the Vatican," said Ackerman. "Could be any one of them. There must be a hundred American monsignors in Rome alone." He paused for a second and then asked, "Why are you calling me?"

Nate raised his eyebrows and tapped the desk with a pencil. He paused for a moment to think. He had not told Ackerman that Tochi had specified the source as an American monsignor. Why had Ackerman made that assumption?

"Whoever was the source for this article," continued Nate, "clearly knew a lot about these cardinals. Maybe he had access to their files?"

"What are you suggesting?" demanded Ackerman angrily, almost in a shout. "Bishops' files are confidential. I certainly don't know anything about that article."

For the first time, Ackerman was not friendly or flirty. Nate had touched a nerve.

"I've got to go," said Ackerman. "Ciao."

Nate studied the dead receiver in his hand and sensed he was on to something.

In the files Nate had received from Tracy at their lunch in Georgetown, there had been a dossier on Ackerman. Flipping through the file now, Nate saw Tracy's handwritten note: "Hangs out at Angelo Azzuro, a mob gay bar."

Nate thought for a moment. When people are living a double life, they sometimes let their guard down when they're drinking. They also might say things at night in a familiar place that they would never say in daylight or to strangers. Perhaps Monsignore Anonimo had been talking to someone at Angelo Azzuro.

It's worth a field trip, thought Nate. He searched Angelo Azzuro online. It was within walking distance of the Columbus Hotel, in the Trastevere section of Rome.

Gay nightlife, the world over, starts late. Being a New Yorker, Nate knew that, so he didn't even bother getting dressed until after 9:00 p.m. He slipped on a pair of loafers, a pair of jeans, a white linen shirt, and a Giorgio Armani sport coat. He wore no socks. He wanted to attract attention. Looking good was always an asset, but in a gay bar it might get people talking.

Finding Angelo Azzuro on a tiny side street in Trastevere was a challenge. And at 10:00 p.m. on a Tuesday, there were few other places open. He asked directions from an English-speaking waiter at a café in Piazza Santa Maria. "Straight ahead, two streets, then turn right," said the waiter. Once he was close, Nate just followed the trickle of men entering a door under a blue neon angel. From fifty paces away you could feel the pulse of the music.

Nate's white shirt glowed under the purple black light on the stairs. He unbuttoned the second button of his shirt as he descended the steps. If he was going to exploit his assets, he might as well go all out.

At the bottom of the steps, the bouncer unclicked the velvet rope and let him in with a smile. "*Buona sera signore. Prego entrare.*"

Nate headed for the bar. Everyone talks to bartenders, so they are almost always good sources of information.

There were no stools at the bar. Patrons just leaned up against the Lucite-topped counter. The lighting cast everyone around the bar in a flattering aura.

The bartender was a muscular Italian from what seemed to be a Sylvester Stallone look-alike contest. He nodded at Nate as a sign that he was ready to take his order.

"Do you speak English?" asked Nate.

"Yes, a little," smiled the bartender, extending his hand across the bar to shake hands. "I'm Stefano. What would you like?" His smile became a grin, fully aware of the double entendre of his question.

"You mean to drink?" asked Nate. He knew how to play the game. He was from New York, after all. The verbal volley was fun.

"To drink for now," said the bartender. "Afterward, who knows?" Another smile flashed across the glowing bar.

"Whiskey and water with ice," said Nate. The bartender served it up in a heavy crystal glass, not the usual cheap bar glass. Nate had already achieved favored-client status.

He took a sip and leaned against the bar for a while, surveying the crowd. A young man came over and stood at Nate's right hand.

"Do many Americans come to this bar?" Nate asked the bartender.

"Yes," said Stefano. "Some come here once. Some come here more than once. I hope you are the second kind." Then he said with mock chagrin, "Are you only looking for Americans?"

"I'm looking for a particular American," said Nate. "Do you know Matthew Ackerman?"

The bartender paused his glass washing and looked up. He seemed to be considering his response. The young man next to Nate, obviously drunk, jumped into the conversation with a leering smile. "Everybody knows Monsignore Matteo. Even the *giornalisti*. He loves to talk to everyone."

Now Stefano was stuck. If Ackerman were a regular, Stefano could hardly deny that he knew him. So, he said simply, "Yes, I know him."

"Do you think he will be here tonight?" asked Nate, a little anxious that he might run into the monsignor.

"Maybe not," said the bartender warily. "He usually comes on Wednesdays or Sundays."

"Ask his friend Donato," offered the young man. "He always comes with him."

"Who is Donato?" asked Nate. The young drunk was proving more useful than the bartender.

"He's over there," said the helpful stranger, obviously trying to make himself indispensable to Nate. The young man pointed across the room to an alcove where a short man, who looked to be in his early forties, was leaning against a pillar. The man in the alcove was talking to no one and had a bored expression on his face.

The bartender was annoyed with the talkative volunteer. "*Stai zitto*," Stefano said to the young stranger. There was nothing nice in his tone.

"Who is Donato?" asked Nate.

"I don't know," said the bartender. "He works with Matteo, I think."

"No, he doesn't work with Matteo," interrupted the tipsy young man, determined to be part of the conversation. "He works at the Banco Vaticano." The young man was clearly proud of his insider knowledge. "I hear he carries bags of gold to the vault, if he likes you. But he never carried a bag of gold for me," said the smiling young man with a touch of drunken self-pity.

Nate remembered that Ackerman had mentioned a Donato in their conversation at the Columbus Hotel.

Maybe this was the same guy.

"*Stai zitto, finochio*," said Stefano, picking up the serrated paring knife he used for slicing lemons and waving it at the young man. "*Oma.*" There was that Mafia word again. The young man had obviously given away some information Stefano thought imprudent, but he was too drunk or too infatuated with Nate to care about the threat.

"Why do you care only about the monsignori?" pouted the young man. "*Gli laiaci* are not good enough for you?" He was beginning to get obnoxious, even though he had been helpful.

"Does he come here all the time with Monsignor Matteo?" asked Nate.

"Ask him yourself," said Stefano, obviously done with the conversation. Stefano turned again toward the young drunk.

"*Tu—va via*," Stefano said. He pointed into the crowd, ordering the young man to leave. The young man obeyed as he disappeared onto the dance floor.

Nate walked away from the bar. He crossed the room toward Donato and leaned against one of the tall bar tables, hoping to strike up a conversation. Donato obliged, eventually looking Nate's way and smiling. Nate smiled back. Bingo, he thought.

Donato moved over to the table and flirted. *Ciao, bello.* He extended his hand toward Nate, palm partly up. Nate did not know whether to kiss it or shake it. So he gave it a shake.

"*Ciao,*" said Nate. "That's the end of my Italian, I'm afraid. I'm an American."

"Oh, I love Americans," gushed Donato. "You do things so quickly and efficiently in America. My name is Donato. It means 'gift,'" he said with a smile. "But I'm not free."

Nate was a little overwhelmed by his aggression.

"I was here to meet another American," said Nate coyly.

"Really?" asked Donato. "Who might that be?"

"Matthew Ackerman," said Nate. "Do you know him?"

"Yes," said Donato. "Everyone in this bar knows Matteo, but he won't be here until tomorrow. He always comes here on Wednesdays."

"And what do you do, Donato?" asked Nate.

"I'm in finance, private finance, very private finance," said Donato. He appeared a little uncomfortable now that work was being mentioned. Nate was now sure this was the Donato from the Vatican Bank. Very interesting that a bank official would be hanging out in a Mafia-run bar without any fear of discovery, Nate thought.

"And you?" asked Donato, shifting the focus. "What do you do?"

"Oh, I'm a lawyer," said Nate casually.

Just then Nate's cell phone went off. He could not hear it, but could feel its vibration. He fished the phone out of his pocket as he held up a hand to Donato, relieved that he had an excuse to stop the conversation for a second. "*Scusi,*" said Nate, moving away.

The screen on his phone showed Tracy's number. Nate answered the phone covering his other ear with his free hand, as he crossed the bar and headed for the exit. The music was too loud to hear much, so he shouted into the phone, "Hang on, Bill, 'til I can get outside."

"Where are you?" asked Tracy. "Sounds like a disco."

"It is. I'm doing research," said Nate. Tracy did not pick up on the remark. Nate headed for the exit upstairs. Once he was out on the quieter street, he said to Tracy, "OK, Bill, go ahead."

"I'm just calling to confirm our meeting at 10:00 a.m. a week from this Friday," said Tracy. "I'll be staying at the Hassler, near the Spanish Steps. It's only a couple of blocks away from the Knights of Malta Embassy on the Via Condotti. "

"I'll find it," said Nate. "I'm beginning to connect the dots here. I'll tell you when I see you. I think you'll find it very interesting. Who else will be at the meeting?"

"A man from Interpol and a representative from the Italian police, the Carabinieri. I think we need to keep this close to the vest for now," said Tracy. "But we may want some official police help."

"Good," said Nate. "I'm not sure who we can trust at this point."

"Only a few days in Rome and lost your faith already?" asked Tracy sarcastically.

"No, just seeing things in a different light," said Nate. "Anyhow, I'll see you a week from Friday. Bye."

The walk back to the hotel was invigorating. The cool night air felt good. In a strange way, Nate had actually enjoyed the evening. It had even been fairly productive.

He had learned a little about Ackerman, including that he talked to journalists and was a pal to a Vatican Bank official. There was a high probability that Ackerman was Monsignor Anonimo.

Nate was not at all shocked to discover that priests hung out in a gay bar, although it did sadden him a little. He actually felt sorry for people like Ackerman and Donato. They were just lonely, pathetic men who had locked themselves in a closet that had no exit.

Nate didn't think that anybody expected perfect chastity anymore. Most people he knew thought that celibates were either crazy or liars. Brigid didn't believe anybody lived their vows. And if they did, she didn't think it made them holy.

Nate chuckled as he remembered a favorite quote from G. K. Chesterton, one of his Catholic heroes: "The worst temptation of the most pagan youth is not so much to denounce monks for breaking their vow as to wonder at them for keeping it."

As a lawyer, Nate knew that the dangerous and destructive thing about the priests' behavior came from their need for secrecy. It made them do reckless and dangerous things. It made them drink. It made them vulnerable to blackmail, extortion, and worse. It bound them together in a conspiracy of secrecy and a confederacy of evil. Who knew what they might do to preserve their mutual secrets? Nate had seen it with public officials.

It all seemed so unnecessary. To people of Nate and Brigid's generation, sex was good. It was a part of life, but only a part. And of late, thought Nate, only a very small part of his life.

As he turned the corner off the Lungo Tevere, the great dome of St. Peter's came into view at the end of the Via della Conciliazione. Nate was struck with the grandeur and romance of the city. It was easy to fall in love with the place, and it was an easy place to fall in love. Perhaps Ackerman and Donato had fallen in love with Rome.

However, thought Nate, it's better to fall in love with a person. A wave of emotion swept over him. He missed Brigid powerfully. Rome would have been better had she been there to share it with him.

As he reached the door of the Columbus Hotel, he suddenly felt a chill, not from the air of the cooling summer evening, but from within himself. It was the same chill he had felt a month ago, as he stood at the top of the steps with Tracy in Georgetown. It was a shudder of evil.

15

THE UNRAVELING

MONSIGNOR ACKERMAN'S MOBILE PHONE RANG AT 9:00
a.m. as he was leaving the American parish of St. Agnes on Piazza
Navona. Ackerman had gone there to celebrate the morning Mass for
half a dozen pilgrims. The call was from Stefano, the bartender from
Angelo Azzuro.

Ackerman was shocked to hear Stefano's voice on the phone. The only
place he had ever spoken to him was in the bar. How did he even get the
number? But then Ackerman remembered whom Stefano worked for.

The bartender's voice was serious. "Matteo, we have to meet right now.
I'll be at the *capolinea* of the 64 bus in fifteen minutes. Meet me there."

Ackerman demurred. "But, but I have work."

"Screw work," said Stefano. "Fifteen minutes. Be there." The call
ended. Ackerman started walking. He picked up his pace as he crossed
the Ponte Sant'Angelo. When the Mafia said, "Be there," they meant it.

As Ackerman got to Piazza Pio XII, just outside the Vatican wall
and across the street from his office, Stefano was already there, leaning
against the bus shelter. Ackerman had never seen him in daylight before.
He was surprised that Stefano looked so much older. And today, there
was no trace of the bartender's smile.

"Get on the bus," Stefano told Ackerman as he handed him a ticket. They climbed on just as the doors closed. They got seats at the very back. After a few stops the bus would fill up with passengers, but for the moment it was nearly empty.

"We've got a problem, a big problem," said Stefano in English. He wanted to leave no chance for misunderstanding. "And you are a big part of it. There was an American lawyer in the bar last night, asking questions about you. That silly fairy Antonelli was also at the bar, and he told him all about you and Donato and the bank."

The whine of the bus engine drowned out their conversation. At each stop more passengers got on the bus, with the blank faces common to commuters everywhere. They paid no attention to Stefano and Ackerman. In fact, they paid no attention to anything.

"Matteo, you talk too much. You've been seen talking to this lawyer at the Columbus." Ackerman remembered the waiter who told him to shut up. "He has been coming to your office. Now he comes to the bar looking for you. He knows too much."

Ackerman started to speak, but Stefano held up his hand to silence him. "He is not just a lawyer," breathed Stefano. "He is an investigator for the Holy See. He is here to discover who is killing all the *cardinali*. Remember, Matteo, you are in this. You were the source for the article in *Panoramio* that gave my friends the names for the targets. Your article said who might close the bank to us. *E la culpa tua*. It's all your fault." Stefano stuck his finger in Ackerman's chest. The bartender was almost spitting as he whispered, "We would not have known who to target if it weren't for you and your people."

"My people?" said Ackerman, trying to deflect the charge. "I didn't tell you to target anyone. I just gave information to the writer. It was in *Panoramio*, for God's sake."

"*Si*, your people, Matteo," said Stefano. "Your two cardinal *amici*, who have been making money from the Camorra for years." Stefano made a point of using the *Napolitano* name for the mob. "They knew what they were doing. They became rich men because of us. You got

your share. Now they owe us something. Now you owe us something."
Stefano repeated himself for emphasis.

The bus lurched to a stop in Largo Argentina.

"You call your cardinal friends and tell them to stop this investigation
or . . ." Stefano made a pistol gesture with his thumb and index finger,
pointing the gun at Ackerman's heart.

"I will go see them tomorrow," said Ackerman.

"No *domani*," said Stefano angrily. "*Oggi*. You go today! You get
this lawyer to stop the investigation now! If he is not on a plane to the
United States tomorrow, I will call my *capo*. Then it is out of my hands,
monsignore. The *capi* are not nice people, if they think their interests are
in danger. You remember what happened to Roberto Calvi when he
cheated my *capi*? It could happen to you, too. It could happen to me.
Then I am dead along with you. No more talking to this lawyer. *Zitto!*"

They rode on in silence. Ackerman wanted to jump off the bus and
run away, but by this time it was absolutely full. Besides, what difference
would it make? There was no running away from the Camorra.

So Ackerman stayed put. Panic set in. What was he going to do? This
was what he had always been afraid of. When you dance with the bear,
you may get eaten.

He tried to recall how it all started. Ackerman had gone to Angelo
Azzuro out of loneliness and boredom. Stefano had been nice to him
at first. He gave him free drinks and introduced him to elegant men.
Then Stefano offered him a way to turn his Vatican contacts into
money and excitement. Ackerman liked to be useful. He wanted the
money. Even more, he wanted to have the attention from someone
like Stefano.

All Ackerman had to do was carry messages to his friends at the
Vatican, especially to Cardinal Luciano Crepi, who ran the Vatican
City State.

Soon Ackerman recruited Donato to greet these special depositors at
the door of the bank. Donato needed no coaxing.

It was Donato who introduced Ackerman to Julio Salazar, the

Colombian cardinal from Cali. Salazar had many friends who needed a way to dispose of huge amounts of cash. The Cali drug cartel was the largest in Latin America. They made giant deposits, arriving with suitcases full of cash. Donato carried their bags for them too, parading up the steps in his cassock. There was nothing illegal about it. No one asked any questions about the money.

The cardinals and priests told themselves that the Vatican needed the money. "The Church could do a lot of good for people all around the world," they said.

"Besides," they told themselves, "it is only justice."

After years of working for the Vatican, Donato and Ackerman were still poor. They owned no houses or cars. Instead, they lived in dormitory rooms.

"It was only fair," they said to themselves. They even reminded each other that there was a provision in Church law that allowed priests to take "occult compensation" if they were underpaid. *Occult* in Latin simply means hidden.

"Would canon law provide for it if this hidden compensation were not just?" they asked themselves.

But the talking to journalists was Stefano's idea. It never would have occurred to Ackerman.

Stefano had introduced Ackerman to the reporters at the bar. That also seemed like fun at first. Suddenly, Ackerman was the expert, the big shot, the insider, Monsignore Anonimo, at the Vatican. He loved the attention.

What Ackerman hadn't realized was that some journalists worked for the mob. Their articles were a way of communicating secret information to certain readers, hidden in plain sight, published for millions to read.

It had all been a game, but now the game had turned deadly. All I did was carry a few messages and talk to a few people. I did less than all of them, thought Ackerman. Now I'm in danger!

Then Ackerman thought about his friend Donato. That stupid fool. Donato was not even subtle about what he was doing. He would override the lay director of the bank. God only knows how many millions of dollars had been run through that bank. To Donato especially, it was all a game. With the money he was paid, he got to be a Roman playboy. The Mafia's money was spilling out of their bags and into Donato's pockets.

Stefano's voice jerked Ackerman out of his thoughts and back to reality. "Remember," warned Stefano. "We paid you. And we paid Cardinale Luciano and Cardinale Julio. They all got rich taking our money. We helped them with their projects. They wanted no change in the Church, so we helped them with their enemies. We even paid that crazy priest in Belgium to cause trouble, so the liberals would look bad. You took our pay, now you work for us. You stop this investigation today, *oggi*, and tell the cardinals that you won't be the only one to hang from a bridge if this thing falls apart."

Ackerman gulped and stared at Stefano. It was as if he were staring at a stranger.

"One more thing," said Stefano. "We don't want to see you at the bar again. No more."

Stefano reached for the signal to stop the bus. It labored up the Via Nazionale for a couple of more blocks and slowed to a stop in Piazza della Repubblica, across from the ancient ruins of the Baths of Diocletian. Stefano swung down the bus stairs and disappeared into the crowd. Ackerman wanted to raise his hand to say good-bye. He had always thought of Stefano as a friend, but now he knew better.

Monsignor Ackerman was numb with fear.

He rode the bus a few more blocks to the end of the line at Stazione Termini, the great train station of Rome. Everyone else had gotten off the bus before he moved. All life was completely drained from him.

He walked across the piazza to the taxi stand, where a long line of tourists was waiting in the taxi queue. Drivers and tourists were shouting and waving their arms impatiently, as part of the typical Roman chaos. Ackerman felt terribly alone. He sat down on a bench at the edge of the piazza and did something he had not done spontaneously in a long time. He prayed.

16

SIAMO IN CRISI

THE TAXI TOOK ACKERMAN TO THE PORTA SANT'ANNA, the same Vatican gate that Cardinal O'Toole had passed through after learning of Manning's death. Ackerman had entered that gate thousands of times, but now he felt like a tourist visiting a strange land. Suddenly, it all seemed surreal—a place of fear, not security.

The Swiss guard recognized him and saluted smartly as he passed through the gate. Ackerman remembered the excitement he had felt as a young seminarian when he entered the Vatican for the first time. He had been so full of innocence, devotion, and enthusiasm. What happened to that naïve young Midwesterner? He had been so confident of his faith and so much in love with the Church.

At the visitors' office, near the guardhouse, Ackerman stopped to use a Vatican phone reserved for visitors. He dialed the number for the receptionist in the Pontifical Commission for Vatican City State, Cardinal Luciano Crepi's office. He wanted to see if the Cardinal was in his office before he made the long walk from the gate.

"Yes, Monsignor, His Eminence is here," said Crepi's secretary cheerfully.

"I would like to see him," said Ackerman.

"His Eminence could see you next week," said the secretary.

"No," said Ackerman. "*Ora!* Now! It's urgent. Tell him it concerns Donato." Ackerman surprised himself by almost shouting at the receptionist. He knew that Crepi would see him if it involved Donato, Crepi's right-hand man at the Vatican Bank.

After a few seconds, she came back on the line. "The cardinal can see you now."

While the pope is officially the monarch of Vatican City, Crepi was the real governor of the mechanics of the 108.7 acres that form the smallest sovereign state on earth.

Cardinal Luciano Crepi was a cigar-smoking manager who would have been at home in the Chicago mob. He enjoyed his job. He took special relish in chewing out subordinates. He was the classic "kiss up" and "kick down" petty tyrant. It was fair to say that he did not carry a spiritual aura about him.

His office was as spectacular as a museum. In fact, it was a sort of annex of the Vatican Museums. As the governor of Vatican City, he had access to all its storehouses, workshops, and exhibits. Behind Crepi's desk hung Raphael's *Transfiguration of Christ*, depicting Jesus rising up into the clouds with Moses and Elijah. Crepi could get anything he wanted, including art from the Vatican Museums. He chose carefully, conscious that the right art would both impress and intimidate a visitor.

Crepi's portfolio included all the departments of any country, albeit in miniature. The Swiss Guard is a tiny one hundred-man army. There is a post office, a police department, a court system, and a printing office. There is also a supermarket and a gas station. These are very popular with Romans, because purchases made there are exempt from Italian sales taxes. Crepi's jurisdiction also included a health office and a small fire department with complete EMT service.

The Vatican has some things that even some large countries do not have, like world-class museums, a famous library, and a laboratory of archaeological research. Despite the Church's persecution of Galileo, there are even two working astronomical observatories, one in the suburbs of Rome and the other, oddly enough, in the mountains of Arizona.

But the real prize in Crepi's Vatican collection was the Vatican Bank. Although there was a lay board of experts and a group of cardinal directors, Crepi was its day-to-day lord, and Donato was his vassal.

Ackerman hustled up the stairs to Crepi's office in the *Governatorato*. He opened the giant door of the outer office and walked right past the receptionist and into Crepi's high-ceilinged, frescoed office. The cardinal was on the phone.

Ackerman did not wait for him to finish. "*Eminenza*," said Ackerman, "*abbiamo un problema.*"

Crepi looked up, annoyed. He broke off his conversation with a hurried *arrivederci* and hung up the phone.

They spoke excitedly in Italian.

"Matteo, what do you mean by coming in here like this?"

"We are in deep shit," said Ackerman. "I had a visit this morning from the Camorra. They threatened me. They said I could end up like Roberto Calvi if I don't get this investigation of the deaths of the cardinals called off. There is an American lawyer here, Nate Condon, who is investigating . . ."

The cardinal held up his hand to stop Ackerman. "I know," said Crepi. "I had to approve his expense account. Nothing much goes on around here without my department." He was, as always, full of himself.

"Well, then," said Ackerman, "you may already know that the American lawyer was out at the Angelo Azzuro last night asking questions about me and Donato. He also wanted to know who was talking to *Panoramio*. I think he knows that I was the anonymous monsignor who talked to Tochi. I only talked to Tochi because the Camorra set it up. I did what they asked."

Ackerman was really agitated now. "Stefano, the bartender at the Angelo, tells me that the list I gave them in the article was a hit list! We said those cardinals were curial outsiders. That's all! You were the one who gave me that list. I had no idea the Camorra was reading the article to know who to kill."

He continued, practically hysterical. "Stefano also told me that I wouldn't be the only one to end up like Calvi. His *capi* want Nate on a plane to the United States tomorrow, or you and Cardinal Salazar might also be swinging from a bridge."

That got Crepi's attention. He stood up. Crumbs from his morning snack of coffee and cornetto pastry fell to the floor with his napkin.

"He threatened us?" Crepi asked, using the royal "we."

"Yes," said Ackerman despondently. "I am a dead man. You, too. This is the Camorra we are playing with. They have killed children."

Crepi took charge of the conversation. "Matteo, go home and stay there. Tell the bishop's office that you are sick. Maybe we can get you on a plane out of the country tomorrow. I will call Salazar." Crepi paused, his barked orders ceasing.

Ackerman started to leave.

"And Matteo, one more thing. For God's sake, shut up! No more talking to this American!"

Ackerman left the office, badly shaken. There was no offer of protection from the cardinal, nothing but a plane ticket. What good would that do? The Mafia had contacts in St. Louis and everywhere else in the States. They could find him wherever he went.

The gravity of the situation had settled in. Ackerman went into a private bathroom in the hallway and vomited his guts out.

* * *

Crepi called Cardinal Salazar on his cell phone. Salazar was at his office in the Apostolic Penitentiary. "Julio, meet me at your apartment now! We have to talk."

Salazar was stunned. "*Perche?*"

"Don't ask questions," said Crepi. "Just meet me. Ten minutes."

He hung up.

Crepi was nervous, but not panicked. He had known this day would eventually come, when his kingdom might come down around him. He thought, I hope that weakling Julio can hold it together.

Crepi did not start out as a cynic. He started out as a romantic in life, but cynics are often disappointed romantics.

As he hurried out of his office, Crepi thought about his situation. The problem is, he thought, I made myself into God. St. Thomas Aquinas said the foundational sin was pride. That's exactly what I did.

He surprised himself at how much theology he could remember from his seminary days.

Salazar's apartment was on the top floor of a Vatican-owned building that faced St. Peter's. It had a spectacular view of St. Peter's Square. CNN regularly rented out its balcony, at an exorbitant price, to supply the background for standups from Rome, whenever there was a big event at the Vatican.

The terrace was big enough to roller-skate on. The floor of the large reception room was covered with oriental rugs, the walls with damask silk. The hallways and parlors were decorated with priceless works of art and precious antiquities from the Vatican storehouses and museums.

It took half an hour for Crepi to reach Salazar's apartment. He was an old man, after all, and a heavy smoker.

Once he settled in Salazar's living room, Crepi got to the point. "That Monsignor Ackerman came to see me. The Camorra has made a threat against him and against us. They want this investigation of the deaths of the cardinals by the American lawyer called off."

Salazar knew about Nate's investigation. There were few real secrets in the Vatican. Everybody was gossiping about the deaths of the cardinals. It was in all the papers. Nate and his investigation were hardly a secret.

"It's all coming apart," said Salazar. "We never intended for it to come to this. We were only doing some financial favors for friends and trying to help our own families. I never thought they would kill our brother cardinals. Why?" Salazar started to moan and cry.

"Oh, stop it," said Crepi coldly. Salazar continued to moan.

Crepi was not sympathetic. "You knew the risks. You wanted the money. Your house on the cliff at Positano, your BMW, your first-class air tickets, they all came from the money we ran through the Vatican Bank. Of course they are going to kill over this. The bank is too valuable to them."

"But we never asked them to kill anybody!" protested Salazar. "I never thought it could get us killed!" Tears were running down his cheeks.

Crepi pressed on. "We asked them to eliminate our rivals, so we could stay in charge of the Church. Who did you think we were dealing with? Your friends are the Cali Cartel, for God's sake. They kill for sport. We were doing business with the Camorra. They kill judges in their own courtrooms. We knew the risks, and we wanted the benefits. Don't start crying like a woman."

They went silent for a moment.

Then Crepi started up again. "We still have one more card to play. We control the Vatican Bank as long as Pope Thomas is alive, and we can control who is chosen in the conclave after he dies. The Mafia wants to keep us around until then, so they can be sure nothing changes at the bank."

"Do they know about the priest in Belgium?" asked Salazar.

"Oh, goddamn it, Julio—they paid for the priest in Belgium. We wanted to make the liberals look bad, so they would have no support in the Church. So that's what we did."

"But," said Salazar, "we wanted to make it look like they were responsible for the cardinals' deaths. We could still use that."

"Julio," answered Crepi, "the Mafia knows who is responsible. They did the killings. I am not worried about the stupid press or liberal Catholics. I am worried about the Mafia. They don't care who runs the Church. They only care who runs the bank."

That was the most honest part of Crepi's statement. Despite the prohibition in tradition and canon law, Crepi and Salazar had already been politicking votes for the next conclave. They planned to elect a man who would do their bidding. O'Toole was on their list.

The two men might have been believers at one point, but they had long since stopped doing any real religious work. They just used the institution to feather their own nests, just like in the days of the Borgias and the Barbarinis.

Considering the importance of the favors Salazar and Crepi had done for the Mafia and the Cali Cartel, the cardinals were actually working cheap. They got a house here and a car there. A few hundred thousand euros were chicken feed to organized crime.

"Oh, Luciano, what have we done?" said Salazar, starting to cry again.

"Oh, just shut up!" said Crepi. "We have to be strong. We have to be sure that Ackerman doesn't do any more talking, or perhaps the Camorra will take care of that for us."

Salazar stood up. "I need air," he said.

He went out on his terrace overlooking St. Peter's Square, whining.

"*O Dio, O Dio,*" he kept saying. It was the most praying that Salazar had done in years. Crepi followed him onto the terrace.

"We have to think about the next conclave," said Crepi. "We still have a little time, as long as the pope's health holds up. The Mafia wants us around to guide the hand of the Church in the selection of the next pope. We might be able to bargain our way out of this and then retire in peace."

Salazar calmed down. "*Giusto.* You're right, we might have a chance." At seventy-five, Salazar was just weeks away from retirement. He hoped his Cali Cartel friends would leave him alone and let him die in peace. He had amassed enough money.

Just then Crepi's mobile phone rang. It was his secretary. The EMTs from the Vatican Fire Department had been dispatched to the pope's apartment in the Belvedere Palace. "The pope is having another heart incident," said the secretary urgently.

"*Va bene. Vengo subito,*" said Crepi.

It didn't look like Salazar and Crepi would have to wait long for the next conclave. It was the third incident in a month. Time was no longer on their side.

17

DEATH OF A POPE

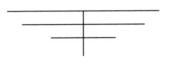

POPE THOMAS WAS UP AT 6:00 A.M. TO DRESS FOR MASS.
Every day it got harder and harder. Just two days before, the pope had
fainted and EMTs had been summoned. Today he was moving slowly.

Living in the papal apartments is very much assisted living. Every
octogenarian should be so fortunate. The papal butler, Antonio, awak-
ened him gently with the line "*Laudatur Jesus Christus.*" Praised be Jesus
Christ. The pope replied, "*Semper Deo gratias et Maria.*" Thanks to God
and Mary always.

Antonio helped the aged pope to the toilet, then sat him on the plastic and aluminum shower chair for a sponge bath. The old man's skin
hung loosely, and his thin haunches gave him the look of a cadaver.

Then the butler wheeled the shower chair into the pope's changing
room, basically a large walk-in closet. He handed the pope each item of
clothing. The old man needed extensive cuing. "Now put on your shirt.
Lift your foot, Holiness, so I can put on your sock."

At that point, the pope always reminded the butler, "Pull the toe."
The pope hated tight socks.

After he was dressed, it was time for medication. There was a raft of
pills: blood pressure, a diuretic, cholesterol, and all the other ailments of
old age. Every day the pope asked, "What are all these pills for?" And

every day the butler replied the same way: "Doctor's orders, Holiness." Even the Vicar of Christ, the Patriarch of the West, and the successor of St. Peter has to obey his doctor.

Then the pope was wheeled out of his apartment on the top floor of the Apostolic Palace and down the hall to his private chapel. It was absolutely silent in the apartments, but the sound of Roman traffic drifted through the open windows.

In the chapel was his personal secretary and friend Monsignor Mario Ranieri, already seated in one of two chairs behind matching kneelers positioned to face the tabernacle in the alcove at one side of the chapel. He rose to his feet as the pope entered.

They said their morning prayer together in Italian.

"*O Dio, vieni a salvarmi.*" Oh, God, come to my assistance.

"*Signore vieni presto in mio aiuto.*" Lord, make haste to help me.

Despite their being staunch conservatives, who advocated an almost complete return to Latin at every opportunity, when it came to their own prayer, they prayed in their own language.

It was a Friday, the day Christ died, according to tradition. Friday is the penitential day in the Church. Like priests and nuns around the world, the pope and his secretary said Psalm 51, David's lament for his sin.

> *Have mercy on me, O God, in your kindness,*
> *In your compassion blot out my offense.*
> *O wash me more and more from my guilt*
> *And cleanse me from all my sin.*

It is a moving psalm, which ends with a call to personal conversion and a put-down of temple worship.

> *For in sacrifice you take no delight,*
> *Burnt offering from me you would refuse,*
> *My sacrifice a contrite spirit,*
> *A humble and contrite heart you will not spurn.*

After fifty years of saying it, they no longer had to look at the page.

Monsignor Mario then wheeled the pope into the little sacristy nearby to vest him for Mass. An antiquarian, Pope Thomas loved the splendor of the brocade vestments, lined with watered silk. The hierarchy might talk a lot about solidarity with the poor, but there was precious little evidence of it in their daily lives. The cost of the pope's Mass vestments could have built an old folks' home for the poor in Nicaragua.

The Mass began as usual with the sign of the cross. The pope was seated in his wheelchair. These days, when there was no one looking, he was always in his wheelchair. Now, he labored through the opening prayers and penitential rite: "Lord, have mercy. Christ, have mercy. Lord, have mercy."

At the readings, he began to slump. He signaled to his secretary to read the gospel, a story of Jesus' challenge to the Pharisees, the religious leaders of His time. The pope closed his eyes during the reading.

At the consecration of the Mass, the pope began slurring his words, and his face had become an expressionless mask. He struggled to lift the host after the words of consecration. "This is my body." His hands trembled.

He couldn't lift the ornate chalice after the consecration of the wine—"This is my blood"—so Monsignor Mario lifted it for him.

Then the pope slumped over in his wheelchair. His secretary pulled an emergency signal cord on the wall. EMTs from the Vatican Fire Department came running from their office near the Vatican gate.

* * *

Pope Thomas was wheeled back to his bedroom. Antonio, his butler, gently lifted the vestments over his head and wrapped him in a wool shawl.

About that time, the EMTs came through the door and made a move to lift him into bed. But the pope signaled that he wanted to be seated in his favorite chair, near the window. They complied, but not before starting an IV of Heparin, to combat blood clots. They tried to start him on oxygen, but he waved the mask away.

The pope was clearly dying.

In his home village of Sant'Agata sui due Golfi, people always drank the same medicinal tea for any health crisis. Mario arrived now with a mug of that same hot tea, just like their mothers would have done.

"Paolo," he said, "*un puo di te*," a little tea. He offered the cup to the pope, but he could not hold it. He was too weak. Mario lifted the cup to the pope's lips, so he could take a sip.

Sitting there in a collarless shirt, a baggy pair of black slacks, and a woolen shawl, Pope Thomas did not look like the Vicar of Christ and Patriarch of Rome. He looked like a little old man in a nursing home.

"I am dying, Mario," said the pope. "I hope the Lord forgives me."

"Of course the Lord forgives you," said Mario, "but I'm not sure about our mothers." They smiled.

"*Si*, Mario. Remember when we stole the biscotti from my mother's kitchen? Mama chased us all the way down the hill. We ran to the top of the cliff overlooking the Bay of Naples and ate the cookies there."

Mario began to cry. "They were the best cookies ever, weren't they, Paolo?"

The pope smiled and reached out to embrace his friend, causing the cup of tea to slip from Mario's hands and fall to the floor. Mario reached out to return the embrace, as the old man slumped over into his arms. The Bishop of Rome was dead.

Everyone dies the same way. In the end, it is not the offices held or the honors accumulated that matter. In the end, it is love that matters. It is the little intimate memories of personal moments that really matter.

Holding his dead friend, Mario was filled with memories and yearning for days long gone. "Paolo, we should never have left the village."

The EMTs carefully lifted the pope's body into his bed.

Cardinal Crepi's cell phone rang. As the camerlengo, the cardinal chamberlain, of the papal household, by tradition, Crepi had a central role in the ritual of a pope's death. His first duty was to declare the pope dead. Crepi came running, as much as his girth and age allowed, arriving breathless at the papal bedroom door.

Tradition took over.

The camerlengo no longer tapped the pope on the head with a silver hammer three times, as they once did, to ascertain whether he was dead. But he did place a *fazoletto*, a handkerchief, over the pope's face and called to him three times by his baptismal name. "Paolo, Paolo, Paolo." There was no response.

Other cardinals and high-ranking prelates began to arrive. Crepi then declared the pope dead and called the Vicar of Rome, the bishop who runs the daily activity of the diocese of Rome.

A hammer was now brought. Crepi removed the Fisherman's Ring from the pope's finger and smashed the seal to symbolize the end of his reign.

Once the pope's body was removed to the Vatican morgue, Crepi ordered everyone out of the papal apartments. The rooms were locked, and Crepi affixed a seal to the door. He did this to secure the pope's personal things. In the past, the looting of the papal apartments was a common practice.

The pope's death was an electric shock to the employees of the Vatican and around the world. The Holy See is a monarchy. In some ways it is a dictatorship. All the power is vested in one man. When the pope dies, it is like an earthquake in that tiny kingdom.

By custom, mourning would last for nine days, the *novem dies*. Cardinals from around the world would assemble. The little hotel in the Vatican, the Casa Santa Marta, would be vacated so that the 120 cardinal electors could be housed together.

By Church law, the conclave was to begin fifteen days after the death of the pope. *Conclave* means with key. Since the thirteenth century, the cardinals have been locked up for their deliberations, not so much for secrecy as to force them to make a decision on the successor.

* * *

Cardinal Crepi realized that he had only fifteen days to consolidate his position with the other cardinal electors. He had to maneuver to secure a sympathetic successor onto the Throne of Peter.

Crepi's plan was to protect himself by protecting the power of the Roman Curia and his own position in it. To do that, he needed to freeze out any outsider cardinals, not just the progressives, but all outsiders. Nothing must change, he thought. Nothing must change.

The greatest danger to men like Crepi was not the political left or right, but the radical extremist groups, like the Soldados. They would mount a takeover of the Vatican Curia and put all their own people in every position of power and authority. Marcelino may have been in prison, but his éminence grise, Cardinal Mendoza, was free to move about. If the Soldados took over, they would be in charge, and Crepi and his crowd would be out.

Eventually, Crepi wanted to retire with his wealth. But for now, he wanted to protect his position and himself. To accomplish all this, he needed allies, especially Salazar.

Crepi called Salazar on is his cell phone. "*Julio, il papa e morto. Dobiamo parlare.*"

18

IT IS FINISHED

ON SATURDAY MORNING, THE DAY AFTER THE POPE DIED, Nate boarded a tram to the church of San Lorenzo, "outside the walls" near Piazza Risorgimento. Rome still has a few decrepit, dark green, pre–World War II trams in service. They are slow and uncomfortable, but the city keeps them around for movie shoots. Tourists love them, but the Romans hate them.

The winding ride out to San Lorenzo gave Nate some time to think. Ackerman had called Nate from a borrowed cell phone, asking for a meeting. The monsignor sounded desperate.

Ackerman had told Nate that he feared going home to his rooms at the Villa Stritch, so he was staying in a friend's apartment near the University of Rome, La Sapienzia. "He's away on vacation," said Ackerman. "I had to beg him for the key. I'm feeding his cat for a few days. He lives just down the Viale Regina Elena from San Lorenzo.

"I need to meet with you right now," Ackerman breathed into the phone to Nate. "It's a matter of life and death. We can't meet at my office, or anywhere near the Vatican. We will be seen. Meet me at 10:00 a.m. in the cloister near the sacristy of the Church of San Lorenzo. It's near the big cemetery, Campo Verano. Take the tram."

San Lorenzo is one of the seven pilgrimage churches of Rome, but it is probably the least visited. When Romans say something is *"fuori le mura,"* they mean outside the old city walls built by Emperor Aurelian in the third century. Romans have a long frame of reference.

In ancient Rome, cemeteries had to be located outside the city walls. The church of San Lorenzo is at the gate of the largest cemetery of Rome, Campo Verano. This "summer field" is a giant city of the dead, peppered with the elaborate tombs that the Italians love. Because of it, San Lorenzo has become the funeral church of Rome.

The church itself is an odd hybrid. In fact, it is really two churches grafted onto each other. The first one, erected over the tomb of St. Lawrence the Martyr, was built by Emperor Constantine in 330. The second was built in the 400s. Sometime in the early 1200s they were joined, and a medieval bell tower and front porch were added. It makes for an odd-looking building.

During World War II, San Lorenzo was the only church in Rome that sustained serious damage from Allied bombs. It was rebuilt after the war. Just outside the restored church stands a statue of Pope Pius XII, pleading to the heavens to stop the bombs.

Nate hopped off the tram as it pulled into the piazza in front of San Lorenzo. Not very impressive, he observed as he looked at the church. He chuckled to himself at the thought of what an "expert" he had become on all things Italian, after only two weeks in Rome.

Luigi Barzini, the famous Italian journalist, once observed that after only two weeks in Italy, Americans think they understand everything, but after two years they are sure that they understand nothing.

Nate crossed the piazza to the front porch of the church. A funeral was just getting started. There was a hysterical scene around a Mercedes hearse. A black-clad widow threw herself on the coffin, sobbing. The mourners gathered around, beating their breasts and crying. As Nate slipped through the side door to the right, he thought of something he had read in a guidebook: "When you live in Rome, you don't live in a city; you live on the stage of an opera."

Once inside the church, it took Nate a few seconds to get oriented. Light entered the building from the upper-story windows, but down below it was dim and cool.

Ackerman had chosen well. Apart from the mourners at the door, there was nobody around.

Nate walked down the side aisle to the sacristy. As an altar boy, he had learned the layout of churches. Sure enough, the sacristy, where priests vest for Mass, was in front by the altar. It was a large room with cabinets along one side and a huge vesting table. He found himself alone in the room.

Nate paused for a minute. He thought, I wish I were wearing a wire. Then it occurred to him that his smartphone was also capable of recording. He slowed his steps as he entered the sacristy and set the phone to record. Then he continued toward the open door at the far end of the sacristy, which led out to the enclosed cloister of the Franciscan friars, who staffed the church.

He found himself in a lovely, walled courtyard. On his right, as he entered the garden, were pieces of ancient Roman ruins plastered into the wall. The ruins had been found around the church buildings. The cloister was enclosed by the two-story convent. A barrel-vaulted colonnade surrounded a formal garden with roses and a little fountain.

On the far side of the courtyard, away from the sacristy, Nate saw Matt Ackerman, partially hidden in the shadow of an arch. He was not dressed as a priest. Ackerman looked like any tourist in slacks and a polo shirt.

"Hello, Monsignor," said Nate. "You certainly picked a location with atmosphere."

"Yes," said Ackerman. "Nothing like a necropolis to focus one's mind on the shortness of life."

"Why are you thinking about the shortness of life?" asked Nate.

"My life is in danger," said Ackerman. "You have to call off this investigation. The pope is dead now. You don't have a mandate anymore. If you keep on with this investigation, you may uncover things you don't want to know about the Church. You will almost certainly get more people killed. And you will most certainly get me killed." When people are scared, they talk. Ackerman was clearly scared.

Nate saw an opening. "What do you mean?" he asked. "Why will I get you killed?"

"Stop playing coy," snapped Ackerman. "I know you were at the bar. You talked to Stefano, the bartender, and to Donato, the monsignor from the bank. Stefano told me."

Nate was a bit taken aback by Ackerman's anger. "Sure, I was there," he said to Ackerman. "It's part of the investigation."

"Well, then, you should know what's been going on," continued Ackerman. "Cardinals Crepi and Salazar have been laundering money for the Mafia, and the Latin drug cartels have been laundering money through the Vatican Bank. Donato was the bag man. I know he's talked to you."

"Will you testify to that at trial?" asked Nate.

"If I do, I'm a dead man," said Ackerman.

"People have been killed for less. With Crepi in charge of the bank and Salazar going back and forth to Colombia all the time on a diplomatic passport, they could protect the mob from anyone, except maybe a new pope or a nosy reporter.

"Crepi and Salazar knew this pope would not last long. If he died, the music might stop. So they began eliminating any cardinals who would not be well disposed to their 'arrangements.'" Ackerman made little air quotations with his fingers around arrangements.

"Murder seems a high price to pay for money laundering," said Nate, prodding Ackerman to say more.

"It was cheap," said Ackerman. "Especially for Salazar and Crepi. The mob owned them."

"What do you mean?" asked Nate.

"Scandal," said Ackerman. "The Church is all about appearances. The mob knew something about Crepi and Salazar that they didn't want public. It was not your everyday scandal. It was something far worse, I guess. I don't know the details. You're the investigator. You look into it."

Ackerman paused to let his revelation about the cardinals sink in, then he started up again. "The Camorra doesn't care about the Church. They just liked having an in-house bank that is beyond investigation. It was easy for them to convert narco dollars to legitimate currency."

"So, how did the mob know who to kill?" asked Nate.

Ackerman nervously lit a cigarette.

"Crepi and Salazar, and maybe a few others, gave them the list. At first, it was just about protecting the bank. But then Crepi and Salazar saw an opportunity to settle a few scores within the College of Cardinals and the Church. They could eliminate their enemies. The mob didn't mind doing a favor or two for their faithful cardinals." Ackerman took another deep drag of his cigarette. "Those two, Crepi and Salazar, really don't care about the Church either," said Ackerman. "They just care about themselves. They're old men. They just want to die in comfort. Then the whole thing can come crashing down for all they care. But with the pope dead, they may now be out in the cold. They want to be sure that the next occupant of the Chair of Peter is friendly to them."

A Franciscan friar walked by and looked at Nate and Ackerman, as if wondering why these two men were engaged in such a long conversation in his garden.

"Let's go for a walk in the cemetery," suggested Ackerman. They went out a side door that led to the Via Verano and the cemetery. Ackerman walked fast. He clearly didn't want to say any more until they reached an area where the tombs were close together and the shade trees provided cover.

Once they reached the tombs, Nate asked, "So, where do you come in?"

"I was the messenger. I didn't even know it at first. I communicated with the Camorra by way of the bar. I took messages to Stefano. Sometimes, I met a journalist at the bar who wrote articles in *Panoramio*. Stefano set up the meetings for me. At first I thought I was just serving as a leak for articles that would go after the liberals in the Church. But eventually,

I figured out Crepi and Salazar's interest. In one article I talked to *Panoramio* about how I think that any cardinal that Crepi and Salazar told me to identify as papabile became a target. I guess I was fingering targets for those two scumbag cardinals."

"Why are you telling this to me now?" asked Nate. "You know that this information could be used against you."

"You've got to help me," said Ackerman. "I'm a dead man if all this comes out. Call off the investigation, or at least get me some protection."

"I can't let it go," said Nate. "I have a mandate from the pope, even if he is dead. I also have an obligation to the truth. I'm an officer of the court in the States. This money laundering is mostly US currency. It's a crime back home. I can't just walk away from this evidence. You decided to be a part of this scheme. That's not my fault. People are dead because of you, Monsignor."

Ackerman seemed tired. They walked over to a bench in a shadowed area of the cemetery and sat down. Ackerman lit another cigarette, chain-smoking his nerves away.

Nate felt a surge of anger. Like most believers, he had never really examined his faith or questioned the Church. This past couple of weeks had challenged his most basic beliefs about the Church and its goodness. He felt betrayed by what he had learned.

"Let me ask you something," Nate said to Ackerman. "How did this happen? How did you get involved in all of this shit? You're supposed to be a priest, a moral example. Look at yourself. You're laundering money. You're a messenger for the mob. You're hanging out in gay bars, drinking yourself to death. What kind of priest are you?"

"You don't think I know what I've become?" said Ackerman. "That's why I drink. I can't stand it. I can't stand myself."

"But why?" asked Nate more insistently. "Why do it in the first place?" Still feeling the fury. This was not just an investigation. This was personal. The investigator in him wanted the truth; the Catholic in him wanted an apology, an explanation, some justification for the betrayal of a lifetime of trust.

"I don't know," said Ackerman. "Boredom, maybe. No, not boredom. Really, it was more like anger, maybe self-pity. I don't know. But it all seemed better than nothing."

Nate snorted in disgust. But he knew he needed to keep Ackerman talking, to record as much as he could for the sake of the investigation. He tried to keep the anger out of his voice as he said, "Tell me more."

There was silence for a moment, then Ackerman continued. "I didn't start out this way. I came here an innocent kid from the Midwest, full of idealism about the Church, about life. I wanted to be a great priest and a holy man. I wanted to be somebody my mother would be proud of."

"You mean you couldn't tell her you were gay?" asked Nate.

"It's not that simple," said Ackerman. "She probably knew. Lots of priests are gay. The problem is not being gay. The problem is being celibate. Celibacy turns us all into liars. Gay or straight, we all have to pretend that we don't need human love. The whole thing is built on mendacity." He repeated the word again, as if contemplating it. "Mendacity.

"Lies! Lies!" yelled the priest.

Nate was startled by the priest's shout.

"When I applied to the seminary, the vocation director told me not to tell anyone I was gay. I had to rewrite my biography essay, so that I basically lied about myself. I said I had a normal dating life, which was nonsense. I have never even been on a normal date.

"The vocation director wanted vocations. The truth was a small price to pay to keep the bishop happy. Get warm bodies into the seminary. That was the goal. They didn't care if I lied." He crushed out another cigarette. "Once I got to the seminary in Rome, I discovered that keeping up appearances was a way of life. We pretended we were celibate. We also pretended we were happy when, in fact, we were really lonely as hell." Ackerman wiped sweat from his brow with a handkerchief. Then he continued. "Why do you think so many bishops had no problem covering up the pedophiles? It was easy for them. They were already experts in mendacity."

"Don't you think you're making too big a deal out of this?" asked Nate. "Lots of people are celibate."

"It's not about sex," Ackerman snapped back. "It's about love. I missed love. That's the whole point of life, and I missed it."

Now Ackerman was almost talking to himself.

"The Church wants me to love a God I cannot see, but I was never supposed to love a person I could see. I never in my whole life said I love you to any living person, except my mother. And nobody, but my mother, ever said it back to me," said Ackerman quietly. "I hardly ever even said it to her either." He wasn't angry, just reflective.

Monsignor Ackerman stood up and started to walk again. It was as if he had to walk off a cramp. Really, what he wanted to walk off was his life. Nate followed along. The priest talked, almost to himself, again.

"I've never met a priest who was not diminished by celibacy. Never. Don't let them tell you that they love in the abstract or love in general. That's bullshit. That's their rationalization. It's their way of avoiding real love. It's their way of avoiding commitments."

He picked up a rock by the path and threw it against a tomb.

"Celibacy leaves a wound. Some people kid themselves into thinking it doesn't, but it does. You try to compensate, but you are never really whole. Some priests drown their sorrows in alcohol or pills. A lot of them overeat and get obese. Food is a great drug."

Nate had noticed that a lot of priests were obese, but he had never really thought about why.

Ackerman was growing agitated again, and there was no stopping him. "Some guys travel all the time to escape. Others take secret lovers. Some redecorate the rectory over and over again. That's a classic clerical tradition, decorating. Just look at all the frescoes in the Vatican. It's a kind of retail therapy that's been going on for centuries."

"What are they trying to compensate for?" asked Nate.

"It's all really just a pitiful compensation for the lack of love," said Ackerman. "Celibates are all trying to make up for the one thing they tell everybody else is the reason for living—love. We tell everybody that God is love, but we don't have any in our own lives."

Nate thought Ackerman was just over the top.

"Spare me your self-pity," said Nate. "Lots of people live all or part of their lives without sex. What about all the sick or handicapped? What about widows? They're celibate. Even married people don't have sex all the time." He thought of his own marriage.

"Is that what you think I'm talking about?" asked Ackerman angrily. "Sex? Grow up! I'm not talking about sex. I'm talking about love."

He turned to Nate, almost screaming. "I don't have to take that from you, Nate Condon. Look at you. Life comes easy to you. You're handsome. You're rich. You're athletic. You're smart. You're respected. Everybody loves YOU!"

He poked his finger at Nate with each staccato declaration. "The world is your oyster. You never wake up and look in the mirror and hate what you see. There's no conflict in the life of the Nate Condons of this world. It's different for me. I hate what I see in the mirror."

Nate was silent. He had never thought of himself as privileged. But he guessed Ackerman was right. Life had given him some challenges, but no internal conflicts.

"I married myself to Holy Mother the Church, and she hates me. She tells me every day that there is something wrong with me. Mother Church tells me that I am 'intrinsically disordered.' What does that mean? I'm told that my deepest desires and yearnings, which hurt no one, are my path to hell. Basically, my own Church tells me I am a freak. It tells me that God has made some ghastly mistake."

Ackerman stopped walking for a moment. A sob came out of him from somewhere deep inside. A lady down the path in the cemetery heard it and looked in their direction. Nate knew she probably assumed that Ackerman was grieving someone who had died. He was: himself.

Ackerman sat down on a stone bench. His sobbing stopped, which was a relief to Nate.

Ackerman started talking again. "Sex and lies are not really the biggest clerical sins. John XXIII thought ambition was the real clerical sin. We use it as a substitute for love and affection. Look at the bishops. They don't fool me! I read their dossiers all day, every day. They're nothing but a bunch of peacocks preening themselves in hopes of getting noticed by the next guy up the ladder. Peacocks, all of them!"

Ackerman stood up again and kicked at the gravel in the path, sending it flying. He was full of furious energy now.

"Yes, Your Excellency! No, Your Eminence! Where else in the whole goddamn world do grown men expect to be called excellent or eminent? But they know the truth. They're just like all these poor slobs buried here." Ackerman gestured toward the array of tombs stretching off into the distance. "We all share the same demons. They're no more excellent than the next guy."

Nate interjected, "There must be some healthy and happy priests."

"Sure," said Ackerman. "But they aren't over here in Rome.

"Plenty of good guys get ordained, but they don't stay here. They go home to Iowa or Missouri or wherever." He gestured off toward the horizon. "They go back and become ordinary parish priests. If they are lucky, they fall in love with their parishes, and if they are really lucky, their parishioners fall in love with them. But they never look back. That's what I should have done."

"So, why didn't you just go home and become a parish priest?" asked Nate, looking Ackerman straight in the eye. "You could have had a good life."

"You want the truth? I didn't want it. I was too proud. That was my real sin. I was too proud to do the ordinary crap of being a parish priest."

Nate looked at Ackerman.

"Don't look at me like I'm some kind of freak. I'm not the only one who was too proud for ordinary parish work. Just look at these bishops. None of them, truth be told, ever wanted to be ordinary parish priests. They all say they did, but they didn't." He paused for a few seconds. "They didn't want the endless confessions, depressing nursing homes, stinking prisons, and daily onslaught of hospital rooms and funerals, crazy people, and endless problems any more than I did. It bored me. It bores most bishops. I wanted what most bishops really want. I wanted to be in charge."

"Did you get what you wanted here?" asked Nate.

"Does it look like I got what I wanted?" responded Ackerman, gesturing toward himself. "I'm a pathetic bureaucrat who drinks his nights away in dark bars, pretending to be someone else. I hate my life. I got nothing. It all turns to ashes in your mouth."

Once more he kicked the gravel in the path and snorted.

"It's ironic," he said. "This is actually the most honest confession of my life, and you aren't even a priest. You can't give me absolution, can you, Father Condon?" Ackerman made the sign of the cross in the air, as if blessing the graves.

Ackerman turned toward Nate and looked straight into his eyes.

"What do you think cardinals like Crepi and Salazar really believe? Anything? Do you think they believe in God? Do you think they believe in Jesus Christ? Do you think they believe in carrying their cross, self-sacrifice, humility, and being a servant of others? Nonsense! Hell, they won't even wash women's feet on Holy Thursday. They want people to serve them. That's it—nothing else! Especially those two, Crepi and Salazar. They are as corrupt as they come. Like I told you, look into them. The Camorra has something on them. I've heard that for years.

"Something happened down in Napoli, thirty or forty years ago. That's what I hear. They were involved in somebody's death. A man or boy fell off a ferryboat or something like that. The Camorra saved their asses. So, now they owe them forever, just like Faust. Go down to Naples and see for yourself. It must be something big for them to finger their own pals for assassination and launder money for drug lords."

"I'll look into it," said Nate. "If there is something there, I will find it."

Ackerman attempted to laugh again. Instead, it came out as a half scream and ended as a snort.

"Me and my petty little sins can't hold a candle to Crepi and Salazar, especially that sniveling little Colombian." He broke a branch off a nearby tree and started hitting a monument. "They are all a bunch of goddamned Pharisees," he said, smashing the stick on the stone. "They got what they wanted, places of honor at banquets and titles of respect. Everything Jesus preached against."

The stick Ackerman was smashing on the tomb was in splinters now. "Are you jealous of them?" asked Nate.

"Ha!" answered Ackerman, throwing his stick. "Not anymore. It's all crap. Nobody cares about them and their endless pretensions. People here in Italy laugh at them—the 'men in dresses,' they say.

"No, I don't want what they have. All I really want now is to be Matt Ackerman, just plain old Matthew Ackerman from St. Louis, Missouri. But it's too late for that. I lost myself, my soul, in Faust's bargain here in Rome. "

Nate could see tears running down Ackerman's cheeks. For the first time, he really felt sorry for the priest. Nate repeated his earlier question. "So, why didn't you just leave?"

"I don't know, for a lot of reasons, I guess. I was afraid that I couldn't make a living doing anything else. Remember what the bad steward in the gospel says, 'To beg, I am ashamed. To dig ditches, I am not able.' It doesn't make any sense now, but I was afraid. What would I do? Where would I go? Who would have me, a balding middle-aged gay guy with no skills and no money? Fear kept me here. I was stuck. And now I'm finished."

It occurred to Nate that this was more than a confession. It was a valediction.

Ackerman suddenly stopped in front of a stone mausoleum with a crest over its door that looked like an American eagle. The inscription under the crest in Latin abbreviations read "*Pont. Col. Amer. Sept.*"

Curious as to why they had stopped, Nate asked, "Whose tomb is this?"

"This is the mausoleum for the North American College," said Ackerman. He was suddenly calm, as if he were a tour guide. "I suppose I could be buried here.

"In the old days," the priest explained, "if a student at the NAC died over here in Rome, they didn't ship his body home to America. They buried him here. Now they fly you home in a box, but there are still a few guys who would rather be buried here. They don't even go home when they're dead."

"Seems strange," said Nate. "I guess they lose connection with their homes."

"No," said Ackerman, "they lose connection with themselves." Ackerman turned to Nate and asked, "Are you going to help me?"

"I do feel sorry for you, Monsignor, but I have to follow the investigation where it leads," answered Nate. "I'm not stopping now. Besides, even if I did stop this investigation, there is no guarantee of safety for either of us. I'm sorry."

"Then I am a dead man," said Ackerman. "There is nowhere to hide from these people."

Ackerman asked Nate quietly, "If I die before you leave Rome, would you make sure that my ashes are sent home to Missouri? Maybe there I can just be Matt Ackerman again."

"Yes," answered Nate, touched by the request and aware that it was no idle thought. They stood there a moment as if frozen. Then Nate said, "I'll pray for you, Monsignor."

"Good," said the priest. Then Matt Ackerman turned and walked silently off into the City of the Dead.

19

NAPOLI, MATER DOLOROSA

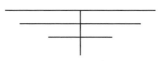

THE TRAIN WHEELS DID NOT MAKE THE USUAL CLICKETY-clack. The Frecciarossa, or red arrow, trains operate on welded rails, gliding noiselessly along at speeds of up to two hundred miles per hour. They travel from Rome to Naples—140 miles—in only an hour and ten minutes. As the towns flew past Nate's window—Anzio, Gaeta, Falciano, and Casoria—he thought, Why doesn't Amtrak have something like this?

Nate was following up on Monsignor Ackerman's accusations against Crepi and Salazar, made during their walk through the cemetery at San Lorenzo the day before.

Ackerman had been so insistent that Nate didn't waste any time following up on the lead. While still on the tram coming back from the cemetery at San Lorenzo, he called his assistant. "Please do some research on Cardinals Crepi and Salazar," he said. "See what you can find out about them from thirty or forty years ago—newspaper articles, police reports, anything."

Miss Orsuto was superefficient. In the half hour it took him to get back to his little office near the Vatican, she managed to find a newspaper article in the online archives of *Il Mattino*, the Naples daily. It was from June, forty-two years earlier.

The article reported that there had been a tragic accident on the overnight *traghetto* from Naples to Palermo. It said that a young boy, Gianluca Luppino, age seventeen, had fallen overboard and drowned. It mentioned that two priests, monsignors from the Vatican, Crepi and Salazar, had been witnesses. They had seen him go overboard. There was a photo of the two young priests looking very serious. The boy's body had been retrieved from the water, and the harbor police in Sicily had pronounced it an accident.

A follow-up article a few days later showed a photo of the boy's mother, Giulia Luppino, age thirty-nine, at the funeral in Naples. She had collapsed from grief at the boy's funeral and had been taken to the hospital. The paper reported that the whole city had been captured by her sad story. Thousands of flowers had been sent to her hospital room at Ospedale Cardinale Ascalesi. The Napolitani are a bighearted people, and they are nothing if not emotional at other people's suffering.

Giulia Luppino was still alive forty-two years later, now age eighty-one. Sandra had tracked her down. She could find anyone. With a few phone calls, Miss Orsuto made contact with her. The old woman still lived just north of Naples, in Scampia. Her apartment was in the most crime-ridden and drug-infested housing development in all of Italy, maybe in all of Europe, a place called the Vele, the sails. It got its name from the triangular shape of the gargantuan concrete buildings that, from a distance, had the look of enormous sailing ships.

Sandra told Nate that there had been a movie made about Vele a few years before. The film, *Gomorrah*, was about the ultimate in degraded modern human life in a concrete desert.

Living in the Vele was beastly and monochromatic, a real-life film noir. The only time Napolitani visited the Vele was to buy heroin. Miss Orsuto said it was known as the heroin capital of Europe.

Sandra made up a file of clippings about the incident forty-two years earlier and about the Vele. When Nate got back to the office, he asked her to make arrangements for him to visit the dead boy's mother in Naples.

So, the day after his walk with Ackerman, Nate and Sandra were headed south to Naples on the Frecciarossa to interview Giulia Luppino.

Sandra Orsuto was going along to translate and facilitate. In a very short time Nate had really come to rely on her. She was not only efficient, but also discreet and thoughtful. Her language skills had been opening doors for him all over Rome.

The train pulled into Naples Central, a dirty and giant old structure in the heart of chaotic and criminal Napoli.

Napoli is a city one either loves or hates. It has one of the most spectacular urban settings in the world on the Bay of Naples. As a port city, it has all the squalor and tawdriness of any sailor's town.

The American Seventh Fleet is home ported in Naples. American sailors know it well. Navy officers say that Naples has the weather of San Diego and the ambiance of Calcutta.

Everything is crowded in Naples, especially the area downtown near the train station. Nate and Sandra detrained at the central station and went directly to the taxi stand in front.

Miss Orsuto asked several taxis in the queue to take them to the Vele in Scampia. When the taxi drivers heard the address, they wagged their fingers at them and spat an emphatic "No." Sometimes, they just laughed out loud.

One taxi driver said to her in Napolitano dialect, "You're crazy, lady, you and your man in his fancy Armani suit. You don't want to go there, unless you are buying heroin."

Finally, one driver outside the normal queue agreed to take them. His vehicle had no taxi medallion or license displayed. Sandra had agreed to pay him the equivalent of one hundred dollars, the price of their luxury train tickets to Naples. The "taxi" driver also agreed to wait for them and bring them back after their visit.

They climbed into the taxi, a filthy and decrepit Fiat Panda, the workhorse of the Italian poor. There was no air-conditioning. All the windows were rolled down to let in air in the stifling heat and humidity of a Naples summer day. It had been a long time since Nate had ridden in a car with no air-conditioning.

They inched along, street by street, through the traffic fumes of Napoli *centro*. They had barely gone four blocks when a boy reached in the open rear window and tried to snatch Sandra's purse. Nate leaned over and grabbed the boy's arm and nearly broke it. The boy retreated, but not without her purse. Luckily, Miss Orsuto, knowing the ways of Naples, had put her money and identification in her shoulder bag, which was on the floor of the car, firmly fixed under her foot.

Eventually, the taxi freed itself from downtown traffic and climbed up and out of central Naples. The streets became wider, the landscape more desolate. There was trash along the roadside. Plastic bags were caught in the scrawny tree limbs and clung to the bus stop signs. Nate started getting nervous. This was uncharted territory for foreigners.

Whenever you are in a strange country where you don't speak the language, there is a feeling of helplessness. It's like being a child again. He was glad that Miss Orsuto was along to translate it all for him.

The taxi came to a stop on a long concrete parking area. A few abandoned cars in the *parcheggio* appeared to have been totally stripped. One car had even been torched.

Sandra and Nate climbed out of the taxi. As soon as the door was closed, the driver said, "Ciao," and took off. They stood there open mouthed for a second, realizing that they had just been abandoned.

A concrete bridge led across a kind of moat that surrounded the apartment building before them. They crossed it.

Sandra pointed to a huge vinyl sign, yellow with black lettering, that someone had hung above from the balconies of the top three floors of the building. She read aloud, "*Quando il vento dei soprusi sara' finitio, le vele sarranno spieagate verso le felicita.*" She translated, "'When the wind of the oppressors is done, the Vele will be pushed toward happiness.' That's so Napolitano. They are always poetic, even in the most depressing of circumstances," she said wryly.

Before them, along the ground floor, were some abandoned shops. A few women had set up tables in the corridors that ran the length of the building. They were selling nothing but condoms and syringes.

As Nate and Sandra stood there, a big black SUV cruised through the parking lot and came to a stop at the end of the bridge. A little kid ran out with a paper bag, tightly wrapped around what appeared to be a block or brick. The Camorra was collecting its drug money. Every two or three hours they cruised through to make their collections.

Nate and Sandra stepped around the syringes at the entrance of the Vele and made their way to a long open corridor that ran the length of the giant building. A little child's toy motorcycle, a wheelie toy for riding, was smashed at the entrance. Garbage was everywhere. The odor was stifling in the summer heat.

The corridor was in a kind of atrium. Back in the 1970s, this ultra-modern design had won awards. It might have looked nice on paper. People could look over the balconies and see who was coming and going. They could also drop crap down on them, which it appeared they had done.

The elevators were, of course, broken, and long since boarded up, so they took the stairs. At the bottom of the staircase was an iron gate. Miss Orsuto told Nate that these gates were not put there by the housing authority, but by the Camorra. They could be locked by drug dealers to slow down the policemen. This was a city of thieves.

Sandra got out her cell phone and called the number for Mrs. Luppino. She got directions to the apartment, which was on the tenth floor. The staircases looked like something out of the fantastical imagination of Salvador Dali. They crisscrossed between wings of the building in flying forms, open and dangerous. Each floor of the Vele was set back from the floor below to create a large terrace. It was a design idea gone horribly wrong. It gave the buildings the look of a Babylonian ziggurat, but there were definitely no hanging gardens. They were platforms for danger, fights, and drug use.

When they got to the tenth floor, Giulia Luppino had come out to the staircase to greet them. She was a friendly, grandmotherly woman, short and wide. Her gray hair was pulled tightly in a bun. She wore black from head to toe and walked with the help of an aluminum cane that had four little feet on the bottom. The cane stood up by itself when she let go.

"*Benvenuti*," she said to them perfunctorily. She led them down the corridor-balcony to her apartment, past a number of other apartments, all of which appeared to be abandoned, their doors wide open. The three entered through a metal-reinforced door that had a security gate of iron bars.

Italy is a nation of public squalor and private splendor. The contrast between the corridor-balcony outside and the apartment's neat interior couldn't have been greater. Outside all was chaos and filth. Inside all was order and cleanliness.

The floor shined from washing and waxing. The glass on the windows was sparkling clean. The furniture was covered with lace doilies. On the wall hung an olive-wood crucifix, probably brought back from the Holy Land by a church pilgrimage.

The small sitting room opened into a tiny kitchen. On the wall in the kitchen Nate could see holy cards and other images taped to the wall near the Formica table, which doubled as an altar for the household shrine. Very near the table were two cheaply framed prints of saints, one of Padre Pio, the patron saint of Southern Italy, the other of St. Francis, the poor man of Assisi. According to Catholic lore, both Padre Pio and St. Francis had received the stigmata, the marks of the open wounds of Christ. Consequently, they were the great patrons of people who suffer and the natural patron saints of these apartments in the Vele.

There was also a holy card of St. Anthony taped to the wall, holding the child Jesus. In Italy, St. Anthony is the go-to saint for impossible or difficult causes. He is considered so powerful in the Italian Catholic pantheon that they just call him *il Santo*, the Saint. No further explanation needed. If you need something, just ask "the Saint."

Nate quickly looked around the apartment like a police investigator, noticing the family photos in a display case in the corner of the living room. There was a wedding photo with a young Giulia, standing next to a handsome man in uniform.

There was also a smiling photo of a teenage boy on a beach. The boy was suntanned and strong, in the prime of life. Nate walked over to the display case and looked at the photo, but he did not touch it.

Mrs. Luppino watched him carefully. "*Mio figlio, Gianluca,*" she said to Nate.

Nate nodded. "Handsome," he said to Sandra, who translated. "*Bello il tuo figlio.*"

Giulia motioned for Sandra and Nate to sit down on the over-stuffed living room sofa. She went into the nearby kitchen and came back with a tray on which she had put a bottle of mineral water and a little espresso coffee pot in the Italian style. She poured the water into glasses and the espresso into dainty ceramic cups that she took from her china cabinet. She offered them sugar for the coffee. Then she sat down in a worn easy chair opposite them. In the corner of the room a flat-screen TV perched on a small stand was playing at a high volume. Sandra asked permission to turn it off, so they could talk. "*Si,*" said the lady of the house. "It's nothing," she said in Italian, waving her hand at the TV as if to dismiss it.

Talking through Sandra's translation, Nate explained that he worked for the Vatican and that he had come to Mrs. Luppino to learn about the events that took place forty-two years ago. Mrs. Luppino nodded slowly and swallowed hard, her face expressionless.

"I'd like to ask you about the circumstances around the death of your son, Gianluca," Nate explained.

"Luca," corrected the old lady. "We always called him Luca. Only Luca."

"Tell us about Luca," said Nate.

Her eyes filled up. Clearly after all this time, it was still painful for her. "He was my boy," she said. "What can I say? He was my only son. He was the moon and the sun of my life. He was a good boy, always happy, always singing." Her voice trailed off. Sandra stopped translating.

Her eyes were also filling up with tears. Nate paused for a moment. He felt ashamed to be pressing on such a painful memory.

"Tell us about that night he went on the ferryboat to Sicilia," said Nate.

"Luca was in my little trattoria near the port. He worked there, waiting tables. I did the cooking. My husband, Giogio, wasn't there. He was in the merchant marine and always away on ships. So, it was mostly just me and Luca.

"The restaurant was crowded that night. I was busy. Those two monsignori came in. They sat at the table near the door and had quite a bit of wine. They seemed happy. The captain of the *traghetto* was also in the restaurant that night.

"The two priests were talking to Luca. They told him they were going to Sicilia on the overnight ferry. Luca always wanted to go to Sicilia. He wanted to visit his cousins there. I never would let him go. It was too expensive, too dangerous. I never had time to take him. His father was always away, and when he was home he never wanted to go back out on a ship again.

"The priests offered to take Luca. 'He will be safe with us,' they said. Luca begged me. 'Please, Mama. Please, Mama,' he said. 'Please let me go! I never go anywhere!'

"I wouldn't have done it, but the captain said, 'Oh, Giulia, let the boy go.' He was the captain of the *traghetto*. He promised he would bring Luca back in a few days. I never should have listened. Never! Never! Never!

"So, I said, '*Va bene.*' But you stay with your uncle and come back after two days.' Luca was so happy. He ran to get his things. He kissed me and kissed me. I gave him a rosary for his pocket. *O Dio! O Dio! O Dio!*"

Giulia Luppino was now rocking back and forth in her chair. Tears streamed down her cheeks. She was back in the events of forty-two years ago, reliving the nightmare, trying to take back her awful decision.

"What did they tell you happened onboard the ship?" asked Nate gently.

"They said he fell overboard late at night. But I know that was a lie! A lie!

"Luca was not a drinker. He was not stupid. He grew up here in Naples. He was always on boats and around the water. He was a great swimmer. He was very strong. Look at his photo. You can see how strong he was. He never would have fallen off the ship, and he never would have drowned. I don't believe it. I don't believe it. I never believed it!

"The captain came to see me. I never saw those two priests again. They never came back to see me. They didn't come to the funeral. The whole city of Napoli was at the funeral, but not those two. *Bastardi! Bastardi!*

"The captain said it was an accident. That they pulled Luca out of the ocean and that he was dead. But when I saw my boy, there were marks on his neck. Marks like someone had bitten him. Blood marks.

"The Camorra came by and paid me two million lira." Miss Orsuto guessed that was about ten thousand dollars at that time. "They told me that they appreciated my silence.

"I didn't know what to do. When the Camorra tells you to be silent in Naples, you are silent. But I knew that Luca did not drown." Mrs. Luppino paused and looked blankly at the wall behind Nate, as if staring at a distant object.

"Two years later, I went down to the funeral home. I asked to see the records. The *signore* there said he had no records, but I didn't believe it.

"I left the funeral home and went down to the medical examiner's office *in centro*. The man there also said he had no records, but I knew there must be something. A lady in the office remembered me from the newspaper articles and the stories on TV.

"After the medical examiner left the room, she told me to call the reporter from *Il Mattino* who had written about Luca's death. She said the reporter had a copy of the examiner's report at the time and that he might still have it.

"So, I called the reporter. He met me at a café *in centro*.

"He said yes, he still had his notes, but he had not brought the files with him. He gave me only a clipping from the paper that I already had. But he told me one important thing I did not know before. He said there was no water in Luca's lungs, according to the medical examiner. I wasn't sure what that meant.

"A few weeks later, I asked a friend about no water in the lungs. He didn't know what it meant either, so we called the doctor at the clinic here in Scampia. The doctor said it meant that Luca did not drown. My boy was already dead when he fell in the water. They killed him. Then they threw him in the water. That's what those bastards did. Killed him! *O Dio. O Dio.*"

Now Giulia was rocking back and forth, not sobbing but moaning.

"My son, my son," she moaned.

Sandra sat there for a little while and let the poor woman grieve.

"What do you think happened, *signora*?" she asked.

"They killed him. Those two devils. Those two priests. And they killed me at the same time. Luca was a good boy. He was everything to me. They never even called me. They never even offered a Mass for my son.

"After he died, I could not go on. I closed the restaurant. My husband left me. We separated, no divorce. The Church does not approve, so he just left me. He said he could not stand the memory of Luca either. He blamed me!"

She paused, sobbing. She wiped her eyes with a paper napkin, then she continued.

"Years later, when my husband died, we were still married, so I got his pension from the merchant marine. That's how I live. They send me a check every month. I still wear black. People think I'm mourning for my husband. The widow Luppino, they call me. But it's not for him, not for my husband. It's for Luca I mourn."

Nate noted the black dress of a traditional widow. This little woman had spent most of her adult life in mourning.

Nate asked her, "What would you like to see happen to those men, *signora*?"

"Suffer," she said. "I want them to suffer as I have suffered."

There was a pall of sadness over the room. Sandra asked to use the bathroom and excused herself. Nate could hear her crying on the other side of the bathroom door. Nate pulled a kitchen chair over to the old lady and sat there holding Giulia Luppino's hand in wordless communication.

After a minute or two Sandra came back in the room, wiping her eyes with a handkerchief. Nate stood up. Sandra and Nate stood facing the mother who was still weeping. Nate suddenly thought of all the victims of child abuse and their families. "We will try to get you justice, *signora*. I will see to it that these men are punished."

Then Nate looked at the photo of Luca. "*Signora*, could I have a photo of Luca?"

"*Si, certo*," said the old lady. "Take that one. I have many copies." She pointed to a photo in a small metal frame on the end table near Nate. He put it in his coat pocket.

As they made preparations to go, Sandra remembered that the taxi had left them. They were stranded.

When Sandra explained, Giulia said, "Don't worry. I will ask my neighbor to drive you to the *centro*. He has a car. He would be glad to do it."

Then she added, "You are the only people who have ever come by to see me about Luca in more than forty years. *Grazie*. I feel closer to him just talking about it. I'm glad someone remembers."

Before they left the apartment, Nate stood in front of the grieving mother. She was still seated in the easy chair, a real-life Mother of Sorrows. His eyes filled up with tears again. When he tried to speak, nothing came out, so he leaned over and kissed Giulia on the top of her head and squeezed her hand gently.

They rode downtown in the neighbor's car. Neither Nate nor Sandra spoke. It was not until they were on the train back to Rome that Nate was able to speak.

"I'm going to fry their fucking asses, Crepi and Salazar. I'm going to see to it that they rot in a hell worse than where that poor old lady lives."

He held the picture of Gianluca tightly in his hand, looking out the window as Naples flashed by.

20

TWO STEPS DOWN

"TWO STEPS DOWN," SAID SISTER PERPETUA IN A HIGH-pitched voice with a heavy Italian accent. She was dressed in a black Benedictine habit, a plastic bag on her head to keep her veil dry from the water that dripped from the roof of the catacombs. Sister was tired. It was the last tour of the day.

She carried a rolled umbrella, which she used as a pointer, and she held it over her head to lead her tour group of giggling American school-girls through the Catacombs of Priscilla.

Sister Perpetua was annoyed. "Please, girls, stay with the tour. There are forty miles of maze beneath these streets. If you get lost, you might never be found."

She pointed a bony finger at the errant girls. That sent the girls into paroxysms of hysterical laughter, which only made Sister Perpetua even more annoyed.

The Catacombs of Priscilla are located underneath the modern Via Salaria, perhaps the oldest road in the city of Rome. It runs from the Adriatic Sea to the Sabine Hills. It is called *salaria* because it was the path of the salt trade between the Sabine people and the Romans.

Ancient Romans valued salt for food preservation and cooking. For a time, they even paid their legionnaires with salt, as a form of currency. Hence, the word "salary."

On either side of the tunnel, the tufa walls were lined with niches; in neat rows, three or four levels high from floor to ceiling, ancient Christians had been entombed there during the years of persecution. The niches, once covered with stone façades, were now open and empty, like shelves in an unused pantry.

Students on field trips test boundaries. Despite the nun's admonitions, three girls wandered off from the tour, down a dimly lit tunnel. After about fifty meters, the escaping students turned a corner and found themselves in a small, dark room. Now they were disoriented and had to feel their way along the walls looking for an exit. One of the girls reached into a dark recess, thinking it might be a door. Her hand touched something damp and slimy. She let out a scream and pulled her hand back. As she did so, the slimy object tumbled out onto the floor.

Sister Perpetua came running with her umbrella in one hand and a flashlight in her other. The dim light revealed that the slimy object was a naked corpse. The body was so bloody and disfigured that its sex was not immediately apparent.

The girls grew hysterical. Sister Perpetua made the sign of the cross and began praying. The school chaperones ushered the girls quickly out of the catacombs.

Even in jaded Rome, the discovery of a bloody body in an ancient catacomb is big news. Within minutes, satellite trucks from Rome's news channels had arrived at the entrance to the catacombs on the Via Salaria. The evening news showed a body bag on a gurney, being lifted into a police van.

Later that night, the police received an anonymous call from a disposable mobile phone. "The body from the catacombs is a priest who could not keep his vow of *omerta*." The caller hung up.

It took the medical examiner about eight hours to positively identify the body. Monsignor Ackerman was dead.

* * *

Early the next morning, Nate received a courtesy phone call from the Italian police, telling him that the monsignor had been murdered. Nate had mentioned to the police at the Questura that he would be meeting with Ackerman at the Columbus. Nate immediately telephoned Cardinal O'Toole, who was at breakfast in his apartment.

"Your Eminence, have you heard the news? Monsignor Ackerman is dead. They found his body in the catacombs, badly beaten."

"Oh, God," said the cardinal. "What the hell is happening? Do they know who did it?"

"Nothing yet," said Nate. "But they have reasonable suspicions. The police got a call, saying he broke his vow of *omerta*."

The cardinal grunted.

"Can you come over here now?" asked O'Toole. "I don't want to talk about this on the phone."

"I'll be there in half an hour," said Nate.

He threw on his jeans and a polo shirt and grabbed his laptop. It was a fifteen-minute walk from the Columbus Hotel to the cardinal's apartment, down the Via della Conciliazione, past the entrance to St. Peter's Square, and a block over to the Piazza Leonina.

On his way over, Nate began to wonder about O'Toole's safety. Six cardinals may have already been killed, and now Monsignor Ackerman? I should get him some security, thought Nate. Maybe even have his food and mail screened.

The cardinal's housekeeper buzzed Nate into the apartment house lobby. He took the creaky elevator up to the third floor, and the nun let him in. Not much security here, Nate thought.

O'Toole was sitting in an easy chair in his study, staring at the wall.

He looked at Nate. Without greeting him, he said, "What happened?"

"I don't know yet," said Nate, "but I think we'd better get you some protection from now on. In fact, it wouldn't be a bad idea for all the cardinals to get some protection."

"OK," said O'Toole, "whatever you think." He didn't seem to care very much. He seemed preoccupied. "But what about Matt? What happened to him?"

Nate thought the cardinal was asking about how Ackerman died. Actually, he was wondering more about how Ackerman had lived.

Nate realized the cardinal wanted to talk. O'Toole gestured for him to sit in the overstuffed chair across from him.

"All the American priests in Rome pretty much know each other," began O'Toole. "I used to see the monsignor at the Thanksgiving dinner up at the NAC and at our Fourth of July barbecues. I saw him change over the years. I knew he was in trouble. But you know how it is. We're all busy. I thought he'd pull himself together." Nate wasn't sure just how much O'Toole knew about Ackerman, but then the cardinal continued. "There were rumors about him hanging out in gay bars and staying out late, but he was always at his desk in the morning. I guess that's all I really cared about, him getting his work done."

"Unfortunately, there was more to it than that, Your Eminence. He was acting as a messenger for the Camorra. He may have been involved in fingering targets for the Mafia."

The cardinal looked at Nate. His mind was somewhere else. Nate wondered if O'Toole had even heard what he was saying.

"I should have been a better priest to him. I was the senior guy among the Americans here in Rome. I should have been there for him."

Nate wanted to be consoling. "Well, you did what you could."

"No, I didn't," O'Toole said dismissively. "I've seen this before. I've seen these young guys come here full of idealism and end up drinking themselves to death. We let them die. We even help it along."

Nate raised an eyebrow, curious. "What do you mean?"

"A priest I know from back home—Father Jack McClendon—told us a story once when I was in the seminary. It always stayed with me."

O'Toole looked out the window, ruminating.

"Back in 1946, I think, *LIFE* magazine ran a story about some foxes. It's a true story, I guess. I used it once in a homily.

"Seems like there were these foxes living in the woods outside some town in Ohio. They ate mostly mice and crickets. Sometimes, they also ate a chicken or some quail. This made the people of the town mad. So, one Saturday they organized a foxhunt. They got maybe six hundred men, women, and children with sticks. They formed a big circle, a mile across. Somebody shot a gun as a signal. Then they started walking through the woods and fields, yelling and baying to frighten the foxes out of their holes. As the circle closed in on them, the foxes ran back and forth. They were frightened."

O'Toole paused, and Nate could see the story affected him. "So, what happened?" asked Nate.

O'Toole said, "It's almost hard to believe." There was a catch in his voice. "Sometimes, a fox would have the guts to snarl back, but it would be killed on the spot. Some foxes stopped in their anguish and even tried to lick the hands of their tormentors. They wanted to stop the killing. But the townspeople had no mercy. They killed the affectionate foxes, too. They just smashed them with their sticks. The photos showed the foxes standing there with their wounded and dying friends. The foxes had more compassion than the people. Finally, as the circle grew smaller and smaller, the few remaining foxes went to the center of the circle and just lay down. They just gave up. They didn't know what else to do. But the townsfolk knew what to do. They killed them. They hit the dying and wounded until they were dead. They even taught the children how to do it."

Tears were running down the cardinal's face.

This is about more than Ackerman, thought Nate.

O'Toole got up and walked to the sitting room window, looking out toward the Vatican. "We have our own foxhunts in the Church," he continued. "We call them inquisitions or inquiries. We persecute people who disagree with us. We frighten them into doing what we want. We call them horrible names like heretic or apostate. We say they are intrinsically disordered. We say they are immoral. We say they are defective— all because they disagree with us. We have the power, so we crush them by humiliating them. That's what we do to our own people. People like Ackerman. We crush them."

O'Toole gestured out the window toward his left. "Look out over these rooftops. Not even a mile from here, we burned Bruno at the stake in Campo de' Fiori. We accused Galileo of heresy and put him under house arrest in a tower on the other side of the Vatican. We silenced him, but we knew he was right, so we let him continue his research. We've silenced some of our own greatest philosophers and theologians. Look at how we treated Chardin, John Courtney Murray, and even Charlie Curran." Nate had no idea who those people were.

The cardinal finished his thought. "We launched the Crusades from St. Peter's with the mandate to kill tens of thousands of people we labeled as infidels. Who the hell do we think we are?"

The cardinal suddenly fell quiet.

Nate was at a loss for words. The silence consumed him, forcing him to seek comfort in sound wherever he could find it.

He exhaled slowly and focused on the clock in the hall ticking. He turned his head. Traffic was picking up in the square outside.

21

AVANTI A DIO

ROME WAS WAKING UP TO ANOTHER DAY.

The news of Ackerman's death ricocheted around the city and the world. "The Vatican in Disarray" was the headline on CNN International. People were enthralled.

Sitting on his rooftop terrace, Cardinal Luciano Crepi picked up his copy of *Il Messaggero*, the Roman newspaper, from a silver tray that had carried his breakfast. He scanned the headlines. He dropped his morning cappuccino to the floor when he saw the headline of Ackerman's death. Immediately, the cardinal knew that his life, too, was over.

Crepi loved luxury. All his life, he had surrounded himself with things of beauty. As the governor of Vatican City, he was, in effect, the landlord. As the landlord, he could live just about anywhere in the Vatican. He made an apartment for himself on the top floor of the Palace of the Governor of Vatican City. Originally that building had been built in the 1930s to be a Franciscan seminary; the Governatorato is one of the more modern buildings in the Vatican. It is much photographed by tourists standing at the dome of St. Peter's, because the driveway in front has a papal crest made out of hedges and flowers.

The top floor of the palace boasts a giant rooftop terrace. On the terrace is a loggia, or covered porch, with dramatic arches rising twenty feet above the roof. The loggia is topped by a statue of St. Francis of Assisi. Cardinal Crepi loved the loggia, but he had nothing in common with the poor man of Assisi.

That rooftop terrace was marvelous for receptions. It had one of the most dramatic views in Rome. Cardinal Crepi liked to take his breakfast on the roof in nice weather. It allowed him to sit at the table and see all of Vatican City, master of all he surveyed.

Luciano Crepi was, above all, a realist. He knew that if Monsignor Ackerman was dead, probably at the hand of the Camorra, then his own death was probably not far off. He had outlived his usefulness to the Mafia, and now he was a liability.

With the dramatic murder of Cardinal Manning in New York, in plain view, no one seemed safe. It was only a matter of time until the trail of blood led to his door.

The cardinal resolved not to wait. If he were to die soon, he wanted to die on his own terms. Certainly he did not wish to be stuffed ignominiously into a tufa niche in the catacombs below the Via Salaria, like some slaughtered animal.

Crepi put down his newspaper on the silver tray and stood up with deliberation. He reached inside his cassock pocket for his mobile phone and called his office. "I'm not coming in this morning," he said. "I will be working in my apartment. Please see to it that I am not disturbed."

"*Va bene, Eminenza*," the receptionist said.

His movements were calm and deliberate now.

Crossing the giant terrace, he walked down one flight of stairs to his apartments. The walls of the corridors were covered with Flemish tapestries of hunting scenes.

Before going to his bedroom, he walked into his large reception room. With a single tap to his smartphone, the quintessential Roman opera, Puccini's *Tosca*, filled the apartment. It was his favorite opera.

He turned the volume up as loud as it would go. The music drifted outside, serenading the gardeners as they clipped the hedges around the papal seal, which was created by thousands of multicolored flowers.

He opened the doors of his cedar closets and began to lay out his choir robes, all custom made for him by Gammarelli, the papal tailors.

He dressed himself in his choir cassock made entirely of scarlet watered silk, with silk piping and buttons.

Around his waist he put a silk fascia, a wide sash that was supposed to be a symbol of his devotion to Christ. As Jesus said to Peter, "Someone would fasten his belt and take him where he would not go." The scarlet fascia, by custom, is worn only during the *sede vacante*, the vacancy of the papacy.

Over all this, he draped a delicate lace surplice that covered him from his shoulders to his knees.

Around his neck he placed, with a reverence usually reserved for a royal coronation, a jeweled pectoral cross that had once belonged to Alexander VI, the Borgia pope, the most notoriously bad pope in Roman history.

On his head he placed a red silk *zucchetto*, a skullcap that looks like a yarmulke. Over that, he put a red silk hat called a *biretta*. It was supposed to recall a shepherd's cap, though no shepherd ever wore anything remotely like that. It has three little peaks or "horns" to grab during ceremonies.

His hat had been presented to him by the pope when he was made a cardinal. It was a sign that he would defend the papacy, "even to the shedding of blood."

Around his shoulders, he draped a thirty-foot-long cape, made of scarlet watered silk, called a *cappa magna*. Originally, it was designed to cover a horse's ass when the cardinals rode a horse in procession. The long train would have been carried by a servant in procession; now, he double-draped it over his own arm.

With the strains of the opera still playing, he wandered around his apartment, caressing all the things he had accumulated in a lifetime of clerical prominence. There were ivory animals made from illegal elephant tusks. He touched the photos taken with popes, kings, presidents, and diplomats who had passed through the Vatican.

He opened the cabinet of his collection of writing pens and antique napkin rings. All useless things, but things of beauty, covered with jewels and fine gold.

He stroked all the tapestries and paintings on the walls.

He took a crystal tumbler down from a mirrored cabinet in his dining room and poured a glass of Benedictine brandy. As the opera was coming to its third act, he walked over to an oak chest at the end of his study and lifted out a polished wooden box. Inside was a pearl-handled revolver, said to have belonged to Benito Mussolini, the Italian dictator. Crepi was a fascist, politically, and secretly admired Mussolini. He slowly loaded the gun.

He took the elevator back up to the rooftop terrace. The strains of the opera could be heard through the open windows. Tosca's lover had now been shot by the firing squad. Just as the music came to the point where Tosca threw herself off the parapet of the church of San Andrea Della Valle, Luciano Cardinal Crepi stood up on the parapet of the Palace of the Governor of Vatican City. He looked out one more time at the great dome of St. Peter's, which was itself a reminder of the corruption of the papacy, financed through the sale of indulgences.

Crepi looked around at his kingdom here on earth. He waited for Tosca to start singing the final aria. "O Scarpia, Avanti a Dio!" "O Scarpia, we meet before God!" Then, just at the moment in the opera when she hurls herself over the edge, Cardinal Crepi, governor general of Vatican City, raised the pistol gently to his temple and blew his brains out.

The gun flew out of his hands and fell into the bushes near the building. His body fell with the same drama as Tosca's. His great red *cappa magna* made a delicate silk streamer like in a Chinese opera. It billowed out in the wind as his body fell the ninety feet to the ground below. The cardinal landed in the driveway, just beyond the papal seal.

Tourists standing at the base of the dome of St. Peter's thought it was some sort of dramatic show. They snapped pictures as Crepi fell, considering themselves lucky to have caught such an unusual and colorful event.

When his body hit the pavement of the driveway below, Cardinal Crepi bounced a few inches from the impact. Then, he lay motionless in a slowly growing pool of his own blood. The Vatican gardeners, who were clipping bushes around the driveway hedges, came running.

Cardinal Luciano Crepi departed this world on his own terms.

22

UN BEL' CANTO

THREE HOURS LATER, CARDINAL JULIO SALAZAR WAS JUST about to sit down to his midday *pranzo* when the telephone rang. It was Monsignor Donato calling. The cardinal's housekeeper called him to the phone. "The monsignor sounds *molto agitato*."

"Your Eminence, horrible news. Cardinal Crepi is dead."

"*O Dio*," gasped Salazar. "*Perche?*"

"We don't know for sure," said Donato, "a suicide, possibly. He fell from the terrace of the Governatorato, but there was a bullet in his head. No gun has been found yet, so we don't know who shot him, or if he shot himself."

"*O Dio, O Dio*," Cardinal Salazar kept repeating. "What is happening to us?" Julio Salazar, always an emotional man, became hysterical.

Donato had his own worries. "First Ackerman, now Crepi. Perhaps it is our associates from the bank," he said. Donato did not dare to refer to the Camorra on the telephone, but Salazar knew whom he meant. "We have to disappear. We might be next," said Donato.

He hung up without saying good-bye.

Julio was frozen with fear. He stood motionless in his living room, the telephone receiver still to his ear. He thought, the Camorra killed Ackerman and Crepi. There is nowhere to hide. They have contacts everywhere.

Salazar began pacing back and forth like a caged animal. He went out onto his terrace overlooking St. Peter's Square. Then he realized that was a bad idea. If the mob were after him, a sniper could be anywhere. He hurried back inside and pulled the drapes closed.

The best thing, he thought, is to call Franco. He knows me. He will tell me what is going on.

Don Franco Virgilio, a *capo* in the Di Lauro clan, the most vicious of the Naples Mafia, was Cardinal Salazar's contact at the Camorra. He was known as a jovial man and a ruthless killer. His hand shaking badly, Salazar fumbled with his Rolodex. At last, he located the number.

"Don Franco Virgilio, *per favore*," he said when someone answered. "Tell him it's Cardinal Julio Salazar."

Virgilio always took Salazar's calls. People always answer the phone calls of those who have made them money.

"I am very sorry, Your Eminence, Don Franco is not available to talk to you. But tell us where you are, and he will get back to you. Can I tell him where you are?"

Salazar got the picture. Suddenly, he was persona non grata. He certainly was not going to tell the mob where he was.

"Is there a message for Don Franco?" she asked.

"*No. Non importa. Arrivederci*," said Salazar. He hung up before they had a chance to ask any more questions. Now, he was really panicked. Virgilio had never refused his calls before. This was a very bad sign.

Salazar knew he could not stay at his apartment. Virgilio could have someone outside his building in a matter of minutes, if he was next on the Mafia hit list.

Salazar was in a panic, trying to figure out what to do. He knew he needed protection, and he needed it fast.

Like a child looking for monsters, the aging Colombian cardinal peered out between the drapes of his balcony window, toward the dome of St. Peter's. For so long he had felt safe in the shadow of that dome, but now he felt exposed.

Below his apartment balcony, in the Piazza San Pietro, across the street, crowds of tourists were gathering. Television news trucks were setting up their huge satellite dishes, in anticipation of the papal funeral.

The city of Rome always kept police stationed just outside the entrance to St. Peter's Square. There was always some problem, with thousands of tourists coming and going. A couple of police cars and an armored police van were routinely parked at the end of Bernini's colonnade. Practically every morning, Salazar greeted those policemen as he walked to his office in the Vatican.

Salazar had an idea. He knew an inspector with the city police. He fumbled again with his Rolodex, found the number and, giving in to his panic, pleaded with the policeman as soon as he came on the line.

"Inspector, I'm in trouble. I need your help. Please, help me." Salazar was almost sobbing. "Send the armored car from the piazza over to my apartment."

"Wait a minute. Slow down, Your Eminence. What is the problem? Why the armored car?" asked the inspector.

"I need protection. I'm next. You know about Cardinal Crepi. You know about the monsignor dead in the catacombs. I think I'm next, you understand. I'm next!"

The inspector was cautious. "OK, I'll send a police car to pick you up."

"No, no," said Salazar, almost hysterical, "you must send the armored car. My door is on the Via Rusticucci. It is a very narrow street. The armored car will block the whole street. No other car will be able to get by. You know these people. You know the Camorra would not hesitate to shoot a police car." Salazar could hardly believe that he had actually spoken the name of the mob into the phone, but it was worth the risk. The inspector agreed to send the car.

"*Va bene, subito arriviamo*," said the inspector. "I'll send the armored car and a police car right away. Don't worry, Your Eminence. We will take care of you."

The inspector was covering himself. Rome was talking about the killings of two high-ranking Vatican officials. He did not wish to have a third dead body on his hands today. He certainly did not want to be responsible for the death of another cardinal.

"Eminence, we'll be at your door in two minutes. Be in lay dress," ordered the inspector.

Two minutes later the armored van, with police cruisers in front and behind, roared up to the entrance of Salazar's apartment building. They blocked the short, narrow street. Policemen jumped out, dressed in armored vests, with semiautomatic Uzis in hand. It looked like a hostage situation or the protection of a foreign diplomat.

The apartment house door opened, and a frightened little old man emerged, dressed in black slacks and a blue shirt. Flanked by two armed police officers, Salazar literally ran from the door of his apartment house to the waiting van. The rear door of the armored vehicle slammed shut. For the moment he was safe. The van immediately took off, trailing a cloud of diesel fumes.

Salazar rode in silence, and then he asked, "Where are we going?"

"The Palazzo de Giustizia," said the policeman. The Palace of Justice houses the supreme court of Italy. In its basement, in addition to a labyrinth of prison cells, there are accommodations for the protection of high-profile witnesses, politicians, and judges during trials.

The van turned onto the Lungo Tevere, the road that runs along the Tiber River. The Palace of Justice is an elaborate Beaux-Arts building. A huge statue of Winged Justice, riding in a Roman chariot pulled by four galloping bronze horses, graces its roof.

The police van bounced down the ramp of the subterranean entrance at the rear of the Palazzo de Giustizia, and up to a loading dock, where two Carabinieri were taking a smoking break.

Salazar was glad to see the Carabinieri, who by reputation are much less likely to be on the payroll of the mob than the local police. He allowed himself to hope that he would be safe there.

Salazar stepped down from the vehicle. The police escorted him into the building and down the hall to a barren, windowless room—empty but for a square table between two chairs. There was a water cooler with paper cups in the corner. Salazar helped himself to a drink of water and sat down. Thirty minutes later his friend, the police inspector, arrived with a detective from the Carabinieri.

They had hardly entered the room when Salazar began to wail. "My life is in danger!"

"*Calma ti, calma ti*. We agree," said the inspector.

"Don't tell me to calm down!" screamed Salazar. "My life is in danger!"

"We know," said the inspector, putting his hand on Salazar's shoulder and directing him back into a chair. Salazar sat, but was not calm. He said to the inspector, "There is an American in Rome investigating the deaths of cardinals around the world. I forget his name. Call him. I need to talk to him."

"I know who he means," said the inspector. "He has been in our office at the Questura looking at files. We will find him." The police left the room. An hour later the door opened suddenly. Salazar flinched. He did not know what to expect. It could have been the Camorra.

* * *

Nate walked in with a briefcase and a digital recorder. He popped open the briefcase, put the recorder on the table, and turned it on.

"OK, Your Eminence," said Nate. "I have a few questions for you." Nate was all business. Cardinals are accustomed to deference. They like to set the agenda. They are not accustomed to being interrogated, especially by laypeople.

"I'm not here for questioning," objected Salazar. "I came here for protection." He spoke in English. He obviously did not need a translator. After all, he had been a diplomat.

"You don't tell us what you came here for," said Nate, "and you certainly don't set the agenda here. This is a police investigation, not a social call. You cooperate, or you will not get protection." Nate was clearly in charge of this encounter.

Salazar glared back.

"May I have some water?" asked Salazar.

"In a minute," said Nate. "First, answer some questions.

"We know that you and your buddy Crepi were laundering money for the drug cartels. We also know that you brought narco dollars to Rome from Latin America and ran them through the IOR," said Nate, using the initials for the Vatican Bank.

"If you know so much, you don't need me," said Salazar sarcastically.

"Mind your manners," snapped Nate. "Maybe we don't need you, but you need us. We could just as well put you back out on the street. If you prefer, we could call the Camorra and let them know you are strolling down the Lungo Tevere. Or you could just answer the questions."

Salazar fell silent.

"Tell me," said Nate, "about your connection to the Camorra. Why were you naming papabile in *Panoramio* magazine?"

"That was Crepi's idea," said Salazar. It was clear he was going to blame everything on his dead friend. "At first we just wanted to protect the bank. The Camorra was doing a lot of business with us and the bank.

"But then, we started to get worried about Manning in New York and some of the others. Manning was the biggest threat. He was on the board of the bank, and he had many contacts among American bankers. He talked about bringing them over to supervise our operations. Manning could have ruined everything.

"But then Luciano had the idea that we could also solve some of our other problems in the Church, ones that had nothing to do with the bank or the Camorra."

"So, you marked cardinals to be killed?" asked Nate.

"No," protested the cardinal. "We never intended for people to be killed. We thought we were just telling the Camorra who they had to worry about. Killing was their idea. Things just got out of our control.

"Luciano said many times that we were riding the tiger, and that we should be careful or we'd end up inside the tiger. But we did not want people to be killed. We just wanted them silenced. We thought the Camorra would just frighten them into silence and make them cooperate."

"But you were playing with Don Franco and the Di Lauro clan. You knew they were violent. What did you expect?" asked Nate.

"I don't know," answered Salazar, sweating. "Can I have some water now?" Nate waved his finger in a gesture of refusal. No.

"What cardinals did you name for the magazine?" asked Nate. "Did you give them other names besides Manning's?"

"Well, let me see," said Salazar evasively. He was not sure what Nate knew. He did not want to reveal too much.

"We were worried about Cardinal Alfonse Lohrman of Santiago. He had a lot of contacts with Chilean bankers. He was very critical of the bank."

"Nobody else?" asked Nate.

"Well, we talked about the cardinal from Milan, Antonio deCapo. He also had many friends, and he knew everything about Italy. Luciano was always suspicious of him. We gave his name to *Panoramio*."

"What about the cardinal from Manila?" asked Nate.

"Who?" said Salazar. "You mean Mody." Salazar was clearly on a first-name basis with most of the other cardinals.

"I don't know anything about his death. I heard that was just a traffic accident. It was just traffic in Manila. That's what we heard."

"Did you mention Cardinal Garcia from Guadalajara?" asked Nate.

"Ignacio? No. Certainly not! Ignacio was a good friend. And certainly no threat to Crepi or me. We all went to the Academia together. We all became diplomats the same year. And he had nothing to do with the bank.

"We heard many stories about what happened to Ignacio. Some people said it was just the drug cartels, but I never heard that from any of my friends in the Zetas. There were other stories—maybe someone in the Church. I don't know."

"Tell me what you know about the murder of Cardinal Manning," said Nate.

"Manning was a friend. I liked him very much. I never wanted him killed. That was *puro* Luciano."

Salazar's friend was not even dead twenty-four hours, and he was already dumping him in the Tiber.

"Luciano had problems with Manning. He said Manning was the biggest threat to the bank. If he came to Rome with his banker friends, they would see immediately what was happening. Then everything would collapse, and Crepi and me with it."

"So, you had him killed?"

"No, no," screamed Salazar. "We had no one killed. We just identified friends and enemies for our friends in the Mafia. We just named the reformers and the papabile. The ones who wanted to change everything."

Salazar was talking with his hands. "The Camorra made decisions on their own. I knew nothing."

"Did you communicate the names through Monsignor Ackerman?" asked Nate.

"Yes, yes. The names of the reformers. We gave them to Ackerman to pass along through journalists or through that bartender friend of his. It was the Camorra who made all the decisions, not us. Luciano and I couldn't run things, much less that pathetic faggot Ackerman." Salazar was derisive. "Ackerman was a fool. He worked for drinks and a few euros."

Nate was increasingly disgusted by Salazar. "It seems like Monsignor Ackerman served you well. Yet you show him very little respect for it."

Salazar shrugged.

"So, who else was involved with all this?" asked Nate.

"Hundreds of people," said Salazar. "Donato opened bank accounts. He received the cash deposits, no questions asked."

"How did you get the money into Italy?" asked Nate.

"We used diplomatic pouches from Latin America and around Europe to bring in cash. Every week at least, sometimes every day. There is a pouch from the larger nunciatures. No one can stop a diplomatic pouch at customs."

"Wait," said Nate. "What do you mean diplomatic pouch?"

"Couriers from the nunciatures carry them, but they have no idea what is inside. Couriers have immunity. Anything can be put in there. Since our letters were coming from cardinals, no one asked any questions. Mostly the pouch carries letters and documents. Sometimes it carries checks for the bank, money that is being routed to missions. But sometimes we could have an envelope full of cash. It could be only ten thousand or twenty thousand dollars, not huge amounts. But if you do that every day, from Colombia or Mexico, it mounts up."

Salazar was almost relishing the details of his operations with Crepi. It was as if he were actually proud of their complex scheme. They were the untouchables.

"Luciano's office was in charge of the Vatican mail. The secretary of state was involved in the diplomatic pouches, but we could control everything with the right people here in Rome. It was flawless," he said with pride, "unless, of course, Interpol or the Federal Reserve asked too many questions."

Nate flinched at the mention of the Federal Reserve. He thought of Brigid. She could have stumbled on to this scheme.

Salazar paused. "May I have some water now?" he asked.

Nate signaled to the Italian policeman, who brought a cup of water. Salazar took a long sip.

"So, tell me who else was involved, besides the diplomatic corps," said Nate.

"Dozens of people were involved," said Salazar. "Employees at the IOR handled deposits. They made loans and advanced expenses for all sorts of charitable and religious projects. It was not too hard to convert the narco dollars to legitimate currency. Once the money is legitimate, you can use it anywhere in the world.

"Many people benefited, so many people knew," said Salazar. "Occasionally, we had to reward some people in the bank who suspected what we were doing. That is nothing unusual here in Italy. We call it *la mancha*."

"How did you get involved with the Camorra? When did it start and why?" Nate was thinking about Signora Luppino in the Vele in Scampia.

"You and Crepi didn't just wake up one day and decide you were going into business with the mob. The Mafia must have had some power over you."

Salazar thought for a moment. A lifetime of silence and hiding is not easily thrown away. "Yes," said Salazar. "They had some power over us."

"Just tell me the whole story," said Nate.

The cardinal hesitated. Nate pulled the other chair up to the table and sat down, his face just inches from Salazar's. "Tell me the truth now, or I'll call Don Franco at the Camorra, tell him where you are, and let him know that you have been very helpful to us."

"So," said Salazar, seeing that he was at an impasse, "Luciano and I graduated from the Academia about forty years ago. Forty-two, to be exact. We had just finished our exams. It is a hard program of study. We were very tired, but we were happy to be finished. We got our first assignments. I was assigned to Kenya. Luciano was going to Mexico, both as assistants to the nuncios. We decided to go to Sicily for a few days of vacation before our assignments began. We had two weeks. We spent one night in Naples, before we took the *traghetto* to Palermo. We were in a good mood. We had dinner on the Lido in Naples, where all the fish restaurants are. We had wine with dinner. We were, as you say, tipsy. The boy waiting on us was very handsome and so polite. He kept saying *'Grazie Monsignore!'* and *'Si Monsignore.'* He was young, but he knew how to flatter, like all of the *Napolitani.* They use flattery to get money out of you, but we loved it. We were young, drunk, and excited about our first diplomatic post."

"All right, I get the picture," said Nate, almost shouting. "What happened next?"

"Well, that boy," said Salazar. "He was so beautiful and young. All night he kept flattering us. I thought he was flirting with us. He really was flirting with us!"

Nate flinched, thinking of the old lady's description of her innocent boy, and said, "Just cut the shit, you asshole, and get on with the story."

For the first time in the interview Salazar looked surprised and scared.

"I told Luciano, 'We should bring this boy with us to Sicilia.' But he said, 'No, Julio. He is too young, even for you.' Luciano knew my weakness." Salazar lowered his eyes. "I still remember his name, Luca. We called his mama over and asked, 'Why don't you let Luca come to Sicilia with us? We can show him the island. It will be a wonderful time.'

"She hesitated. 'He is only seventeen,' she said. But the captain of the ferryboat was sitting close by in the restaurant. He heard us talking and said to her, 'Signora, why not let the boy go with these two *monsignori*? What a wonderful opportunity for the boy.' I think Luca knew him. His mama said to us, 'These people, they run everything here, the restaurants, everything.' So, we said, 'We will take good care of him.' Luca was happy to come with us. It was fine at first. We had beautiful first-class cabins. We were all drinking on the *traghetto*, even the boy. Luciano passed out on his bed. Luca and I kept on drinking. One thing led to another. You know."

Salazar waved his hand in little circles as if gesturing toward something that was obvious.

Nate said, "No, I don't know." He was not going to make this easy for Salazar. He had absolutely no sympathy for pedophiles, none.

"What happened then?" Nate demanded.

"Nothing more," said Salazar. "That was it. Then Luca got up and went out. He fell overboard later. I didn't see him. I was in the cabin."

"You told the police that you saw the boy fall overboard," said Nate.

Salazar suddenly realized that Nate already knew something about that night.

Nate pounded his fist on the table so hard the digital recorder in front of them bounced two inches. He yelled, "I want the goddamned truth!"

Nate opened his briefcase that was sitting beside his chair. He threw the photo of Luca that Mrs. Luppino had given him on the table. Salazar flinched.

"Did you have sex with the boy?" Nate yelled, breathing into Salazar's face, his saliva spraying onto the cardinal's cheeks.

"I got a little rough with him. It was a game."

Nate was disgusted. "A game!" he screamed.

Salazar continued, "Suddenly he just stopped breathing. He stopped moving. I thought he had passed out. I don't know what happened. Then he vomited. It was like a seizure. I didn't know what to do. Like I said, then he stopped breathing. I tried to wake him up. I panicked. I woke Luciano. The boy was dead."

At this point Nate couldn't even look at Salazar. His back was turned to him. "You told the police that he fell overboard."

"That was Luciano. He said, 'We can't tell. We can never tell. We'll be thrown out of the diplomatic corps and the priesthood. We will go to jail. The boy is underage.' Lucio said we should go to the captain. The Camorra ran the *traghetti*. We thought they could fix everything. The captain came. We told him the story. The boy was already dead."

"So, you threw him overboard?" Nate asked with disgust.

"The captain left for a while," continued Salazar. "Then he came back with two men from his crew. He said he could make it look like an accident. One of the men had a camera. He kept taking pictures. The Camorra had pictures of everything. They could release them at any time. They even got a picture of us in the room. The captain said he would take care of things, but that maybe we could do him or his friends a favor one day."

Salazar wiped his brow and looked at Nate, who motioned for him to continue.

"We asked him why they were taking pictures. The captain said for insurance purposes. Then they put the boy's clothing on and carried him out. We followed them up onto the deck. Then they threw the boy's body overboard. We saw it. I think we were the only witnesses. The captain sounded the general alarm, and the ship stopped.

"They sent divers overboard and found the body. The story in the papers said that the boy had been drunk and that he fell overboard and drowned. They made it look like an accident. When the press came to us for the story, that's what we told them.

"We canceled our trip to Sicilia and flew back to Rome from Palermo. The captain told the boy's family that there had been an accident at sea. He took responsibility. The *traghetto* company paid the boy's mother and family. They said it came from insurance. It was in the newspapers." Salazar paused. His face was flushed, and he was almost out of breath. "They did not suspect us. Later, I think, the family was told by the Camorra that their silence would be remembered.

"We escaped, but what a price! *O Dio*, it was a terrible price!"

Salazar was weeping hysterically now. He stopped for a moment.

Nate picked up the cup of water and threw it in the cardinal's face. "Spare me your grief, you asshole. I went down to Naples yesterday. I met Luca's mother. She knows what you did."

Salazar was shaking now. Decades of lies crumbled around him.

"We had no choice," said Salazar. "Luciano and I. We had no choice."

Nate interrupted him. "You had a choice, you piece of shit. We all make choices. You made your choices."

Salazar was almost talking to himself now.

"It was small things, at first. We carried letters in the diplomatic pouch. We ran messages, did errands. No one stops a diplomat and nobody questions a priest, especially not a monsignor from the Vatican. But gradually, they wanted bigger and bigger things.

"They helped us, too. They made donations to church projects. They arranged letters of recommendation. We became prominent with their help and were noticed by our superiors. We moved ahead." Salazar was talking more and more slowly, almost in a trance.

"You moved ahead on the blood of a seventeen-year-old boy who had never been out of Naples," said Nate. "You never sent a word of condolence. You never even visited his mother. You took that innocent young boy, who trusted you because you were priests, and you got him drunk and raped him. Then you threw his body overboard like a piece of trash and lied to the police and to his mother. Then you willingly went to work for the mob. Some messenger of Christ you were!"

Nate slammed the palm of his hand on the table. "You disgust me."

"Every time we thought about getting out," said Salazar, "we got a visit from the Camorra with the pictures from that night. We paid and paid. Now Luciano has paid with his life. They killed him."

Nate realized it was useful for the time being to let Salazar think that Crepi had been killed by the mob. "That's enough for now," said Nate.

"Can you protect me?" pleaded Salazar.

"No promises," said Nate. "It depends on your cooperation. I can tell you right now, though, that you won't be getting immunity. You'll be going away for a long time."

Salazar bristled, his arrogance still not quenched completely. He thought he had one more arrow in his quiver. "You tell your patron O'Toole that he better watch his step. He's made plenty of enemies. I still have friends in the Vatican. His medicine can turn to poison."

Nate thought it was a strange remark, but he attributed it to the bluster of a desperate man.

On his way out of the room, Nate told the policeman, "Put this piece of garbage in a regular cell. His days of privilege are over!"

The policeman smiled and locked the door behind Nate.

Salazar, once a prince of the Church, had become a prisoner of the State.

23

HEAT WAVE

THE BIG APPLE WAS IN THE MIDST OF ITS FIRST SUMMER heat wave. Temperatures soared into the nineties in Central Park. New Yorkers were fleeing to area beaches, pools, and neighborhood fire hydrants.

Brigid Condon arrived into the noontime summer heat from Belgium. Her stay in Brussels had been extended from four days to ten as the work dragged on. Taxi service from New York airports is spotty at best. Whether it's snow in winter or heat in summer, taxis seem to be nonexistent. So she took the Port Authority AirTrain into Manhattan.

When she got to Penn Station, she had to stand in a long taxi queue on 8th Avenue. She had time to check her messages, which she could hardly hear over the roar of midtown traffic.

Brigid was unaware that both men and women gave her second glances as they passed by. She was one of those unself-consciously beautiful people. Despite the heat, she looked cool. Ironically, Brigid did not think about her looks. But Nate did.

The street noise made it impossible to hear her voice mail, but she saw she had a dozen text messages from Nate.

Eventually, a taxi freed up, and the dispatcher opened its door for her. The driver threw her bags in the trunk. Of course, the air-conditioning was not working, and so with the windows open, it was still too noisy to check her messages.

In less than an hour, she was upstairs in their apartment. Finally settled on her bed, she checked her voicemail. There were several messages from Nate.

"Brig, this is Nate. Call me."

"Brig, it's me. Call me."

"Brig, it's your lonely husband. Call me."

"So, where are you? Belgium must be fascinating. Call me."

"What do I have to say to get you to call me?"

Brigid decided to call him. She looked up the number for the Columbus Hotel in Rome. European phones have that funny long ring. It even sounded far away. A few seconds later, she got through to his room.

Somebody in Rome picked up the phone and said, "*Pronto.*"

"Nate, is that you?" said Brigid, perplexed. She didn't think Nate knew any Italian.

"*Si, sono io,*" said Nate, recognizing her voice and deciding to have a little fun with her.

"Speak English," said Brigid.

"*Non parlo inglese,*" said Nate.

"Speak English or I'm hanging up," persisted Brigid.

"OK," said Nate. "That's really the extent of my Italian anyway. After two weeks here I'm still at sea, but I'm beginning to find my way around. What's up in New York?"

"It's sweltering here. Wish I were back in Belgium," said Brigid.

"Did you get to Bruges?" Nate asked.

"Yes, it was very interesting. I met a nun there."

"Wait, wait, wait. What did you say? You, *you*, met a *nun*? Will wonders never cease? How did this all happen that you met a nun?"

"Are you sitting down? I even went to Mass. At least it was a sort of Mass. A Mass without a priest. This Church of yours has sides I knew nothing about."

"I'm finding out the same thing here. What are you doing now?" said Nate.

"Running a bath. Then meeting Drew and Sophie for drinks at Papillon."

"Say hello to Sophie for me and watch out for Drew."

"Well, I am lonely." They both laughed.

"Come to Rome, babe. It's beautiful here this time of year. And we can go to the funeral of the pope. That's not an offer you get every day."

"Well, you are wearing me down. How can I resist a dead pope?"

"I'm pulling out all the stops. Even a dead pope," said Nate. "Is it settled, then?"

"Hmm . . . Let me get back to you on this one. Throwing in the dead pope was a good play on your part. By the way, how is the investigation going?"

"OK, I guess. But I'm learning a lot about the Church. Stuff I wish I never knew. People say if you come to Rome, you'll lose your faith. But you should come anyway. Rome would be good for us."

"OK. You're starting to convince me. Let's talk more tomorrow. You know I love you, Nate," said Brigid.

"I know. I love you too, babe. Ciao," said Nate.

When they hung up, Brigid stared at the phone for a few seconds. Jet lag was catching up with her. She needed a hot bath and a good nap before she would be ready to meet her friends at the bar. She lay down and was asleep in seconds.

An hour later, Brigid was up, dressed, and walking over to Papillon. She was an extrovert, so being with friends always gave her energy. She was anxious to share her experience in Belgium.

Drew and Sophie were sitting under the clock at the bar. By the time Brigid arrived, the evening happy hour crowd had just about filled the place. Drew stood up and hugged Brigid when she found them at the barstools.

"Don't get too close, Drew," joked Brigid. "Nate told me to watch out for you. He's in Rome, so he can't fight back."

"Ah, when have I ever listened to him?" smiled Drew.

"Never," said Brigid. She turned to Sophie and gave her a socialite's kiss on the cheek.

Sophie flattered Brigid. "Oh, Brig, despite a transatlantic flight and a New York heat wave, you still look fabulous as ever!"

"Thank you, darling Sophie," said Brigid. "You're insincere as always, but I love your lies." Brigid's conversation with her New York friends was a little like a Noel Coward script—arch sophisticated.

The bartender came over and smiled at the ladies.

"I'm going to make it easy for you," said Drew. "We're all drinking the same thing: double shots of Glenfarclas, straight up." The bartender nodded. Such an expensive Scotch meant a good tip.

Sophie waved to catch the waiter's eye. "That's Glenfarclas for these two, but just tonic with lime for me."

Brigid raised an eyebrow quizzically. Maybe Sophie is pregnant, she thought. For a moment she felt a twinge of envy.

"So, tell us about Belgium," said Sophie. "Was the chocolate wonderful?"

"Chocolate is always wonderful," smiled Brigid, "but I'll tell you the real wonderful—monk's beer! I went out for a beer with a nun, at a Trappist monastery, if you can believe that!"

"Imagine," marveled Sophie, "you, the champion lapsed Catholic, out drinking with a nun at a monastery. And you thought the Age of Miracles was over."

"Did you have a conversion experience over there?" asked Drew.

"Not exactly," said Brigid, "but it was very interesting. I went to Mass in Bruges with a colleague from the EU Central Bank. That whole town is a medieval jewel. You should go there sometime."

"What's there?" said Sophie.

"Lots of old houses and canals and art," said Brigid. "Sort of like Venice. But the most interesting thing I saw there was a medieval women's compound they called a Béguinage.

"Did you know there were female-only communities in the Middle

Ages? They were single women, but not nuns. They lived together in walled compounds. Some of those communities lasted seven hundred years. They supported themselves with handicrafts. They kicked the men out at sundown. Just beautiful, really."

"Sounds like a delicious idea," said Sophie, looking at Drew. "Most nights, anyway."

The bartender brought the drinks.

"So, tell me about this nun who took you drinking," said Drew.

"Her name is Miriam, Sister Miriam. I don't know. There was just this immediate connection. I felt drawn to her, like a guru or advisor or something. She was calm and pleasant, not angry like a lot of the people here."

"What does she do?" asked Sophie.

"I don't know exactly," answered Brigid, taking a sip of her Scotch. "She's in charge of the convent in Bruges. They work with the poor and local battered women. I was surprised they even have poor people in Belgium, with their social safety net. Her convent has a drop-in center for migrants and gypsies, too."

"Sounds like good work," said Drew over the din of the bar.

"I really liked Miriam," continued Brigid. "She reminded me of my grandmother in a way, a kind person. She was like the nuns I had in school, smart, straightforward—nobody's fool. I liked her."

The bar was getting oppressively noisy, too noisy for conversation. "Let's try the tables outside on the sidewalk," suggested Drew. They squeezed their way through the crowd, trying not to spill their expensive Scotch. They found an empty table. Despite the heat, it was more pleasant.

Brigid picked up the thread of their conversation. "The most amazing thing was, we had Mass at the convent and there was no priest. Miriam said they can't get priests, because there just aren't any. So, they have been saying Mass by themselves for years—no men. How about that?" Brigid was clearly energized just talking about her experience.

"Well, are they thinking of starting a new church or something?" asked Drew.

"If they do, I'll join," said Sophie. "A women's church."

"No, it's not like that," said Brigid. "They're not angry at the old Church. They're just practical. Women can't wait around for men in collars to bring them communion.

"They don't feel they have left the Church. They say the Church has just ignored them. Anyway, I felt more at home with those women than in any parish here in New York."

They all paused for a moment, enjoying the warm June evening. They did some people watching for a while. A mime came by and entertained them with the old "prisoner of the glass" routine. Drew ordered them some bottled water and a plate of cheeses.

When the mime left, Brigid picked up her story again. "I met somebody else over there," she said. "His name is Bernard Willebroeck, an angry ex-priest. Not that he doesn't have good reason to be angry. His nephew was molested by a priest. Even this guy's own bishop confessed to pedophilia."

Drew and Sophie seemed genuinely shocked. "How could anyone continue on with the Church after that?' observed Sophie.

"I don't know," answered Brigid. "This guy runs a group called New Church. I read some of their statements. They gave me the shivers. It goes to show you how divided this Church really is."

"You haven't talked this much about religion in years," observed Drew.

"Well, people evolve. Isn't that what Vice President Biden said once about gay marriage? Seems to me it's only the rigid or the stupid who don't change," answered Brigid.

"Well," said Drew, "tell that to the Catholic Church, right? They don't care that they are wrong, so long as they are consistently wrong."

Brigid and Sophie smiled at Drew's acid tongue.

"Do you think a new pope will make a difference?" Sophie asked. "You said Nate is in Rome. Was he there when the pope died? I didn't know his law firm had business over there."

"They don't," said Brigid. "Oddly enough, he's working for the Vatican. The way Nate explains it, Pope Thomas asked for his help."

"Wow! He knew the pope!" Sophie exclaimed.

"No, I'm kidding, but that was how Nate put it to me when he explained why he was taking time from his firm to spend who knows how long in Italy. He reports to a cardinal, some Boston connection, who asked him to look into the killing of Cardinal Manning. It may be linked to other killings. It's all very murky. I don't know much about it, really." Brigid took a drink of the bottled water. She realized that perhaps she should say less about what Nate was doing. All that talking might actually be putting him in danger.

"Well, when is he coming back?" asked Sophie.

"I don't know. He's been after me to go over there. He's still working on the investigation, but everything will stop for the pope's funeral. It will be something to see. I just don't know. I can't just drop everything and chase Nate around the world. But I do miss him . . . "

"Oh, just go," said Sophie. "You have vacation coming, don't you? June is a slow month in the legal business. You'll never have this chance again to see Rome with your husband.

"Besides," Sophie added, in an intimate girlfriend voice, "It would be good for the two of you. A little hot romance never hurt a marriage."

"Maybe you're right, Sophie," said Brigid.

"Yeah," said Drew, "that's how my first marriage went cold. Then Soph came along."

"Oh, shut up, Drew," said Sophie with a wave of her hand. The conversation was girls only.

Once their Scotch glasses were empty and the cheese was gone, it was time to go.

"We're going to Craft for dinner," said Sophie. "It's a special evening. We have something to celebrate." She sent a look and a small smile over to Drew. "And it's our anniversary, too. June wedding, you know. Would you like to join us?"

"No," said Brigid, "I feel enough of a third wheel here as it is. It was fun meeting you guys for drinks. Go have one of those famous veal meatballs for me. I'm still a little jet-lagged. I think I'm just going to turn in early."

"OK," said Drew, "but do think about Rome."

"Yes," added Sophie. "Go."

Drew and Sophie walked off into the humid June evening, arm in arm. Brigid watched them leave, a little envious. Then she thought, celebrating? Maybe they are expecting.

Warm summer evenings often bring people out onto the streets, but on this particular evening, even diehard New Yorkers were choosing air-conditioning over alfresco dining. The sidewalk café was emptying out.

Brigid headed off in the opposite direction from Sophie and Drew. As she left the café, she noticed a man sitting alone at a corner table. He was dressed completely in black, with long blond hair pulled tight in a ponytail behind his ears. He was smoking, which is forbidden in New York, even outside. She also noticed that he was drinking coffee. It seemed odd for such a warm evening. Like most New Yorkers, she deliberately avoided eye contact.

Brigid headed east on 54th. From the restaurant it was only a fifteen-minute walk back to their apartment on Park Avenue. Brigid prided herself on being a real New Yorker, fearless and confident. She was rarely intimidated by the city. But tonight, she felt differently. Despite the warm evening, she felt a chill, or rather a shudder. It was a sinister presence, similar to what she experienced in her brief encounter with the ex-priest in Bruges.

As she stopped for the light at the corner of 54th and Madison, she turned slightly to her right, almost brushing her shoulder against the man with the ponytail. Suddenly, she was gripped by a fear like she had never experienced before. The man lifted his hand in a threatening gesture toward her. She instinctively jerked back away from him, thinking he was about to hit her or worse. Instead, he pointed his finger at her.

His dark eyes locked onto hers, and with the slightest accent, maybe French or Spanish, he said, "You and your husband should consider this a warning—stop asking questions and digging into matters that could prove very dangerous for the both of you."

With that, the ponytailed man turned right and headed down Madison Avenue away from her.

Brigid's heart was racing. She hadn't said anything. For a moment she was affixed to the pavement, and she stood there unaware that the light had turned green in her crosswalk. Crossing Madison, she quickly reached Park Avenue and almost broke into a jog as she approached her building. She smiled at the reassuring presence of Gus, their doorman.

Back in the safety of her apartment, Brigid was exhausted but had trouble sleeping. She needed to hear Nate's voice. There were times in her life that she really needed him. And this was one of them. She also needed to tell him to be careful over there in Rome.

Nate answered, half-asleep.

"I'm coming to Rome," she said.

"Really? You're coming to see me?"

"Of course," said Brigid. "You and the dead pope, in that order."

24

THE BRUGES CONNECTION

ON HER FIRST FULL DAY IN ROME, BRIGID CAME DOWN TO breakfast, dressed for the summer heat in a sleek, silk blue shirtdress.

Nate was already at a table in the veranda restaurant overlooking the courtyard garden. He was reading the *International New York Times* and poking at half of a grapefruit. "Wow," he said, looking up from his paper. "You look great. This dining room looks a whole lot better with you in it."

Brigid smiled as she slipped into the chair opposite him. "Flattery is always appreciated, even when we know it's flattery," she said, adding "*grazie.*"

A white-coated waiter brought coffee and orange juice to their table.

After nearly a month in Rome, Nate had gotten used to the Hotel Columbus, with its frescoed vaulted ceilings, torch-lit courtyard, and traffic noise outside. He hardly even noticed the endless parade of tourists going past the front entrance on Via della Conciliazione as they headed to St. Peter's.

But to Brigid, all the sights and sounds were delightfully exotic. Before she touched her coffee, she paused for a few seconds, drinking in the setting. The stuccoed walls, the potted palms, the sunlight on the courtyard below, the sound of water from the fountain dripping into the pool, all created an air of timelessness.

Brigid could almost see Cardinal Giulio della Rovere stepping out of his coach in the courtyard. She wondered if he had interviewed Michelangelo in the formal rooms outside the restaurant.

The Eternal City does cast a spell on visitors, especially in the spring and summer. Brigid hadn't anticipated that she would be so impressed by Rome. In fact, she was enthralled.

She took the linen napkin from the table and put it on her lap. "Well, honey, we are in the same city again," she said to Nate. "I never thought you'd get me to Rome, but you did."

"Me and the death of a pope got you here," said Nate. "It took some doing, but I'm glad you're here."

The waiter returned to their table. Brigid spoke to him in English, ordering a cappuccino, a pastry, and a boiled egg. The waiter, well accustomed to American breakfast tastes, answered, "*Eccelente!*" With a slight bow, he glided away.

"What do you have planned for today?" asked Brigid.

"I'm working on my presentation at my temporary office. I'm also going to make reservations for our excursion to Orvieto. Are you going off to tour the city?"

Brigid remembered Sister Miriam. She had mentioned she was going to be in Rome about this time. She needed to warn her about the ponytailed man.

"Maybe later. But first I'd like to try to get in touch with Sister Miriam, the nun I met in Belgium. She mentioned she would be here for a meeting at her mother house."

"There must be a lot of mother houses in Rome," said Nate. "Do you know which one?"

"Not sure, but she belongs to a community that was founded in Belgium. I don't know their name."

"I'll have my assistant check it out," said Nate. "Sandra likes to solve puzzles." Nate got up from the table, took his cell phone out of his jacket pocket, and went out into the hallway to make the call.

After a couple of minutes he came back into the dining room. "Sandra will check it out for you and call you within the hour." Nate liked being a resource for her, even for so small a matter. As Nate sat down at the table, the waiter arrived with their cappuccino and breakfast.

"Thank you for taking care of that," said Brigid. "And for making all this possible."

They ate for a few moments in silence. Nate took a drink of his cappuccino and handed her the paper. "There's a lot on the pope's funeral on page one. We'll probably hear of nothing else for the next few days."

Finishing his breakfast, he stood up and came around to her side of the table. He leaned over to kiss her on the cheek. "I'm so glad you are here," he said.

"I love being here with you," she answered, kissing him back. She watched him walk away through the dining room. The thought occurred to her that he was just as handsome as George Clooney in *The American*.

Soon after, Brigid received a call from Sister Miriam in her room. "That was fast!"

"Your husband's assistant is quite efficient," said Miriam. "I'm so thrilled you are here. Why don't we meet this morning? We could go for a walk in the Villa Borghese gardens."

Brigid thought this would be a good time to mention the ponytailed man who followed her in New York. Miriam listened without interrupting as Brigid relayed the details of her strange encounter.

"Miriam, it's difficult for me to believe that all this is connected in some way to that group in Bruges. Maybe more is going on here than just hurt feelings and angry Catholics."

Brigid took a deep breath. "Sister, we have so much to catch up on."

There was a moment of silence. Then Miriam stated, "Take a taxi to Piazza del Popolo, and I will meet you at the top of the steps to the Pincio, where the park begins."

* * *

Brigid got a cab at the front door of the hotel. Traffic was terrible. She could have walked in the hour it took her to go a couple of miles. From the circular piazza, she climbed the mountain of steps. Miriam was waiting there at the edge of the Piazzalle Napoleone, a huge promenade where Roman mothers walked their babies in strollers and little boys bounced soccer balls off their heads to each other.

The two embraced and let out a dignified squeal.

"Brigid, so good to see you here in Rome," said Miriam.

"Oh, Sister, I am so thrilled to be here," said Brigid.

Sister Miriam looked almost exactly the same as she had back in Bruges: plain light brown dress, sensible walking shoes, black shoulder bag. Brigid noticed again the simple little cross, pinned to the left shoulder of her dress. Apart from the cross, you would not have known that she was a nun. You would have figured that she was a poor, but dignified, older woman, which of course she was.

Brigid and Miriam stopped to admire the view from the Pincio. A hundred feet below they watched the people crossing the Piazza del Popolo and circling the huge obelisk in the piazza center. Off in the distance they could see the huge dome of St. Peter's set against an azure sky. It was warm but not hot. Behind them were the smells of the pretzel vendors. The ice cream vendors could be heard ringing the bells on their carts, selling Algida ice cream bars.

There could not have been a clearer or more vibrant morning. The two women were delighted to just be in each other's company. They stood there in silence, taking in the moment.

After a while Miriam said, "Let's walk back into the park. There is a little folly called the Temple of Aesculapius that I want you to see. It looks like a miniature Greek temple. We can sit and talk over there."

"Who was Aesculapius?" asked Brigid.

"A minor Greek god, I think," said Miriam. "I remember on a pilgrimage I took to Turkey there were centers of healing dedicated to him. He was the Greek god of healing, especially of the emotionally disturbed. Maybe that's why they built a temple to him here in the park. People come here for a little peace."

The two women walked arm in arm. There were too many tourists around to speak of Bruges, so Miriam continued the small talk.

"Tell me about that husband of yours," said Miriam. "When am I going to meet him?"

"Soon enough, Miriam. If you are going to the pope's funeral, maybe we could go over together."

"That would be great. I hate being in big crowds by myself. Most of our sisters here in Rome are too elderly to go to an event that big."

"Fine," said Brigid. "Then it's settled. Come by our hotel tomorrow before the funeral. We are at the Columbus. It's right by the Vatican."

"It's a famous hotel," said Miriam. "I always wanted to see the inside. That would be great."

There was a café in the park. They grabbed a coffee and took it to one of the nearby tables, in the shade of a tree.

"What do you think will happen in the conclave?" asked Brigid.

"I don't hope for much," said Miriam thoughtfully. "They don't have much to choose from.

"Pope Thomas was a well-intentioned man, but weak. He wanted to reform things, but he was overwhelmed. I met him once a few years ago. People were impressed by his simplicity, but I think the curia here is so entrenched that it was all too much for him." Miriam looked at Brigid. "What are you hoping for? Anything?"

"I don't know, really," said Brigid. "I don't feel like I'm a Catholic most of the time, but somehow when it comes to the election of a new pope, I suddenly care about what's going on. Seems strange that in the twenty-first century there's not a single woman who has a voice in choosing the leader of a billion people."

"Not just strange," said Miriam. "Immoral."

Brigid chuckled and nodded. To a schoolgirl from Long Island, it still seemed strange for a nun to talk that way about the Church.

"The conservatives in the Church don't think we should even get our feet washed on Holy Thursday," said Miriam. "They certainly are not going to let a woman into the room when it comes to voting for the pope."

"Well, the world is leaving them behind," said Brigid. "Nobody really cares what they do. Among my friends in New York, half of them were raised as Catholics, but almost nobody pays any attention to what the Church says."

"Nobody but your husband," said Miriam.

"True," said Brigid. "But this investigation may be weakening even his ties to the Church. He seems a little bit repulsed by what he's seeing. I guess the closer you get to the internal workings of the Church, the more you dislike it. Sort of like that ex-priest we met in Belgium. He certainly was turned off by the Church."

"Not turned off," said Miriam. "Angry. There is a difference. Bernard is certainly not indifferent to the Church. He hates it.

"By the way, I went to a meeting in Bruges the other day. Bernard and others from New Church were there. Bernard and I didn't speak. In fact, he avoided me. But some of New Church people let me know they were not happy about our visit. They especially are not happy that your husband is making inquiries into their business. They seemed to know all about it. After the meeting, some people told me some disturbing things about Bernard. Your husband might want to know about them.

"I always thought New Church was just talk, but now I don't know.

"The difference is, your friends in New York just walk away from the Church. Bernard wants to throw a firebomb on his way out the door," Miriam said as she finished her coffee.

"Why is he so angry?" asked Brigid.

"Let's walk around the pond a little," said Miriam, checking to see if anyone was eavesdropping. "I'll tell you what I know of his story. Maybe it would be useful to your husband in his inquiries."

The two women got up and walked along the carefully tended gravel path toward the little pond. On an island there was a perfectly round little reproduction of a Greek temple dedicated to the Greek god Aesculapius. They found a bench near the pond and sat down.

Miriam looked again to see if anyone was watching them. When she saw they were alone, she stated softly, "Evidently our visit really upset Bernard. He wouldn't even speak to me the other day. But once he found out that he was the target of Nate's investigation, it made him livid. He even called the convent and told me that you and your husband had better stay away."

"Do you think he is dangerous?" asked Brigid.

"No one is angrier at the Church than an ex-priest. His anger has roots that go way back," said Miriam.

"I've known Bernard for years. When he was young, he was one of the brightest and most attractive young priests in the diocese of Bruges. I knew his family. His mother was very devout. He was one of eleven children. He wanted to be like Damien of Molokai. He was full of idealism. He was going to change the world, and he thought the Church was his vehicle to do it.

"He always wore his hair long. He was very handsome and charismatic. As they say, all the women wanted to be with him, and all the men wanted to be like him."

"I know the type," said Brigid, thinking about Nate.

"In those days," continued Miriam, "devout Belgium had way too many priests. It seems hard to believe today, but we used to say that the principal export of Belgium was priests and nuns. You may have heard of a famous movie called *The Nun's Story*. That was about a Belgian nun who went to our colony in the Congo. To Catholic youth in Belgium, raised on pious stories of great adventure in the Belgian Congo, there could be no better place to set about the liberation and reformation of the world. Bernard finished his seminary training in the early seventies, just after the Second Vatican Council, about ten years after Belgium gave up its colony in the Congo. Reform was in the air. He requested permission for an assignment in the missions. Even though war was raging down there, the Bishop of Bruges gave him permission to go."

"Did something happen down there to make him so angry?" asked Brigid.

"I think so," said Miriam. "I only know the rumors, but since our visit, I have made some more inquiries."

She looked into the distance.

"Like many young priests in the missions, he soon grew very lonely. He became very close to a beautiful African woman who had studied medicine in Belgium. I'm told that her European name was Immacule. I think there was a pregnancy. She was out in the bush working as a women's doctor. She did not get good medical care herself. The bishop, who later became a cardinal, demanded that Bernard leave the country to avoid scandal. I know Bernard was angry about that. I've heard him say as much. He said that if he had been an African priest, there would have been no problem. The bishops did not expect the Africans to live their vow of celibacy. It was well known that many African priests had women and families. But with Europeans, it was a different story. They were expected to remain celibate, and certainly not to share their bed with an African woman."

"What happened to the woman and the baby?" asked Brigid.

"I hear that Immacule died in childbirth, preeclampsia, probably. The baby survived and was given up for adoption. Bernard went back and searched for the child, but did not find it. A boy, I think."

"That's quite a story," said Brigid. "I can see why he is so angry, especially at bishops and the Church."

"But that's only half the story," said Miriam, raising her hand as if taking an oath. "When Bernard came back to Bruges in the eighties, he was assigned to a parish where one of his sisters lived. After a few years, Bernard discovered that his nephew had been molested by the parish priest. Bernard was ready to kill the man.

"But instead, he went to the bishop about it. The bishop told him to keep quiet, and he would do something about it. However, nothing was done. The molesting priest was just moved to another parish."

"It's become a familiar story," said Brigid.

"About ten years ago, it came out in the papers that the bishop had been molesting his own nephew during those years when Bernard had gone to him. The bishop's nephew is now suing the diocese of Bruges and the bishop. The bishop appeared to think it was all in good fun. He said the boy appeared to like it at the time. That it was just rough play."

"Wow," said Brigid. "What happened to the bishop?"

"Nothing," said Miriam. "He just resigned in disgrace, but so far nothing. No criminal charges. The case is still pending, and the bishop still receives his pension.

"Bernard is in his early seventies now. He left the priesthood more than twenty years ago, but I don't think his anger has ever cooled. He is bitter about the woman he loved and the double standard for African priests, but he is especially bitter about his nephew and the hypocritical bishop."

"Do you think he would do anything violent?" Brigid was suddenly concerned about Nate.

"Well," said Miriam, "Bernard and his group have been much more aggressive in the past year. They have held more demonstrations. They threw eggs at the bishops when they came out of a meeting. They have disrupted some Masses and probably sprayed graffiti on Church buildings. Last year, they disrupted the Holy Blood procession in Bruges with some street theater and loud speakers playing hip-hop music."

"What is the Holy Blood procession?" asked Brigid, incredulous at the strange arcana of the Catholic world.

"A lot of medieval silliness, if you ask me," said Miriam. "The bishop parades around Bruges with a vial that they claim contains Christ's blood. They keep it in a church off the town square in Bruges. It's big for tourist business in Bruges."

"Oh, that's right. Maria mentioned that," said Brigid. "Has Bernard's group ever been charged with anything serious?"

"Not so far," answered Miriam. "They have been arrested for nuisance things like the Holy Blood procession. However, I wouldn't put it past them. In the past year, there were some Church arsons in parishes around Belgium and Ireland where there had been pedophile priests. Remember when we mentioned this to him? He said he was cleared of all charges." Miriam paused for a second and continued. "Somebody even planted a bomb in the cathedral in Bruges, but it was found before it exploded. Bernard's group is getting increasingly angry, and they're funded by someone. Probably someone from outside Belgium. Bernard has many close ties to people in Italy. He comes here frequently. So, I wouldn't say it was impossible that he would be violent."

Brigid nodded. "Maybe I can find out who is funding them," she said.

Miriam paused a moment and lowered her voice. "About a year ago, the old cardinal in Kinshasa, Patrice Musaku, who had transferred Bernard out of the Congo, died in a fire. Some people told me that Bernard seemed very pleased when he heard about it and that he seemed to know many details about the fire. Nothing was ever proven. I hate to even think such a thing, but I wouldn't say it was beyond the realm of possibility." Brigid nodded.

The women sat in silence for a few seconds, contemplating the seriousness of the charge. They watched a school of ducks paddle past on the little pond nearby. The ducks swam out to the little island on which stood the faux temple of Aesculapius. The ducks ignored the sign forbidding their climb at the water's edge, *Vietato Salire*, and hopped up on the shore of the little island.

"Look at that," said Miriam to Brigid. "Even mother birds know how to protect their young. It's hard to believe that Holy Mother the Church didn't protect her young.

"Maybe if there were some women bishops or priests, the Church would have a different attitude about this," said Miriam. "The fact is, the men who get to be bishops these days are more worried about protecting their careers and the Church, as an institution, than they are about protecting their people. For them it is all about career and power. It's not about shepherding. And you know, Brigid, as strange as it may seem, Bernard has always been a shepherd. I think he has an almost pathological hatred for shepherds who have betrayed their people.

"The scandal that started in America added fuel to the fire that has been burning inside Bernard for all these years." Miriam paused in reflection.

It was getting a little cool sitting in the shade. Brigid suggested they walk around the park. They headed in the direction of the great riding center called the Galoppatoio. The Italian national police were practicing for an equestrian show there, vested in their formal livery. The two women joined a small crowd watching the white horses, the policemen in their red plumed hats and their blue capes with scarlet lining. It was a mixture of color, elegance, and danger.

Brigid remarked, "If this is typical of Rome, it is not hard to see where the Church gets its love of show. It seems ingrained pretty deep in the Italian culture. Look at these policemen."

"Have you been to Rome before?" asked Miriam.

"No," said Brigid.

"Well, you should try to see some of the sights while you're here. Not just the Church stuff, but the historical things like the Roman Forum and the Coliseum. See the catacombs and the churches of the early martyrs. When you study history, you find out that women have been central to the life of the Church all the way along. Many of the martyrs were women. The early house churches were dependent on women."

"What is this meeting that brings you to Rome?" asked Brigid.

"It's called a general chapter for my religious congregation," said Miriam.

"What does that mean?" asked Brigid.

"Well, each province sends a representative to this meeting every few years to discuss our religious community."

"I thought you were a nun," said Brigid.

"I am," said Miriam. "A religious nun."

"Aren't all nuns religious?" asked Brigid.

"Well, what we mean by religious is that we are women who live out in the world, but adopted a religious rule for our lives. We do many different jobs, but we all keep the rule of prayer and self-discipline. Strictly, a nun is someone who lives in a cloistered convent."

"Are there many women left in your religious community?" asked Brigid. Like any good lawyer, she picked up quickly on terminology.

"Not so many anymore," said Miriam. "Each year we are fewer and fewer. I guess we'll die out soon. Some laywomen will have to carry on our witness and life. But something new will come along. There will always be women who want to live together and pray and do good work.

"Shall we keep walking over to the Spanish Steps?" asked Miriam.

"That would be wonderful," said Brigid, who was enjoying her tour and just being with Miriam. "I read in a guidebook that Keats and Shelley used to go to a coffee bar at the foot of the Spanish Steps. We could get lunch there."

The two women wandered off into the street theater that is Rome.

25

NEW PENTECOST

ASKED TO DESCRIBE THE CATHOLIC CHURCH, JAMES JOYCE answered, "Here comes everybody."

Pope Thomas's funeral was on a Saturday, the ninth day after his death. It was a collection of everybody. Heads of state, diplomats, and monarchy were all mixed in with pickpockets, gypsies, street sweepers, and journalists. Just about everybody found a place in St. Peter's Square, even the unbeliever. Whatever one's faith, it was a great spectacle. Romans love the circus.

Nate had received tickets from Cardinal O'Toole's office for the funeral, but their passes only got Nate, Brigid, and Sister Miriam up to the first row of barricades at the foot of the steps leading into St. Peter's Basilica. They squeezed their way up to a spot along one of the wooden barriers in the front of the piazza. Behind them, a crush of humanity sandwiched them all together, leading the nun to remark, "It's certainly nice to meet you, Nate, but I didn't expect it to be this intimate."

Their little pied-a-terre was just to the right of the main entrance of St. Peter's Basilica, in front of the statue of St. Paul. If they looked up at the façade of the great church, they could see one of the giant clocks that faced the square. Apart from mere symmetrical balance, there is really no reason the façade of the Church should have two clocks. Ironically, they never show the same time. One is usually ten minutes ahead of the other. They show that the Church is completely unconcerned with the correct time. Just like the Queen of Hearts in *Alice in Wonderland*, the time is whatever time they say it is. If you asked the cardinals and bishops processing into the funeral, they would say the correct time was the twelfth century.

Nate had promised to hold a spot for the Tracys, who had just arrived in Rome the night before, but finding it impossible to keep his promise, Nate called Tracy on his cell phone. "Bill, we're in front of the statue of St. Paul, but I don't know how you will find us in this crowd. We'll connect with you later at the hotel."

"OK," said Tracy. "We're too tired to push our way to the front. See you later."

Papal funerals are held in St. Peter's Square to allow half a million people to attend. While everyone may be physically present in the square, they do not all have the same experience. Some can see and hear virtually nothing, while others are caught up in the details of the liturgy.

A pope's funeral, while gigantic in scale, is basically the same funeral that any Catholic receives. There are, however, a few odd wrinkles.

For one thing, the cardinals vest themselves in red. At most funerals, the priest wears white or purple or, in days gone by, black. The red signifies the blood of the martyrs, an irony that escapes most cardinals.

Oddly, there is no pall placed on the papal casket as there would be at most Catholic funerals, where the casket is draped with a white cloth intended to signify Christian baptism. Papal caskets are bare, following a much more ancient tradition, intended as a sign of simplicity.

On top of the pope's casket, the presiding cardinal places an open book of the gospels, a reminder that the pope was called to preach the gospel.

Customarily, the pope often gets three coffins. First, a simple wooden coffin, made of cypress, is used at the funeral. Then, just before the interment in the crypt under St. Peter's, the wooden coffin is placed inside another made of zinc, meant to prevent tampering. Finally, both coffins are placed into a third casket made of walnut, which is engraved with the deceased pope's coat of arms.

The simple cypress casket is meant to show that at least in death, if not in life, the pope was a poor man. When Catholics stand before their maker, they would much rather that God think of them as poor than rich. After all, as the Bible states, "It is easier for a camel to go through the eye of a needle than for a rich man to enter the kingdom of God."

Just about the last prayer said at every Catholic funeral recalls the story of the poor man, Lazarus, who starved to death at the gate of the rich man. In the story told by Jesus, Lazarus went like a shot to the bosom of Abraham in heaven, while the rich man suffered the torments of hell. In the mind of Jesus, poor was better than rich.

*   *   *

The funeral for Pope Thomas took place on a splendid June morning, with hardly a puff of cloud in the sky. A breeze cooled the crowd standing in the bright sunshine. It was a perfect Roman morning.

Brigid, Nate, and Miriam could hardly make out the words coming from the loudspeakers, but they did have the benefit of little booklets with the prayers and readings, distributed by the Vatican Press. Readings were in French, Portuguese, or Swahili, as well as Italian, English, and Greek. One thing about the Catholic Church; it really is catholic.

Once Mass began, the crowd settled down, but communion time was chaos.

Up on the platform, where the royalty and heads of state were seated with the cardinals, people lined up in orderly queues to receive communion. But down in the "mosh pit" of St. Peter's Square, the crowd was much more Italian, every man for himself. Nuns in habits were the most dangerous. Under their skirts, they carried concealed umbrellas, which they wielded like weapons as they approached the body of Christ.

Observing the scramble, Brigid said to Sister Miriam, "I thought papal Masses would be more reverent."

Miriam smiled. "Reverence at a papal liturgy is more an aspiration than a fact."

Hundreds of priests fanned out into the crowd to distribute the Eucharist. Like those around her, Brigid went for communion. Nate was surprised to see her receive the host. But then, everybody else received communion, including Hollywood starlets and atheist politicians, who were notoriously opposed to the Church back home. There seems to be a special dispensation for papal liturgies.

Giving communion to half a million people takes a long time. During the interlude, the temperature dropped and the wind picked up.

Even before all the priests had returned from distributing communion, the Dean of the College of Cardinals intoned the prayers of final commendation and farewell. Then the patriarchs of the Byzantine churches came forward in their crowns and incensed the body of the pope with clouds of smoke. Just as they concluded their ritual, a microburst of wind swept into the piazza with the force of a mini tornado. The more pious in the crowd might have thought it was the movement of the Holy Spirit.

The swirling wind nearly leveled the row of elderly cardinals lined up for the final commendation. Lifting their vestments over their heads, the wind sent their miters flying through the crowd. Their little red zucchettos followed the miters, airborne like silken Frisbees.

Blinded by the wind, with their vestments wrapped around their heads, the bishops staggered around like a flock of drunken penguins.

Little children in the crowd caught the miters and the zucchettos and put them on their heads, pretending to be bishops. These newly minted "bishops" began dancing around with their fancy hats on their heads. Embarrassed parents grabbed at the children and tried to get the miters back.

As quickly as the wind had arisen, it died away. Then the heavens above the square opened and let loose a drenching downpour, sending the crowd of half a million running for cover. The people in the best seats, like the diplomats and the heads of state, were in the worst position to find cover, since they were far from Bernini's colonnade. Umbrellas proved useless. In a few minutes, the high and the mighty were soaked to the bone.

The papal casket was hurried inside, while the cardinals and patriarchs, drenched to the skin, struggled to walk in their clinging vestments, heavy with rainwater.

Nate, Brigid, and Miriam were so quickly soaked that it was useless to run. Besides, at her age, Sister Miriam was not about to sprint anywhere. They let everyone else flee ahead of them and walked in the rain the half mile or so back to the Columbus Hotel.

Once in their suite upstairs, all three changed into hotel bathrobes. They sent Sister Miriam's simple brown dress to the hotel laundry to be dried and ironed and had hot tea sent up to the room as they sat reviewing the events of the morning.

"Well," said Brigid, "every time Nate goes to a funeral, something dramatic happens. At least no one died this time."

"Maybe the Holy Spirit was trying to get our attention," said Miriam. "The scripture says that God makes the rain fall on the just and the unjust." She was positively giddy with the irony of the events of the morning.

As soon as Miriam's dress was returned, all dried and pressed, she prepared to leave. "I want to get home to the mother house and share this moment with my sisters. We have been praying a long time for a movement of the Holy Spirit; I think we got it today. It makes for a wonderful story."

As she went out the door, Miriam said, "You know, I think this is a new Pentecost." She kissed them both. "Ciao," said Miriam cheerfully. "Thanks for a wonderful morning." She laughed to herself as she went down the long hotel corridor.

Nate and Brigid found themselves alone in the room.

Nate asked, "More tea?"

Brigid raised her eyebrows and said, "I have something else in mind."

* * *

Around 3:00 p.m., the phone in their room rang. Nate picked it up. It was Tracy. "Do you want to meet Peggy and me for dinner at Alfredo's?" he asked.

"Brigid and I are renting a car and driving up to Orvieto for a romantic evening. Do you and Peggy want to come?"

"No, thanks," answered Tracy. "At our age, Peggy and I are more interested in a bowl of fettuccini and a bottle of wine than romance. Have a nice time."

"Thanks," answered Nate. "I'll call you when we get back. See you at the presentation on Monday."

"Ciao," said Tracy.

While Brigid was in the shower, Nate went downstairs with the luggage to the concierge desk to see about the rental car he had reserved.

The day before, when he reserved the car, Nate had specified, "I want something fast and sexy."

"Every car in Italy is fast and sexy," said the concierge with a smile.

When Nate got to the desk this afternoon, he asked, "Is my car ready?"

"It's right outside," said the concierge, pointing to the little courtyard. Nate was immediately drawn to a red Alfa Romeo 4C convertible. It was definitely fast and sexy.

Nate called Brigid from the phone in the lobby. "The car is here. I'll wait for you in the bar."

A few minutes later, Brigid came into the bar dressed in an off-white linen skirt and an apricot silk blouse. Everybody in the bar turned as she entered. She came up to Nate and said, "Are you my driver?"

He was in love again.

Getting out of Rome during rush hour is always a challenge, but getting out of Rome on the day of a pope's funeral is nearly impossible. It's a good thing that Alfa Romeos look good standing still, because for the first couple of miles, they were mostly standing still.

Once they reached the autostrada, they opened up the car and it flew. With the top down, Brigid turned up the radio. They got lost in a ballad by Tiziano Ferro, "*Il Regalo Piu Grande.*" They had no idea what the words meant, but like everything in Italian, it was sensual.

In two hours they arrived at Orvieto, a hilltop town of romantic dreams.

Built on a pedestal of volcanic rock, it was once a papal fortress in the days when the popes ruled Umbria and all of central Italy. It hasn't changed much since the Middle Ages. It couldn't. There is absolutely nowhere to grow.

The little plateau on which Orvieto stands, sits atop steep cliffs. The only way to reach one end of the town is by funicular.

The jewel of Orvieto is its cathedral, with zebra-striped courses of white and black rock. It took three hundred years, thirty-three architects, one hundred fifty-two sculptors, ninety mosaicists, and sixty-eight painters to complete. It practically bankrupted the town, but today nobody counts the cost, since the cathedral is what draws the tourists.

Nate and Brigid arrived about six that evening and checked into a room at La Badia outside Orvieto, a former monastery turned hotel, with stone walls eight feet thick and a medieval tower. Their room had French doors that opened out to reveal a view of the town on the neighboring hill.

Before supper, Brigid and Nate took a walk through the maze of little alleys and streets inside the old city walls and took the funicular up to the town.

Deliveries in Orvieto are made with three-wheeled *ape* trucks, which are really modified motorcycles, with a little flat bed on the back. The word *ape* means bee in Italian. They're called bee trucks because of the buzzing sound their two-stroke engines make when toiling up and down the hills. The Condons had to step into doorways to allow the *apes* to pass.

Their walk led them to the Piazza del Duomo, the cathedral square. In the light of the June sunset, the façade of the cathedral actually appeared to glow as the orange light struck the hundreds of thousands of bits of gold in the mosaics. They stood there in silence, transfixed for a minute by the sight of the shimmering cathedral.

Brigid broke the silence. "What kind of faith and love motivates such art?" she asked rhetorically.

"I don't know," said Nate. "Sometimes we lose sight of the miracles of our own religion. It is easier to find miracles in things that are strange. That's why Westerners turn to Buddhism, and Asians turn to Christianity."

They tugged on the front doors of the cathedral, but they were already locked for the night. Inside was the cathedral's prize relic, a bloodstained napkin called a *corporal* from the miracle of Bolsena. Legend has it that a twelfth-century priest, who doubted the transubstantiation of the bread and wine into the body and blood of Christ, saw the host bleed. The bloodstained corporal was preserved and brought to Orvieto. For centuries, hundreds of thousands of pilgrims have come to see it. Even today, they come. Whether the pilgrims are faithful, curious, or merely gullible, what they see is in the eye of the beholder.

As they walked back to the hotel, Brigid took Nate's arm. "I have to tell you something that Sister Miriam told me yesterday. When I was in Bruges, I visited that guy Bernard Willebroeck, the one you asked me to see. Sister Miriam tells me that our visit really upset him. He was even more upset to learn that some Vatican investigation was focused on him. Miriam thinks he might be dangerous. His group has been responsible for demonstrations in Flanders and maybe even a few cases of arson. Apparently, this guy had been a priest in the Congo, where he got a woman pregnant. He was sent home, and she died in childbirth. He always had it out for the cardinal who sent him home. The retired cardinal died in a fire not too many years ago, and people say that Bernard may have been responsible. Miriam thinks this Bernard fellow has even more reason to be angry at bishops, because his nephew was molested by a priest and the bishop did nothing. Then it later came out that the bishop himself was molesting his own nephew."

They stopped walking. Sometimes, news is so shocking it is necessary to stop to take it in.

"Whew," said Nate. "I had no idea when I first started turning over rocks in this investigation what kind of vermin I would find living underneath. It really shakes your faith. I wonder if I've made a mistake putting my faith in the Church all these years."

Brigid could see that all the scandal was actually painful to him.

"Well," she said, "our faith was never in this Church anyway. It was always in something bigger and more mysterious than any institution, no matter how old. It was in God, I guess," she said, "and in each other."

"I'm really happy to hear you say that," said Nate.

"What, the part about God?" asked Brigid.

"Yes, but more the part about each other," said Nate.

They stepped into a darkened doorway, and he pulled her to him.

They ambled back to the hotel, hand in hand. They hadn't walked that way in years. In the room, looking out at the floodlit walls of the Cathedral of Orvieto, Nate said, "I'm glad you came over."

"So am I," said Brigid.

26

THE AUTOSTRADA

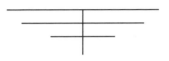

GOING BACK TO ROME, THE TRAFFIC ON THE AUTOSTRADA
was terrible. Sundays are the worst days to drive in Italy, because Italians
vacate their cities every weekend for houses in the mountains or at the
seaside. The return is pure gridlock.

Brigid and Nate were reluctant to leave Orvieto, but Nate had a presentation to make on Monday to Cardinal O'Toole, Tracy, and the police.
The cardinal needed to hear the results of the investigation before the
conclave began on Thursday.

Once on the autostrada, surrounded by noisy trucks and speeding
cars, it was not very pleasant to have the top down on the Alfa, so they
stopped at the Autogrill to put the top up and to buy gas. Brigid went
into the gift shop and bought a half-kilo bar of Torrone, a super-sweet
nougat bar loaded with nuts. "In the States we can only get these at
Christmas," said Brigid when she came back to the car.

As Nate was pumping gas, Brigid noticed two men leaning against a
black Mercedes, parked at the entrance of the Autogrill. They seemed to
be looking in their direction. One of them had a ponytail. Looks like that
guy, Bernard, thought Brigid. The other had a shaved head and big arms
like the guy who broke into their room at the Four Seasons.

Once back on the autostrada, cars were at very close quarters. Italians tailgate recklessly and drive incredibly fast. In Europe they say that Germans drive fast because they are in a hurry. But Italians drive fast because it is fun.

Nate mostly played it safe, staying in the poky lane on the right-hand side as they headed south. After they had traveled only a few kilometers on the highway, the black Mercedes they had seen at the Autogrill started keeping pace with them, to their left, in the passing lane.

"Why doesn't this damn guy just pass?" wondered Nate.

"I saw those two guys back at the rest stop," said Brigid.

Just then, the man in the passenger seat near Nate rolled down his window and pointed a long black object at them.

"Oh, God, he's got a gun," screamed Brigid. Nate later said it was a nightstick or a piece of black pipe.

Just then the Mercedes seemed to swerve into their lane. It hit the left fender of the Alfa. Nate jerked the wheel to the right, and the Alfa veered onto the shoulder. There was no way to stop, because cars were bearing down on their tail.

When the Mercedes hit the Alfa, the man in the passenger seat made a jerking motion with a stick, as if he were going to shoot them. Nate was trying to control the car, but Brigid got a good look at them.

Nate got the car under control and brought the Alfa to a stop on the shoulder. Brigid was screaming, "Oh, my God! Oh, my God!"

Nate's heart raced, but he said nothing. He got out to inspect the damage. There was a gash in the left front fender, but the tire was intact. They were shaken, but there was no serious damage to them or the car.

"What was that about?" yelled Brigid out the window.

"I don't know," said Nate as he got back in the car. "I think someone is trying to send us a message."

"They could have killed us," said Brigid.

"If they had wanted to kill us, they would have," said Nate. "I think this was just a warning. Get out your cell phone and call the police."

"I don't speak Italian," said Brigid.

"Doesn't matter," said Nate. "They can trace our location from the cell phone. Just keep saying 'help, accident, autostrada.' They'll figure it out."

While they were waiting for the police, Brigid told Nate, "I think I saw the man who was in the passenger seat back at the rest stop. He looked sort of like that guy Bernard that I met back in Bruges."

Ten minutes later, two Italian traffic police officers arrived on their Moto Guzzi motorcycles. They took an accident report, but there was nothing to do. Nate called his contact at the Carabinieri in Rome and asked him to do a little investigating.

"Somebody in a black Mercedes just tried to run us off the road. It was a big car, probably E class. It had EU plates, but I couldn't get the number. See if you can check this out for us."

"*Va bene*," said his contact and hung up.

After the traffic police left, Nate pulled the car back onto the roadway. The Alfa roared up to 120 kilometers in a matter of seconds.

"Who was it?" asked Brigid.

"Not sure," said Nate. "Maybe the Mafia, but I don't think so. They would not hesitate to pull the trigger."

"I wonder if it was the Bruges crowd," said Brigid. "Miriam said they were pretty angry about our visit. But why would they do that? They could have killed us."

"Somebody may want to silence me," said Nate. "There is a lot more at stake than a few reputations."

* * *

The dome on St. Peter's was lit up by the time they got back to Rome. As they turned onto the Conciliazione, they were glad to get back to the safety of the hotel.

"I don't look forward to dealing with the insurance on this car," said Nate. "From what I hear of Italian insurance bureaucrats, I'll probably have two years of paperwork just to get this dent repaired."

"I'll leave the paperwork to you," said Brigid. "I want a hot bath."

* * *

Nate's presentation to the panel that would review his investigation was Monday morning. He was up early and off to his office before Brigid was awake.

Preparations were already underway for Thursday's conclave to elect a new pope. Cardinal O'Toole needed the report before the conclave began, so that an explanation could be made to the other cardinals.

Nate packed up like he was going to court. He had a big briefcase, like lawyers carry to court, plus his laptop and some background material on each of the deceased cardinals.

Just as Nate loaded up his briefcase, Brigid walked through the door. "Surprise," she said. "Just thought I would wish you well." Nate beamed and gave her a big hug.

His assistant, Sandra, interrupted. "The captain from the autostrada police is here," she said. "He has some information about the accident."

A tall policeman stood in the doorway behind her. Nate motioned him into the room.

"Good morning," the captain said in English, tipping his hat toward Brigid.

Nate noticed the gesture and said, "Oh, *scusi*, this is my wife, Brigid." The policeman said, "*Piacere signora.*"

Nate asked, "What have you got for us?"

"I have some information about your accident yesterday on the autostrada. We ran the plates on the black Mercedes that hit you on the A1. It is registered to a Mexican national, a Jorge Carillo. He works for the Collegio degli Soldados de Cristo in the Via Aurelia. That's the seminary of the Soldados de Cristo.

"We went to the car owner's home on the grounds of the seminary. There we found the Mercedes, with some damage on the right front fender. Red paint, too. Could have been from your Alfa."

"We interviewed the owner of the car and another man with a pony-tail who matched the description you gave us. We took them down to the Questura and charged them with leaving the scene of an accident. We also gave them a citation."

"So it evidently wasn't your Bruges crowd," said Nate to Brigid. "Looks like it was the Soldados. You know the Soldados, that group Bill and Peggy are so fond of." Nate chuckled to himself. "Odd," he said. "I've been threatened by the mob, but never by a couple of guys working for a seminary. Rome is surreal."

The police officer opened a leather case and placed two photos on Nate's desk. "Do you recognize either of these men?" he asked.

Walking over to the desk, Brigid said, "We didn't see the driver."

Picking up one of the photos, she said, "This is definitely the passenger. The guy with the ponytail." Then, picking up the second picture and raising her voice, she said, "Look, Nate, this is the guy from Washington. The one with the big arms who was with Peggy at the hotel, and in the picture in *The Times*."

The police captain said, "*Grazie*, we will prepare the papers for the complaint and get back to you." He packed up his briefcase, made a little bow toward Brigid, and left the office.

27

THE PRESENTATION

NATE HAD RESERVED THE LIBRARY OF THE KNIGHTS OF
Malta on the Via Condotti for his presentation. It was a twenty-minute
ride in morning traffic through central Rome.

Nate was the last to arrive. When he entered the high-ceilinged
room, the representatives of the police, Bill Tracy, and two cardinals
were already seated in high-backed leather chairs arranged in a semicircle facing a screen. There was a projector sitting on a table in front of
the screen.

Besides Cardinal O'Toole and Bill Tracy, the group included the head
of the Vatican police, a regional inspector for Interpol, the commandant
of the Swiss Guard, an Italian magistrate who was in charge of investigating the Camorra, and Cardinal Paolo Santini, the vice camerlengo of
the Vatican. He ran the mechanics of the Vatican after Crepi's suicide.

After introductions, Nate went right into his presentation.

"Gentlemen, we are here to review the findings, thus far, of the Holy
See's investigation into the murders of Cardinal Manning from New
York and five other cardinals of the Roman Catholic Church.

"As you know, these deaths have been widely reported in the news
and have been the focus of an enormous amount of official and unofficial
investigation. To our knowledge, no other investigation is attempting to

link these deaths to one another, but we believe they may be connected. We are also investigating two other deaths, the suicide of Cardinal Crepi and the murder of Monsignor Ackerman, which are related to this investigation. A brief report and biography on each of the six murdered cardinals, as well as crime-scene photos, if we have them, were distributed to you as you arrived."

Nate switched on the projector, and photos of the dead cardinals appeared on the screen as Nate called each name.

"The six murdered cardinals are Cardinal Alfonse Lohrman, the Archbishop of Santiago, Chile, who died in a clinic in Santiago where he had gone for a routine outpatient operation.

"Cardinal Ignacio Garcia of Guadalajara, Mexico, who died at the airport in Monterrey, Mexico, where he had gone for a meeting of the Bishops' Conference of Mexico. He was caught in the crossfire of what appeared, at the time, to be a fight between two drug cartels.

"Cardinal Modesto Rondo, Archbishop of Manila, who died in a horrific ten-car pileup on an expressway in the Philippines. Two other people were killed in that accident.

"Cardinal Patrice Musaku from Kinshasa in the Congo, who died one year ago in a fire at his cottage on the grounds of the provincial seminary.

"Cardinal Antonio deCapo, Archbishop of Milan, who apparently died from food poisoning three months ago after dining at one of Milan's finest restaurants.

"And finally, the Cardinal Archbishop of New York, Francis X. Manning, who was assassinated about one month ago at St. Patrick's Cathedral just as he began a funeral for the former US attorney general, Frank Sullivan.

"Of course, you are all aware of the details surrounding the suicide of Cardinal Crepi and the gruesome murder of Monsignor Ackerman, which have been widely reported in the media here in Rome.

"The question for the Holy See is twofold: Are these deaths related and, if so, what group or groups are responsible?"

"There is another question," interjected the head of the Swiss Guard, Klaus Speirman. "How do we protect the cardinals in the conclave next week?"

"I'll leave that question for you," said Nate. "My portfolio only extends to who and why. The police are investigating these deaths in each of their home countries, and we have used their investigations in our own inquiries. Here is what we know so far about these various cases."

Nate clicked the projector again, and the picture of Cardinal Musaku reappeared on the screen.

"We can eliminate two cardinals from the list of criminal or suspicious deaths: Musaku and Rondo.

"It appears that Cardinal Patrice Musaku died in an accidental fire when his retirement cottage on the grounds of the seminary burned to the ground. The cardinal was a heavy smoker, and there was evidence that he fell asleep while smoking in bed. There was no evidence of arson or foul play, despite persistent rumors that a group called New Church in Belgium may have been behind the fire. New Church is headed by ex-priest Bernard Willebroeck."

Nate pressed the projector's remote control, and a picture of Bernard appeared on the screen. "Authorities are continuing to monitor Willebroeck and his group. There also seems to be some connection of this group to the Mafia, which sent him substantial sums through international wire transfers.

"Since he has violated money-laundering statutes in the European Union, we have requested his arrest by the authorities in Belgium. I understand that was accomplished this morning. His computers and communications equipment have been seized. If his group is a threat to anyone, it has been neutralized for the present."

"Good," said Tracy.

O'Toole nodded, apparently satisfied. "What about Cardinal Rondo? He was such a young man. You said his death was not suspicious. What happened to him?"

"Well," said Nate, "sometimes a traffic accident is just a traffic accident, and that seems to be the case here. The traffic in Manila is notorious. Visibility was very poor in a rainstorm on a divided highway. Cardinal Rondo was driving in a small car, a Hyundai Accent. There were ten cars involved in the accident. Cardinal Rondo's car was sandwiched between two larger trucks, and he was killed instantly. In my estimation, it was just an accident."

"There's the argument for a big car," interjected Tracy with a chuckle. The others turned and looked at him. They did not see any humor in the moment.

Nate looked in Tracy's direction and cleared his throat. "The deaths of the remaining four cardinals are suspicious, as are the deaths of Crepi and Ackerman. Our investigation has uncovered evidence definitively linking Cardinal Crepi and Monsignor Ackerman to the Camorra. It also appears that the deaths of three cardinals, Manning, Lohrman, and deCapo, may also have been related to Mafia activity. All three of these cardinals served on the board of the IOR. It has been suspected for years that the Mafia has been using the Vatican Bank to launder money."

Nate clicked to the slide of Lohrman's face. "Cardinal Lohrman was a reformer. He wanted to clean up or close the bank. But he was compromised by his cooperation with the Chilean generals in the 1980s. Perhaps the Mafia used his vulnerability to pressure him to allow the IOR to continue laundering money. In any case, it appeared he wanted to stop it, so they might have wanted to kill him."

Nate popped up another slide, showing Lohrman's body and head, bluish and discolored. Nate saw the attendees grimace at the corpse.

Nate continued, "The forensic toxicology tests showed levels of various toxins in his system. Lohrman was known to have an allergy to some types of anesthesia. It was recorded on his pre-op admission form. It was either gross negligence, or the drug was intentionally administered. The anesthesia that he was allergic to was administered in a lethal dose. This caused the cardinal to go into cardiac arrest on the operating table."

"Did they try to revive him in the clinic?" asked the Interpol captain.

"They tried," said Nate, "but it was a small surgery clinic, not a hospital. They did not have much of a staff. An ambulance came, but by the time it got there, he was dead.

"Chilean officials are still investigating, but it was clearly not a simple error. There had to be multiple violations of protocol in the clinic. And the anesthesiologist has disappeared. It seems that he has family members connected to a Colombian cartel."

The audience in the library shook their heads but reacted little. They were not easily shocked.

After a brief pause, Nate picked up the thread. "The evidence points to the murder of Cardinal Lohrman by organized crime, probably agents of drug cartels interested in continuing their money laundering. If he was getting out, that may have been enough to kill him.

"It is probable that Cardinal Salazar may have tipped off the Camorra here in Italy that Lohrman was a loose cannon. He used Ackerman as the go-between. Ackerman talked to a reporter from *Panoramio*, and the reporter wrote stories that identified who the Camorra should kill."

The Italian magistrate shook his head. "I'm not surprised," he said. "These people have connections everywhere. Money is their passport."

Nate agreed. "One thing is for sure, they certainly did not want to lose the IOR as a money laundering outlet. Cardinal Salazar has talked to us about that. Salazar and Monsignor Donato Scarpini, the assistant manager at the bank, are both currently under arrest by the Italian police. They have both given detailed accounts of their connection to money laundering for the Mafia and for the Latin American drug cartels. It also appears that Cardinal Crepi and Monsignor Ackerman were deeply involved in all of this."

"*Madonna Santa*," said Cardinal Santini, a longtime friend of Cardinal Crepi.

"Why would Luciano be involved in such things?"

Nate looked at the cardinal. "Shame," he said.

"Shame and scandal. The Camorra knew details from Crepi's past. Actually, details involving both Cardinal Crepi and Cardinal Salazar," responded Nate. He flashed a slide of Gianluca up on the screen, along with a slide of a newspaper article from the time of the boy's death.

"It seems that Salazar and Crepi had a sexual relationship with this young man on a ferryboat from Naples to Sicily. The boy died in their room, as an accident, or was killed. We are not sure. In any case, the Camorra threw his body overboard and made it appear to be a drowning. From that moment on, Crepi and Salazar worked for the Mafia as much as the Church."

Nate flashed the newspaper photo of Crepi and Salazar, standing on the dock in Palermo. O'Toole was surprised to see how these two men had looked more than forty years ago.

Nate paused. There was an inward taking of breath that could be heard from all of the listeners. Even these worldly men were shocked.

Nate took a drink of water from a glass on the table nearby and picked up the presentation again.

"It seems that in light of recent scandals, the board of the IOR was discussing possible changes in the operation of the bank, or perhaps even closing it. The three murdered cardinals were all strong advocates of these changes. The Mafia may have murdered them to stop the bank reforms."

"So, Manning, deCapo, and Lohrman were on the board of the IOR," said Tracy. "What happened to deCapo?"

"Poison," said Nate. "The toxicology shows high levels of opiates in his bloodstream and stomach. He probably ingested it while having lunch. He had respiratory problems in the restaurant and was disoriented and slurring his words, according to the police report. They thought he had too much wine. Certainly the wine and the drugs could have been lethal. It was no accident.

"But what I can't figure out is why the mob or drug cartels would kill three members of the board of the IOR. Was there some urgency about reform? Was the goose going to stop laying golden eggs?"

"I think I know why," said O'Toole. "Pope Thomas was weak. If any one of those three were elected the new pope, the IOR was going to be reformed. The Mafia wanted to be sure that no insider at the IOR would be able to move against them."

"The death of Pope Thomas," said Nate, "has given new urgency to the question of bank reform. Somebody new will be in charge after the election of the new pope. Cardinals Crepi and Salazar, who had been helping the Mafia, wanted to preserve the status quo regarding the bank so their friends could continue laundering money. But they could see their days were numbered."

The head of the Vatican police raised his hand to ask a question. "So, why did Cardinal Crepi commit suicide?"

"It appears that my investigation sent the Camorra into a panic," said Nate. "Monsignor Ackerman was killed because he was unable to get this investigation terminated. In simple terms, the Mafia thought he talked too much. For years he had been acting as a go-between for Cardinals Crepi and Salazar and the Camorra. Monsignor Ackerman used the press and his contacts at a gay bar here in Rome to communicate with the Mafia. They suspected he had violated the code of *omerta*. That's why they killed him. The code of silence is even more important than their money laundering. *Omerta* is the glue that binds the Camorra and the Cosa Nostra and all the other branches of the Mafia together. They could not overlook the violation of their code.

"After Ackerman was murdered, Crepi knew that his service to the Mafia could be exposed and that his usefulness to organized crime might be coming to an end. The cardinal was a methodical man and a realist."

"That is true," interjected the head of the Swiss Guard.

Nate nodded. "Rather than live a life stripped of all his comfort and privilege and looking over his shoulder in fear, Crepi chose death."

"His final act of pride," said O'Toole. Nate nodded again and returned to his slides. He put up an image of Ackerman.

"Before Monsignor Ackerman died, I spoke to him about his own involvement with Crepi and Salazar. I recorded the conversation. He verified everything we have heard so far about money laundering. He also said that his leaks to a journalist for *Panoramio* helped identify who the Mafia should kill, though Ackerman did not know at the time, that these leaks would lead to murder.

"Ackerman also gave me a lead to follow regarding Cardinals Crepi and Salazar and the death of the boy in Naples forty-two years ago. I went down to Naples and interviewed the boy's mother, who informed me that the medical examiner found no water in the boy's lungs. He was clearly dead when he hit the water.

"Cardinal Salazar confirmed this and that the Camorra helped the cardinals cover up the boy's death. They were faithful lieutenants for the Mafia. But eventually, of course, they also received some substantial financial rewards. They were very attached to the money the Mafia gave them."

The Italian magistrate interjected, "Of course they were. Money was their real god."

Nate put up slides of two faces. "Arrests have been made. Don Franco Virgilio of the Di Lauro clan and a bartender from a Mafia-operated gay bar have been arrested." A slide of Stefano appeared.

"Other related people are being rounded up by the Italian police, thanks to the inspector here." The Interpol inspector nodded in acknowledgment.

"Unfortunately," said the Italian magistrate, "this will hardly put a dent in their operations. They will probably be out of jail before the end of the week."

"That may be true," said Nate, thinking of Giulia Luppino, the mother of the dead boy in Naples. "But the arrest of the *capi* will lead us to people lower down. Maybe there will be a brief interruption in the Mafia activities on the local level. Perhaps even in drug-infested Scampia.

"One thing that even the Mafia seems shocked at is child molesters. They might take retribution on their own on those who covered up the death of a young boy, even if it was more than forty years ago."

Nate paused again to take a drink of water. He thought to himself that maybe the gates of the Vele would stay open for a while and maybe the nightmare that started forty-two years ago for Giulia Luppino would come to an end.

"But there seems to be one more cardinal you did not discuss," said the head of the Swiss Guard.

"Right," said Nate. "Cardinal Ignacio Garcia of Guadalajara. Cardinal Garcia died in the crossfire of what appeared to be a shootout between rival drug cartels at the Monterrey airport in Mexico."

Nate projected some images of Mexican newspaper headlines. "You may have read about the horrific and public killings done by the drug cartels in Mexico that have claimed innocent bystanders. There was one shooting at a gambling casino in Monterrey earlier that year that killed over forty innocent people. At a ranch just north of Monterrey on the way to Matamoros, more than a hundred bodies were found. Sometimes the cartels have stopped buses and killed everyone on the bus, even children who just happened to be on the bus, when they only wanted one person. They did not want to leave any witnesses.

"But," said Nate deliberately, "I don't think this was the case with Cardinal Garcia. He was not an innocent bystander. He was the target."

"Why do you think that?" asked Cardinal Santini. "Who made him the target?"

"As shocking as it may seem," said Nate, "I think he was targeted by people within the Church." There was an audible gasp from the two cardinals and the employees of the Vatican in the room.

"Who?" they demanded.

"The evidence points to the Soldados de Cristo," said Nate. Bill Tracy jerked uncomfortably in his chair and opened his eyes wide. Nate paused for a moment to let the accusation sink in, and then he continued.

"Cardinal Garcia was a longtime opponent of the Soldados," said Nate. "He was especially suspicious of their founder, Monsignor Marcel Marcelino. It is now well known that Marcelino was sexually, financially, and morally corrupt. Garcia was an outspoken critic of the Soldados, who could not and would not risk the possibility of him becoming pope. Just a week before his death, Garcia preached the last in a series of four homilies, criticizing fanatical groups in the Church. He especially singled out groups led by despicable and corrupt men, who had little appreciation of the gospel of Christ. It was obvious he was referring to the Soldados. They could not abide such criticism."

O'Toole interrupted the flow of Nate's presentation. "Garcia's reputation for reform was gaining notice, not only in Mexico, but also here in Rome. He was pretty clearly a leading papabile."

"Precisely," said Nate. "The Soldados had motive and means to kill Garcia. They wanted him out of the way, because it was too big a risk for them that he might be elected pope. A Mexican pope who was opposed to the Soldados would have been a mortal threat to their existence."

Nate flashed a portrait of Cardinal Garcia on the screen.

"I interviewed the cardinal's secretary," said Nate. "He told me that Garcia had received threats in the weeks leading up to his death."

"Yes," said the Interpol inspector. "We had reports of that. I've brought them along."

Nate projected up on the screen images of newspaper articles with pictures of Cardinal Garcia and accounts of his sermons.

Nate projected photos of Marcelino on the screen next, followed by photos of his mistresses, children, and homes. He gave some of the details about Marcelino's extensive corruption.

Tracy covered his eyes as Nate probed the more lurid details.

"The Soldados founder had not one, but two secret mistresses and families he supported with money from the religious order. He regularly had sexual relations with seminarians in his order and swore them to silence. He also used undue influence to induce vulnerable widows to give up their fortunes to him." Nate looked over at Tracy and thought about Peggy.

"All of this has been well documented," said Nate. "Monsignor Henry Rodriguez has been assigned by the Holy See to investigate the Soldados and to oversee their operations. He has, at times, been concerned for his own safety."

"But why would anyone stage a shootout at the airport?" asked the Italian magistrate. "Why not kill him quietly?"

"Reputation," answered Nate. "The shootout at the airport was not just a killing. It was character assassination. The cardinal's killers wanted to make it look like Garcia was involved with the drug cartels, maybe even on their payroll. Shootings like that were so common in Mexico, they knew that it would hardly be investigated. If it really were a drug hit, the police would just leave it alone."

Nate projected news photos of the cardinal's corpse, lying askew, half-dismounted from his black Lincoln, in the departure ramp of the Monterrey airport.

"Even the murder of a cardinal would be just another drop in the sea of blood. It was well known that the drug cartels would not hesitate to kill a priest or a bishop. So, why not a cardinal?

"If they had killed judges, police chiefs, prosecutors, and journalists, a cardinal would only be one more dead man. The shooting did not just attack Cardinal Garcia's body. It also attacked his reputation. People just assumed that he must have been involved in the dirty drug wars of Mexico. So, the Soldados didn't just rid themselves of their enemy. They also ruined his reputation. It was a public relations bonus.

"After all, if Cardinal Garcia was a target of the drug cartels, it implied that he was somehow involved with them. If he was in league with the cartels, then the Soldados' chief critic would have been neutered."

Nate flashed up headlines from Mexican papers showing that the cardinal was suspected of drug dealing.

"Cardinal Garcia was an honest man. The Soldados made him into a drug dealer," said Nate.

"But why would the Zetas or some other cartel shoot a cardinal on behalf of the Soldados?" asked the Interpol inspector.

"Easy," said Nate. "Money. They are assassins for hire, just like the Mafia that killed Manning in New York. It was the ideal crime for the Soldados.

All they had to do was pay the money to the cartels to do the crime. The drug cartels got the blame, but they didn't care. The Zetas or the Sinaloa cartels are happy to do any crime if you pay them enough."

"The Soldados have many people working in Rome," said O'Toole. "In some ways, they are a bigger threat to us than the Camorra. We can close the bank and even close the diplomatic corps. That would make the Church a lot less useful to the Mafia. But it is a lot harder to deal with a religious order as big and as worldwide as the Soldados."

Cardinal Santini nodded in agreement. "They are more like a movement than a community. They have their lay group, Regnum Dei. They have money and houses and lots of fanatical followers.

"Even though we have arrested Marcelino and a few others, they still have their acolytes."

O'Toole agreed, for the first time becoming visibly agitated. "They want to take us back to the ultramontane church of the 1800s, when the pope was an absolute monarch and the Church was a cultural fortress."

"Even if we arrest the ones who are responsible for the crimes, we cannot turn off the movement," said Santini. He added, "The Soldados are always comparing themselves to the Jesuits in their early days. Maybe we should treat them just like we treated the Jesuits in the eighteenth century and suppress them for seventy or eighty years."

Santini and O'Toole chuckled. The reference was lost on Tracy and Nate; even though they had gone to Jesuit schools, they didn't know that the Jesuits were once suppressed by the pope.

"What should we do about Mendoza?" asked the head of the Swiss Guard. It was his job to guard the conclave, and his tone of voice was serious.

"We begin the conclave in three days. How can we have a cardinal in the conclave who may have been involved in the murder of his fellow cardinal and countryman?"

Nate thought about the police report he had received from the police captain just before the meeting.

"The Soldados are nervous about this investigation," said Nate.

"They were responsible for an attempt on the life of my wife and me on the autostrada yesterday."

O'Toole interrupted. "The Italian police can arrest the guys who attacked you on the autostrada, but the Church can't keep Mendoza out of the conclave. We don't have any proof against him. Even if we did, he has not only a right, but also an obligation, to be in the conclave. That's his duty as a cardinal. We have to let him in." O'Toole continued, "The Soldados are an even bigger problem than the Camorra."

The Italian magistrate raised his eyebrows. "That's something I don't hear too often, that somebody is a bigger problem than the Camorra," he said.

They sat there in stunned silence for a minute or so. These revelations about the extent of corruption in the Church and the threat presented by the Soldados de Cristo were a lot to take in, even for sophisticated men.

"But what about the murder of Manning?" asked O'Toole. "Who was responsible? That's how this whole investigation got started."

Nate picked up the thread again. "The investigation thus far indicates that it was the Mafia behind the murder of Manning, but they used New Church to carry it out. They got New Church to use a Belgian contact working at Rockefeller Center in New York to leave the door to a balcony across from the Cathedral open. The Mafia was able to come in and set up a remotely controlled gun.

"They were all using each other: New Church, the Mafia, and their friends in the hierarchy. Only the Camorra had the money and the connections to make Manning's murder happen. New Church was their unwitting co-conspirator. They thought they were working for a like-minded Church reform group."

"But why would the Mafia want to make it look like New Church murdered Manning?" asked O'Toole.

"The Mafia wanted to deflect attention from the bank. If they could make it look like the people who were angry about pedophilia were behind Manning's murder, there would be no outcry to reform or eliminate the bank. By implicating New Church, they would send any investigation down a rabbit hole.

"Bernard Willebroeck and his group were a useful cover for the Mafia."

Nate concluded the presentation and switched off the projector.

"That's the extent of my investigation. There is a lot to be concerned about. We are dealing with a threat that is so dangerous, the reputation and future of the Church are at stake."

Everyone but Nate and Tracy left the library in silence.

As Nate packed up his case, he said to Tracy, "Bill, I want to show you something." He pulled out the photo from *The New York Times*. "This is the man that Brigid saw with Peggy at the Four Seasons in DC."

He also pulled out a copy of the photo that the Italian police captain had shown him earlier in the morning. "This is the same man who attempted to run us off the road yesterday. What the hell is going on here?"

Tracy was obviously flustered. "With God as my judge," he said, "I never saw this man before. We do have friends in the Soldados, but I don't know anything about this. Peggy and I would never be involved in any of this shit."

Nate looked him directly in the eye. "I want to believe you, Bill, but I can't let it stop here. I have to follow the evidence where it leads. You know the drill."

Tracy put his hands up in disgust. "Damn it, Nate. Do whatever you have to do." He turned on his heel and walked out.

On his way back to the the Hotel Columbus, Nate told the taxi to pass by the FedEx office near the Stazione Termini in the Via Tiburtina. He told the driver to wait while he ran in with a package addressed to *The New York Times*.

The young man behind the desk asked, "Do you want insurance with this?"

"Yes," said Nate with a smile. He thought to himself, Well, in a way this package *is* my insurance.

28

O'TOOLE AND MCCLENDON

THE JESUITS HAVE SEVERAL HOUSES IN ROME, BUT THE biggest and draftiest is called the Bellarmino, named after St. Robert Bellarmine, the "Hammer of Heretics." Everyone who spends a winter at the Bellarmino catches a cold, but by June the corridors are unbearably hot.

Cardinal O'Toole arrived at the Jesuit house just before 1:00 p.m., the hour of *pranzo*. His boyhood friend from Salem, Jim Kelleher, S.J., and his old pastor and spiritual director, Jack McClendon, were already in the dining room. The rector of the house jumped up from his spaghetti to greet the cardinal, but it was Jim and Jack who got a hug from His Eminence.

"Mike, you look good. Are you ready to become pope?" asked McClendon as he embraced O'Toole. It was a struggle for him to get out of his chair. His arthritis was getting worse.

"No talk like that, Jack. We don't want to scandalize these holy Jesuits," said O'Toole, raising his eyes to the ceiling as if imploring heaven.

As a Jesuit, Kelleher felt very much at home in the big, impersonal Jesuit house. As Voltaire said of Jesuit community life, "They come together, they don't know each other, they live together, they don't love each other, they die, and they don't mourn each other."

One thing about old friends: the passage of time does not seem to matter. Jim Kelleher and Mike O'Toole had grown up together in Salem. When they got together, their Boston accents grew more pronounced, and they called each other "Mike" and "Jimmy," as they had when they rode their bikes up and down Essex Street.

After lunch, O'Toole suggested they go back to his apartment. "I have to pack my things to move over to the Casa Santa Marta. You're going to have to move over there too, Jack. Why don't you spend the night at my place? Then we can move over there together tomorrow."

"That's a good idea," said McClendon. "I'll get my bag."

"What's the matter," asked Kelleher, "afraid of Jesuit hospitality?"

"Nah," said McClendon, "but at my age I can only take one Jesuit at a time."

The three men piled into a taxi and headed toward O'Toole's apartment near the Porta Sant'Anna.

Cardinal O'Toole had asked Father McClendon to come to Rome to be an English-language confessor for the cardinals in the conclave.

For the period of the conclave, all the cardinals live together at the Casa Santa Marta. The only people permitted inside those living quarters, besides the cardinals, are confessors for various languages, doctors, and personal aides to the invalid cardinals. But even they cannot enter the Sistine Chapel for the conclave itself. Those doors are sealed.

McClendon was the kind of senior priest who would be respected by the cardinals. It was an extraordinary honor for him and an unusual opportunity to have something to say to the men who would elect the next pope.

Back at the apartment McClendon headed for the bathroom. "The old man's curse," he said. "Never pass a working bathroom."

They watched him shuffle slowly down the hallway.

O'Toole looked at Kelleher and said, "Jack sure has aged a lot. I saw him only three weeks ago, and he seems to have aged five years since."

"Well," said Kelleher, "he is eighty-six."

"But he doesn't seem well to me," said O'Toole. The cardinal's housekeeper brought in coffee. Over coffee, O'Toole gave the two priests a summary of Nate's report.

At the end Kelleher whistled. "Wow, who would have thought it could be so bad?"

Jack McClendon had rejoined them and caught up with the conversation. He was philosophical. "The effects of original sin are still real, Mike. Clericalism breeds pride, and pride breeds hubris. Maybe this is a chance for the Church to really do something about clericalism."

"Like what?" said O'Toole, genuinely curious about what should be done.

"Like admit that we are sinners just like everybody else," said McClendon. "Let's get away from the crazy idea that we are different from everybody else. What was that idea we were taught in seminary, that somehow we were 'ontologically changed' by ordination? Priests are just like everybody else, or maybe worse, because we pretend to be better."

The three Bostonians spent the rest of the afternoon catching up on news from home and recalling old times. Kelleher walked back to the Bellarmino for dinner.

As evening came, Jack fell asleep on the sofa. O'Toole got up and covered him with a blanket. It actually felt good to do an ordinary act of service for someone else. Most of the time, other people waited on him.

O'Toole woke Jack up for dinner. "What do you want for dinner, Jack?"

"Just soup and bread," said Jack. "I don't suppose you have any clam chowder around here."

After dinner, they sat in the cardinal's study and O'Toole drew an envelope out of his coat pocket. "Let me read you something that I got today from Nate Condon. You remember Nate. He's Brendan Condon's son from Charlestown."

"Oh, yeah," said McClendon. "I became close to his father back home. Looks like he's turned up a lot in his investigation"

"Yeah, a lot," answered O'Toole, putting his eyeglasses on his nose and adjusting the reading light by his chair.

"Anyway, he gave me this letter from the mother of a monsignor who worked here in the Vatican and who was murdered last week here in Rome."

"I read about it in the papers," said Jack. "Very tragic, so sad. He was found in the catacombs, wasn't he?"

"Yeah. That's the one. I want to share it with you, Jack." O'Toole leaned on the arm of his easy chair opposite McClendon and read softly.

> Dear Mr. Condon,
>
> I want to thank you for making the arrangements to send my son's ashes home to me.
>
> Not a day has gone by in almost thirty years that I haven't prayed the rosary for my son Matthew. I will continue to pray for him, as I always have, until God calls me home too.
>
> My son was not perfect. He was what the years, and the Church, made him. There were times when I was so angry at him. Matthew got into many things over there in Rome that I never understood. His work didn't seem to have much to do with the Church that I love.
>
> I know this. I gave the Church my young boy, filled with a love for Christ and an enthusiasm to make the world a better place. I know he had a desire to be just a good priest.
>
> The Church gave me back the ashes of a self-loathing alcoholic . . . a man broken, bruised, and defeated. Despite all, he is still my son. Whatever he did, he is still my son. And I love him.
>
> I will always be grateful to you, Mr. Condon, for your kindness to me and my boy.
>
> Sincerely,
> Louise Ackerman

The two men sat there in silence, devastated by the sadness of the letter.

Jack leaned forward in his chair. "What have we done to these poor men God gives us? You have to be a spokesman for this poor woman, Mike. Somebody has to speak for her and all the people who are hurt or disappointed by the Church."

Jack paused for a second, then asked, "What was his problem, Mike?"

"He was lonely, I think. And like lots of guys here, he was ambitious. He hated himself because he was gay. He hung out in bars and became an alcoholic. He started doing desperate things. He felt he was unloved and unlovable. Ackerman was not a bad guy, really. He was just lost."

"How sad," said Jack, "but let's be honest with each other, Mike. We both know there are thousands of priests just like him. Many priests and bishops are gay, more than we want to admit. They live in terrible isolation. They can't be honest with anyone, not even themselves. You have to do something about it, Mike."

"What can I do?" asked O'Toole, somewhat irritated.

"For one thing, we can end mandatory celibacy," said McClendon.

"What would that do?" said O'Toole.

"Well," said Jack carefully, "it would take away the safe haven for gays. It makes us all be more honest. Celibacy isn't the real problem here anyway. The real problem is honesty.

"Celibacy is part of a much bigger problem of dishonesty about sex and sexuality in the whole Church. We can't ask people to be celibate all of a sudden after ordination."

"But we give them a long time to think about celibacy in the seminary," responded O'Toole. "They have five years. We tell them to think about it carefully."

"Sure," Jack answered, "but just because you think about it carefully doesn't mean you really understand it. How can you say with certainty when you are twenty-five years old that you are really going to be chaste and celibate for the rest of your life? Maybe you could promise for a few years, but your whole life?

"We have the same problem with marriage. When people say, 'I do' at the altar, half of them really don't. They don't know what is ahead."

"But they still promise," said O'Toole.

"They promise," agreed Jack, "but often they don't deliver." He continued, "Celibacy is even harder than fidelity in marriage. Some people can't be celibate, no matter how much they think about it. Some people can be celibate for a while, but then loneliness or desire overwhelms them. It's an inhuman and unnecessary request to make of people who want to be ministers of the gospel."

"But we have been doing it for millennia," interrupted the cardinal.

"No, we haven't. It has only been the official policy of the Church for eight hundred years, and we know that it has been more honored in the breach than in the observance. Look at what Chaucer says in *The Canterbury Tales*."

"Lots of people keep their vow of celibacy," said O'Toole.

"And plenty more don't," answered Jack. "The Church says something that is basically untrue about ordination. We say that at the moment of ordination men suddenly get the grace to be celibate. They don't. It doesn't come that way. It's a process. Everybody is called to be celibate at times in their lives, but almost nobody is called to live without sex for their entire life. Besides, it really has nothing to do with the priesthood. We already admit many people to the priesthood who are not celibate. Look at the Eastern churches. Their priests aren't celibate. Look at the Anglican and Lutheran clergy. We let them in, even if they are already married. We already have a married clergy. Look at the deacons. We don't require them to be celibate. Maybe we should just drop this charade. It keeps good people out and distorts the people who are in."

"Sounds like you're trying to rewrite our whole sexual ethics," said O'Toole.

"Maybe you've forgotten what it's like in the parish, Mike. Nobody is paying much attention to us on sex or marriage anyway. Couples are living together before they are married. They have babies out of wedlock. They get divorced and get married again, and they don't care about an annulment from the Church. Gay people are not ashamed of who they are anymore. Nor should they be. Most of my nieces and nephews didn't get married in the Church. They don't care what the Church thinks. They won't stay in bad marriages either, just because we expect them to. No, we don't have much influence these days.

"Maybe if we did away with the demand of celibacy, we would free priests to be more honest with themselves and with the Church. If we allowed people like Ackerman to come out of the closet, they might be healthier men. Then they might be better able to serve others without the weight of shame bearing down on them."

"Oh, Jack, I'm too tired for this discussion now," said O'Toole.

"I'm tired too," said Jack. "And I'm old. So, let's get some sleep."

The two men stood up and gave each other a hug.

"I love you, old man," said the cardinal, "and I'm so glad you're here."

"I'm glad to be here with you, Mike." Then, thinking of his beloved dog back home, he added, with a smile, "but I'd rather be home with Chocolate."

The cardinal looked at him with surprise. "Just kidding, Mike," said Jack.

"I know," said O'Toole. "I can't really compete with Chocolate anyhow."

He added, "Tomorrow we move to the Casa Santa Marta to get ready for the conclave. Much to do."

* * *

In the morning, just about the time that McClendon and O'Toole were checking into the Casa Santa Marta, Nate and Brigid were temporarily checking out of the Hotel Columbus, but they weren't leaving Italy. They were headed to Venice for a second honeymoon.

The Condons had decided that several more days in Italy might help them remember why they'd fallen in love with each other in the first place. Rushing back to New York and a life that seemed to drain them of passion made no sense after the week they'd had. Somehow it was easier to be passionate in Italy, and the Condons were rediscovering their love together.

For the first time in a long time, they found themselves compassionate and caring with each other. They were more engaged. Nate wanted to reignite what had begun in Orvieto. What could be more romantic than Venice? he thought. He had made arrangements for them to spend a few days at the Hotel Danieli on the Grand Canal in Venice.

Brigid told Nate, "It will be our long-delayed honeymoon."

She was already there by imagining the two of them drinking wine on the hotel balcony overlooking the Grand Canal, looking out on the water taxis and *vaporetti* plying the canal. Maybe they could feed the pigeons in the Piazza San Marco or go for a gondola ride and snuggle up on a red velvet cushion while the gondolier sang Verdi.

It is said that Venice invites *dolce far niente*, the sweetness of doing nothing. The Venetians have been idle for hundreds of years. Brigid was hoping that kind idleness would be what their marriage needed.

Nate called the desk to reserve a car. While they were waiting for it to be brought around, Brigid suggested that Nate call Cardinal O'Toole and let him know they were delaying their return by a few days. "We should at least wish him well," she said. "After all, he is preparing to elect a new pope."

Nate called the cardinal on his cell phone.

O'Toole was thrilled that they were staying. "After the conclave I'll have a chance to show you the bits of Rome that most tourists never see," he said.

"I also want to thank you, Nate, for everything you have done for the Church," said O'Toole. "I think your investigation will have far-reaching implications." He paused for a second and added, "You're a good man, Nate Condon. Your father would be proud of you."

"Thank you, Your Eminence," said Nate. "God bless you, too."

29

THE GENERAL CONGREGATION

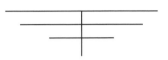

AS SOON AS CARDINAL O'TOOLE HUNG UP THE PHONE WITH
Nate, he called the Vatican transportation office to request a car to trans-
port him and Jack McClendon the few city blocks from his apartment to
the Casa Santa Marta, inside the Vatican walls.

The Casa Santa Marta is a guesthouse used by official visitors to the
Vatican. The term "guesthouse" is a misnomer. It is actually more like
a small hotel, with about 140 rooms, a large dining room, and a chapel
that can accommodate a few hundred people. Each of the residential
rooms has a private bath, and most of them are small suites with a sitting
room as well. The hotel was built in the 1990s, on the orders of Pope
John Paul II.

Most of the time, it serves as a short-term residence for clerics who
work in the Vatican or for visitors on some official business. During the
election of a pope, however, the regular residents are evicted to make
room for the cardinals who will elect the pope and their immediate staff.

Prior to the construction of the casa, the Vatican workmen used to
construct cubicles for the cardinals in the hallways of the Vatican Museums, just off the Sistine Chapel. Those lodgings were uncomfortable,
drafty, and difficult for the elderly men who might be locked up there for
days in the conclave. All those old men had to shuffle down the hallways

to common bathrooms. For men of a certain age, who found it necessary to get up several times per night, it was quite a procession.

So, John Paul II ordered a place built that was equipped with modern plumbing, heating, and air-conditioning.

Conclaves are an oddity of the Catholic Church. In Catholic parlance, a conclave refers to the meeting to elect a new pope.

Cardinal electors are cut off from the outside world during the election. They are not allowed to have radio or television, cell phones, or Internet access. They are transported back and forth from the casa to the Sistine Chapel in buses with curtained windows. Vatican employees are not allowed to signal or contact the cardinals, and cardinals are not allowed to communicate with the outside world.

Locking the cardinals up is designed more to keep unwanted influence out than to keep the prelates in.

Conclaves are nearly eight hundred years old. In centuries past, many cardinals functioned more as a proxy vote for kings or lobbyists for rival factions in the Church. The kings of Spain and France and the Holy Roman Emperor once had veto power over who was elected pope. Influence-peddling in papal elections was once rife. Benefices and offices were traded back and forth to guarantee someone's election or to buy someone's support. The most corrupt pope in history, Alexander VI, the infamous Rodrigo Borgia, ascended to the papacy the old-fashioned way: by bribery.

For the first five centuries after Jesus, the Bishop of Rome was chosen by a vote of the clergy and the people of the city of Rome, just like bishops elsewhere. Gradually, only the deacons, priests, and bishops of the city and the surrounding suburbs of Rome were allowed to vote. These men were generally incardinated in the diocese of Rome; that is, they had faculties to function in Rome. In 1059, voting in papal elections was restricted to cardinal electors alone.

Not all cardinals were clerics. There were lay cardinals, and even a few boy cardinals, one as young as seven years old. As the papacy increased its power, the election of a pope became more and more contentious. Some cardinal electors represented outside interests like kings and countries. Elections could drag on for months, even years. By the Middle Ages, cardinals were locked in, with a key, to force them to come to some sort of conclusion.

The first true conclave was in 1241. It included only ten cardinals.

The longest conclave on record took almost three years, from 1268 to 1271. Back then, the conclave was usually held in the same town where the pope had died, in that case Viterbo, just south of Rome.

Twenty cardinals were locked in a little castle while deliberations dragged on for three years.

The frustrated townspeople gradually reduced the cardinals' rations to bread and water. Still the cardinals haggled and dithered. Finally, the enraged townspeople went up on the roof and began to remove it, plank by plank. The old men inside still refused to compromise. Three of the twenty cardinals died from exposure. One cardinal resigned in disgust.

In the end, they elected a layman, Teobaldo Visconti. He was immediately ordained a priest and a bishop. So much for the need for pastoral experience.

Things have changed over the years. Conclaves are not so violent or dramatic. In the past 200 years, no conclave has lasted more than a week or so. Most of the politicking is done before they enter the Sistine Chapel.

Prior to the conclave, the cardinals meet for five or six days to discuss the state of the Church in what they call general congregations. Conclaves are secret, but the congregations are public. It is in the course of these deliberations that the real politicking takes place.

These upcoming congregations promised to be painful. Mike O'Toole was dreading them. He had been asked to give one of the meditations to the assembled cardinals. These are intended to set the tone and direction of the conclave.

He knew that all the dirty linen of the Church would be aired. Things could get rough. As diplomats might say, it would be a "full and frank exchange of views."

With the leak of Nate's report to *The New York Times*, there was no papering over the problems of the Church. It was in crisis. The relentless drumbeat of bad news made it the worst crisis since the Reformation. The local Roman newspaper, *La Repubblica*, asked in a headline, "Is the Barque of Peter Sinking?"

If it was not sinking, it was certainly taking on water at an alarming rate.

A black cloud had settled over the cardinals. It was in this atmosphere that Jack and Mike checked into the Casa Santa Marta. Mike went off to the meetings, and Jack to his room.

"I'm feeling very tired," said Jack. "Maybe I'll take a nap before lunch." He looked pale.

The Synod Hall is a large modern theater in the Vatican, with a few hundred seats. In the arm of each seat are a headphone jack and a set of controls, so that listeners can receive simultaneous translations. Its technological amenities were in stark contrast to the rest of the Vatican.

As a truly global organization, the Catholic Church needs a way to make everyone understood at these meetings. Some people called it the Pentecost Hall, because like the hearers of the apostles on Pentecost, each person hears in his own language.

Now that Pope Thomas's funeral was behind them, the electors would focus on the conclave ahead. What the cardinals said would determine the future of the Church and their own futures.

Mike O'Toole had been chosen as one of the two cardinals to present a meditation on the seriousness and importance of the upcoming conclave. To the insider crowd, he seemed a safe choice. He was, after all, one of them. But Cardinal O'Toole had always had an independent streak.

After the opening prayer, he made his way to the dais at the front of the theater, took a drink of water, and began to speak.

"My brothers, we are in crisis.

"The crisis is of our own making. We are charged with preaching the gospel of our Lord Jesus Christ. That is our mission. We have not been faithful to our mission. Instead, we have gone off after other things.

"Over the next few days, as we approach the conclave, the world will experience a tsunami of images from Vatican City. What picture will the world have of us? Will they see humble servants of the man from Galilee or princes of a worldly power?

"We Catholics, who love our Church and see it as the body of Christ made visible, should step back from the pomp and power of these meetings and consider what image we project.

"What would Jesus say of us? Would he say to us that we are blind guides who strain the gnat and swallow the camel?

"Let me make a confession here.

"I have been a priest and bishop for nearly half a century. In all those years I have seen in the Catholic Church more corruption than I care to admit. In truth, I have also been part of that corruption.

"I know that I have devoted most of my time to the machinery of running the Church as an institution and very little of my time to the preaching of the gospel.

"I know that I have spent most of my life in association with the rich and the powerful and very little in contact with the poor and the suffering.

"I know that I have been more concerned with my prerogatives and titles than I have been with proclaiming good news to the poor, liberty to captives, or bringing sight to the blind.

"I know that I have sought to protect our power and wealth and prestige, and as a result have served not God, but mammon.

"I know that I have made our customs and traditions more important than the spiritual needs of our people. Today, we have priests who toil with as many as ten thousand faithful in their care, and no one to help them. In my own country, more than three thousand parishes have no pastor.

"Worst of all, I know that I have allowed wolves to attack our flock, rather than be the good shepherd who lays down his life for his sheep.

"Bishops have not protected the children in their care, and instead have protected their own image and power. Instead of consequence or punishment, they have been given the reward of prominent positions."

There was an audible gasp in the hall at the clear reference O'Toole was making to the former Archbishop of Boston, sitting just a few feet in front of him.

O'Toole continued anyway. "We are in crisis.

"One of our brothers has committed suicide because of corruption.

"Another of our brothers is in prison, accused of the most horrific crimes.

"People are not coming to the sacraments or hearing the voice of Christ, scandalized by our behavior.

"Many people feel that the Church does not love them, indeed that it scorns them. Many people think we offer no mercy, only judgment.

"Ours is an old and large house, elaborately furnished, but one that needs cleaning.

"For all our sins and failures, there is much good in this Church of ours.

"Here we have met Christ.

"Here we have heard his voice and known his presence.

"Here we have found community and shared love.

"Here we have experienced forgiveness and known peace.

"In the days to come, we must recapture what is best in our tradition and have the courage to dismiss that which is sinful or harmful.

"This is not an easy task, but it is a necessary one.

"We have only one purpose, to continue the ministry of our Lord Jesus.

"As St. Paul said, 'I count everything as rubbish except the surpassing value of knowing our Lord Jesus Christ.'

"'Forgetting what lies behind, but straining forward to what lies ahead, we continue our pursuit toward the goal, the prize of God's upward calling in Christ Jesus.'"

Mike O'Toole, the Catholic boy from Salem, Massachusetts, the boy who served early morning Mass, the prefect of his class in the seminary, the obedient son of the Church, sat down exhausted, feeling weak at the knees.

The eyes of all in the auditorium were on him.

He looked up toward the back row of the auditorium and saw his friend Jim Kelleher sitting in the seat on the end. Jim gave him a thumbs-up.

Cardinal Alejandro Mendoza of Mexico, head of the Sacred Penitentiary and a member of the Soldados de Cristo, stood up and abruptly walked out. He was followed by four other members of the Soldados de Cristo who had been seated in the gallery. Clearly not everyone was pleased with Michael O'Toole.

30

CONCLAVE AND CONFESSION

AFTER MORNING MASS IN ST. PETER'S BASILICA AND LUNCH at the casa, the cardinal electors walked in procession to the Sistine Chapel, identically dressed in scarlet silk cassocks and white lace surplices, with short scarlet capes called mozzettas draped over their shoulders. On their heads, they each wore little red zucchettos and square stiff birettas. Individually, they looked ridiculous. But together, they were strangely impressive.

Just before they entered the chapel, the cardinals were required to turn in all their electronic devices: mobile phones, pagers, laptops, iPads, and anything else that could be used to communicate with the outside world. Most cardinals handed them to their secretaries or assistants. O'Toole handed his cell phone to Father Jim Kelleher, who was acting as his assistant, as he boarded the bus to go over to the Sistine Chapel.

At the entrance to the chapel, they processed down a long corridor to the chapel door, while the Sistine choir sang the ancient litany of the saints, a hypnotic chant.

"Saint Peter, Saint Paul, St. Andrew," the choir intoned in Latin.

At each saint's name, the cardinals answered the choir in a haunting refrain, "*Ora pro nobis*," meaning pray for us. There were a lot of saints, because the procession took twenty minutes to fill the chapel.

Like prep school boys, the cardinals lined up in order of seniority, senior to junior. As they entered the Sistine Chapel, each took his place at four rows of tables, two rows on each side of the center aisle of the chapel. The tables were draped with skirted wine-colored velvet and covered with white tablecloths.

On the ceiling above them in the center panel was Michelangelo's depiction of *The Creation of Adam*, showing God the Father's crooked finger touching Adam and bringing him to life. In the neighboring panel, Adam and Eve were shown weeping at their expulsion from the Garden of Eden.

On the front wall of the chapel, above the altar, was Michelangelo's fresco of *The Last Judgment*. The cardinals looked up at the last judgment each time they came forward to the altar to cast their votes. It was a stirring reminder of the gravity of their decision. They would have to account for themselves and their vote when they stood before the judgment seat of the Lord.

Michelangelo included only one cardinal in his representation of the final judgment—the notorious Cesare Borgia, who at the time was the Archbishop of Valencia, in Spain. He is shown being ferried off to hell by the Greek god Minos.

Borgia was hardly an edifying reminder of the lineage of cardinals. He was the role model for Machiavelli's scheming prince. He was the illegitimate son of his even more notorious father, Rodrigo Borgia, Pope Alexander VI, who was elected pope in that very chapel, fifty years before Michelangelo completed his famous painting.

Pope Alexander VI shocked even jaded Renaissance Europe with his behavior. He had multiple mistresses and fathered nine illegitimate children, including Cesare. One wonders how any conclave could have chosen the scandalous Rodrigo as pope.

This conclave promised to be more abstemious than the conclave that elected the Borgia pope.

In the middle of a long line of electors, Cardinal O'Toole proceeded slowly to his assigned place. Once at their seats, the cardinals took off their birettas and placed them neatly on their desks next to their name-plates. They were, after all, products of Catholic schools and like everyone trained by the nuns, valued order in everything.

Together, they lifted the little leather-bound prayer booklets, which had been placed at the center of their red leather blotters, also embossed with the Vatican seal. In unison, they said the midday prayer together.

At the end of the conclave, the cardinals could keep their blotters, prayer books, and nameplates as souvenirs. They were sort of papal door prizes.

Their prayers at an end, the cardinals came forward one by one to take an oath of secrecy, promising never to reveal the deliberations of the conclave. Each cardinal approached a podium set up in the center aisle of the chapel, to add his signature to the book that contained the words of the oath.

With all the preliminaries over and the cardinals back in their seats, the master of ceremonies for papal liturgical functions issued a stern order in Latin, *Extra Omnes!* Everybody out!

The aides to the cardinals, the monsignors, the television people, and everybody except the cardinals filed out. Then the chapel doors were gently closed and locked; the Swiss Guards, in ceremonial dress, were posted just outside the chapel doors, to keep out all intruders.

Suddenly, the conclavists were alone. In that moment of isolation O'Toole felt the weight of his conscience and of history. He took a deep breath. Be with me now, Holy Spirit, he thought. Momentarily the balloting would begin.

The first ballot is merely a beauty contest. Cardinals voted for one another as a courtesy to an old friend or an honor to an important figure. Many names received a few votes, but they were not serious candidates. The second ballot was a more radical winnowing out of the real papabile.

There were two ballots in the first afternoon session. No cardinal got more than forty votes on either ballot. Votes were roughly divided among two blocs of cardinals, one bloc from the Southern Hemisphere and the other from cardinals of the Roman bureaucracy.

Each cardinal was supposed to disguise his handwriting as he wrote the name of his candidate on a ballot, but it really didn't matter much, since the ballots were burned after they were counted. After the ballot was filled out, they proceeded by order of seniority to the altar to cast their votes. O'Toole was in the middle of the pack.

As he approached the altar, O'Toole raised his hand holding the ballot high over his head, so all could see he had only one ballot. He declared in Latin, "I call as my witness Christ the Lord, who will be my judge, that my vote is given to the one whom, before God, I think should be elected."

Michael O'Toole, the fireman's kid from Boston, placed the twice-folded ballot on the gold plate that rested on top of a twenty-five-inch-tall gold chalice that stood at the center of the altar. He looked up at Michelangelo's *The Last Judgment* and then turned over the plate, allowing the ballot to drop into the chalice. He turned and walked back to his seat. He had cast a safe vote, for Cardinal Santini, the camerlengo, just another faceless Vatican bureaucrat. But he knew that vote was just a placeholder until he could see which way the wind was blowing in the conclave. For a church so deeply mired in crisis, a safe vote would not be enough. Once again he felt afraid. This time not for himself, but for the Church.

After all the ballots were cast, the three scrutineers counted the total number of ballots, to be sure it was exactly the same as the number of cardinal electors. Then they opened and recorded the actual votes on tally sheets maintained by each scrutineer. The last of the three vote counters read aloud, in Latin, the names written on the ballot. It was almost hypnotic. Johanem Cardinalem Kluger. Paulus Cardinalem Kilgari.

The first and second rounds of voting went smoothly. The only sounds were the calling of the names by the scrutineers and the hushed talking among the cardinals. The conclavists weren't supposed to keep their own totals, but some of them made discreet coded notes on their blotters to keep track of the voting. O'Toole was surprised to hear his own name a score of times. Michael Cardinalem O'Toole. He assumed that these votes were courtesies from mission-country cardinals who had benefited from his assistance.

As evening drew near, the scrutineers burned the ballot cards from the two rounds of voting together in the potbellied stove in the corner of the Sistine Chapel, near the door. They added some coal tar to make black smoke to indicate that Rome had not yet elected a new pope. In the piazza outside, twenty thousand people were waiting. They were disappointed, but not surprised, when they saw the smoke was black.

After the votes were burned, everyone broke for dinner.

The conclavists piled onto three buses with curtain-drawn windows and made the five-minute drive across the Vatican to the Casa Santa Marta. There was little talking even to the staff. Inside the casa, the cardinals were like monks in an abbey, only there was no abbot.

For some reason, O'Toole felt absolutely exhausted when he arrived at the dining room.

In theory, the electors are prohibited from making any deals. But men are men, and a lot of politicking took place at mealtime.

There was no assigned seating. Dinner was served on a long buffet table, to keep staff to a minimum. The meals were bland. For men accustomed to the finest food in the world, the simple fare was an incentive to get down to business.

Mike O'Toole filled his plates with pasta and salad and made his way to a table in the far corner of the room, where three other cardinals were already seated. They were all English speakers from Australia, the Philippines, and Kenya, so he felt comfortable in their presence.

The conclavists tended to sort themselves out by language. Polyglot cardinals were at a distinct advantage. They had many more potential dinner partners. Americans were often at a distinct disadvantage, because they were linguistically challenged. Americans were derisively known as the silent cardinals because of their lack of language skills.

Actually, language was only recently a problem in papal conclaves. Before the 1970s, pretty much everybody spoke Italian.

Just beyond the table where Mike O'Toole sat down, two cardinals were seated at a smaller table, locked in what seemed to be an intense debate.

The Mexican, Alejandro Mendoza, leaned forward over his plate of pasta, knife in his right hand and fork in his left. He glared across the table at a more reserved and quieter Frenchman, Cardinal Jean Louis Amiot, the Archbishop of Paris. Mendoza was visibly angry.

"The problem is Vatican II," he said, practically shouting at Amiot in Italian.

"Nonsense," returned Amiot. "The problem is that the reform started at Vatican II was never finished."

"You idiot liberals," seethed Mendoza. "The last legitimate pope was Pius XII, and the last valid council was Vatican I. All the rest is apostasy."

"Are you saying that three thousand bishops of the Roman Catholic Church were in heresy at Vatican II?" challenged Amiot, half-amused and half-shocked.

"I'm saying that they betrayed the Church and sold out to the corruption of our age. You liberals destroyed the Church," said Mendoza, pointing his knife menacingly at Amiot and practically spitting.

The Archbishop of Paris was not accustomed to being accused of being a liberal. Back home, Parisians thought of him as a conservative. Amiot's usually timid openness to modern French culture passed for modernity in this dining room full of reactionaries.

The argument between Mendoza and Amiot was beginning to attract the attention of the other cardinal electors. It was getting loud.

"You idiot reformers. You ruined everything. Before that fat man, John XXIII, sat his ass on the Throne of Peter, the Church was just fine. The seminaries were full. The nuns were obedient. Women knew their place. There was no talk of divorce. It was illegal in most Catholic countries, which does not include France." Mendoza was landing as many rhetorical blows as he could.

"And all this nonsense talk about religious liberty—that's the fault of you French and your revolution. We never should have adopted that stupid declaration of religious liberty. *Dignitatis Humanae* indeed. How can we say that people should be free to choose their own religion? People should only be free to choose the truth. The truth, I tell you!" Mendoza was red faced. It seemed he had delivered this diatribe before.

Energized by the attack, Amiot was not backing down.

"You Latins. What would you like? Another inquisition?" he shouted back. "You want to go back in time to your childhood. You want the Church to go back to 1955 and your beloved Pius XII. Well, you can't!

"It doesn't matter if you get every priest in the world to wear a cassock, you can't take the Church back to 1955. We don't live there anymore. Even if *we* had not changed, the *world* has changed. People won't listen to our arrogant breast-beating about the 'truth.'"

Mendoza countered, "If we were confident of our faith again, we could get people to listen to us. Your friends sold us out to the world. You whine about wanting to be relevant to the age. Relevant? You pushed relevancy so far, we became irrelevant!"

Everyone in the room put down their forks and focused on the dueling Mexican and Frenchman. It was a show worth watching.

"You French are a bunch of airheads. Tell me, why is it that every French priest has written a book on spirituality and nobody in France goes to church? Why should anybody bother to listen to your relevant Church?" Mendoza's tone was openly mocking. "You have nothing to say to the world, and the world does not care to have an echo of itself."

Amiot stood up and threw down his napkin as if challenging Mendoza.

"*Mon Dieu*, apologize!" said the Frenchman, more in a hiss than a shout.

"You Latins, with your Opus Dei and your Soldados de Cristo, you won't be content until you bring back the auto-da-fé, the rack, and the thumbscrew! You want the burning of heretics? Maybe we should burn a few liberal nuns and moral theologians, just like we did Bruno! Is that what you want? Another bonfire in Campo de Fiori?"

Everybody in the room was openmouthed by now. They would not have been the least bit surprised if either cardinal had pulled a pistol out of his cassock. These tensions simmer beneath the surface of every Church gathering, but they seldom come out so dramatically.

Amiot was not done. "The problem with Vatican II was that we didn't go far enough. People today are not children. They read books. They know science. They have thoughts. We can't just pat them on the head and tell them what to think and what to do.

"People today engage with other religions and cultures. We have more practicing Muslims in France than Catholics. Your fifteenth-century world is gone forever, Alejandro. There is no going back. Women work today. They are educated. They don't need men telling them what to do. They don't need marriage to survive.

"You talk about France and change, what about your precious Mexico? The Mexicans invented birth control, and they certainly have embraced it. Mexico City legalized gay marriage long before we French made it legal. Change has already come to Mexico, and you don't see it. We lose ten thousand Catholics a day to evangelical churches in Latin America, and your Soldados do nothing but cultivate rich widows. So, where was your witness to the Catholic faith? *Merde*."

O'Toole felt dizzy as he listened.

"Let me tell you something, Alejandro. Sure we made some mistakes at Vatican II. But the Church does not exist in a hermetically sealed bubble. We have to change, and we always have, even though we don't admit it.

"Once we condemned Galileo. Then, four hundred years later, we said we were sorry. Believe it or not, sometimes the Church is just wrong. We've changed on a lot of things. Once we practiced capital punishment; now we oppose it. Once we participated in the slave trade in the Americas; now we condemn it. Once we said usury was a mortal sin; now we have priests who are bankers. Once we turned Jews over to the torturers; now we call them elder brothers. We were wrong. We had to change." Amiot was waving his arms now, practically swinging at Mendoza.

"But you conservatives are so convinced that you are always right. Your certitude makes you cruel. Maybe it is your certainty that you possess the absolute truth that makes you so cruel."

Then the Archbishop of Paris got personal. "You conservatives are a bunch of frauds. Look at your order, the Soldados—so conservative! You condemn everyone else as a sinner. But you were started by a pedophile philanderer and a thief. How many children did your founder sire? How many boys did he take to his bed? Remove the beam from your own eye before you try to pluck the splinter from your neighbor's eye."

Amiot was intoxicated with his fury. There was no restraining him now, though he would regret his outburst in the morning.

He continued. "You condemn homosexuals—'intrinsically disordered,' you call them. But your order is absolutely full of . . ." Amiot stammered for a moment. "How do they say it in English? Closet queens." He was actually spitting his words out.

"You are *toujours gai*. You make the Church stink with hypocrisy. Clean out your own house before you point fingers at mine!"

Mendoza looked stunned at this onslaught. Amiot pressed his advantage. "What do you have to say to the modern world? Women back to your kitchen! Gays back to your closet! Nuns back to your cloister! Muslims back to Arabia! Blacks back to Africa! Protestants, off with your heads!"

Everyone was breathless. One thing about the French that you have to admire—they have a way with words, no matter what language they are speaking.

It was all too much for Mendoza. He grabbed the water glass on the table in front of him and tossed its contents into Amiot's face.

"I am no queen," shrieked Mendoza in an octave that seemed to undercut his point.

Mendoza pointed his finger at the drenched Amiot and said, "We will see where this conclave takes us tomorrow. I predict your day is finished."

With the rigid pride of a bullfighter, Mendoza straightened himself up and made for the door. His movement was impeded, however. During the debate with Amiot, the Mexican cardinal's sash had entangled itself in the arm of his chair. Unaware that he was tethered to the chair, Mendoza pulled it along behind him as he tried to make an indignant exit. The chair bumped along for a couple of steps, until it wedged itself under the lip of one of the dining room tables. The other cardinals began to giggle at the sight of the trailing chair. Mendoza fell to the carpet.

The pratfall broke the spell of the argument. The dining room erupted in spontaneous laughter. The Cardinal Archbishop of Rio De Janeiro laughed so hard he almost choked on his tiramisu.

Cardinal Amiot stepped forward to help Mendoza up, but the bull-fighter in the fallen cardinal asserted itself. He was too proud to accept assistance from his opponent. He took a swing at the Frenchman instead. Once back on his feet, Mendoza extricated his sash from the arm of the offending chair and made a rapid exit.

Dinner was over.

O'Toole felt like he was in a bar back in Southie. His first thought was "I have to tell Jack." He went straight up to McClendon's room on the top floor of the casa, where the confessors and support staff were lodged. Mike knew he could find a drink there. Jack had doubtless smuggled a bottle of vodka into the casa.

"Jack," he said when the old man opened the door, "you'll never believe what just happened at dinner. It was a real fight: Amiot from Paris and Mendoza, the Soldado. They really went at it. It was almost like being in a schoolyard." O'Toole looked around. "You have a drink here?" he asked.

"In the bathroom," said Jack. "There is ice in the trash bag. You won't believe how hard it was to find ice in this place."

O'Toole poured himself a vodka and came back into Jack's bedroom. They each took a seat in the armchairs near the window.

O'Toole was emotionally exhausted.

"I don't know, Jack. The wheels seem to be coming off the Church.

Two cardinals practically got into a fistfight over the direction we are taking. You know, the usual stuff. Mendoza wants to roll back Vatican II. Amiot thinks Mendoza is a fraud and a hypocrite. It seems like we're heading for a schism rather than a renewal."

Jack could see that his friend and protégé was really hurting. "Mike, maybe the schism already exists. We haven't agreed for years now. Maybe it has to come out in the open."

"Well, I can't see how two cardinals practically duking it out in the dining room helps anything."

"A false agreement doesn't help anything either," said Jack. "It is only a façade of unity, not real communion."

O'Toole leaned toward his old friend and confessor. "Can we treat this like a confession?" he asked.

"It's under the seal," answered Jack, making the sign of the cross in blessing. "That's why I'm here."

For a moment he felt just like little Mike O'Toole, the idealistic college kid going to friendly old Father McClendon for confession during his summer vacation.

"Father, I think I have been a fraud and hypocrite, just like Amiot accused Mendoza. I have been ambitious. Many times I have remained silent for the sake of my career. It was my pride. I wanted to hold high office, but I did nothing once I got a red hat. I just took care of myself."

Jack wanted to be soothing to his old friend. "Did you do what you thought was right?"

"No, that's just it. I did what I knew was wrong sometimes. I did only what I thought I needed to do to advance in the Church."

"What for?" asked Jack.

"Nothing, just to climb up the tree." Cardinal O'Toole chuckled to himself. "One of the missionary bishops told me they have a saying: 'The higher the monkey climbs, the more ass he shows.'"

They both laughed.

"Do you think your ass is showing?" asked McClendon.

"Sometimes," said O'Toole. "None of this stuff has anything to do with preaching the gospel. Look at me. I'm investigating cardinals who might be killing cardinals. That bright boy from Charlestown, Nate Condon, gave us a report that would curl your hair. We have cardinals who are pedophiles. We have cardinals who launder money for the mob. We have cardinals who get assassinated because they oppose the Soldados de Cristo." He paused and took a sip of his vodka.

Crepi and Salazar came to his mind as he continued. "I knew years ago that Crepi was a scoundrel. I let him go on stealing. I suspected Salazar was on the take from the drug cartels, and I knew that he had a love for young boys. I never did anything, though. I just let the rot spread. And what about me? All I did was keep the whole engine going. I worshiped the Church, not God."

"Silence in the face of evil is a sin," said Jack, affirming O'Toole's confession. "Sometimes our sins of omission are more damaging than our sins of commission."

O'Toole nodded. After a pause he resumed his confession.

"Look, Jack, I've sent a lot of money to African bishops. I know full well that the only reason the African bishops go along with celibacy is because they need money from Rome. I know, and they know, that few of their priests are actually celibate. They have wives and mistresses on the side. But we all just go along, pretending."

"Not everyone," interjected Jack.

"Well, no, not everyone, but practically everyone," answered Mike. "The whole thing is like a giant mutual fraud. We pretend to believe what we are saying. They pretend to accept our preaching. We know they don't pay much attention to us, and they know that we don't really care, so long as they keep up appearances. The Church just keeps on going. Nobody is really listening to us on things like birth control. Look at the Italians. They have the lowest birth rate in the world.

"We don't really believe what we are saying ourselves. They go along with us, because they just like being in church on Sunday morning. It gives them a feeling of belonging. They like singing, I guess."

"I guess," said Jack. "Or maybe they don't have anywhere else to go for spiritual nourishment."

There was a long pause. O'Toole took another sip of vodka. Confession is easier with a vodka, he thought. Then he continued.

"Why didn't I say the obvious, years ago? When I was in the parish back home, I talked to a woman who had six kids and an alcoholic husband. They had no food in the fridge. I told her to go home to her husband and be obedient to the bastard. 'It's your duty,' I told her. She couldn't use birth control, because we said so. Sex was supposed to be total self-giving, we told her. What nonsense! There was no self-giving in that alcoholic husband of hers, only taking. A few weeks later I prayed over her in the morgue." O'Toole covered his face with his hands. Jack reached forward and put his hand on Mike's shoulder.

"I sent a few women back to their alcoholic husbands," continued the cardinal. "I loaded them up with guilt. I should have told them to pack up the car and get the hell out.

"Even in confession I toed the company line, even when it destroyed people. You know that gay boy I did the funeral for back in Charlestown? You remember that, Jack?"

Jack nodded sadly.

"He was a good kid. But let me tell you something else. I did the funeral, not because I was a good priest, but because I felt guilty. I felt guilty, because I was hiding my own secrets. I knew that boy was gay, because I had seen him out at a bar in Boston. I was there in the bar. I don't really know why I was there. I was out with some friends for the evening, and out of curiosity we went to this bar. That's where I saw him. I don't know if he saw me or not. At least that kid was honest about himself. I was the fraud, Jack. I was the fraud."

"You weren't a fraud," said Jack. "You are just an ordinary human being."

"I don't even know what my sexuality is," said O'Toole. "Sad to be sixty-five years old and not even know what your sexuality is."

There were tears running down Mike O'Toole's face. He seemed like a teenager again—vulnerable, teachable. There was silence for a long time as both men realized that this was the most honest moment of a fifty-year friendship.

Jack broke the silence. "We did what we were told. We trusted the ones who told us. That does not excuse us, but it helps explain us. "

Then Jack added, "We were obedient sons to Holy Mother the Church. We always want to support our mother, even when we know she is wrong. She's your mother, after all. You never want to admit that she drinks or fools around, so you paper over the problems and put a good face on the family. But in the long run, it would be better if you admitted that mom was a drunk and got her help."

"Are we a dysfunctional family?" asked Mike.

"All religions are dysfunctional families," said Jack. "The problem with us Catholics is that we are a close-knit dysfunctional family. We hug our neurosis tight, like a security blanket."

They both laughed.

"Is there a way out for me?" said O'Toole.

"Yes," answered Jack, "more of a way out for you than for me. My day is over, but you are still on the field. In many ways, I lost my chance. Don't lose your chance now.

"You can't undo the past, but from now on, the unvarnished truth will be your best friend. Speak the truth in love, but resolve to speak the truth, even when it embarrasses us."

"You were never afraid to speak the truth," said O'Toole, looking at Jack with admiration. "I remember when you went down to Selma to march on that bridge, even though all the racists in Southie wanted the cardinal to excommunicate you. You even confronted the racists in Boston in the school desegregation riots. You could have been killed. You marched with Martin Luther King, and you demonstrated against the Vietnam War. You made us look at poverty. I never thought that you were afraid of anything, Jack."

"That stuff was easy," answered Jack. "It's easy to reform other people's houses. I never did much within the Church, though."

"You spoke out about celibacy and birth control," offered Mike.

"Weakly," said Jack, "and not often enough. And not at any expense to myself."

The intensity of the confession had exhausted them both. They leaned back in their chairs.

"I'm not sure if I should give you absolution or whether you should give it to me," said Jack. "Maybe we should absolve each other."

"Let me kneel down for an act of contrition," said Cardinal O'Toole. "I wish I'd been half the priest that you have been over the years."

The cardinal-prince of the Church knelt down in front of his old pastor and said a child's act of contrition. "Oh, my God, I am heartily sorry for having offended thee." Tears streamed down the faces of both confessor and penitent.

When O'Toole finished his prayer, Jack spoke the words of absolution over his kneeling friend.

"Through the ministry of the Church, may God grant you pardon and peace. I absolve you of all of your sins, in the name of the Father, the Son, and the Holy Spirit."

The two old friends struggled to their feet and embraced.

"There won't be many more times together," said Jack. "As soon as this conclave is over, I'm back to Gloucester."

"I know," said O'Toole. "That's why I wanted you here now."

After O'Toole went downstairs to his room, Jack got ready for bed. Just before he turned out the light, he went to the window and looked out on the Roman night sky. Up on the Gianicolo Hill, in the big city park, lovers were making out in cars parked along the road that overlooked the city. A mile away in the late-night cafes near Piazza Navonna, people were drinking coffee and liquor and arguing politics. Families were going for late-night strolls to get gelato. There was ordinary life.

Somewhere in the distance Jack could hear a dog barking.

31

THE ELECTION

THE NEXT DAY, MIKE O'TOOLE WAS UP EARLY, BUT JACK, enervated by a terrible fatigue, slept in.

When the buses arrived to take the cardinals to the Sistine Chapel for the next session of the conclave, the mood among the electors was tense. Mercifully, Amiot and Mendoza rode on separate buses.

The day's session began with midday prayer. Friday, the day Christ died, is the penitential day, a time to recall our sinfulness. O'Toole recalled the argument the night before between Amiot and Mendoza as they listened to the day's reading from Philippians:

> "Maintain your unanimity, possessing the one love, united in spirit and ideals. Never act out of rivalry or conceit: rather let all parties think humbly of others as superior to themselves, each of you looking to other's interest rather than his own."

As he looked around at the splendidly arrayed "princes of the Church," he thought that perhaps they should have started the session with the words of Psalm 146:

> *Put not your trust in princes,*
> *in mortal men in whom there is no help.*

Take their breath and they return to clay,
and their plans that day come to nothing.

The specter of Crepi lying dead in the Vatican gardens and Salazar languishing in an Italian jail hovered over the chapel. So did the memory of the fury of the argument the night before at dinner.

The balloting continued just as the day before, with the scrutineers calling out the names. They had two ballots in the morning. Then, just before lunch, they burned the ballots in the potbellied stove with some coal tar to make black smoke. The people waiting in the square were again disappointed.

Nobody talked much on the buses back to the casa. It was clear to everyone that the field was narrowing and that Cardinal O'Toole was a contender. His name had received more than forty votes in the morning session, clearly more than a "courtesy vote" from mission countries.

Perhaps the cardinals identified Mike as a safe choice. As a curial cardinal he was seen as an insider, not a threat to the established order. But as an American, he was seen as something new. Perhaps he would be a better manager than Pope Thomas had been. Maybe he could douse the flames of scandal swirling around the Church.

O'Toole noticed that Jack was not in the dining room for *pranzo*, but there was no time to check on him.

After lunch, the cardinals took a brief nap. Italians call it a *pisolino*. Americans might call it a power nap.

O'Toole went by Jack's room after his *pisolino* and tapped on the door. Hearing no response, he pushed the door open a bit. Jack was asleep in the easy chair. Good, he thought, the old man is resting.

At 3:00 p.m., the cardinals were once more on buses, headed for the Sistine Chapel. By 4:00 p.m., they were casting the first ballot of the afternoon. It was clear that coalitions were forming.

Three cardinals received a substantial number of votes. The Archbishop of Nairobi received thirty votes. The Archbishop of Sao Paulo received thirty-six votes. And Michael O'Toole garnered forty-two votes. Perhaps the taboo against electing an American was weakening.

The atmosphere was tense as they prepared for the second ballot of the afternoon. If there were to be a decision that day, it would come now. They repeated the ritual of the previous ballots.

After everyone had voted, the three cardinal scrutineers came forward and took their seats at the table near the altar. They collected the ballots and began to count them.

The calling of names fell into the rhythm of a litany.

Sitting at his place, Cardinal O'Toole kept his own tally. Two-thirds were needed for election. Since there were one hundred twenty voting cardinals, eighty was the magic number.

O'Toole was gaining votes, probably because the African and Asian votes were moving his way. All those years of distributing mission money and visiting their dioceses had made O'Toole a familiar and friendly face.

The litany continued. O'Toole, O'Toole, O'Toole. The revisers examined each ballot. Michael O'Toole began to sweat. Sixty-five, sixty-six, sixty-seven.

He thought of his father, who'd left the Church in anger. He thought of his mother, who died at the age of ninety-three, a daily communicant until just before she died.

Memories overwhelmed him. He thought of the times he rode his bicycle up Commonwealth Avenue to serve early morning Mass, moved by the mystery of it all. He thought of the Dominican sisters from his parish school, filing into a darkened church for the 6:30 a.m. Mass in their white habits and black veils. They had seemed stern and tender at the very same time.

In his distraction O'Toole lost count. Was it seventy-five or seventy-six? He didn't know. Eighty-one, eighty-two. The singsong continued.

Suddenly, he was aware that the other cardinals were on their feet applauding. They were looking at him. The revisers confirmed the vote: eighty-three for O'Toole.

Michael O'Toole realized he had been elected the Bishop of Rome, the Vicar of Jesus Christ, Prince of the Apostles, Supreme Pontiff of the Universal Church, Primate of Italy, Metropolitan of the Roman Provinces, Sovereign of Vatican City, and Servant of the Servants of God.

In short, he was the pope.

He sat frozen at his place. "Oh, God, be my help," he prayed under his breath.

The Dean of the College of Cardinals came to him and asked, "*Accepi electio Pontifex Maximus*? Do you accept your election as Supreme Pontiff?"

O'Toole stood, dry mouthed. He stared at Cardinal Amiot, with his mouth open. Finally, he said quietly, "*Accipio.*"

The Dean then asked, "What name do you wish to be called?"

Michael O'Toole had not thought about what name he wanted to be called if elected pope, at least not seriously. He looked down at the table. Then he looked around the room. His eyes were drawn to the fresco over the altar of the Last Judgment. He saw the Archangel Michael with sword drawn.

"Michael," he said weakly. "My father's name was Michael. It is the name my parents gave me at my baptism. I started my journey with that name, and I will end my journey with that name. I will be Michael."

Already he was breaking with tradition. No pope in a thousand years had chosen to keep his baptismal name, but so be it. Michael it was.

Pope Michael was led out of the chapel and into the so-called "room of tears," where new popes are vested. There, on hangers, were three white cassocks: large, medium, and small. He put on the large one and looked in the mirror, shocked to see himself dressed as the pope.

He was immediately led back into the chapel so the cardinals could line up to make their obeisance.

It was an awkward moment. They had entered the Sistine Chapel as equals, but now he was their superior. Mike O'Toole did not like the feel of it. Instead of sitting in the chair that had been positioned for him on a raised dais, he merely stood in front of the altar and embraced each cardinal as he came forward, both men standing, so they could look each other in the eye.

The ballots were burned in the stove, this time with chemicals to make white smoke. In the piazza, people saw white smoke billow from the little chimney, and a huge cheer went up from the crowd.

It's a long walk from the Sistine Chapel to the balcony on the façade of St. Peter's that overlooks the piazza. All the cardinals were fairly old men, so it took a good half hour to reach the balcony.

The cardinal deacon came to the microphone on the balcony. The sound system squealed as the microphone was turned on. He was not a very good public speaker, and he did not project his words well. He also did not speak directly into the microphone, so his words were garbled. His hand shook as he read the prescribed Latin announcement from a card:

Annuntio vobis gaudium magnum, Habemus Papam, Eminentissimum ac Reverendissimum Dominum, Dominum Michael, Sanctae Romae Ecclesiae Cardinalem, O'Toole qui sibi nomen impsuit Michael.

It was hard to hear over all the background noise. Besides, hardly anyone in the square really knew Latin. The people in the crowd looked at one another for a few seconds, confused.

"Who?" they asked.

* * *

Sitting in his room at the Casa Santa Marta, Jack McClendon was saying his evening prayers when he heard the roar of the crowd in St. Peter's Square. He got up and went to the window. It could be the election, thought Jack. At the very least, the crowd is reacting to the smoke.

Jack's window at the casa looked out on the rear of the great basilica. It was hard to tell what was happening on the other side of the huge church. There were no televisions or radios in the guesthouse, so Jack was at a loss. Perhaps it is the new pope, he thought.

Searching for confirmation, he went out into the hallway to find someone who might know what was going on. There was nobody on his floor, so he took the elevator down to the lobby. A man dressed in a white coat, probably the porter or a waiter, came running through the front door of the casa.

"What's going on?" asked Jack. "I heard noise in the square."

"We have a pope!" said the porter excitedly.

"Who?" asked Jack.

"O'Toole," answered the porter, struggling with the name, which sounded strange to Italian ears. "*Un americano*," he added.

Jack steadied himself on the counter of the registration desk in the lobby.

Poor Mike, thought Jack, he's never coming home again.

Jack went back up to his room, suddenly overcome with fatigue. He sat down in the easy chair and reopened his breviary to finish evening prayer, but he was too distracted to concentrate.

His old prayer book was stuffed with prayer cards, articles, and quotes that he had come to treasure over the years. Really, he no longer needed to read the words of most of the psalms. He knew them by heart.

Jack took out a card with the words of Mary's prayer, the Magnificat. He held it loosely between his thumb and forefinger, not really looking at it. He recited the words from memory.

> *My soul proclaims the greatness of the Lord,*
> *My spirit rejoices in God my savior*
> *For he has looked with favor on his lowly servant.*

As a young priest, he had thought of the Virgin's prayer as just a poem of simple praise. But as he got older, he understood it as a very revolutionary poem, about upsetting the powerful and raising up the powerless. He heard the words with new ears:

> *He has cast down the mighty from their thrones and lifted up*
> *the lowly.*
> *He has filled the hungry with good things*
> *And the rich he has sent away empty.*

He has come to the help of his servant Israel,

For he has remembered his promise of mercy,

To Abraham and his children forever.

As he finished the Magnificat, the card slipped from Jack's fingers and fell to the floor.

*   *   *

In their suite at the Hotel Danieli in Venice, Nate and Brigid watched in stunned surprise as Cardinal O'Toole stepped out onto the balcony of St. Peter's in a white papal cassock. Neither knew what to say. Brigid broke the silence first.

"My God," she said, giddy with excitement, "we actually know the new pope!"

Nate gestured for her to be quiet while O'Toole was preparing to address the crowd in the square. The immense crowd in front of the new pope was both jubilant and curious. Nate wondered if O'Toole would be speaking in English, but he spoke only in Italian, a Boston-accented Italian.

"I'm afraid for him," said Nate, "after everything I've learned about the Church."

"He's nobody's fool," said Brigid.

"Nobody's fool," said Nate with a shrug, "but maybe somebody's target. After all, someone tried to run us off the road just because I was investigating. What do you think they will do to him, now that he has the power to actually threaten them?"

Brigid and Nate watched the television as the new pope turned and walked back behind the red velvet curtain of the balcony.

The reporters from Rai 1 appeared on the screen to give their spin on the papal election. Not understanding what they were saying, Brigid stood up and walked out onto the balcony overlooking the Grand Canal. It was a beautiful Venetian evening.

Nate switched off the TV and fixed them both a drink from the mini-bar. Then he joined her on the balcony. The late summer evening, the lights reflecting on the water of the canal, and the gondolas gliding by silently made them forget about the election.

After a sip of his Campari and soda, he set the drink down on the railing and pulled Brigid toward him. He wrapped her in his arms for a while, stroking her back and hair. Just as he bent down to kiss her, he heard a "pop," like the sound of a rifle. A glass pane in the French doors behind them shattered, and a bullet buried itself into the wall of their hotel room.

Nate pushed Brigid down behind the balcony railing, and a second bullet whizzed overhead and shattered another pane in the door. They lay there safe for a moment behind the brick wall of the balcony rail, terrified. Brigid started screaming. Then she started cursing. "This god-damn Church is going to get us all killed," she yelled.

Nate covered her mouth. "Be quiet. We need to figure out where it is coming from." From the delayed sound of the gunfire, the shooter was some distance away.

They lay there for a minute or two. No more bullets came. Nate whispered to Brigid, "Let's crawl into the room and get to the bathroom. There is a phone in there."

Once in the bathroom, they called the desk. "Call the police," Nate told the desk. "Someone is shooting at us."

"*Subito*," said the man at the desk.

32

ORPHANED

TO EVERYONE'S SURPRISE, O'TOOLE BOARDED THE BUS back to the casa along with the other cardinals, foregoing the customary limo. The papal apartments, sealed up after Pope Thomas died, remained sealed. The new pope's toothbrush, medicines, and clothes were all back at the casa, so he returned with the boys on the bus.

In the dining room, all the cardinals were in high spirits. Cardinal Amiot was positively giddy. A few cardinals, notably Mendoza, were absent from dinner.

O'Toole found himself embarrassed as cardinal after cardinal rose to propose a toast to him during dinner. Pope Michael did not get back to his room until well past 11:00 p.m. He was emotionally and physically exhausted. He hooked up his CPAP machine and fell into a deep sleep.

The next morning was a Saturday. The phone in Pope Michael's room rang while he was shaving. It was Jim Kelleher.

"Good morning, Your Holiness," he said.

O'Toole was taken aback for a second by the title of address. "I'm still Mike to you, Jim."

"I have bad news, Mike. Jack is in the hospital. He had some kind of heart incident last night. They found him sitting in the easy chair in his room this morning. I called the desk at the casa when he didn't answer his phone. Jack was always an early riser, so I knew something must be wrong."

"Where is he?" asked O'Toole.

"The ambulance took him to Gemelli an hour ago," said Kelleher. "I'm going up there now. It looks pretty bad, because Jack told the EMTs in the ambulance that he wanted last rites. Jack would never use that term unless he knew it was the end. I'm sure he wants to see you."

"I'll go with you," said the new pope.

Kelleher was incredulous. "You can't do that," he said. "You're the pope. You can't just run off to the hospital. Besides, you have things to do, don't you?"

"There are people here who will take care of all the planning," said O'Toole. "If Jack thinks this is the end, then it is the end. I would never forgive myself if I didn't see him. Come to the casa and pick me up. I'll call the gate and tell them to let you through. What are you driving?"

Kelleher had to ask somebody what kind of car they had there at the Jesuit residence. "I'll be driving a little Fiat 500, Mike. Hardly fit for the supreme pontiff."

"Bullshit," said O'Toole. "Pick me up! We'll go together. Tell them at the gate that you have some important papers for me from America. Ciao."

After they hung up the phone, O'Toole felt a little disoriented. He had known Jack McClendon since he was a teenager. Jack had always been there for him.

O'Toole still thought of Jack as the strong young priest who had arrived in Salem fresh out of the seminary. He was the curate who took the altar boys swimming in the cold ocean at Devereux Beach in Marblehead. Now Jack was dying. The pope called the gate to alert them for Kelleher and then got dressed.

Absentmindedly, O'Toole dressed himself in his ordinary black suit and clerical collar. He hung his pectoral cross around his neck and stuck it in his jacket pocket, just like any other bishop. Then he remembered the white cassock in the closet. Oh, crap, he thought, I'm pope now. I'll wear what I want. It was a freeing thought.

Pope Michael went down to the lobby to wait for Kelleher. The porter was sitting at the front desk reading *La Repubblica*. He was so startled to see the pope that he spilled coffee all over his newspaper. Running over to O'Toole, he asked breathlessly in Italian, "Can I do anything for you, Holiness?"

"No," said O'Toole. "I'm waiting for a car."

The poor man was completely flustered. He didn't know if he should stand there with the pope or keep a respectful distance. His anguish was relieved a moment later when a bright red Fiat 500 pulled up to the front door. Kelleher got out and stood by the driver's door, looking over the car toward the main entrance of the casa. Pope Michael emerged from the building and ran down the stairs. "Let's go," he said to Kelleher.

"What, no white cassock?" asked the Jesuit.

"Oh, stuff it," said O'Toole. "Not my style."

"Do you want to call a police car to take you up to the hospital, Mike?" asked Kelleher. "I don't think this is safe. You should probably have some sort of escort, or a bulletproof car, or something." Kelleher was clearly worried.

"Who's going to know I'm in this car?" asked O'Toole. "Let's just go. This may be my only chance to see Jack. Drive. I'll tell you how to get there."

The official title of the hospital is the Hospital of the Catholic University of the Sacred Heart, but everyone calls it Gemelli Policlinico after the name of its founder, Agostino Gemelli, a Franciscan monk who was both priest and doctor.

The Gemelli Policlinico is only a couple of miles from the Vatican, but the winding road up Monte Mario makes it seem farther. Kelleher drove like a madman. Since it was still early on a Saturday morning, the streets were fairly deserted.

Gemelli is not the closest hospital to the Vatican. Just a few hundred meters from St. Peter's Square is the ancient Ospedale di Santo Spirito. Parts of Holy Spirit Hospital were built in the twelfth century to house wounded crusaders returning from the Holy Land. Today, Roman wags insist that the hospital has not been substantially remodeled since the Middle Ages. Romans say, "If you want to die, go to Santo Spirito."

When Pope John Paul II was shot in 1981, the ambulance carrying the pope roared right past Santo Spirito and went straight up to Gemelli. So did the ambulance that picked up Jack, squealing around the hairpin turns that lead to the top of Monte Mario.

O'Toole hung on to the sissy bar, the handle above the door in the Fiat, as Jim Kelleher careened around the curves and headed up the hill. Kelleher had to keep downshifting the Fiat to coax it up the slope.

Halfway to the hospital, Kelleher noticed that they were being followed by police cars. Evidently someone had seen the new pope leaving the casa and had alerted the *vigili*.

On the way up, Kelleher handed Mike a little metal case, called a pyx, containing one consecrated host. "This is for Jack," he said.

When they reached the top of the hill, the car roared down the Via delle Pineta Sacchetti, weaving in and out between the cars, and shot through the hospital gate labeled *Ingresso*. As they pulled up to the main entrance, security guards came running from the guard booth at the gate, wondering why the car had not stopped.

The pope unfolded himself from the tiny car and headed for the hospital lobby, leaving the door open.

"Wait, Mike!" Kelleher shouted. "Take the oils!" The pope ran back.

Through the open passenger door he tossed the pope a little leather case containing a vial of blessed olive oil and a small purple stole. He also reached the glove compartment of the car and handed him a ritual book for the anointing of the sick, in English. Kelleher had thought to bring them from the Jesuit residence.

"Thanks, Jim," said O'Toole. "I guess I've been a bureaucrat too long."

By this time, the security guards were converging on Pope Michael. Kelleher yelled to O'Toole, "You go up to Jack's room. I'll deal with these guys." O'Toole ran for the front door and disappeared into the hospital. Just as O'Toole passed through the hospital doors, the trailing police cars came squealing into the hospital driveway.

Inside, O'Toole had to ask directions. The lady at the hospital information desk did not recognize him. After all, popes don't usually make sick calls at hospitals.

Jack was in the cardiac ICU, a glass-walled section at the end of a seemingly endless corridor on the fourth floor. It was the place where they brought the sickest heart patients. Jack's cubicle was one of a dozen or so that opened out onto a central nurses' station.

Once he found the proper cubicle, Pope Michael slid the glass door closed behind him and pulled the privacy curtain. The nurse at the desk said nothing. A priest visiting a Catholic hospital was commonplace.

Jack was hooked up to all the latest telemetry. A screen above his bed registered his heart rate, oxygenation, blood pressure, and temperature. Jack had an oxygen tube under his nose and an IV in his arm. His breathing was shallow. O'Toole pulled a chair next to the bed.

He touched his friend's hand and said, "Hi, old man. Did you plan to leave without saying good-bye?"

Jack turned and smiled weakly. "Michael O'Toole, I'm surprised you could come. Aren't you the pope now? That's what I heard."

"I guess I am," said O'Toole. "Hard to believe that a boy from the North Shore could get elected pope."

"Look what you did to me," said Jack. "You gave me a heart attack." Both men laughed a little, then both started crying.

"Can you anoint me?" asked Jack.

"Yeah," said O'Toole. "Jim Kelleher gave me the oils when I got out of the car. I never would have remembered."

"I can tell you're not a parish priest," said Jack with a smile. "But I guess the Bishop of Rome will have to do for now."

O'Toole put on the purple stole and opened the green plastic-covered ritual book. He was unfamiliar with the prayers, and he fumbled a bit, crying.

"Oh, forget the book for now," said Jack. "Just give me absolution first."

"For what?" said O'Toole.

"For a lifetime of sin," said Jack.

The Bishop of Rome raised his hand over his friend's head and gave him absolution, ending with the words "I absolve you from all your sins, in the name of the Father, Son, and Holy Spirit."

They said the Lord's Prayer together. The pope gave the priest Holy Communion from the little pyx that Kelleher had given him.

Then O'Toole found the right page in the ritual book and opened the vial of oil. He prayed, "God of mercy, ease the sufferings and comfort the weakness of Your servant, Jack, whom the Church now anoints with this holy oil, through Christ our Lord."

Mike put a few drops of oil on his thumb and made the sign of the cross on Jack's forehead, saying, "Through this holy anointing, may the Lord in His love and mercy help you with the grace of the Holy Spirit."

Then he turned Jack's hands palms up, and anointed each of them with oil, saying, "May the Lord, who frees you from sin, save you and raise you up."

Quiet descended on the room as they prayed silently. The only sound was the sound of the monitors beeping and the intravenous pump whirring away.

O'Toole recited the words of Psalm 23: "The Lord is my shepherd." He choked back tears when he got to the words "Even though I should walk through the valley of the shadow of death."

With the psalm complete, Jack looked at his spiritual son for a moment and struggled to speak. "Mike, you are the pope now. A lot of hopes and prayers are riding on you—especially mine. This is your opportunity to open the windows of the Church again, like John XXIII."

"Don't talk about all of that now," said O'Toole.

"No," said Jack with some force. "Now is the time. I'm dying. We won't get another chance. God has called you. Don't forget that."

Jack paused and swallowed.

"Mike, what you do now matters. It matters to millions of people like your father who left the Church and your mother who kept going to daily Mass, despite all the scandals. For them, use this chance that God has given you."

For a moment, both their thoughts were back in Salem. The tears started again.

Jack took a little sip from the cup of water on the tray table beside his bed. He continued, "Mike, they are going to call you Holy Father now. Be a father, a real father, not just to the Church, but to the world. Love the world, Mike. Love it like a father would. The world needs a father more than it needs a lecturing professor."

Jack's voice was becoming weaker and weaker. "The Church is in crisis. The wheels are coming off. We've known that for years. Think of your nieces and nephews. They don't go to church. Why? Think of most of the Catholics you grew up with back in Boston. Most of them don't go anymore either. We can't go on like this. The Church back home is dying. Even in Africa there are problems. You know that better than anyone."

O'Toole nodded. He had always pointed with pride to the growth of the Church in Africa, but he knew it was a mile wide and an inch deep. In another generation, all the problems that plagued Europe and North America would surface there. Human nature is the same everywhere. The problems are the same.

"I want to do something to bring things back," said Mike.

"Not things," said Jack. "People. Bring people back to the Church.

"You know," continued Jack with considerable difficulty, "back home they have that Shaker village out near Pittsfield. It was once a living, breathing religious community, but now it's just a museum. Don't let the Church die like that. We are not some kind of museum, with saints under glass. We are a hospital for sinners. Our work is not about keeping traditions, it is about changing lives and saving souls."

"What should I do?" asked O'Toole. He was so accustomed to asking advice from Jack that it did not seem strange to him that the pope should be asking an aged parish priest for answers.

"We've been talking about these things for years," said Jack. "You know the problems. The Church has been in the deep freeze of winter for twenty years. If you bring the spring, people will start coming back to life when things thaw a bit. Just love people first. Then you can lead them."

The new pope nodded. "I'll do my best, Jack."

"The Church has literally become a scandal. We stand in the way of people coming to the faith with our pompousness and our lavish wealth."

"I know," said O'Toole, thinking of his many trips to impoverished Africa.

"I love the Church," said Jack between short breaths. "The Church has been my home all my life. I love her like my mother or a wife. But maybe we should have a church that loves us back. Try it, Mike. That's what Jesus did. He told people good news. His harsh judgments were reserved for the Pharisees and the priests."

Jack stopped and pointed to his tattered prayer book. The binding had been taped with duct tape. "I want you to have my breviary, Mike. Your name is in it, along with your mother's and your father's and that boy you buried in Charlestown."

O'Toole took the worn breviary from the table beside the bed. Very few things in a priest's life are more personal than his prayer book. It is full of cards of people they have buried, friends who have been ordained, and memories of the past.

"Just remember, Mike, you are not the ruler of God's people. You are their servant. If you remember that, you'll be OK. And so will the Church."

Michael O'Toole looked at Father McClendon. Suddenly he was a student again, listening to the teacher. "I wish I was as good a priest as you are, Jack," said Pope Michael.

"Stop that nonsense," said Jack. "You are. You're a great priest. Just have some faith. All the certitude of the hard-liners does not show faith. It shows their doubt. They are afraid. Afraid of the future. Afraid of the Holy Spirit."

Jack pointed to his breviary again. "Look in the back cover. I think I wrote something there by Reinhold Niebuhr. Read it."

Mike fumbled with the fat book. Cards fell out. "Read it out loud," said Jack.

O'Toole found the handwritten quote from Niebuhr: "Frantic orthodoxy is never rooted in faith, but in doubt. It is when we are not sure that we are doubly sure."

"Turn the page," said Jack. "There is something else you need to read from two saints, Benedict and Francis de Sales."

Mike found two typewritten quotes pasted into the index page. Under Benedict's name the passage read:

> *Unity in necessary things,*
> *Freedom in doubtful things,*
> *And love in all things.*

Under the name of St. Francis de Sales, there was another quote:

> *We must begin with love, continue with love, and end*
> *with love.*

"That's it, Mike. It's all about love. It's about relationships, not laws. Relationships to Christ and to each other."

Jack's sentences were getting shorter. His eyes closed for a while, then opened again.

"I don't know for sure that heaven exists," said Jack. "But I know that the ideal heaven will be a full place, full of people. I don't need to imagine damned souls to make me happier in heaven. I hope we can all complete the circle of our lives and see the face of God."

Jack looked at O'Toole and said, "I love you, Mike. I have since you were a kid."

"I love you, too," said O'Toole.

Just then Kelleher tapped on the glass wall and slid open the door. He stepped into the room.

"Hiya, Jack," said Kelleher to the dying man in the bed.

Jack looked at him. That was all the greeting he could manage.

The pope was now at a loss for words. Tears dripped down his cheeks. Kelleher put a hand on O'Toole's shoulder. Jack's breathing was getting more and more shallow. He stopped trying to speak. Then, without any sigh or shudder, his breathing just stopped.

The lines on the monitor went flat. It let out a loud, continuous squeal. Responding to the alarm, the nurse came running in. She checked Jack's pulse. Then she stepped outside the door and called the doctor.

Death is not very often dramatic. It is usually just a silent passage, like stepping through a doorway, from one room to the next. Jack stepped away from this world quietly to whatever world lies beyond.

"He's gone," said Kelleher, making the sign of the cross over Jack.

The Bishop of Rome and Vicar of Christ felt like a spiritual orphan.

33

A HAND IN THE DARKNESS

O'TOOLE AND KELLEHER STOOD THERE IN THE ICU ROOM for few minutes, neither wanting to leave. O'Toole picked up Jack's breviary and turned to the prayers for the dead. He read Psalm 130:

> *Out of the depths I cry unto you, oh Lord*
>
> *Oh Lord, hear my voice,*
>
> *Let your ears be attentive to the voice of our pleading.*
>
> *If you, O Lord, should mark our guilt, who would survive?*
>
> *But with you is found forgiveness, for this we revere you.*

While they were still praying the psalm, a doctor from the ICU came in and pronounced Jack dead. He signed a certificate, checking his watch for the time.

A nurse came in and disconnected Jack from the tubes, wires, and monitors, all useless now.

Both the doctor and the nurse looked at O'Toole, but neither said anything. Perhaps they didn't believe their eyes. The sight of a priest in a hospital room at death is not unusual, but the sight of the pope is unheard of.

After the doctor and nurse finished their short, secular liturgy of death, they left the room, pulling the curtain and sliding the glass door closed behind them.

O'Toole and Kelleher were alone with Jack's lifeless body.

They sat down and waited in silence for a good five minutes. Neither wanted to leave Jack alone, even though they knew he had already left them.

Finally, Kelleher spoke. "What now?" he asked.

"I don't know," said O'Toole. "I need some time alone. I want to go somewhere just to think."

"We could go back to the Vatican," said Kelleher.

"No good," said O'Toole. "People press in on you there. They will say they just need a minute, and then they will take an hour. Let's go somewhere that we can talk." He paused. "Maybe we could go up to the grounds at the NAC. I could call the rector and tell him I need a private place for a bit."

The pope got out his cell phone. Kelleher chuckled. "The pope's cell phone number! Now that's a number the world would love to have."

Before they could make the call, a distinguished-looking man about age fifty in a tailored Italian suit slid open the glass door and came into the room. "*Con permesso, Santo Padre*," he said formally to O'Toole. "I am Luigi Giuliani, the administrator of the hospital. It is an honor to have you here."

They shook hands all around. Guiliani bowing slightly to the pope.

Then Giuliani said, "*Dunque*," which means "now then." Italians always say *dunque* when they are about to say something of consequence.

"It's a madhouse downstairs. The press knows that you are here. They have surrounded the main entrance and your little car."

He looked at Kelleher. "You cannot get out without going through the paparazzi. I'm afraid you are trapped."

"Is there another way out?" asked Kelleher.

"There is an elevator just outside this unit," said the hospital administrator. "We use it only for patients going to surgery and for transporting bodies to the morgue in the basement. It has an override button to prevent it from making any stops, so that people don't get on the elevator when we are transporting a body to the morgue. You could take that elevator down to the ground floor and then follow the corridor to the loading dock."

"But what about the car?" asked Kelleher.

"I'm afraid you will have to leave it for the moment," said Giuliani. "But my car is parked near the loading dock. I would be honored to drive, Your Holiness, wherever you would like to go. We could cover you in the backseat with a blanket. No one would be looking for you in my car."

"Thank you so much, Signor Giuliani. We appreciate this kindness," said the pope.

The three men stepped toward the door, but O'Toole turned back for a moment. He leaned over Jack's dead body and kissed him on the forehead. "Good-bye, old man. I'll see you in heaven," he said. Then he turned to the others and said, "*Andiamo.*"

Now it was Kelleher who paused. "Wait," he said. "Let's take off our collars and just go out in something else. The press will be looking for the pope."

"*Un momento,*" said Giuliani. He went to a linen room on the other side of the ICU and came back with two blue technicians' smocks and a hospital blanket. O'Toole and Kelleher put on the smocks and headed toward the elevator, hoping that no one called the lobby to alert the press.

The old elevator smelled bad. When it whirred to a stop in the basement, they walked down a long corridor and emerged onto a loading dock. Delivery trucks were parked along the dock.

Giuliani led them down a side staircase into a covered parking garage. The director's car was parked very near the garage entrance in a reserved spot. It was a huge Lancia, the car of the upper middle class in Italy.

The pope got in the backseat and lay down. Kelleher and Giuliani covered him with a blanket. Then they got in the front. Giuliani drove the three of them out of the hospital grounds. It looked like a hospital technician and the hospital director going out on an errand.

As they exited the hospital grounds, Kelleher looked back at the scrum of reporters and a dozen television trucks clustered near the main entrance. They ignored the anonymous Lancia leaving through the gate. A few blocks away, Kelleher turned to the backseat and said, "We're out."

The pope sat up, blinking in the sunshine.

"*Dove andiamo?*" asked the administrator.

"*Al Gianicolo,*" said the pope.

O'Toole got out his cell phone and called the rector, William Tourigney, at the North American College. He had a little trouble getting through. The porter at the college didn't seem to believe that it was the pope calling.

Finally, the rector came on the phone.

"Bill," said O'Toole. "This is Cardinal O . . . This is Pope Michael." It felt strange to refer to himself as the pope.

"I need to come up to the college for a little while. I need to talk privately with a priest from the States. I would like absolute privacy. Is that possible?"

The pope put the call on speaker so they could all hear the rector. "Anything you want, Your Holiness. I'll tell the porter at the gate to let you through."

The Lancia made its way down Monte Mario, past the Vatican, and then up the Gianicolo Hill to the North American College. The seminary sits on a fairly large tract of land overlooking the Vatican and the city of Rome.

The Gianicolo Hill, like Monte Mario, is not one of the seven hills of the ancient city, but it is historically significant. The Gianicolo takes its name from the Latin name for the Roman god Janus, the two-faced god. The month of January takes its name from him too.

Janus is the Roman god of transitions, the god of beginnings and endings. All the statues of Janus have two faces, one looking forward to the future and the other looking backward to the past. The two faces also make Janus the god of good and evil, of truth and hypocrisy. The ancient Romans invoked Janus when they were going to war or making peace. O'Toole caught the irony of going to the hill of Janus at this transitional moment.

When they pulled up to the gate of the North American College, Giuliani honked the horn on the Lancia. By this time they had put their Roman collars back on. A clerical collar would help them get in the gate.

The porter looked out the window. He saw two priests in a big black Lancia with a driver and probably thought nothing unusual. He pressed the button to open the heavy steel gate. After it slid open, the car pulled into the cobblestone courtyard of the American college. The gate closed behind them. They were safe from prying eyes.

O'Toole recalled vividly the first time he went through that gate forty years before, when he arrived as a seminary student. He remembered how much the seminary looked like a prison. In fact, the local Roman *ragazzi* called the fascist-style building Sing Sing, after the famous New York prison.

The car pulled across the large cobblestone yard to the main entrance. The two priests got out and thanked the hospital administrator profusely, who, in turn, thanked them profusely.

O'Toole and Kelleher walked up the three red marble steps to the formal entrance hall. In the stone floor was the crest of the college. Inscribed under the crest was the Latin motto of the college, *Firmum Est Cor Meum*, which literally means "Strong is my heart," but generations of seminarians applied it to their bishops and translated it as "Hard is my heart."

Standing alone in the college lobby for a moment, they heard the rector, Monsignor Tourigney, come running breathlessly down the corridor.

"Holiness, Holiness, welcome," he said, patting his forehead with a white handkerchief. "What an unexpected honor to have the new American pope visit the American College on the first day of your papacy. This is truly historic."

The rector was the classic ambitious Roman monsignor, unctuous and flattering.

"Is there a place where Father and I can talk privately?" asked the pope.

"My suite, of course, Holiness. It would be my honor," said the rector.

"Fine," said the pope, interrupting the rector. "That's perfect."

"I'll send up some refreshments," said the monsignor.

"Just coffee and pastries would be fine. One more thing, we don't want to be disturbed." Holding up his finger to the rector for emphasis, he said, "No one, you understand, Father?"

"Certainly," he said. "I'll bring up the refreshments myself."

The rector pushed the button for the elevator. The doors on the Art Deco elevator opened. It carried them up two floors to the level of the rector's suite. Once inside the suite, they crossed the living room to a large tiled terrace with upholstered porch furniture.

When they were settled on the terrace, Kelleher and O'Toole took a deep breath. Both men were still a bit stunned. Jack had died hardly an hour before. O'Toole had been elected pope less than twenty-four hours before. So much had happened in the past day, and so much more lay ahead.

The view from the terrace was lovely. It looked out onto a mani-cured lawn and a garden bordered by an ancient wall, built in 275 AD by Emperor Aurelian to fortify the city. It provided a fortress-like barrier for the college. People speeding by on the other side of the wall had no idea of the green oasis a few feet away.

Along the walkways of the garden were tall umbrella pines, oddly trimmed in the Roman fashion with all the branches at the top. These were the "pines of Rome," memorialized in music by Respighi in his concerto.

Everywhere there were flowers.

"Jim," said O'Toole, "I'm shell-shocked."

"I know," said Kelleher. "We've both lost someone we loved very much."

"Yes," O'Toole said, "and someone who loved us very much."

He paused for a moment. "I feel disoriented, like I did when my mother died."

Kelleher could see that the new pope needed to talk, so he let him talk.

"What should I do now?" asked O'Toole rhetorically. "The curia is a mess. Cardinals are killing cardinals. We have a sex abuse scandal that never stops. While the curia lives in regal splendor, we close parishes and hemorrhage membership around the world."

O'Toole fingered Jack's breviary. He pulled out a newspaper clipping that Jack had stuck on the inside front cover.

After a moment, he said to Kelleher, "Listen to this. It's an interview with Cardinal Martini before he died. Jack must have saved this for me." Then he read:

"'The Church is tired. In Europe and America our culture has become old, our churches and our religious houses are big and empty. The bureaucratic apparatus of the Church grows and grows. Our rites and our dress are pompous . . .'"

O'Toole paused and scanned down the page, then began again.

"'Where are the heroes who can inspire us? . . . The Church is two hundred years behind the times. Why doesn't it stir? Are we afraid? Is it fear rather than courage? In any event, the faith is the foundation of the Church. Faith, trust, and courage.'"

Just then Monsignor Tourigney arrived with coffee, water, and pastries. He put the tray down and left the two men alone. A good servant knows when it's time to disappear.

O'Toole and Kelleher took their snack, momentarily enjoying the Roman sunshine and listening to the Vespa motor scooters toiling up the hill on the other side of the ancient wall.

"This garden is kind of a metaphor for the Church," said the pope. "Here we are behind our ancient walls. Everything is beautiful and serene, but just on the other side of that thick stone is a living, pulsating, turbulent city. We are completely unaware of ordinary life."

Kelleher nodded his head. "It is even worse than that. Sometimes when we go out into the world, we are afraid, and so we retreat behind the wall again."

"Do you think we are as bad as all that, Jim?" asked the new pope.

"Yes, sadly, I do."

After a pause O'Toole started to speak again.

"You're right, Jim, but remember how excited and enthusiastic we were as seminarians and young priests? It wasn't just because we were young and inexperienced. It was more about the possibilities for the Church. That's what Vatican II provided. The Church felt young, hopeful.

"Hope! Hope was that great gift that Christ gave us. Hope to be better. Hope to dream. Hope that mercy would always trump justice. And hope that as weak and sinful as we are, we can always get better at being human."

O'Toole seemed strangely energized by his own *ferverino*.

Jim jumped in. "God knows, Mike, in the past fifty years there's been enough talk, enough scholarly papers, and endless committee meetings. The issues of celibacy, married priests, woman priests, gay rights, and authority have been dissected and pulled apart over and over. It's time to act, Mike. To do something big. Something bold. We've been discussing these things for decades. Time to stop talking and start moving."

O'Toole picked up this thought. He sounded enthusiastic, even young again. "You're right, Jim. Jack felt that Catholicism was dissolving right around us. These so-called issues need to be settled, so we can get back to proclaiming some good news."

O'Toole looked tired, but there also seemed to be a new resolve in the way he spoke. "Jack used to say that he didn't know with any certainty whether heaven existed, but that he chose to believe that it did, because it makes life easier to live. You know, Jim, I feel the same way about the future. I have no certainty about the outcome of what I need to do now, but I believe that it is the right thing. I'll leave the rest to the Holy Spirit."

He paused and took a drink of water.

"St. Augustine said that faith is like a hand stretched out into the darkness. That's the type of faith we will need on this journey." The pope finished his coffee and stood up. "Time for me to get back, Jim. I want you to stay here in Rome for a while, if you can. I need you. I need your advice. I need your honesty. Most of all, I need your friendship."

"I'm with you," said Kelleher. "Let's go."

* * *

Two days later, Pope Michael was installed in a simple ceremony. St. Peter's Square was not quite full. The taint of scandal hanging over the Church kept many of the dignitaries and even some common folk away.

Nate, Brigid, and Sister Miriam were once again in the square, but this time they had seats at the top of the steps, in the second row, just behind the heads of state. Pope Michael had arranged the seats, partly to honor them and partly to protect them.

Brigid and Nate were pleased with the pope's installation, but not elated.

After the incident in Venice, they now had a police bodyguard and a bulletproof Lancia to ride around in. When they returned to Rome, they didn't check back into the Columbus Hotel. Instead, Nate called a friend at the Justice Department in Washington who pulled some strings to let them stay in a safe house on the grounds of the American Embassy on Via Veneto.

As Pope Michael was delivering his homily, Nate's mind wandered back over the preceding few weeks. He thought of Monsignor Ackerman, frightened in the cemetery. He thought of Signora Luppino, in Naples, crying for her son. He thought of Cardinals Crepi and Salazar and their sleazy, self-centered lives. He thought of the corruption that Monsignor Rodriguez told him about.

Nate trusted O'Toole as a good man, but he no longer believed in the goodness of the Church bureaucracy. He saw it as just as corrupt as any bureaucracy. "Two months ago, I would have been thrilled just to be here in the square. Now I keep looking over my shoulder."

Brigid agreed. "As soon as we get back to New York, I will relax a bit. But it will be a while before I stop wondering if someone is watching us."

Sister Miriam was cautious.

"Something new is being born, at least I hope so. Pope Michael might be different. Maybe this time grace will be allowed to build on human nature. That's the way it has to work anyway."

34

THE FUTURE

POPE MICHAEL WAS NERVOUS.

It was only three days since his installation. He had asked the cardinals to remain in Rome for a consistory. Given the crisis of the moment and the corruption unearthed in Nate's investigation, he saw no reason to put things off. Previous popes had tried caution. He would try candor.

Before his speech to the consistory, Pope Michael sat in a little conference room, just outside the Vatican Synod Hall. He had a plastic cup filled with water on the table beside him. Next to the cup was a leather folder containing his speech. In his hands, he held Jack's old breviary. He needed a moment of prayer and he needed the presence of Jack.

The only other person in the room was Monsignor Henry Rodriguez. Pope Michael had named the Mexican American priest to be his personal secretary. From Nate's investigation he had learned that Father Rodriguez was fearless enough to finger the Soldados for the murder of Cardinal Garcia. That was the kind of man the pope needed for an assistant. Rodriguez stood guard at the door of the conference room to give the pope a few moments of privacy.

For centuries the word consistory meant a mandatory meeting of the College of Cardinals, presided over by the pope. But today's meeting would be different. This consistory would include not only cardinals but also priests, nuns, monks, and representatives from various religious orders. Sister Miriam was in the audience representing her religious order. The pope had thought to include a few laymen and women. Something never done before.

Even the setting was different. Instead of the ornate grandeur of the Sala Clementina, the papal throne room, Pope Michael gathered the consistory in the Vatican Synod Hall. It had the look of a university lecture hall, except that it had the capacity for simultaneous translation, each one understanding in his own tongue. Pope Michael wanted a new Pentecost.

The pope's speech was printed on heavy vellum. The new leather folder already had his official seal affixed to the cover. At the bottom of the speech was a decree. He signed his name and then affixed the initials P.M. for Pontifex Maximus. This inscription was the title of the ancient pagan high priest of Rome. It meant supreme bridge builder.

The Pontifex Maximus was supposed to be the bridge builder between heaven and earth. Pope Michael hoped he could be a bridge builder between factions in the Church and between the past and the future.

If the pope's anxiety was high, the stakes were even higher. Catholics were divided more than at any time in a thousand years, and Pope Michael knew it. In an earlier age, people would have called it a schism. Nobody was ready to call it that, yet.

Lots of people would be unhappy with Pope Michael, no matter what he said at this consistory. Some would be furious, but would stay. Others would be furious enough to leave.

On the other hand, if he gave even a sliver of daylight to Catholics hoping for reform and renewal, the Church might have a chance at rebirth. A great many people would be happy, some deliriously so.

People around the world were pessimistic about the prospects for a rebirth in the Church. A friend of Nate's at an investment bank in New York had been asked by *The New York Times* to rate the Catholic Church as if it were a potential investment. The reporter asked, "Would you rate the stock as buy, sell, or hold?" Without hesitation the banker said, "I'd say sell now."

Despite the fact that Catholicism claimed more than a billion baptized souls, fewer than half of them ever darkened the door of a parish church. Membership had been hemorrhaging for a generation, especially in Latin America.

The Church wasn't even doing its job at administering the sacraments. Parishes were unmanned. Some parishioners never even saw a priest. Year after year, the Church ordained only half as many priests as it needed. Fewer people came to communion, got baptized, or got married. Even fewer got buried each year.

Some of the maladies of the Church were self-inflicted—the wounds of scandal. No pope had ever really dealt with the rot at the top.

Leaning forward, Pope Michael cupped his face in his hands, his elbows resting on his knees. He prayed, "Come, Holy Spirit, kindle in me the fire of your love."

He opened Jack's breviary, looking for Psalm 63, which had always been one of his favorite psalms. He found it among the Sunday prayers.

> *Oh God, you are my God, for you I long*
> *For you my soul is thirsting*
> *My body pines for you like a dry weary land, without water.*

He paused and looked at the cover of the breviary. With his finger, Pope Michael slowly and deliberately traced the faded gold cross embossed on the cover. Then he closed his eyes and imagined that Jack was sitting there, guiding him. It occurred to the pope that the faded cross in the leather cover was like the Church, worn and faded but still imprinted on the hearts of millions of believers.

Pope Michael stood up. Monsignor Rodriguez opened the door to the passageway that led to the hall. The pope gathered his papers and walked out slowly. Rodriguez followed.

When he entered the aula, the members of the consistory sat frozen for a moment, not knowing what to do. They were surprised to see that he was not dressed in the white cassock traditionally worn by popes. Instead, he was dressed in a plain black clerical suit, like any priest or bishop would wear. His only mark of office was the pectoral cross that hung around his neck. There was a little murmur in the audience. The simplicity of his dress was in dramatic contrast to the cardinals in the front few rows, who were resplendent in silk and lace. But his dress was very similar to the priests and laity seated in the back of the auditorium. Even in their clothing, there was a schism in the consistory.

After a moment of hesitation, nearly everyone stood as the pope made his way to the dais. There were a few people who remained seated, indicating their disapproval. O'Toole mounted the stairs to the center of the raised dais and stood behind the lectern. There was a chair behind him, but he did not sit down. Rodriguez took a seat to the pope's right at a lower place on the platform.

Behind Pope Michael, the wall was covered in plain fabric, designed to absorb sound. Above his head on the rear wall hung a large wooden crucifix. He hoped their eyes were fixed on Christ, not him. But he was under no illusions.

Still standing, the pope said in English, "Let us pray." By speaking in English, he broke another precedent. Popes had traditionally addressed the cardinals in Latin. Then the pope said nothing. They just prayed in silence, like the disciples in the upper room waiting for their Pentecost, as they collectively invoked the Holy Spirit.

After thirty seconds or so of awkward silence, O'Toole silently made the sign of the cross on himself and then motioned for everyone to be seated. He remained standing at the podium. This, too, was a break with tradition. People do not sit while the monarch stands, but Pope Michael wanted it clear that this pope was not so much a monarch as a shepherd and teacher. In his black suit he looked more like a Jesuit professor at the Gregorian University across town than the Monarch of Vatican City.

"Esteemed brother bishops and dear sisters and brothers in Christ," he began.

He looked out at the crowd in the room and nodded toward the women, including Sister Miriam, as an acknowledgment of their presence.

"We in this room, and the members of the Church around the world, are collectively the human vessels of a divine gift that has been entrusted to us to be good news for all men and women.

"In our Church, humanity finds home and hearth. Countless good men and women around the world have entrusted to us their faith and hopes. In the Church they hope to find the light that will guide them to happiness in this world and in the world to come.

"It falls to us to bind up wounds, heal the brokenhearted, bring light to the darkness, and joy to the sorrowing.

"Above all, it falls to us to show love to the whole world. To show love to every man and woman, but especially to those who feel forgotten, oppressed, marginalized, and abused.

"It falls to us to show love to sinners and to lead them to holiness.

"We must say frankly that we have at times forgotten our tasks and strayed from our purpose.

"It is no secret to anyone that the Church is in crisis. In the past few months prior to the death of my beloved predecessor, Thomas, the Church has been convulsed by scandal and consumed by its own worries.

"Even in the College of Cardinals, we have been touched by corruption, murder, and suicide."

He paused for a moment and looked around the hall. He wanted this to sink in, especially his oblique acknowledgment of Crepi's suicide. People certainly noticed the change in papal tone. Eyebrows were raised.

"As we speak, there are members of the College of Cardinals who are confined to prison by civil authorities for unspeakable crimes. These crimes have touched at the integrity and dignity of the Church. They have discredited her witness everywhere.

"Indeed, all around the globe the Church has been wounded by crimes against her own young people. These crimes were committed by men who should have been shepherds of souls. They were covered up by bishops

more interested in their careers and our institutional image than our
Christian witness or the safety of the children of God.

"We have seen these sins before. Sin is no stranger to humanity or to
the history of our Church. Scripture tells us that our first parents sinned
and despoiled the garden of happiness given by God.

"While the Catholic Church was instituted by our Lord Jesus Christ,
it has ever since been run by ordinary sinners. We are men—subject
to the same immorality, sinfulness, biases, mistakes, and corruption of
other men."

Again, eyebrows were raised. Was the pope admitting to fallibility?

Pope Michael swallowed before continuing.

"Scandal is no stranger to our Church, nor are the efforts to cover it
up. Today I stand before you and the world to confess our sinfulness and
to ask pardon from our people.

"This is a new moment. We cannot continue as before. We cannot
regain the moral authority of the Church by pretending that there is
nothing wrong with her. Such claims would not be believed, even if we
were to make them. Our only recourse is truth.

The pope looked right at the cardinals and said, "The Book of Prov-
erbs says, 'Six things the Lord hates; seven are an abomination to Him:
haughty eyes, a lying tongue, hands that shed innocent blood, a heart
that plots wicked schemes, feet that run to evil, and a false witness who
utters lies.' For those who were counting, that was six."

The pope paused and then added, "And He hates those who sow dis-
cord among the brothers."

His eyes met Mendoza's. Mendoza looked angry, even a bit unhinged.
His jaw moved back and forth as he ground his teeth.

The pope continued, "What if Christ were speaking to us here in this
room today? What would He say? How would He react to us, who claim
to be His Church?

"He, who told us to take nothing for the journey, not even a purse or
a second tunic. What would He say about our vestments of watered silk
and lace?

"He told us that we cannot serve both God and mammon. What would He say about our Vatican Bank, with its scandal and corruption? What would He say about our immense treasury of art and piled-up wealth of buildings?

"Would He tell us again the story of the rich man in the gospel who built bigger barns to hold his wealth? Would He say again to us, 'You fool, this very night your life will be required of you. To whom shall all this piled-up wealth go?'

"Would He compare Vatican City to the ancient temple of Jerusalem and say again, 'All that you see here, the days will come when there will not be left a stone upon stone, because you did not recognize the time of your visitation.'?

"Our Lord said we should not seek titles of honor. What would He say to us who demand to be called Holiness, Excellency, Eminence, or Monsignor? Would He say, as He did to the Pharisees, 'You hypocrites, you white-washed sepulchers, you kill the prophets and then build them tombs. You widen your phylacteries and lengthen your tassels.'?

"Jesus said to us that we should render unto Caesar the things that are Caesar's and to God the things that are God's. What would He say to us when we told Him that we have become Caesar, taking our place among the nations of the earth and pretending earthly power? Would He say to us, 'My kingdom is not of this earth,'?

"What would He say to bishops and priests more preoccupied with expensive architecture and vestments and art and antiquities than we are with the hungry and the poor of the world? Would He say, 'You blind guides, you will fall into the pit yourselves. You strain out the gnat and swallow the camel.'?"

O'Toole paused for effect before he made the most serious accusation.

"Jesus said to us that it would be better for us that a millstone be hung around our necks, and we were cast into the sea, than we should give scandal to one of the little ones entrusted to our care. What would He say to us who harmed children and scarred lives and then, even more scandalously, covered up those crimes to protect the image of the Church?

"Would the Lord weep over us as He wept over ancient Jerusalem? Would He say to us what He says at the last judgment, 'Depart from me, you accursed ones.'?"

People were shifting in their seats. There had never been a consistory like this. No pope had ever spoken so much like a prophet and so little like a bureaucrat or academic.

The pope looked around the room and then back down at his text. He looked up again. He really didn't need the text, as he was speaking from the heart.

"The time for talk is past. In the next few days I will issue several *motu proprios* to accomplish by decree some things that are long overdue."

Kelleher, sitting in the back of the audience, noticed that Michael did not use the royal we used by other popes.

"I will close the Vatican Bank within one year. Other international organizations function without a bank, and so can the Church.

"I will abolish the Vatican diplomatic corps and close our embassies, except for our embassies to international organizations and to Italy. We can no longer be compromised by maintaining diplomatic relations with tyrants and dictators who abuse their people and use the Church to enhance their prestige. Priests should be in the vineyard, not in embassy receptions.

"I will issue a new law for papal elections. The college of electors will not only include cardinals, but also laymen and -women and all the archbishops of the world. My successor will be chosen, as were all the bishops of Rome for the first five hundred years, by the people of God. Today that means the Universal Church and men and women from around the world.

"I will reassign all bishops and cardinals working in the Vatican to ministry in their home dioceses or in parishes. Those who are over seventy years of age will retire. From now on, there will be no bishops working in the bureaucracy of the Vatican. It should be clear to any observer that the central administration of the Church is its servant, not its master.

"Recognizing the extreme shortage of priests around the world, I will issue a *motu proprio*, permitting local bishops, if they so choose, to follow the ancient customs of the Eastern Church and ordain married men to the priesthood.

"I will convene a synod of bishops next year to discuss the question of ministry in the Church, specifically the question of ordaining women to the diaconate or even to the priesthood."

There was a gasp in the hall.

"I will transfer the art treasures of the Vatican to an independent board of laymen and -women to be kept in trust for all humanity. They will no longer be an asset of the Holy See. People will no longer be scandalized by our wealth.

"I will recommence our dialogues with our separated brothers and sisters in any Christian communities who wish to dialogue with us. We will meet them as equals, and we will renew our hope for unity, especially with the churches of the East.

"I will ask each bishop in the world to establish a committee to review the wealth of each diocese. We need only what is necessary for ministry. All else belongs to the poor.

"I will appoint women to head the Congregation for the Religious and laypeople to head the Congregation for the Laity and the charitable work of the Church done by Caritas. I also will appoint women to the ecclesiastical tribunals here in Rome.

"The time is long past for the Church to hear the voices of women and to include them at every level of our councils. It is not enough for us to patronize them with words alone. We cannot let our praise of the Mother of Jesus be a way to avoid treating the mothers of the world with dignity.

"Recognizing that we have made the granting of annulments a legal ordeal that consumes years and paralyzes lives, I will issue a decree entrusting the whole question of marriage annulments to pastors of souls in local dioceses and parishes, without a legal process. No decision should take more than a few weeks. No one should have to wait years for the decision of the Church. Appeals to Rome will be confined solely to those circumstances required by scripture. Divorced Catholics should be allowed to receive communion after reflection with their pastors.

"Most importantly, to end the scandal of child abuse and its cover-up, I will ask that each diocese in the world establish an independent investigation run exclusively by laypeople who will report back to a commission here in Rome within one year. Should any bishop be found to have covered up or ignored child abuse in his diocese, he will be removed immediately. I will also ask for the immediate resignation of any bishop convicted of any civil crime related to shielding or protecting child abusers.

"In some of our religious orders, we have been plagued with scandal. The situation of the Soldados de Cristo is well known after years of investigation. I will issue a decree suppressing that religious congregation and placing their members under the jurisdiction of a special administrator to find them places in other religious communities or return them to the lay state."

There was another gasp in the room. Cardinal Mendoza's face was as crimson as his garments.

"Finally, the Bishop of Rome is not a monarch. He is a bishop, a colleague among colleagues.

"Jesus said His kingdom was not of this earth. Neither should His vicar be treated as a king. The Bishop of Rome presides in love, not in power, over the other churches. Our Church should be more collegial and less hierarchical.

"Wherever possible, the local churches should make their own decisions, laity and clergy together.

"All of these reforms that I have announced are *ad intra*, focused on our household. But the Church must eventually stop looking inward. We need to get these things behind us, so we can create a much more important witness to the world. A church that gazes only at itself does not have its eyes on God or on the needs of humanity.

"Our church cannot continue to ignore the wider world as if it does not matter and as if it has nothing to teach us.

"We must enter into dialogue with non-Christians. We must open ourselves more fully to the insights of the natural sciences. We must strive to see what is good in people, even those with whom we disagree. We must love even our enemies, as the Lord told us.

"The starting point for all of our ministries must be the starting point of the ministry of our Lord when he spoke in his own synagogue in Nazareth.

"'The spirit of the Lord is upon us, and it has anointed us to bring glad tidings to the poor, liberty to captives, recovery of sight to the blind, to let the oppressed of every kind go free, and to proclaim a year acceptable to the Lord.'

"Our trust is in the Lord and His teaching, nothing else. Our help is in the Lord who made heaven and earth, and no one else. Our spirit is in the Holy Spirit, poured out on the Church at the first Pentecost and with us still."

The pope stopped talking. People looked stunned. At first, people were not sure he was finished. They were dumbfounded by the scope of his talk. For nearly a minute, no one moved.

During this silence, the pope thought about the parade of people he had seen in the past few weeks.

From the back of the auditorium, Jim Kelleher nodded his affirmation to Pope Michael. Suddenly, people were roused from their stunned silence. Nearly everyone rose to their feet and started to applaud. The applause grew louder and mingled with some cheers. Even the cardinals sitting in the front rows, hesitant at first, began to applaud.

But not everyone was happy.

Cardinal Mendoza stood abruptly, not to applaud, but to accuse. His body was stiff with anger. Mendoza pointed a finger at the pope, in a gesture both menacing and accusatory. Then, almost lost among the other people applauding, Mendoza stood still for a few seconds, glaring at the new pope.

Then he opened his mouth in a breathless scream that echoed throughout the hall. At the same time he pulled a small pistol from beneath the layers of watered silk and lace that so garishly identified him as a prince of the Church.

With a shaking hand he aimed the pistol in the direction of the pope.

Rodriguez, sitting to the pope's right, had been facing the audience throughout the speech and had particularly been watching the reactions of his old nemesis Mendoza. When Mendoza raised his hand, Rodriguez realized what was happening and leapt up from his seat, up the two steps, toward the pope. He shoved Pope Michael down into a chair on the dais and stood where the pope had been.

Two shots rang out. Within seconds the non-uniformed Swiss guards, who were standing just below the dais, rushed toward Mendoza.

For a second after the shooting, there was an eerie silence throughout the hall. The cardinals around Mendoza were frozen in place, too frightened to move or speak. They seemed like schoolchildren waiting to be rescued or just hoping to be told what to do. Rodriguez felt a burning pain as a bullet ripped through his coat and shirt and penetrated his chest, just above the heart. His aorta had been nicked. The other bullet grazed Rodriguez's forehead, causing blood to pour down his face. Monsignor Rodriguez fell backward onto the lap of Pope Michael, who was seated in the chair behind him. Mendoza didn't move. The Swiss guard wrestled him to the ground and pounded the revolver out of his hand, breaking some of his fingers in the process.

With blood pouring out of Rodriguez's chest and head, O'Toole lay his secretary's body down on the dais. He knelt down beside him and started to pray. By now the Swiss guard had reached Pope Michael. They intended to pull him out of the hall and away to safety. But the pope refused. He continued to kneel beside his wounded secretary and wiped the blood off his face, making the sign of the cross on Rodriguez's forehead in a kind of anointing.

By now Mendoza was in handcuffs and being dragged out of the Synod Hall. EMTs were pushing in through the panicked audience. The pope was now cradling the motionless body of his secretary. With a final effort, Rodriguez reached his right hand up to grasp the pectoral cross that hung around Pope Michael's neck, and used the chain of the cross to pull the pope closer to him.

He whispered to Pope Michael, "Listen to me. These are evil men. They will never, ever give up until . . . "

Monsignor Rodriguez closed his eyes and was gone. Pope Michael rested his head on the dead priest's chest and cried. By this time Father Kelleher had pushed his way down the auditorium aisle and knelt beside Pope Michael at Rodriguez's head. The pope tried to wipe the blood from Rodriguez's now lifeless face. Kelleher pulled the pope's hand away from Rodriguez and helped him to his feet.

Pope Michael was covered in Rodriguez's blood.

For two or three seconds they stood surveying the chaos around them. People were screaming. Some cardinals still in the front row had rosaries, while others held cell phones to their ears. The Swiss guard then pushed the pope and Kelleher out the side door of the Synod Hall to safety in the conference room.

Once in the conference room, Pope Michael turned toward Kelleher and said matter-of-factly, "The schism has begun."

Epilogue

GENERATION

NATE AND BRIGID WERE FINISHING THEIR SUNDAY MORN-
ing jog. Nate knew that this was one of those inexplicable make-sense
moments that, no matter how long he might live, would never be
forgotten.

It was autumn in New York, and Central Park was never more beautiful than it was at that time of year. New Yorkers were sharing one of
those rare fall days with breathtakingly crisp air. Always in late Octo-
ber, the beautifully elegant leaves of the gingko trees go from green
to gold and almost instantly fall to the ground, creating pathways of
golden snow.

It was their favorite time of year. Brigid felt a special connection to
the park and especially to this spot at the Bethesda Fountain, where they
ended their run. They shared a few moments stretching and just soaking
in that wonderful high that made the ten miles more than just a necessary inconvenience.

Central Park was more than a place. For Brigid it was a state of mind.
Nate could never bring up the topic of Central Park without stating that
this grand space, smack-dab in the middle of a great city, allows you to
get away without actually being away.

They could hear the sound of the bells announcing the many Sunday services at the great churches and cathedrals that lined the perimeter of the park.

The events of the past several months left Nate and Brigid in very different places regarding their own spiritual journeys. Places that neither had ever expected to go.

Nate needed time away from the childhood security rooted in the religion of his youth. Brigid found that she was more open to spiritual things than she had ever thought she would be. Her blossoming friendship with Sister Miriam was not only an inspiration, but also a source of comfort and hope.

As Nate got up from the concrete bench that circles the fountain, Brigid gripped his hand and pulled him back toward her. Brushing his hair back with her fingers, she gently kissed him on the lips and whispered in his ear, "We're pregnant."

ABOUT THE AUTHORS

Monsignor John Myslinski was born in Salem, Massachusetts, and was raised in the Boston area, where he attended Catholic schools and university. He received his BA from Boston College and then joined and remained a member of the Jesuits (New England Province) for eight years. John served as a federal officer with the Capitol Police in Washington, DC, prior to entering the seminary at Mt. St. Mary's, where he received his MA in Divinity.

He was ordained to the priesthood for the Archdiocese of Washington. As the "TV priest" for the District of Columbia, he was the host of the program *Real to Reel* for six years and celebrated the television Mass for the Washington metropolitan area for eight years. John served as a chaplain in the Air Force Reserves, and was the pastor of St. Mary's Parish in Rockville, Maryland, for over a decade. John spent many years working with and for the homeless community in the DC area.

He has the double honor of being named Washingtonian of the Year by *Washingtonian* magazine in 1993 for his work with the homeless, and being named a Monsignor by Pope John Paul II in 2005. In a letter to John on the occasion of his honor by the magazine, President George H. W. Bush wrote, "I commend you for your selfless commitment to those in need, and I thank you for helping to make our Nation's Capital a better place to live."

* * *

Father Peter Daly grew up on the South Side of Chicago, one of eight children. He attended Catholic schools throughout high school and then the University of Virginia in Charlottesville, where he received his BA in Religious Studies. For five years after college, he built housing for poor and handicapped people in the Blue Ridge Mountains of Virginia through a small non-profit corporation he established.

Peter received his JD from Catholic University and practiced law in the nation's capital. Feeling the call to the priesthood, he entered the seminary and was sent to the North American College in the Vatican, where he lived for five years. He holds an STB degree from the Gregorian University and an STL degree from the Lateran University, both in Rome. He was ordained to the priesthood for the Archdiocese of Washington in 1986.

He has served at various parishes, notably St. John Vianney in Prince Frederick, Maryland, where he has been pastor since 1994. He was a syndicated columnist for the Catholic News Service for twenty years and has written for the *Washington Post* and the *National Catholic Reporter*. He has continued his commitment to housing for the poor, helping to found Safe Nights (a program for homeless men and women) and a major housing project in Nicaragua, which has built more than 220 houses in and around San Juan de Limay.